THE WOMAN OF ROME

THE WOMAN
OF ROME

A Novel

ALBERTO MORAVIA

TRANSLATED FROM THE ITALIAN BY LYDIA HOLLAND
Translation updated and revised by Tami Calliope

STEERFORTH ITALIA
AN IMPRINT OF STEERFORTH PRESS · HANOVER, NEW HAMPSHIRE

ALL RIGHTS RESERVED

For information about permission to
reproduce selections from this book, write to:
Steerforth Press, 25 Lebanon Street
Hanover, New Hampshire 03755

Library of Congress Cataloging-in-Publication Data
is available from the Library of Congress

ISBN 1–883642–80–9

Manufactured in the United States of America

FOURTH PRINTING

PART I

I

*A*T SIXTEEN YEARS OF AGE, I was a real beauty. I had a perfectly oval face, narrow at the temples and widening a little below; my eyes were large, gentle and elongated; my nose formed one straight line with my forehead; my mouth was large, with beautiful full, red lips, and when I laughed, I showed very white, regular teeth. It struck me that I resembled a certain movie star who was very popular at the time and I began to do my hair as she did. Mother said that although my face was beautiful, my body was a hundred times more so; she said that there was not a body like mine in all Rome.

In those days I did not trouble about my body; I thought a beautiful face was all that mattered. But today I must admit Mother was right. I had firm straight legs, curving hips, a long back, narrow waist and broad shoulders. My belly was rather prominent as it has always been, and my navel was so deeply hollowed in my flesh that it almost disappeared; but Mother said this was an additional beauty, because a woman's belly ought to be rather prominent and not flat as is the fashion today. My breasts, too, were well developed, but firm and resilient so that I did not have to wear a brassiere. When I used to complain that they were overdeveloped, Mother said that they were really splendid and that women's breasts nowadays were nonexistent. When I was naked, I seemed tall and well proportioned, modeled like a statue, they told me later on; but when fully clothed, I looked like a slim young girl, and no one could have guessed that I was built as I was. This, I was told by an artist for whom I first began to pose, was because of the proportion between the various parts of my body.

Mother discovered this painter for me. Before she married and became a shirtmaker, she had been a model; then one day an artist gave her some shirts to make and, remembering her old profession, she suggested I should pose for him. The first time I went to his studio Mother insisted on coming with me, although I protested that I could easily go alone. I felt ashamed, not so much at having to undress in front of a man for the first time in my life, as at the things I guessed my mother would say to persuade him to employ me. And, in fact, after she had helped me to slip my clothes over my head and had made me stand naked in the middle of the room, she began to talk enthusiastically to the artist. "Just look what breasts! What hips! Look at her legs! Where else will you find legs and hips and breasts like these?" And as she said these things, she kept on prodding me, just like they prod animals to persuade people to buy them in the market. The painter was laughing; I grew ashamed and since it was winter I felt very cold. But I realized Mother was not talking in this way out of spite but that she was proud of my beauty because she was my mother and, if I was beautiful, I owed it all to her. The artist, too, seemed to understand her feelings and laughed, not from an ulterior motive, but with genuine friendliness, so that I felt reassured and, overcoming my shyness, walked on tiptoe to the stove to warm myself.

The artist must have been about forty and was a stout man with a cheerful, easygoing manner. I felt that he looked at me without desiring me, as he would at an object, and this comforted me. Later on, when he knew me better, he always treated me with kindness and respect, as a human being and no longer as a mere object. I was attracted to him immediately, and I might even have fallen in love with him out of sheer gratitude, just because he was kindly and affectionate toward me. But he never let himself go with me, always behaving like an artist not like a man, and our relationship remained as correct and distant as it was on the first day I posed for him.

When Mother had come to an end of my praises, the painter, without saying a word, went over to a heap of papers piled up on a chair. After having looked through them, he pulled out a colored print and showed it to Mother. "There's your daughter," he said in an undertone. I moved over from the stove to look at the print. It showed a naked woman lying on a bed covered with rich fabrics. A velvet curtain hung behind the bed and two winged cherubs, like two little angels, floated in the air in the folds of the curtain. The woman really did resemble me; only, although she was naked, the textures and the rings she was wearing on her fingers showed clearly that she must have been a queen, or someone important, whereas I was only a common girl. At first Mother did not understand and stared in consternation at the print. Then suddenly she seemed to see the resemblance. "She's exactly like that! It's Adriana! You see how right I was? Who is this woman?" she exclaimed excitedly.

"It's Danae," replied the artist with a smile.

"Danae who?"

"Danae — a pagan goddess."

Mother, who had expected to hear the name of a real person, was rather disconcerted, and in order to hide her embarrassment began to explain to me that I had to do what the painter wanted — lie like the figure in the print, for instance, or stand or sit and keep still all the time he was working. He said laughingly that Mother knew more about it than he did, and Mother immediately began to talk of when she had been known all over Rome as one of the handsomest models and the harm she had done herself by marrying and giving up her career. Meanwhile the artist had made me lie down on a sofa at one end of the studio and take up a pose, arranging my arms and legs in the position he required. He did this with an ab-stracted, thoughtful gentleness, hardly touching me, as if he had al-ready seen me in the attitude in which he wanted to paint me. Then, although Mother continued to chatter, he began to sketch in the preliminary outlines on a white canvas standing on an easel. Mother noticed he was no longer listening to her, since he was ab-sorbed in drawing me.

"How much will you pay this daughter of mine an hour?" she asked.

Without lifting his eyes from the canvas, the painter named a sum. Mother picked up the clothes I had arranged on a chair and threw them at me.

"Come on! Get your clothes on — we'd better be going," she said to me.

"Now what's the matter?" asked the painter in astonishment, stopping his work.

"Nothing," answered Mother, pretending to be in a great hurry. "Come on, Adriana — we've got a lot to do."

"But, look here," said the painter, "if you want to come to terms, make an offer — what's the meaning of all this?"

Then Mother began to make a dreadful scene, shouting at the top of her voice that he was mad if he thought he could get away with paying me so little, that I was not one of those models nobody wants, that I was sixteen and was posing for the first time. When Mother wants something, she always starts shouting and pretends she is furiously angry. But she is not really angry at all and I, who know her through and through, know that she is as calm as oil un-derneath. But she shouts like the women in the market when a purchaser offers too little for their goods. She shouts most of all at well-mannered people, because she knows their manners will al-ways make them yield to her.

And, in fact, even the artist gave way in the end. While Mother was creating a scene, he kept on smiling and making a gesture from time to time with one hand as if he wished to say something. At last Mother stopped to get her breath, and he asked her again how much she wanted. But she wouldn't say straight out. "I'd like to know just how much the painter who did that picture you showed me gave his model!" she shouted unexpectedly.

The artist began to laugh. "What's that got to do with it? Those were other days — he probably gave her a bottle of wine or a pair of gloves."

Mother seemed as much put out as she had been when he told her the print represented Danae. The artist was having a little quiet fun at her expense, without any malice, of course, but she did not realize it. She started shouting again, calling him mean and boasting about my beauty. Then suddenly she pretended to calm down and told him how much she wanted. The artist argued the point for a while, and at last they agreed on a sum that was only a little less than Mother had asked. The artist walked over to a table, opened a drawer, and paid her. She took the money, looking highly delighted, gave me a few more suggestions, and left. The artist shut the door and then returning to his easel, spoke to me.

"Does your mother always shout?"

"Mother loves me," I replied.

"I got the impression that she loves money more than anything else in the world," he said quietly, as he proceeded with his drawing.

"No, no, that's not true," I answered with vivacity. "She loves me best of all, but she's sorry I was born poor and she wants me to earn a good living."

I've related this matter of the artist in detail, first of all because this was the day when I began to work, although later on I chose another profession, and then because Mother's behavior on this occasion illuminates her character and the nature of her affection for me.

When my hour's sitting was over, I went to meet Mother in a café where she had told me to pick her up. She asked me how it had gone and made me tell every word of the conversation that the artist, who was rather a silent fellow, had carried on with me during the sitting. In the end she told me I would have to be very careful, perhaps this artist had no dishonorable intentions, but many of them employed models with the idea of making them their mistresses. I was to repel their advances at all costs. "They are all penniless," she explained, "and you can't expect to get anything out of them. With your looks you can aim much higher, much higher."

This was the first time Mother had ever spoken to me in this way. But she spoke decisively, as if she were saying things she had been pondering for some time.

"What do you mean?" I asked her in astonishment.

"Those people have plenty of talk but no money. A lovely girl like you ought to go with gentlemen," she answered rather vaguely.

"What gentlemen? I don't know any gentlemen!"

She looked at me. "You can be a model for the time being," she said even more vaguely, "then we'll see — one thing leads to another." But the reflective, grasping look on her face alarmed me. I asked her nothing more on that occasion.

But in any case, Mother's advice was unnecessary, because I was very serious even for my extreme youth. After this artist, I met others and soon became well enough known among the artists. I must say that they were usually tactful and respectful, although more than one showed me what his feelings were toward me. But I repelled them all so harshly that I soon had the reputation of being unapproachably virtuous. I have already said that most of the artists were nearly always respectful; this was probably because their aim was not to make love to me but to draw and paint me. They were accustomed to models, and my naked body, although it was young and fully developed, made as little impression upon them as upon a doctor. The artists' friends, on the other hand, often embarrassed me. They used to come in and begin to chat with the artist. But I soon noticed that, although they did their utmost to appear indifferent, they were unable to keep their eyes off me. Some were quite shameless and would begin wandering around the studio so that they could examine me from every angle. These glances, as well as Mother's veiled allusions, roused my sense of coquetry and made me conscious both of my beauty and of the advantages I might draw from it. At last I not only became accustomed to their tactlessness, but, after a while, I could not help feeling delighted when I saw how excited the visitors became, and disappointed when they were indifferent to me. And so, all unawares, my vanity led me to think that whenever I chose to, I could improve my situation by making use of my looks, just as Mother had said.

My chief aim at that time, however, was to get married. My senses were still dormant, and the men who watched me while I was posing aroused no emotion in me other than vanity. I used to give Mother all the money I earned and, when I was not posing, I stayed at home with her and helped her cut out and sew shirts, our only means of livelihood since my father, who had been a rail-wayman, had died. We lived in a small apartment on the second floor of a long, low building, erected specially for the railwaymen fifty years earlier. The house was situated on a suburban avenue pleasantly shaded by plane trees. On one side was a row of houses exactly like ours, all alike, with two floors, brick facades without any stucco, twelve windows, and a central door; on the other side, the city walls extended from tower to tower, intact at that point and smothered in greenery.

There was a gate in the city walls not far from our house. Near this gate, running along inside the walls, stretched the enclosed site of Luna Park, an amusement park whose illuminations and music enlivened the summer months. If I looked out sideways from my window, I could see festoons of colored lamps, the be-flagged roofs of the various booths and the crowd packed round the entrance under the branches of the plane trees. I could hear the music quite clearly and I often stayed awake at night listening to it and half dreaming, with my eyes wide open. It seemed to come from a world out of reach, at least for me, and this feeling was heightened by the darkness and narrowness of my room. The whole population of the city seemed to have come together at Luna Park, and I was the only one left out. I longed to get out of bed and join them, but I did not move, and the music, which kept up an uninterrupted jangle of sound the whole night through, made me conscious of a definite loss, the consequence of some sin I did not even know I had committed. Sometimes while listening to the music I even began to cry, so bitter was it to be left out. I was

very sentimental at this time and any little thing, a friend's snub, a
reproach from Mother, a touching scene at the movies, made
tears well up in my eyes. Perhaps I would not have been conscious
of a forbidden, happy world if Mother had not refused to let me go
to Luna Park or have any other amusement when I was a child.
But her widowhood, her poverty, and above all her hostility to all
the pleasures fate had denied her, made her refuse to let me go to
Luna Park, or to any other place of entertainment, except much
later, when I was a grown girl and my character was already
formed. I owe to this, in all probability, the suspicion that has remained with me all my life through of somehow being shut out
from the gay, brilliant world of happiness, a suspicion I am unable
to shake off, even when I know for certain that I am happy.

I have already said that at this time I thought only of getting
married, and I can also say how it was that this thought was first
planted in my mind. The suburban avenue where our house stood
led a little farther on to a more prosperous district. Instead of the
long, low railwaymen's houses, which looked like so many dusty,
worn-out old carriages, there were a number of little houses surrounded by gardens. They were not luxurious, clerks and small
shopkeepers lived in them, but in comparison with our sordid
dwelling they gave an impression of a gayer and easier life. First of
all, each house was different; then, they were not all cracked and
stained, with the plaster peeling off, as were our house and others
like it, making them appear as though their inhabitants had long
neglected them through sheer indifference. And finally, the
narrow blossoming gardens that surrounded them created an impression of possessive intimacy, of remoteness from the confusion
and promiscuity of the street. In the building where I lived, on the
contrary, the street penetrated everywhere: into the huge hall that
was like a warehouse, into the wide, bare, dirty staircase, even into
the rooms, where the rickety, casual furniture was reminiscent of
junkshops where the same sort of pieces are exhibited for sale on
the pavements.

One summer evening, when I was out walking with Mother, I
saw a family scene through a window in one of those villas; it im-

pressed me deeply and seemed to conform in every respect with the idea I had of a normal, decent life. It was a clean little room, with flowered wallpaper, a sideboard, and a central lamp hanging over a table laid ready for a meal. Around the table sat five or six people, among them three children between the ages of eight and ten. A soup tureen stood in the middle of the table, and the mother was standing up to serve the soup. It may seem strange, but what struck me most of all was the central lamp, or rather the extraordinarily peaceful and usual look everything had in that light. As I turned the scene over in my mind later on, I told myself positively that I ought to make it my aim in life to live one day in a house like that, to have a family like that and to live in that same light which seemed to reveal the presence of innumerable firm, constant affections. Perhaps many people will think my ambitions very modest. But my situation at that time must be taken into account. That little house had the same effect on me, born in the railwaymen's houses, as the grander, wealthier dwellings in the luxury districts of the city had on the inhabitants of the little villas themselves. One man's paradise is another's hell.

But Mother had made elaborate plans for my future; I soon realized they were plans that put entirely out of the question any such arrangements as the one I desired most. Mother firmly believed that with my beauty I might aim at any kind of success, but not at becoming a married woman with a family like everyone else. We were extremely poor and she looked on my beauty as our only available capital and, as such, as belonging to her as well as to me; if for no other reason than that it was she who had given me birth. I was to draw on this capital as she decreed, without any consideration for appearances, in order to improve our situation. Probably the whole scheme was due chiefly to a lack of imagination. In a situation like ours, the idea of capitalizing on my beauty was the first to occur to her. Mother stopped short at this idea and did not delve any deeper.

At that time I had a very imperfect understanding of what Mother's plans were. But even later, when they were quite clear to me, I never dared to ask her why, with these ideas, she had been reduced to such poverty — she, the wife of a railwayman. I understood from various hints that I was the cause of Mother's failure, since she had had me both unwillingly and unexpectedly. In other words, I was conceived by accident and Mother, who did not dare to prevent my birth (as she ought to have done, she said), had been obliged to marry my father and accept all the consequences of such a marriage. When she referred to my birth, she often used to say, "You were the ruin of me," a phrase that at one time hurt me and was obscure, but whose meaning I understood fully later on. The phrase meant, "If it had not been for you, I would not have married that man, and by now I'd have had my own car." Obviously, as she pondered over her own life in this way, she did not want her daughter, who was so much more handsome, to make the same mistakes and incur the same fate. Today, seeing things from a certain distance, I really cannot bring myself to say she was wrong. A family for Mother had meant poverty, slavery, and a few infrequent pleasures that came to an abrupt end with the death of her husband. Naturally, she considered a decent family life as a great misfortune, and was ever on the lookout to prevent me from being attracted by the same mirages that had led to her own downfall.

In her own way Mother was very fond of me. As soon as I began to go the rounds of the studios, for instance, she made me a two-piece skirt and jacket and a dress. As a matter of fact, I would have preferred some underwear, because every time I had to undress I was ashamed of the coarse, threadbare, often soiled lingerie I displayed, but Mother said it did not matter if I wore rags underneath, what was important was to look presentable. She chose two cheap pieces of cloth of striking color and pattern, and cut out the dresses herself. But since she was a shirtmaker and had never made dresses before, she made them both up wrongly. The one-piece, I remember, pouched in front so that my breasts showed and I always had to pin it up. The jacket of the two-piece was too short and too tight, it pulled across my breasts and hips, and the sleeves did not cover my wrists; the skirt, on the other hand, was too wide and made creases in front. But I thought they were splendid because until then I had been dressed even worse, in blouses, short little skirts that showed my thighs, and skimpy little scarves. Mother bought me two pairs of silk stockings as well: I had always worn short socks and had bare knees before. These presents filled me with joy and pride; I never grew tired of looking at them and thinking about them, and used to walk self-consciously along the streets, holding myself upright, as if I were wearing a priceless dress made by some fashionable dressmaker, and not those poor rags.

Mother was always thinking about my future and before long she began to be dissatisfied with my profession as a model. According to her, my earnings were too small; then, too, the artists and their friends were poor and there was little hope of making useful acquaintances in their studios. Mother suddenly conceived the idea that I might become a dancer. She was always full of ambitious ideas, while I, as I have said, thought of nothing more than a tranquil life, with a husband and some children. She got hold of this idea of dancing when a promoter of a variety company, who put on shows between movies, ordered some shirts from her. She did not think the profession of a dancer would prove to be very profitable in itself, but, as she so often said, "One thing leads to another, and by showing oneself on the stage, there was always the chance of meeting some gentleman."

One day Mother told me she had had a talk with this producer and he had encouraged her to take me along to see him. One morning we went to the hotel where he lodged with the whole company. I remember the hotel was an enormous old palace near the station. It was nearly midday, but still quite dark in the corridors. The impression of sleep being wooed in a hundred rooms filled the air and took one's breath away. We went along several corridors and at last reached a kind of murky antechamber where three girls and a musician were practicing in the sparse light as if they were on the stage. The piano was wedged into a corner near the opaque glass window of the bathroom; in the opposite corner stood a huge pile of dirty sheets. The musician, a broken-down old man, was playing from memory, as though he were thinking of something else or drowsing. The three dancers were young and had taken off their jackets; they stood in their skirts, their breasts and arms bare. They had their arms around each other's waists, and, when the musician struck up an air, they all three advanced toward the pile of dirty sheets, kicking their legs high, waving them to the right and left, and finally turning their backs and waggling their behinds, with provocative movements that produced a most incongruous effect in such a dim and squalid setting. My heart stood still as I watched and saw how they beat time with their feet in a dull and heavy thudding on the floor. I knew that although I had long, muscular legs, I had no gift for dancing. I had already had some dancing lessons with two girlfriends at a dancing academy in our district. They knew how to keep time and kick their legs and swing their hips like two experienced dancers after the first few lessons, but I could only drag myself about, as if I were made of lead from the waist down. I didn't seem to be built like other girls; there was something massive and heavy about me that even music was unable to dispel. Besides, feeling an arm round my waist had filled me with a kind of languorous abandon the few times I had danced, so that I dragged my legs rather than moved them. The artist, too, had said to me, "Adriana, you ought to have been born four centuries ago! They had women like you then. It's fashionable nowadays to be thin, you're a fish out of water. In four or five years' time you'll be a Juno." He was mistaken there, though, because today, five years later, I am no stouter or more Junoesque than before. But he was right in saying that I was not made for these days of slim women. My clumsiness made me wretched and I would have given anything to be slim and able to dance like other girls. But although I ate little, I was always as solidly built as a statue, and when I danced I was quite incapable of grasping the rapid, jerky rhythms of modern music.

I told Mother all this because I knew the interview with the producer of the variety show would only be a fiasco, and I was humiliated at the idea of being turned down. But Mother began shouting at once that I was far more beautiful than all the wretched girls who showed themselves off on the stage and the producer ought to thank Heaven if he could get me for his company, and so on. Mother knew nothing about modern beauty, and honestly believed that the more fully developed her breasts, and the rounder her hips, the more beautiful a woman must be.

The producer was waiting in a room that led out of the antechamber; I suppose he watched his dancers' rehearsals from that room through the open door. He was sitting in an armchair at the foot of the unmade bed. There was a tray on the bed and he was just finishing his breakfast. He was a stout old man, but the excessive elegance of his clothes, his brilliantine, his impeccable tidiness, made a strange effect against those tumbled sheets, in the low light of that stuffy room. His florid complexion looked painted to me, because unhealthy, dark, uneven patches showed beneath the rose flush on his cheeks. He was wearing a monocle and puffed and panted all the time, showing such extremely white teeth that they were probably false. He was dressed very smartly, as I said. I still remember his bow tie of the same pattern and color as the handkerchief tucked into his breast pocket. He was sitting with his belly sprawling forward and, as soon as he had finished eating, he wiped his mouth and said in a bored, complaining voice, "Come on, show me your legs."

"Show the gentleman your legs," repeated Mother anxiously.

I was no longer shy after the studios, so I pulled up my dress and showed him my legs, then stood still, holding my dress up and leaving my legs exposed. My legs are magnificent, long and straight, but just above the knees my thighs began to swell out round and solid, broadening gradually to my hips. The producer shook his head as he looked at me. "How old are you?" he asked,

"She was eighteen in August," replied Mother readily.

He got up in silence, panting a little, and walked over to a phonograph standing on a table among a heap of papers and clothes. He wound it up, carefully chose a record, and put it on the phonograph.

"Now try to dance to this music — but keep your dress up," he said.

"She's only had a few dancing lessons," said Mother. She realized that this would be the decisive moment and, knowing how clumsy I was, she feared the result.

But the producer motioned to her to be silent, set the record going, then with another gesture invited me to begin dancing. I did as he requested, holding my skirt up. Actually I only moved my legs, first left and then right, rather slowly and heavily, and I knew I was not keeping time. He was still standing by the phonograph, leaning his elbows on the table and looking in my direction. He suddenly stopped the phonograph and went to sit down again in the armchair, with an unmistakable gesture toward the door.

"Won't it do?" asked Mother anxiously, already on the warpath.

"No, it won't do," he replied, without looking at her, while he felt about in his pockets for his cigarette case.

I knew that when mother had a certain note in her voice she was going to make a scene and therefore I pulled her by the arm. But she jerked herself free and repeated in a louder voice, while she fixed the producer with gleaming eyes, "It won't do, eh? And why not, if I may ask?"

The producer, who had found his cigarette case, was now hunting for his matches. His stoutness made every movement a great effort.

"It won't do," he replied calmly, but panting as he spoke, "because she's got no gift for dancing and because she hasn't the right figure for the job."

Just as I had feared, Mother began to shout out her usual arguments at the top of her lungs — that I was a real beauty, my face was like a Madonna's, and just look at my breasts, my hips, my legs! He remained quite unmoved, lit his cigarette and went on smoking and watching her while he waited for her to finish.

"Your daughter may make a good wet nurse in a year or two — but she'll never be a dancer," he pronounced in his bored and plaintive voice.

He did not know the frenzy Mother was capable of; it so astonished him that he took his cigarette out of his mouth and stood gaping at her. He wanted to speak but she would not let him. Mother was thin and breathless and it was difficult to tell where all the noise came from. She said a number of insulting things about him personally and about the dancers whom we had seen in the corridor. At last, she snatched up some lengths of silk shirt cloth he had entrusted to her and threw them at him, exclaiming, "Get these shirts of yours made by anyone you like — maybe your dancing girls will do them for you — I wouldn't touch them for all the gold in the world!" He was completely disconcerted by this unexpected conclusion and stood there, amazed and apoplectic, with his body enveloped in his shirt material. Meanwhile I kept pulling at mother's sleeve and was almost crying with shame and humiliation. At last she yielded and, leaving the producer to extricate himself from his lengths of silk, we went out of the room.

Next day I told the artist, who had become my confidant to some extent, all that had happened. He laughed a great deal at the producer's phrase about my potentialities as a wet nurse, and then observed, "Poor Adriana — I've told you time and again! You ought not to have been born in the present age. You ought to have been born four centuries ago. What today is a fault was then considered an asset, and vice versa. The producer was quite right, from his own point of view. He knows the public wants fair, slim girls, with tiny breasts, tiny behinds and cunning, provocative little faces. But you're full, without being exactly plump; you're dark, with a beautiful, round bosom — ditto for your behind! And yours is a sweet and gentle face. What can you do about it? You're absolutely what I want! Go on being a model — then one day you'll get married and have a lot of dark, plump children just like yourself, with sweet and gentle faces."

"That's exactly what I want," I said emphatically.

"Good!" he replied, "And now, lean over a little to one side — like that —" This artist was very fond of me in his way; and perhaps, if he had stayed in Rome and had gone on letting me confide in him, he might have given me some good advice and many things would not have happened. But he was always complaining that he could not sell his pictures, and at last took the occasion of an exhibition that was being organized in Milan to go and settle there permanently. I went on being a model, as he had advised me to do. But the other artists were not so kind and affectionate as he was, and I did not feel inclined to talk to them about my life — which was, after all, an imaginary life made up of dreams, aspirations, and hopes. Because at that time nothing ever happened to me.

2

So I CONTINUED BEING A MODEL, although Mother complained because she felt I earned too little. At that time Mother was almost always in a bad mood; she had counted on my beauty to bring me unimaginable success and wealth. As far as she was concerned, the job of being a model had never been more than a first step after which, as she used to say, one thing would come of another. Seeing I was still nothing more than a model, she grew embittered and irritated toward me, as if lack of ambition had cheated her of certain gain. Of course, she never put her thoughts into words, but allowed her hints, her rudeness, her sighs, the long faces she pulled and all the rest of her transparent play-acting to speak for her. It was a kind of never-ending black-mail; and I understood then why many girls, who are constantly badgered in this way by ambitious, disappointed mothers, end up by running away from home and giving themselves to the first man they meet, if only to escape from such an unbearable state of things. Naturally, Mother behaved like this because she loved me, but it was the kind of love the housewife feels for a laying hen: if it stops laying, she begins to examine it, weigh it in her hand, and reckon whether she would not do better to wring its neck.

How patient and ignorant we are when we are very young! I was leading a wretched life at this time and really never noticed it. I used to give Mother all the money I earned by posing for long, wearisome, boring hours in the studios; and the rest of the time, when I was not naked, stiff, and aching from allowing myself to be drawn and painted, I sat bent over the sewing machine, never lifting my eyes from the needle, in order to help Mother in her work. Far into the night I would still be sewing and in the morning I would rise at daybreak, because the studios were a long way off and the sittings started very early. But before I went to work I made my bed and helped Mother clean up the apartment. I was really indefatigable, docile, and patient, and at the same time serene, cheerful, and even-tempered. Envy, bitterness, and jealousy had no place in my heart; rather I was filled with the gentle, unceasing gratitude that blossoms so spontaneously in youth. And I never noticed the squalor of our apartment.

One huge, bare room served as our workroom; it was furnished with a large table in the middle, always covered with pieces of cloth, while other rags hung from nails in the dark walls where the plaster was peeling off, and a few broken straw-bottomed chairs. There was a bedroom where I slept with Mother in her double bed, immediately above which a huge patch of damp stained the ceiling, and in bad weather the rain used to drip down on us. Also a dark little kitchen cluttered up with the plates and saucepans that Mother, being shiftless, never managed to wash up properly. I never noticed what a sacrifice my life really was, with no amusements, love, or affection. When I think of the girl I was, and remember my goodness and innocence, I cannot help feeling deeply sorry for myself, in a powerless, poignant sort of way, as you do when you read of some charming person's misfortunes in a book and would like to be able to ward them off, but know you cannot. But there you are! Men have no use for goodness and innocence; and perhaps this is not the least of life's mysteries — that the qualities praised by everyone, of which nature is so prodigal, in point of fact serve only to increase the sum of unhappiness.

I imagined at that time that my longing to get married and set up a family life would one day be satisfied. Every morning I used to take the streetcar in the square not far from our house, where among a number of newly erected buildings, I noticed one long, low structure against the city walls that was used as a garage. At that hour there was always a young man about the place, either washing or cleaning his car, who used to stare at me pointedly. His face was dark, thin, and perfectly shaped, with a straight nose, black eyes, a marvelous mouth, and white teeth. He closely resembled an American movie star much in vogue in those days, and that is why I noticed him and, in fact, why I took him at first for something different from what he was. He wore good clothes and had the air of being well educated and decently behaved. I imagined that the car must be his and that he was well-to-do, one of the gentlemen Mother talked so much about. I rather liked him, but I only thought of him when I saw him; then on the way to the studios he slipped out of my memory. But, without realizing it, his looks alone must have seduced me, because one morning while I was waiting for the streetcar, I heard someone obviously trying to attract my attention by making the sort of noise people make to call a cat, so I turned around. When I saw him beckoning to me from the car, I did not hesitate at all, but, with a thoughtless docility that astonished me, walked over to him. He opened the door and as I got in I saw that his hand on the open car window was coarse and roughened, with black, broken nails and the first finger tobacco-stained, like the hands of manual workers. But I said nothing and got in all the same. "Where would you like me to take you?" he asked as he shut the door.

I told him the address of the studio. I noticed he had a quiet voice and I thought him rather pleasant, although I could not help feeling there was something false and affected about him.

"Well, let's go for a ride — it's early — then I'll take you wherever you like," he answered. The car started up.

We left my neighborhood by the avenue running along the city walls, went along a wide road with warehouses and little hovels on each side, and at last reached the country. Then he began to drive like a madman down a straight track between two rows of plane trees. Every now and again he said, without turning around, "We're doing eighty, ninety, a hundred, a hundred and twenty, a hundred and thirty kilometers an hour." He wanted to impress me with the speed, but I was chiefly anxious because I had to go and pose and was afraid that for some reason or other the car might break down in the open country. Suddenly he put on the brakes, switched off the engine and turned to me.

"How old are you?"

"Eighteen." I answered.

"Eighteen — I thought you were older." He really did speak in an affected voice, which occasionally, in order to emphasize some word, dropped as if he were talking to himself or telling a secret.

"What's your name?"

"Adriana. What's yours?"

"Gino."

"What do you do?" I asked.

"I'm in business," he replied quickly.

"Is this your car?"

He looked at the car with a kind of disdain.

"Yes, it's mine," he said.

"I don't believe you," I said truthfully.

"You don't believe me! Well, great —" he repeated in an astonished, mocking tone, without turning a hair. "Well, wondeful — why not?"

"You're a chauffeur."

His ironic amazement became even more apparent.

"Now really, what extraordinary things you say! Just think of that, now! Really — a chauffeur! — what on Earth makes you think that?"

"Your hands."

He looked at his hands without flushing or being embarrassed. "Can't hide anything from this young lady, can I? How penetrating of you. Very well — I'm a chauffeur. Is that all right?" he said.

"No, it's not," I retorted sharply, "and please take me back to town at once."

"Why? Are you cross with me because I told you I was in business?"

I really was cross with him at that moment. I didn't know why; it was as though I could not help it.

"Don't talk about it anymore — take me back."

"It was only a joke. Why not? Can't we even joke anymore?"

"I don't like that kind of joke."

"Oh what a nasty character; I was only thinking: this young lady may even be a princess — if she finds out I'm only a poor chauffeur, she won't even look at me — so I'll tell her I'm in business."

These words were very clever because they flattered me and at the same time showed me what his feelings were toward me. In any case, he said them with a kind of grace that quite won me over.

"I'm not a princess — I work as a model, like you do as a chauffeur, to earn my living," I answered.

"What do you mean, a model?"

"I go to artists' studios, take off my clothes, and they paint or draw me."

"Haven't you got a mother?" he asked pointedly.

"Of course I have! Why?"

"And your mother lets you pose naked in front of men?"

It had never crossed my mind that there was anything to be ashamed of in my occupation, and indeed there was not; but I was glad he felt like that about it. It showed he had a serious moral sense. As I have already said, I was thirsting for a normal way of life, and in his astuteness he had guessed (even now I don't know how) what were the right things to say to me. Any other man, I could not help thinking, would have made fun of me or would have shown an indelicate kind of excitement at the idea of my being naked. So, unconsciously, I modified the first impression his lying had given me and thought that after all he must be a decent, honest young man, just the man I had imagined for a husband in my dreams.

"Mother found me the work herself," I answered simply.

"That means she doesn't love you."

"No, it doesn't," I protested. "She loves me — but she was a model herself when she was a girl, and really, there's nothing wrong in it; lots of girls like me model and are decent girls."

He shook his head, unconvinced, and then, placing a hand over mine, said, "Do you know — I'm glad I've met you. Really glad."

"So am I," I said ingenuously.

At that moment I felt a kind of impulse toward him and I almost expected him to kiss me. Certainly if he had kissed me then, I would not have protested. But instead he said in an earnest voice, protectively, "If I had anything to say about it, you wouldn't be a model."

I felt I was a victim, and a feeling of gratitude swept over me. "A girl like you," he continued, "ought to stay at home and work if she likes, but at some decent job that doesn't expose her to the risk of losing her honor — a girl like you ought to be married, have a home and children of her own and stay with her husband."

That was exactly my way of thinking, and I cannot say how happy I was to find that he thought or appeared to think as I did.

"You're right — but all the same you mustn't think badly of Mother. She wanted to make a model of me *because* she loves me," I said.

"No one would say so," he answered earnestly, with indignant pity.

"Yes, she loves me — it's just that she doesn't understand certain things."

We went on talking like this, seated behind the windshield in the closed car. It was May, I remember, the air was soft, the shadows of the plane trees were playing on the surface of the road as far as the eye could see. No one passed us except an occasional car at high speed, and the green, sunny countryside all around us was deserted, too. At last he looked at his watch and said he would take me back to town. In all that time he had not done anything but touch my hand once. I had expected him to try to kiss me at least, and was both disappointed and pleased by his discretion. Disappointed because I liked him, and, in fact, could not resist gazing at his thin red lips; glad because it strengthened my opinion that he was a serious-minded young man, just as I hoped he was.

He took me as far as the studio and told me that from that day on, if I would be at the streetcar stop at a certain time, he would always take me along since he had nothing to do at that hour. I was delighted to accept, and all that day my long hours of posing passed on wings. I seemed to have found a purpose in my life, and I was glad I could think about him, without any resentment or regret, as a person who not only attracted me physically but had the moral qualities I considered essential.

I did not mention him to Mother; I was afraid she would not have allowed me to become involved with a poor man who had only a modest future. Next morning he came to pick me up as he had promised, and this time took me straight to the studio. The following days, when the weather was good, he took me out, sometimes along the avenues or thinly populated streets on the outskirts of the city, so that he could talk to me at his ease; but he was always earnest and serious in his speech and had a most respectful manner calculated to charm me. My sentimentality at that time made anything connected with goodness, virtue, morality, family affection, stir me strangely, even to the point of tears, which welled up in my eyes on the slightest pretext and gave me an overwhelming and intoxicating feeling of consolation, trust, and sympathy. So, little by little, I came to believe him absolutely perfect. Really, I asked myself sometimes, what faults had he? He was handsome, young, intelligent, honest, serious minded — he could not be said to have any real flaw. I was astonished at this conclusion, because we do not encounter perfection every day of our lives, and I was almost frightened. What sort of man is this, I asked myself, who has no fault, no shortcoming, however much I examine him? In fact, without knowing it, I had fallen in love with him. And we all know love is a deceptive glass that can make even a monster appear fascinating.

I was so deeply in love that the first time he kissed me, in the avenue where we had had our first talk together, I felt a sense of relief, as if I had progressed in the most natural way possible from the stage of an already ripe desire to that of its first satisfaction. Nevertheless, the irresistible impulse that joined our lips in this kiss frightened me a little, because I realized that my actions no longer depended on myself but on the exquisitely powerful force that drove me so urgently toward him. But I was completely reassured when he told me, as soon as we separated, that from now on we were to consider ourselves engaged. I could not help thinking that this time, too, he had read my innermost thoughts and had said the very words I wanted to hear. The uneasiness my first kiss had caused me therefore faded at once; and for the rest of the time we stayed there on the roadside, I kissed him without any reserve, with a feeling of utter, violent, and legitimate abandon.

Since then I have given and received many kisses, and God knows I have given and received them without participating in them, either emotionally or physically, as you give and receive an old coin that has been handled by many people; but I shall always remember that first kiss because of its almost painful intensity, in which I seemed to be expressing not only my love for Gino but a lifelong state of expectancy. I remember that I felt as if the whole world were revolving around me and the sky lay beneath me, the Earth above. In fact, I was leaning back slightly, his mouth on mine, so that the embrace would last longer. Something cool and living pressed against my teeth and when I unclenched them I felt his tongue, that had caressed my ears so long with the sweetness of his words, now penetrating wordlessly into my mouth to reveal to me another sweetness I had never suspected. I did not know people could kiss in that way for so long, and I was soon breathless and half intoxicated. In the end, when we broke away from one another I was obliged to lean back against the seat with my eyes closed and my mind hazy, as if I were going to faint. And so I discovered there were other joys in the world than merely living peacefully in the bosom of one's family. I did not dream that in my case, these joys were to exclude the more homely ones I had aspired to until then; and after Gino's promise of an engagement, I felt sure that in the future I would be able to taste the delights of both, without sinning and without remorse.

I was so convinced of the rightness and the lawfulness of my behavior that that very evening I told Mother everything, perhaps with too much trepidation and delight. I found her at her sewing machine by the window, sitting in the blinding light from an unshaded bulb.

"Mother, I'm engaged," I said, my cheeks burning as I did so.

I saw her whole face screw up in an expression of annoyance as if a trickle of icy cold water were running down her back.

"Who to?"

"A young man I met recently."

"What is he?"

"A chauffeur."

I wanted to continue, but had not the time. My mother stopped her machine, jumped off her chair, and seized me by the hair. "Engaged, did you say? — without telling me anything — and to a chauffeur! God help me — you'll be the death of me!" She was trying to hit me as she said this. I protected myself as best I could with my hands and at last broke away from her, but she followed me. I rushed round the table in the middle of the room, but she was after me, shouting desperately. I was utterly terrified by her thin face thrust out toward me with an expression of agonized rage. "I'll kill you!" she shouted. "I'll kill you this time." Every time she said "I'll kill you," her fury seemed to increase and the threat appeared more actual. I stayed at the end of the table and watched every movement she made, because I knew that just then she was out of control, and was really capable of hurting me with the first thing that she happened to pick up, even if she did not murder me. And, in fact, she suddenly began waving her dressmaking scissors, the large ones, and I was only just in time to dart aside as the scissors passed me and hit the wall. She was frightened herself at this and suddenly sat down at the table, her face buried in her hands, and burst into a nervous choking fit of crying, in which there seemed more anger than sorrow.

"I had made so many plans for you," she said between her sobs. "I wanted you to be rich, with all your good looks — and now you're engaged to a beggar."

"He's not a beggar!" I interrupted timidly.

"A chauffeur!" she exclaimed, shrugging her shoulders. "A chauffeur. . . . You're unlucky, and you'll end up like me." She said these words slowly as if to savor all their bitterness. Then she added after a moment, "He'll marry you and you'll become his servant, and then the servant of your children — that'll be the end of it."

"We'll get married when he has enough money to buy his own car," I said, telling her one of Gino's plans.

"Don't hold your breath! But don't bring him here," she suddenly shouted, raising her tear-stained face. "Don't bring him here — I don't want to see him. Do what you like, see him wherever you like — but don't bring him here."

That evening I went to bed supperless, feeling very unhappy and depressed. But I told myself that Mother was carrying on in this way because she loved me and had made all sorts of plans for my future that were being upset by my engagement to Gino. Later on, even when I knew what these plans were, I could not really blame her. She had received in exchange for her honest, hardworking life nothing but bitterness, travail, and poverty. How could anyone wonder at her hoping for an entirely different life for her daughter? I ought to say, perhaps, that they were not so much cut-and-dried plans as vague, scintillating dreams, which could be cherished without much remorse because of their very brilliance and vagueness. But that is only my own idea; and perhaps, instead, Mother really had reached the decision, through the lifelong dulling of her conscience, of setting me one day on the path that later I was in any case destined to follow on my own account. I do not say this out of spite toward my mother, but because I still do not quite understand what was in her mind at that moment, and experience has taught me that the most contradictory things may be thought and felt at one and the same moment, without one noticing the contradiction or choosing one in preference to another.

She had vowed that she did not want to meet him and for some time I respected her wish. But after Gino had kissed me the first few times, he seemed anxious to have everything open and above-

board, as he put it; and every day he insisted that I ought to introduce him to my mother. I did not dare tell him Mother did not
want to know him because she thought his employment too
humble, so I tried to postpone the meeting with various excuses.
At last Gino realized I was concealing something from him, and
he pressed me so much that I was obliged to tell him the truth.

"Mother doesn't want to meet you because she says I ought to
marry a gentleman and not a chauffeur."

We were in the car in the usual suburban avenue. He looked at
me sadly and heaved a sigh. I was so infatuated with him that I did
not notice how contrived his sorrow really was.

"That's what comes of being poor," he exclaimed pointedly,
and was silent for some time.

"Do you mind?" I asked him at last.

"I'm humiliated," he replied, shaking his head. "Any other
man in my place would never have asked to meet her, would
never have mentioned an engagement — that's what you get for
trying to do the right thing."

"Why worry?" I said. "I love you — that's all that matters."

"I ought to have come with my pockets full of money but no
talk of engagement, of course! And then your mother would have
been delighted to welcome me."

I did not dare to contradict him, because I knew that what he
was saying was absolutely true.

"Do you know what we'll do?" I said after a while. "One day I'll
take you along and we'll surprise her. She'll have to meet you,
then. She can't shut her eyes."

We arranged a day and, in the evening as we had agreed, I took
Gino into the living room. Mother had just finished her work and
was clearing the end of the table in order to lay the cloth.

"This is Gino, Mother," I said as I led him in.

I had expected a scene and had put Gino on his guard. But to
my surprise Mother said shortly, "Glad to meet you," glancing at
him sideways. Then she left the room.

"You'll see, it'll be all right," I said to Gino. I went close to him
and putting my face up said, "Give me a kiss."

"No, no," he replied in a low voice as he pushed me off, "Your mother would be right in thinking badly of me."

He always knew how to say the appropriate words in any situation, and always said them at the right moment. I could not help admitting to myself that he was right. Mother returned and spoke without looking at Gino.

"There's only enough food for the two of us, really — you didn't tell me. I'll go out and —"

She did not finish what she was saying. Gino stepped forward and interrupted her.

"For heaven's sake! I didn't come here to invite myself to supper. Let me invite the two of you, you and Adriana."

He spoke politely like an educated person. Mother was unaccustomed to being talked to in that way and to being invited out, and for a moment she hesitated and stood looking at me.

"As far as I'm concerned, if Adriana wants to —" she then said.

"Let's go to the wineshop down below," I suggested.

"Wherever you like," replied Gino.

Mother said she had to go and take off her apron, and we were left alone. I was full of innocent joy; I felt I had won an important battle, when in reality the whole thing was a play and the only person not acting a part was myself. I went up to Gino and before he could push me away I kissed him impulsively. The relief from all the anxiety that had troubled me for so long, the conviction that from now on the way was open for my marriage, my gratitude to Gino for his polite attitude to my mother, were all expressed in this kiss. I had no hidden purpose, I was entirely wholehearted in my love for Gino; and in my affection for my mother, I was sincere, trusting and naive, like any eighteen-year-old before disillusionment has brushed off the bloom. I did not learn until much later on that very few people like this kind of candor or are moved by it; for it appears ridiculous to most people and above all pushes them to be cruel.

We all three went out to the bar round the corner, just beyond the city walls. Gino took no further notice of me when we were seated, but gave himself up entirely to my mother, with the ob-

vious intention of winning her over. This desire of his to ingratiate himself with Mother seemed perfectly logical to me, and I
therefore paid little heed to the grossest forms of flattery and adu-
lation he was expending upon her. He called her *signora*, a mode
of address that was quite new to Mother, and he was careful to repeat it as often as he could, at the beginning or in the middle of
his sentences, like a refrain. And then quite casually he would
say, "You're so clever, you'll understand —" "You've had experience, there's really no need to tell you some things —" or again,
even more briefly, "With your intelligence —" He even managed
to tell her that at my age she must have been handsomer than I.
"How can you tell?" I asked him, a little annoyed. "Oh! It's quite
plain to see — there are some things one just doesn't need to be
told," he replied, in a genial and flattering tone. Mother, poor
thing, stared at him with her eyes popping out of her head as he
buttered her up in this way; she made radiant, coy, simpering
faces. Then again I would see her lips moving as she silently repeated to herself the fulsome compliments he had showered
upon her. It was obviously the first time in all her life that anyone
had talked to her like this; and her thirsting heart seemed to be
able to drink in his words forever. As far as I was concerned, these
falsehoods seemed to show nothing other than affectionate respect for my mother and kind regard for me; and so I only had to
add one more stroke to the already overcharged picture of Gino's
perfections.

Meanwhile a group of young men had come in and sat down at
a table near ours. One of them, who seemed to be drunk and kept
on staring at me, gave voice to an obscene but at the same time
flattering remark about me. Gino heard it and got up immediately
and went over to the young man.

"Would you mind repeating what you said!" he exclaimed.

"What the hell's it got to do with you?" asked the young man,
who was really drunk.

"This lady and this young girl are with me," said Gino, raising
his voice, "and as long as they're with me their business is my business. Get it?"

"I get it, don't worry — all right, it's all right," answered the young man, intimidated. The others seemed to be hostile to Gino, but did not dare to take their friend's side, while he, pretending to be even drunker than he was, filled a glass and offered it to Gino, who refused it with a wave of his hand. "Won't you drink?" shouted the young tippler. "Don't you like wine? You're wrong — it's good wine. I'll drink it myself." And he gulped it down in one breath. Gino stared at him sternly for a moment, then returned to us.

"Ill-mannered people," he said as he sat down and straightened his jacket with nervous gestures.

"You shouldn't have troubled," said my mother, highly flattered. "They're only rough boys."

But Gino was overwhelmed by this opportunity of parading his chivalry. "How could I have done otherwise?" he replied. "It would have been a different matter had I been with one of those — you, *signora*, will understand what I mean — quite a different matter, altogether. . . . But since I happened to be with two ladies, in a public place, in a restaurant — anyway he realized I was serious, and you see how he shut up."

Mother was completely won over by this incident. Also, because Gino had made her drink and she found the wine as intoxicating as the flattery. But as so often happens to those who have drunk too much, in spite of her apparent surrender to Gino's charm, she continued to harbor ill feelings about our engagement. And she seized the first opportunity of making it plain to him that, in spite of everything, she had not forgotten.

Her opportunity came during a conversation about my occupation as a model. I no longer remember how it was that I came to speak about a new artist for whom I had been posing that morning.

"I may be stupid, I may be old-fashioned, anything you like, but I really can't swallow the fact that Adriana takes off all her clothes in front of these artists every day." interrupted Gino.

"Why not?" asked Mother in a thick voice that warned me, knowing her as I did, of the storm that was brewing.

"Because, in a word, it isn't moral."

I shall not give my mother's reply in its entirety, because it was sprinkled with the oaths and coarse expressions she always used when she had drunk too much or was overcome with anger. But even when I've toned it down, her speech reflects her ideas and feelings about the matter.

"Ah, so it isn't moral, isn't it?" she began to shout at the top of her voice, so that all the people at the other tables stopped eating and turned toward us. "Not moral — what *is* moral, I'd like to know? Perhaps it's moral to work your fingers to the bone all day, wash up, sew, cook, iron, sweep, scrub floors, and then have your husband turn up in the evening so dead tired that as soon as his meal is done he goes to bed, turns his back on you, and sleeps? That's what you call moral, is it? It's moral to sacrifice yourself, never have time to breathe, to grow old and ugly, then croak? Do you want to know what I think? It's that you only live once, and when you're dead, you're dead, and you and all your morality can go to the devil. Adriana's perfectly right to show herself naked if people will pay her for doing it, and she'd do even better if —" A string of obscenities followed that made me writhe with shame because she shouted them all in the same piercing voice as the rest. "And if she were to do these things I wouldn't lift a finger to prevent her — not only that, but I'd help her to it — yes, I would — as long as they paid her, of course," she added, as if struck by an afterthought.

"I'm sure you wouldn't really be able to bring yourself to do it," said Gino, without appearing at all ruffled.

"Wouldn't I? That's what you say! What the devil do you think? Do you think I'm glad Adriana's engaged to a deadbeat like you, a chauffeur? Wouldn't I have been a thousand times happier if she had gone on the streets? Do you think I like the idea that Adriana, with all her beauty that could earn her thousands, is going to be your servant for the rest of her life? You're wrong, utterly wrong."

She continued to shout and with everyone turning their attention on us, I felt dreadfully ashamed. But Gino was not at all disconcerted. He seized a moment when Mother, panting and exhausted, was obliged to stop for lack of breath, to pick up the wine bottle and fill her glass, saying as he did so, "A little more wine?"

Poor Mother could not help saying, "Thanks," and she accepted the glass he offered her. People who saw us drinking together as if nothing had occurred, despite her vehement outburst, went on with their own conversations.

"Adriana, with all her beauty, ought to lead the sort of life my mistress does," said Gino.

"What sort of life?" I asked eagerly, being anxious to lead the conversation away from myself.

"In the morning," he said in a vain and fatuous voice, as if bathing in the reflected glory of his employers' wealth, "she gets up at eleven or twelve. She has her breakfast taken up to bed on a silver salver with heavy silverware. Then she has a bath, but first the maid puts some salts in the water to make it smell nice. At midday I take her out in the car — she goes to have a vermouth or to do some shopping. Then she goes home, has her lunch, lies down and then spends a couple of hours dressing. You ought to see how many dresses she's got! Closets full of them. Then she goes out visiting in her car or has people over. They play cards, drink, put on music. They're awfully rich people! She must have several millions' worth of jewels alone."

Mother's thoughts were as easily distracted as a child's, whom a trifle will put into a good mood. She had now forgotten all about me and the injustice of my fate, and was enthralled by the picture of such splendor.

"Millions!" she repeated greedily. "And is she beautiful?"

Gino, who was smoking, spat out a shred of tobacco scornfully. "Beautiful? She's ugly — thin, looks like an old witch."

They went on talking about the wealth of Gino's mistress, or rather, Gino went on singing the praises of her wealth as if it were his own. But Mother, after her moment of curiosity, had fallen once more into a depressed and dissatisfied mood and did not utter another word all evening. Perhaps she was ashamed of her outburst; perhaps she was envious of all that wealth and was thinking resentfully of my engagement to a poor man.

Next day I asked Gino apprehensively whether Mother had offended him; he replied that although he did not share her ideas, he understood them perfectly, inspired as they were by a wretched life of deprivation. She was to be pitied, he said, and anyway, obviously she only spoke like that because she loved me. This was my feeling, too, and I was grateful to Gino for having understood her so well. Gino's moderation not only filled me with gratitude, but was one more item to be added to the list of his perfections. If I had been less blinded and inexperienced, I would have reflected that only calculated deceit can create such a sense of perfection, and that real sincerity gives a picture of many faults and shortcomings, together with a few good qualities.

The fact of the matter is that I now found myself, in comparison with Gino, in a constant state of inferiority. I seemed to have given him almost nothing in exchange for his patience and understanding. Perhaps my state of mind, as one who had received many kindnesses and felt called upon to reciprocate them, explains why I made no resistance, as I would have done earlier, when his love making became even bolder. But I must also admit, as I have already said about our first kiss, that I felt impelled to give myself to him by a most powerful yet, at the same time, most exquisite force; it was something akin to the power of sleep, which occasionally, in order to conquer our contrary will, induces us to drop off by means of a dream that we are still awake; and so we yield, being convinced that we are still resisting.

I can remember all the phases of my seduction perfectly, because I desired and at the same time repulsed each step taken by Gino; it gave me both pleasure and remorse. Each step, too, was taken gradually. He proceeded neither hurriedly nor impatiently, but as if he were a general invading a country rather than a lover carried away by desire, as he explored my passive body, from my lips down to my thighs. I do not mean to imply, however, that Gino did not really fall in love with me later on, his scheming and calculation did give place to a deep, insatiable desire, even if it was not love.

During our outings in the car, he had been content so far to kiss my mouth and neck. But one morning, while he was kissing me, I felt his fingers fumbling with the buttons on my blouse. Then I had a feeling that I was cold, and looking over his shoulder toward the mirror over the windshield I saw that one of my breasts was uncovered. I was ashamed but did not like to cover myself again. It was Gino who, hastily guessing the cause of my embarrassment, pulled the edges of my blouse together again over my breast and himself did up all the buttons. I was grateful to him for this gesture. But later, when I thought it over at home, I felt excited and attracted. Next day he repeated the gesture, and this time I felt more pleasure and less shame. From that time I became accustomed to this demonstration of his desire, and I think that if he had not repeated it, I would have been afraid he no longer loved me so much.

Meanwhile he talked ever more frequently of the life we would lead when we were married. He also spoke about his family who lived in the provinces and were not really poor, since they even owned some strips of land. I believe he really came, like most liars, to believe his own lies in the end. Certainly his feelings for me were very strong and probably, since we became more intimate every day, they became more sincere as well. As for myself, his talk lulled my uneasiness and gave me a feeling of perfect, naive happiness such as I have never experienced at any time since then. I loved, I was loved, I imagined I would shortly be married. I thought I wanted nothing more on Earth.

Mother realized at once that our morning trips were not exactly innocent and let me see she knew it by such phrases as "I don't know what you and Gino are up to when you're out in that car, and I don't want to know, either," or, "You and Gino are up to some mischief, all the worse for you," and so on. But I could not help noticing that this time her scolding seemed surprisingly mild and ineffective. She not only seemed resigned to the idea that Gino and I were lovers, but also, at heart, to desire it. I am sure now that she was on the lookout for an opportunity to break off my engagement.

3

ONE SUNDAY GINO TOLD ME that his employers had left
for the country, that the maids had all gone off on holiday to
their own villages, and that the villa had been left in charge of
himself and the gardener. Did I want him to show me over it? He
had spoken about the villa so often and in such glowing terms that
I was longing to visit it, and I therefore accepted gladly. But in the
very instant of accepting, a yearning excitement inside me made
me realize that my curiosity to see the villa was nothing more than
an excuse, and that the real motive behind my visit was something
quite different. Nevertheless, I pretended to myself and to Gino
that I believed my own excuse, as we always do when we long for
something and at the same time try not to.

"I know I shouldn't come," I warned him as I got into the car,
"but we won't stay long, will we?"

I was conscious of saying these words in a provocative and at
the same time rather hesitant manner.

"Just long enough to see over the house — then we'll go to the movies," said Gino reassuringly.

The villa stood among other villas in a little street on a slope, in a new and well-to-do district. It was a peaceful day and all those villas outlined on the hillside against the blue sky, with their red brick or white stone facades, their loggias adorned with statues, their glassed-in porches, terraces and verandas blooming with geraniums, and the tall leafy trees in the gardens between each house, gave me a sense of novelty and discovery, as if I were entering a freer and more beautiful world, where it would have been pleasant to live. I could not help remembering my own district, the road running along the city walls, the railwaymen's houses, and I said to Gino, "I was wrong to come here."

"Why?" he asked coolly. "We won't stay long — don't worry."

"You don't see what I mean!" I replied. "I was wrong, because afterward I'll be ashamed of my own house and neighborhood."

"You're right there," he said with relief, "but what can you do about it? You ought to have been born a millionaire — only millionaires live up here."

He opened the gate and led the way down a gravel path between two rows of little trees trimmed into a shape of cubes and rounds. We entered the villa by a plate-glass door and found ourselves in a bare, gleaming entrance hall, with a black-and-white-check marble floor, polished like a mirror. From here we went into a larger hall, light and spacious, with the ground-floor rooms leading out of it. At the end of the hall a white staircase led to the upper floor. I was so scared at the sight of this hall that I began walking on tiptoe. Gino noticed me and told me, laughing, that I could make as much noise as I liked, since nobody was at home.

He showed me the drawing room, a huge place with many mirrors and sets of armchairs and sofas; the dining room, which was a little smaller, with an oval table, chairs, and sideboard made of a beautiful dark and polished wood; the linen room full of white varnished wall cupboards. In a smaller sitting room there was even a bar arranged in a niche in the wall, a real bar with shelves for the bottles, a nickel-plated coffee machine and a zinc counter; it was like a little chapel; there was even a little gilded gateway that shut it off. I asked Gino where they did the cooking, and he told me the kitchen and servants' rooms were in the basement. It was the first time in my life that I had been in a house of this kind, and I could not help fingering things, as if unable to believe my own eyes. Everything looked new to me and made of precious materials — glass, wood, marble, metals, fabrics. I could not help comparing those walls and that furniture with the dirty floors, blackened walls, and rickety furniture in my own house, and I told myself my mother was right when she said money was the only thing that mattered in the world. I supposed the people living among all those lovely things could not help being lovely and good themselves; they could not possibly drink or swear or shout or hit one another, or do any of the things I had seen done in my own home and others like it.

Meanwhile, for the hundredth time, Gino was explaining with extraordinary pride the way life was lived in a place like that, as if he were bathing in the reflected glory of all that luxury and ease. "They eat off china plates; but they have silver ones for dessert and sweets. The knives and forks are all silver — they have five different courses and drink three kinds of wine. The mistress wears a low-necked dress in the evening and the master a black dinner suit. When dinner's over the parlormaid hands round seven kinds of cigarettes, foreign brands, of course, on a silver tray. Then they go out of the dining room and have coffee and liqueurs wheeled in on the little table over there. They always have guests, sometimes two, sometimes four. The mistress has got some diamonds as big as this! and a marvelous pearl necklace — she must have several millions' worth of jewels."

"You told me that before," I interrupted him peevishly.

But he was so carried away he did not notice my irritation. "The mistress never goes down into the basement — she gives her orders by phone. Everything in the kitchen is electric — our kitchen's cleaner than most people's bedrooms. But not only the kitchen! Even the mistress's dogs are cleaner and better off than many people." He spoke with admiration of his employers and with scorn of poor people; and, partly because of the comparison I

kept on making between that house and my own, and partly because of his words, I felt very poor.

We went up the staircase to the next floor. Gino put his arm
round my waist and hugged me tight. And then, I don't know why,
I almost felt as if I were the mistress of the house just going upstairs with my husband, after some reception or dinner, on my way
to spend the night with him in the same bed, on the next floor. As
if he had guessed what I was thinking (Gino was always having
these intuitions) he said, "And now let's go to bed together — tomorrow they'll bring us our coffee in bed." I began to laugh, but
almost hoped it would come true.

I had put on my best dress that day to go out with Gino, and my
best shoes, blouse, and silk stockings. I remember the dress was a
two-piece, a black jacket and a black-and-white-check skirt. The
material wasn't too bad, but the dressmaker in our neighborhood
who had cut it was not much more experienced than Mother. She
had made a very short skirt, shorter at the back than in front, so that
although my knees were covered, my thighs could be seen from behind. She had made the jacket extremely close-fitting, with wide
lapels and such tight sleeves that they hurt my armpits. I felt as if I
were bursting out of the jacket; and my breasts stuck out as if a
piece of the jacket were missing. My blouse was a very plain one,
made of some cheap pink stuff, without any embroidery, and my
best white cotton petticoat showed through it. My shoes were black
and shiny, the leather was good but the shape old-fashioned. I had
not got a hat and my wavy chestnut-brown hair hung loose over my
shoulders. It was the first time I had worn the dress and I was very
proud of it. I thought myself very smart and could not help imagining everyone turned round in the street to look at me. But as soon
as I entered the bedroom of Gino's mistress and saw the enormous
downy bed with its embroidered silk coverlet, embroidered linen
sheets and all those gossamer draperies flowing down over the head
of the bed, and saw myself reflected three times over in the triple
mirror standing on the dressing table at the end of the room, I realized I was dressed like a scarecrow, my pride in my rags was ridiculous and pitiful, and I thought I would never again be able to call

myself happy unless I could dress well and live in a house like this. I almost felt like crying; I sat down on the bed in bewilderment, without saying a word.

"What's the matter?" asked Gino, sitting down beside me and taking my hand.

"Nothing," I said. "I was looking at a peasant I happen to know."

"Who?" he asked in amazement.

"There," pointing to the mirror in which I could see myself seated on the bed beside Gino; and really, we both looked like a couple of hairy savages who had wandered into a civilized house by mistake, but I looked worse than he did.

This time he understood the feeling of depression, envy, and jealousy that was tormenting me.

"Don't look at yourself in that mirror," he said as he put his arms round me. He feared for the outcome of his plans and did not realize that nothing could have been more favorable to them than my present feeling of humiliation. We kissed one another and the kiss revived my courage, because I felt that after all I loved and was loved.

But a little later when he showed me the bathroom, which was as big as an ordinary room, with its white, shining tiles and the built-in bath with nickel-plated faucets; and when he opened one of the closets and showed me his mistress's dresses, packed tight together, the sensation of envy and of my own poverty returned and made me feel quite desperate. I was suddenly overcome by a desire to think no more about these things; and for the first time I wanted, consciously, to become Gino's mistress, partly so as to forget my own condition and partly in order to persuade myself that I, too, was free and capable of doing what I liked, despite the sense of slavery that was weighing me down. I could not wear beautiful clothes or have a house like that, but at least I could make love as the rich did, and perhaps better than they.

"Why show me all these clothes?" I asked Gino. "What do they matter to me?"

"I thought you'd be curious to see what they're like," he replied, rather disconcerted.

"I'm not at all interested in them," I said. "They're lovely, but I didn't come here to look at clothes."

I saw his eyes light up as I spoke.

"I'd rather see your room," I added carelessly.

"It's in the basement," he replied eagerly, "Shall we go down?"

I looked at him in silence for a moment and then asked him with a newly found forthright kind of manner I disliked in myself, "Why are you playing the fool with me?"

"But I —" he began uneasily, in surprise.

"You know better than I do that we didn't come here to look over the house or admire your mistress's dresses, but to go to your room and make love — well, then, let's just go do it then, right now, and stop talking about it."

In this way, all in a moment, through having seen the house, I changed from the shy, ingenuous girl I had been when I entered it. I was amazed at the change and hardly recognized myself. We left the room and began to go downstairs. Gino put his arm around my waist and kissed me on every step — I do not think anyone ever went down a stairway more slowly. When we reached the ground floor Gino opened a doorway concealed in the wall and, still kissing me and holding me by the waist, led me down the back stairs into the basement. It was evening, and the basement was dark. We reached Gino's room at the end of a long passage, without putting on any lights, our arms still around one another, his mouth on mine. He opened the door, we entered, I heard him close it behind us. We stood there in the dark for some time, kissing one another. It was an endless kiss, every time I wanted to stop he started again; and every time he wanted to stop, it was I who went on. Then Gino pushed me toward the bed and I let myself fall on to it.

Gino kept on whispering in my ear, most provocatively, words of endearment and persuasion, with the obvious purpose of bewildering me and preventing me from noticing that, meanwhile, he was trying to undress me. But this was quite unnecessary, first of all because I had made up my mind to give myself to him, and then because I hated all those clothes I had liked so much before, and I was dying to be rid of them. Naked, I thought, I would be as beautiful, if not more beautiful, than Gino's mistress and all the other rich women in the world. In any case, my body had been waiting for this moment for months now, and I felt that despite myself, it was quivering with impatience and repressed desire like a chained and starving animal, which finally, after a long fast, is set free and given food.

For this reason, the act of love seemed entirely natural to me, and my physical pleasure was not accompanied by any feeling that I was doing something unusual. On the contrary, I seemed to be doing things I had already done, I did not know where or when, maybe in another life, just as sometimes certain landscapes seem familiar whereas you are really seeing them for the first time in your life. This did not prevent me from loving Gino passionately, fiercely, kissing him, biting him, crushing him in my arms almost to the point of suffocation. He, too, seemed to be swept away by the same rage of possession. And so we embraced one another violently in that dark little room, buried beneath two floors of the empty, silent house, goading our bodies in innumerable ways like two enemies struggling for life and trying to hurt each other as much as possible.

But as soon as our desire was satisfied and we lay beside one another, drowsy and exhausted, I became terribly afraid that now Gino had had me, he would no longer want to marry me. So I began to talk about the house we would live in after the wedding.

The villa belonging to Gino's mistress had made a deep impression upon me, and I was quite convinced now that there could be no happiness except among beautiful, clean things. I realized we would never be able to own a house or even a single room like that house, but the brightness of the villa even more than its luxury had given me a welter of ideas. I tried to convince Gino that cleanliness could make even ugly objects look beautiful; but what I really wanted was to convince myself, since I was in despair at the idea of my own poverty and I knew that marrying Gino would be the only way out of it. "Even two rooms can be beautiful," I said, "if they're properly kept, with the floors washed down every day, all the furniture dusted and the brass polished and everything kept tidy, the plates in their proper places, the dusters in their proper places, clothes and shoes all in their proper places — the main thing is to sweep thoroughly and wash the floors and dust everything every day. You don't have to judge by the house where Mother and I live — Mother's untidy and anyway, she never has the time, poor thing. But our house'll shine like a mirror, I can promise you that much."

"Yes, yes," said Gino, "cleanliness comes first. Do you know what the mistress does if she finds a speck of dust in some corner? She calls the chambermaid, makes her go down on her knees and pick it up with her hands — as if she were a dog who'd gone to the bathroom in the house. And she's quite right."

"I'm sure my house'll be even cleaner and tidier than that," I said. "You'll see."

"But you're going to be an artists' model," he said to tease me. "And you won't bother with the house at all."

"A model!" I replied sharply. "I'm not going to be a model any more. I'll stay at home all day and keep it clean and tidy for you and cook for you — Mother says that means I'll be your servant — but if you love someone, even being a servant can be a pleasure."

So we stayed chatting for a long time; and little by little my fear dwindled, giving way to my usual charmed and innocent trustfulness. How could I doubt him? Gino not only agreed to all my plans, but discussed the details, improved on them, added others of his own.

After we had rambled on for a couple of hours, or thereabouts, I dropped off to sleep and I think Gino also slept. We were wakened by a ray of moonlight that came in through the basement window and lit up the bed and our bodies lying there. Gino said it must be very late; and in fact the alarm clock on the night table showed that it was a few minutes past midnight. "What on Earth will Mother do to me!" I exclaimed, jumping out of bed and beginning to dress in the moonlight.

"Why?"

"I've never stayed out so late in all my life. I never go out in the evening."

"You can tell her we went out for a ride in the car," said Gino as he got up, "and it broke down right out in the country."

"She won't believe it."

We hurried out of the villa and Gino took me home in the car. I was sure Mother would not believe the tale about the car having broken down; but I did not imagine that her intuition would have led her to guess exactly what had happened between Gino and me. I had the keys of the front door and of the apartment. I went in, raced up the two flights of stairs and opened the door. I hoped Mother was already in bed, and my hope was strengthened by finding the house in pitch darkness. Without turning on the light, I started to go on tiptoe toward my own room, when I felt myself seized violently by the hair. In the dark my mother, for it was she, dragged me into the living room, threw me onto the sofa and began to strike me with her fists, in a tempest of fury, without once giving vent to a single word. I tried to defend myself with my arm, but Mother, as if she could see what I was doing, always found a way of delivering some nasty blow from underneath that got me full in the face. At last she grew tired and I felt her sit down beside me on the sofa, panting heavily. Then she got up, went and lit the lamp in the middle of the room, and came to sit beside me, with her hands on her hips, staring at me. I felt full of shame and embarrassment as she watched me, and tried to pull down my dress and tidy myself up.

"I bet you and Gino have been making love," she said in her usual voice.

I wanted to say yes, it was true; but I was afraid she would hit me again; and now it was light, I was more afraid of the precision of her blows than of the pain itself. I hated the idea of walking about with a black eye, especially before Gino.

"No, we haven't — the car broke down during the trip and made us late," I replied.

"And I say you've been making love."

"We haven't."

"Yes, you have — go and look at yourself in the mirror — you're green!"

"I'm tired — but we haven't been making love."

"Yes, you have."

"We haven't."

What astonished and rather worried me was that she showed no indignation while she kept on insisting like this, but only a strong and by no means idle curiosity. In other words, Mother wanted to know whether I had given myself to Gino, not in order to punish me or reproach me with it, but because, for some hidden motive of her own, she simply had to know. But it was too late; and although I was sure by now that she would not hit me again, I continued obstinately to deny it. All at once Mother stepped forward and made as if to take me by the arm. I raised my hand to protect myself, but she only said, "I won't touch you — don't be afraid. Come along with me."

I did not understand where she wanted to take me, but, since I was frightened, I obeyed her all the same. Still holding me by the arm, she led me out of the apartment, made me go downstairs, and accompanied me into the street. It was deserted at this time of night, and I realized immediately that Mother was hurrying me along the pavement toward the little red light burning outside the chemist's shop where the first-aid station was. I made a last effort to resist her when we were on the chemist's doorstep, and dug my feet in, but she gave me a push and I entered, all of a heap, almost falling on my knees. Only the pharmacist and a young doctor were in the shop.

"This is my daughter. I want you to examine her," Mother said to the doctor.

The doctor made us go into the back room where the first-aid bed was.

"Tell me what's the matter — what must I examine her for?" he asked Mother.

"She's been making love with her fiancé, the little bitch, and she says she hasn't," shouted Mother. "I want you to examine her and tell me the truth."

The doctor began to be amused, his lips twitched as he smiled and said, "But this isn't a diagnosis — it's a matter for a specialist."

"Call it what you like," answered Mother, shouting at the top of her voice all the time. "I want you to examine her — aren't you a doctor? Don't you have to examine the people who ask you to?"

"Calm yourself. . . . What's your name?" He turned to me.

"Adriana," I answered. I was ashamed but not deeply. Mother's scenes were as well known in the whole neighborhood as my own mildness of temper.

"And suppose she has? continued the doctor, who seemed aware of my embarrassment and was trying to avoid making the examination. "What's the harm? They'll get married later on, and it'll all end well."

"Mind your own business."

"Keep calm, keep calm!" repeated the doctor pleasantly. Then turning to me, "You see your mother really wishes it — so take your things off, I won't be a moment and then you can go."

I summoned up all my courage. "All right, then," I said, "I have made love — let's go home, Mother."

"Not at all, my dear!" she said authoritatively. "You've got to be examined."

Resignedly I let my skirt fall to the ground and stretched myself on the bed. The doctor examined me.

"You were right," he then said to Mother. "She has — now are you satisfied?"

"How much?" asked Mother, taking out her purse. Meanwhile I slipped off the bed and put on my clothes again. But the doctor refused to take the money.

"Do you love your fiancé?" he asked me.

"Of course," I replied.

"When are you getting married?"

"He'll never marry her," shouted Mother. But I replied calmly, "Soon — when we've got our papers ready." There must have been so much ingenuous trust in my eyes that the doctor laughed indulgently, gave me a little pat on the cheek, and then pushed us out.

I expected Mother to cover me with insults as soon as we reached home and perhaps even hit me again. But instead there she was, silently lighting the gas and beginning to cook me something.

She put on a saucepan, then came into the living room and, having removed the usual bits of cloth from the end of the table, she laid a place for me. I was sitting on the sofa onto which she had dragged me by the hair a little while before and was watching her in silence. I was very much surprised, not only because she did not scold me, but because her whole face reflected some strangely unrepressed and bubbling satisfaction. When she had finished laying the table, she went back into the kitchen and after a while returned with a dish.

"Now eat."

As a matter of fact, I was very hungry. I got up and went to sit down, rather awkwardly, on the chair Mother was urging me to take. There were a piece of meat and two eggs in the dish, an unusual dinner.

"It's too much," I said.

"Eat — it'll do you good — you need something," she answered. Her good temper was quite extraordinary, perhaps a little malicious but in no way hostile.

"Gino didn't think of giving you anything to eat, eh?" she added after a while, almost without bitterness.

"We fell asleep," I answered, "and afterward it was too late."

She said nothing, but stood watching me while I ate. She always did this — served me and watched me while I ate, then went to eat by herself in the kitchen. For a long time now, she had not eaten with me at the same table; and she always ate less, either my leftovers or some other food not so good as mine. I was a delicate, precious object in her eyes, the only one she had, someone to be treated with every care; and, for some time now, her flattering and admiring servility had ceased to astonish me. But now her calm satisfaction gave me an uneasy sense of anxiety.

"You're angry with me because we made love — but he's promised to marry me. We'll get married very soon," I said after a while.

"I'm not angry with you," she replied immediately. "I was at the moment, because I'd been waiting for you all evening and I was worried — but don't think about it anymore — eat."

Her deceptively reassuring and evasive tone, like the tone people use in speaking to children when they don't want to answer their questions, made me even more suspicious.

"Why?" I insisted. "Don't you believe he'll marry me?"

"Yes, yes, I believe it, but go on, eat."

"No, you don't believe it."

"I do, don't worry — eat."

"I won't eat any more," I said, driven to the point of exasperation, "until you tell me the truth — why are you looking pleased?"

"I'm not."

She picked up the empty dish and took it into the kitchen. I waited until she came back and then repeated, "Are you glad?"

She looked at me for a long time in silence, and then answered, in a threatening, serious tone, "Yes, I'm glad."

"Why?"

"Because I'm quite sure now that Gino won't marry you, and he'll ditch you."

"He won't. He said he'd marry me."

"He won't marry you — he'll have some fun with you, but he won't give you even a pin, penniless as he is, and then he'll leave you."

"Is that what you're glad about?"

"Of course! Because now I'm quite sure you won't marry each other."

"But what does it matter to you?" I exclaimed, hurt and irritated.

"If he wanted to marry you, he wouldn't have made love to you," she said suddenly. "I was engaged to your father for two years, and until a few months before we were married, he only gave me a kiss or two — he'll have a good time with you and then ditch you, you can count on it! And I'm glad he'll leave you, because if he married you, you'd be ruined."

I could not help admitting to myself that some of the things Mother was saying were true, and my eyes filled with tears.

"I know what it is," I said. "You don't ever want me to have a family; you'd rather see me begin to lead a life like Angelina's!"

Angelina was a girl in our neighborhood who had openly begun to be a prostitute after two or three broken engagements.

"I want you to be comfortably off," she replied gruffly. And when she had picked up the plates, she took them into the kitchen to wash them up. When I was alone, I began to think over her words at some length. I compared them with Gino's promises and behavior, and I did not feel that Mother could possibly be right. But her certainty, her calm, the cheerful way in which she looked ahead, disquieted me. Meanwhile she was washing up the plates in the kitchen. Then I heard her put them on the dresser and go into her bedroom. After a while I went to join her in bed, feeling tired and dispirited.

Next day I wondered whether I ought to mention Mother's doubts to Gino; but after much hesitation I decided not to. The truth of the matter was, I was so afraid that Gino would leave me, as Mother had insinuated, that I dared not mention her opinion to him in case I put the idea into his head. For the first time I realized that by giving herself to a man, a woman places herself in his hands and no longer has any means of forcing him to behave as she wishes. But I was still convinced that Gino would keep his promise, and his behavior, as soon as I met him, strengthened me in this conviction.

Certainly I was looking forward to his many attentions and caresses, but I was afraid he would not mention marriage or would only speak of it in a general way. Instead, as soon as the car stopped in the usual avenue, Gino told me he had fixed the date for the wedding in five months' time, not a day longer. I was so delighted that I could not help bursting out, as though Mother's ideas had been my own, "Do you know what I thought? I thought that after what happened yesterday, you would leave me."

"What the . . . !" he said with an offended look. "Do you take me for a brute?"

"No, but I know lots of men act like that."

"You know," he continued, without noticing my reply, "I could have been offended by what you thought about me? What idea do you have of me? Is this how you love me?"

"I do love you," I said ingenuously. "But I was afraid you wouldn't love me anymore."

"Have I shown you in any way so far that I don't love you?"

"No — but you never know."

"Look," he said suddenly, "you've put me into such a bad mood that I'm going to take you straight to the studio." And he made as if to start the car up at once.

Terrified, I threw my arms round his neck and begged him not to. "No, Gino, what's come over you? I was only talking — forget it." I pleaded.

"When you say such things, it means you think them — and if you think them, it means you aren't in love."

"But I do love you."

"I don't love you, though!" he said sarcastically. "I've only been playing with you, as you say, with the idea of leaving you — funny thing you didn't realize it until now."

"But, Gino," I exclaimed, bursting into tears, "why do you talk to me like this? What have I done to you?"

"Nothing," he said, starting up the car, "but now I'm going to take you to the studio.

The car started off, with Gino sitting bolt upright and serious at the wheel; and I let myself go entirely, sobbing as I watched the trees and milestones slipping past the window, and saw the outline of the first houses in the town on the horizon beyond the fields. I imagined how Mother would crow over our quarrel, if ever she came to know of it and found out that Gino, as she had predicted, had left me. Driven by despair, I open the door and leaned out.

"Either you stop or I'll throw myself under the car!" I cried.

He looked at me, the car slowed down and then turning up a sidepath he brought it to a standstill behind a little hillock topped by ruins. He switched off the engine, put on the emergency brake, and then turned to me.

"All right," he said impatiently, "say what you have to say — go on."

Believing he really meant to leave me, I began to speak with a passion and ardor that seem both ridiculous and touching as I look back on them today. I explained how much I loved him; I even went so far as to tell him I did not care whether we were married or not, so long as I could continue to be his lover. He listened to me, sullen-faced, shaking his head and repeating every now and again, "No, no — it's no use today — perhaps I'll have got over it by tomorrow." But when I said I would be content to be his lover he retorted firmly, "No, it must be marriage or nothing." We continued arguing in this way for some time and by his perverse logic he often drove me to despair and made me cry again. Then, little by little, he appeared to change his inflexible attitude; and at last, after I had kissed him and caressed him in vain, I seemed to have won a great victory when I persuaded him to leave the front seat of the car and make love to me in the back seat, in an uncomfortable posture, which in my anxiety to please him, was too quick for me and bitterly exhausting. I ought to have realized that by behaving like this I was not the victor in any sense, but, on the contrary, was placing myself even more in his hands, if only because I showed I was ready to give myself to him, not merely because I loved him, but in order to coax and persuade him when words failed me — which is just what all women do when they love without being sure that their love is reciprocated. But I was completely blinded by the perfect behavior his cunning had taught him to assume.

The date of the wedding had been set, and I immediately began to concentrate on my preparations. I decided with Gino that at first we would go to live with my mother. In addition to the living room, kitchen, and bedroom, there was a fourth room in the apartment, which my mother had never furnished for lack of money. We kept useless, broken junk in it; and you can imagine what useless, broken junk was in a house like ours where everything seemed useless and broken. After discussing the matter endlessly, we fixed our minimum requirements — we would furnish this one room and I would make myself something of a trousseau. Mother and I were very poor; but I knew she had saved something and that she had scraped and saved for me, in order to be prepared, as she said, for any eventuality. What exactly this eventuality was supposed to be was never quite clear, but it was certainly not my marriage to a poor man with an unsettled future.

I went to Mother and said to her, "That money you've set aside is for me, isn't it?"

"Yes."

"Very well then, if you want me to be happy, give it to me now to furnish the room where Gino and I can live — if you've really saved it for me, now is the time to spend it."

I expected argument, discussion, and in the end a blunt refusal. But instead, Mother welcomed the suggestion eagerly, showing once more the same sardonic calm that had so disconcerted me the evening after I had been to the villa with Gino.

"And he's giving nothing?" was all she asked.

"Of course he is," I lied. "He's already said so — but I must give something too."

She was sewing by the window and had stopped her work in order to talk to me. "Go into my room," she said. "Open the top drawer in the bureau, where you'll find a cardboard box. My savings book is in it and also my bits of gold — take both the book and the gold — you can have them."

The bits of gold did not amount to much — a ring, two earrings, a little chain. But ever since I was a baby, that little treasure, concealed among rags and only glimpsed in extraordinary circumstances, had aroused my imagination. Impulsively I hugged Mother. She pushed me away, not roughly but coldly, saying, "Mind — I've got a needle — you'll prick yourself."

But I was not content. It was not enough to have got what I wanted and even more; I also wanted Mother to share my happiness. "Mother," I said, "if you're only doing it to please me, I don't want it."

"Of course I'm not doing it to please him," she replied, taking up her sewing again.

"You don't really believe I'll marry Gino, do you?" I asked her tenderly.

"I've never believed it, and today less than ever."

"Then why are you giving me the money to do the room up?"

"That's not throwing money away. You'll always have the furniture and linen — money or goods, it's the same thing."

"Won't you come round the shops with me and choose the things?"

"Good Lord!" she shouted, "I don't want to have anything to do with it at all. Do what you like, go where you like, choose what you like — I don't want to know anything."

She was quite unapproachable on the question of my marriage; and I realized that her unreasonableness was not due so much to her idea of Gino's character, ways, and means, as to her own way of looking at life. So there was a kind of silent wager on between Mother and me — she wanted my marriage to fall through and me to become convinced of the excellence of her own plans, and I wanted the marriage to go on and Mother to be persuaded that my way of looking at things was right. I therefore clung even more ardently to the hope of being married; it was as though I were gambling my whole life desperately on a single card. I was bitterly conscious all the time that Mother was watching my efforts and hoping to herself that they would fail.

I must mention here that Gino's model behavior never broke down, not even during the preparations for our wedding. I had told Mother that Gino had given me something toward the expenses; but I had lied, because until then he had never hinted at such a thing. I was surprised and at the same time exaggeratedly delighted when Gino, without my asking him, offered me a small sum of money to help me out. He apologized for the smallness of the sum by saying that he could not give more because he often had to send money home. Today, when I think back on his offer, I can find no other explanation of it than that he gloried in being meticulously faithful to the part he had decided to play. Perhaps this faithfulness had its origin in his remorse at having deceived me and his regret at not being in the position to marry me, as he really wanted to at that time. I hastened triumphantly to tell Mother of Gino's offer. She contented herself with saying how small it was — not so little as to make him look cheap, but just enough to throw dust in my eyes.

I was very happy during this period of my life. I used to meet Gino every day and we made love wherever we could — on the back seat of the car, or standing up in a dark corner in some deserted street, or in a field in the country, or at the villa again in Gino's room. One night when he took me home, we made love in the dark on the landing outside my front door, lying on the floor. Another time we made love at the movies, huddled together at the back right underneath the projection room. I liked joining the crowds in the streetcars and public places with him beside me, because people pushed me up against him and I took advantage of this to press my body to his. The whole time I wanted to squeeze his hand or ruffle his hair or caress him in some way, anywhere, even when others were present, and I almost tricked myself into believing it would not be noticed, as we always do when we give way to some irresistible passion. The act of love delighted me, perhaps I loved love itself even more than I did Gino, for I felt myself impelled to it, not only by my feelings for Gino, but also by the pleasure I derived from it. Of course, I did not imagine I could have had the same pleasure from any other man but Gino. But I realized in a dim way that the ardor, the skill, the passion I put into my caresses were not to be accounted for merely by the fact that we were in love. They had a character of their own, as if I had a gift for lovemaking that even without Gino would have shown itself sooner or later.

But the idea of my marriage took first place. In order to save money, I helped Mother all I could and often stayed up late. By day, if I was not posing in the studios, I went round the shops with Gino to choose our furniture and the material for my trousseau. I had little to spend and, for this very reason, I looked about all the more carefully. I even made them bring out things I knew I could not buy, and turned them over at my leisure, discussing their value and haggling over the price; afterward I assumed a dissatisfied air or promised I would return, then left the shop without having purchased anything. I did not realize it, but these frantic expeditions to the shops, this exhausting handling of goods I could not afford, brought home to me the truth of what Mother had said — that there was little happiness to be had without money. This was the first time, after my visit to the villa, that I had a paradise of wealth, and since I felt excluded from it through no fault of my own, I could not help being rather embittered and upset. But I tried through lovemaking to forget this injustice, as I had done at the villa. Love was my only luxury, it alone made me feel I was the equal of many other women richer and more fortunate than I.

At last, after much discussion and research, I decided on my extremely modest purchases; and I bought a suite of furniture in modern style, on the installment plan because I had not enough money to pay for it outright — there was a double bed, a chest of drawers with a mirror, bedside tables, chairs, and a wardrobe. It was common stuff, cheap and roughly made, but no one would believe the passion I felt immediately for these few sticks of furniture. I had had the walls of the room whitewashed, the doors and windowpanes varnished, the floor scraped, so that our room was a kind of island of cleanliness in the filthy sea surrounding us.

The day the furniture came was certainly the happiest in my life. I could hardly believe that a clean, tidy, light room like that, smelling of whitewash and varnish, was my very own; and this incredulity was mixed with an endless feeling of satisfaction. Sometimes when I was sure Mother was not watching, I went into my room, sat down on the bare mattress and stayed there for hours looking around me. Still as a statue, I gazed on my new possessions as if I were unable to believe they were real and was afraid they might vanish into thin air at any moment, leaving the room empty. Or else I got up and lovingly dusted them and heightened their polish. I think that if I had really let myself give way to my feelings, I would have kissed them. The curtainless window looked down onto a huge, dirty courtyard of a prison or hospital, but entranced as I was, I no longer paid any attention to it; I felt as happy as if the room looked out on a beautiful garden filled with trees. I imagined the life Gino and I would lead there — how we would sleep, make love. I had in mind other things I intended to buy as soon as I could — a vase, a lamp, an ashtray, or some other ornament over in the corner. My only regret was that I could not have a bathroom like the one I had seen at the villa, with shining white tiles and faucets, or at least a new, clean one. I was determined to keep my room extremely neat and clean. The visit to the villa had convinced me that a luxurious life began with order and cleanliness.

4

SOMEWHERE ABOUT THIS TIME, while I was still continuing to pose in the studios, I struck up a friendship with
another model called Gisella. She was a tall, well-made girl, with
a very white skin, dark curly hair, small, deepset blue eyes, and a
large red mouth. Her character was quite the opposite of mine.
She was quick-tempered, sharp, and spiteful, and at the same time
practical and self-seeking; perhaps it took these very differences to
unite us in friendship. I knew of no other work she had besides
that of being a model, but she dressed far better than I could, and
did not conceal the fact that she received presents and money
from a man she introduced as her fiancé. I remember how I en-
vied her black jacket with collar and cuffs of astrakhan that she
often wore that winter. Her fiancé's name was Riccardo; he was a
tall, placid, heavily built young man, with a face as smooth as an
egg, which I thought very handsome at the time. He was always
sleek and shining, smothered in brilliantine, and wore new suits;
his father kept a shop for men's underwear and ties. He was simple

to the point of silliness, good-natured, cheerful, and probably quite decent. He and Gisella were lovers, and I do not think there was any talk of marriage between them, as there was between Gino and me. But Gisella, like me, aimed at marriage, without setting too many hopes on it. As for Riccardo, I am sure the idea of marrying Gisella never crossed his mind.

Gisella, who was very stupid but far more experienced than I, had determined that she was going to look after me and set me straight about many things. In short, she had the same ideas as Mother about life and happiness. However, in Mother's case, these ideas were expressed in a bitter and quarrelsome way, since they were the fruit of her disappointment and hardships, whereas, in Gisella's case, they sprang from her obtuseness, allied with her stubborn self-sufficiency. Mother was content simply to formulate her ideas, you might say, as if the statement of her principles mattered more to her than the application of them; but Gisella, who had always thought in that way and did not even dream that anyone might think differently, was astonished that I did not behave as she did. Only when I showed my disapproval, because I really could not help myself, did her astonishment give way to rage and jealousy. She suddenly discovered that I not only refused her protection and advice, but that I might even be inclined to criticize her from the height of my own cherished and disinterested aspirations, and it was then that she planned, perhaps unconsciously, to alter my judgment of her by forcing me to become like herself as quickly as possible. Meanwhile she kept on telling me that I was a fool to keep myself pure; that it was a shame to see me going around so badly dressed, living such a hard life, and that, if I wanted to, thanks to my good looks, I could completely change my whole position. At last I told her of my relationship with Gino, because I felt ashamed to have her think I knew nothing about men, but I warned her that we were engaged and were getting married shortly. She immediately asked me what Gino did and, on hearing that he was a chauffeur, she grimaced. But she asked me, nevertheless, to introduce him to her.

Gisella was my best friend and Gino my fiancé: today I am able to judge them dispassionately, but at the time I was quite blind to

their real characters. I have already said that I thought Gino was
perfect: perhaps I realized that Gisella had some faults, but to
offset them I believed she was warmhearted and very fond of me,
and I attributed her anxiety for my future not to her spite at
knowing I was innocent and her desire to corrupt me, but to an ill-
advised and mistaken goodness. And so I introduced them to one
another in some trepidation. In my naïveté, I hoped they would be
friends. The meeting took place in a café. Gisella maintained a
guarded silence the whole time and was obviously hostile. In the
beginning it looked to me as though Gino was putting himself out
to charm Gisella, because as usual he began to talk expansively,
dwelling on his employers' wealth, as if he hoped to dazzle her
with these descriptions and hide the poverty of his own existence.
But Gisella refused to unbend and maintained her hostile attitude. Then she remarked, I don't quite remember in what connection, "You're lucky to have found Adriana."

"Why?" asked Gino in astonishment.

"Because chauffeurs usually go out with servant girls."

I saw Gino change color, but he was not one to be taken by surprise. "You're quite right," he replied slowly, lowering his voice
with the air of someone considering an obvious fact he had over-
looked until that moment. "In fact, the chauffeur before me married the cook — naturally, why not? I ought to have done the same.
Chauffeurs marry maids and maids marry chauffeurs. Why on
Earth didn't it occur to me before? Still," he added carelessly, "I'd
have preferred Adriana to be a maid rather than a model. I don't
mean," he added, raising his hand as if to ward off any objection
Gisella might make, "I don't mean because of the profession itself
— although to tell you the truth, I can't swallow this matter of getting undressed in front of men — but chiefly because being in that
profession she's obliged to make certain acquaintances, friends
who —" he shook his head and made a face. Then, offering her a
pack of cigarettes, "Do you smoke?" he asked her.

Offhand Gisella did not know what answer to make, and contented herself with refusing the cigarette. Then she glanced at her
watch. "Adriana, we've got to go, it's late," she said. It was late, as a

matter of fact, and when we had said good-bye to Gino, we left the café.

When we were in the street Gisella said to me, "You're about to do something absolutely crazy. I'd never marry a man like that."

"Didn't you like him?" I asked her anxiously.

"Not at all. Besides, you told me he was tall, but he's almost shorter than you — then, he doesn't look you straight in the face — he's not natural at all, and he speaks in such an affected way that you can tell a mile off that he isn't saying what he really thinks. Then all the airs and graces he gives himself, when he's only a chauffeur!"

"But I love him!" I protested.

"Yes, but he doesn't love you — and he'll ditch you one day," she replied calmly.

I was taken aback by this forecast; it was so assured and so exactly like one of Mother's. I can say today that, leaving aside her ill will, Gisella had seen through Gino better in one hour than I did in many months. On his side, Gino's opinion of Gisella was also malicious, but I must confess that later on it turned out to be not ill-founded. To tell the truth, my fondness for both of them, together with my inexperience, rendered me blind: it's only too true that one is nearly always right in thinking badly of someone.

"That Gisella of yours," he said, "is what we'd call a pick-up girl where I come from."

I looked astonished. He explained. "A streetwalker. She's got the manners and the character of one. She's stuck-up because she dresses well — but how does she pay for her dresses?"

"Her fiancé gives them to her."

"A different fiancé every night, I'll bet. . . . Now, listen. It's either me — or her."

"What do you mean?"

"I mean you can do as you like — but if you want to go on seeing her, you can count me out. Either me or her."

I tried to dissuade him, but was unsuccessful. Obviously, he had been hurt by Gisella's scornful contempt for him; but in his indignant dislike of her there must have been something of the same faithfulness to the part he was playing as my fiancé that had made him suggest contributing to the costs of our setting up house together. He was as diligent as ever in the expression of sentiments he did not feel. "My fiancée must have nothing to do with bad women," he repeated inflexibly. At last, being afraid our marriage would go up in smoke, I promised to see nothing more of Gisella, although I knew in my heart that I could not possibly keep my promise, because Gisella and I both worked at the same time, and in the same studio.

From that day on, I continued to see her unknown to Gino. When we were together, she seized every opportunity of referring to my engagement in the most ironic and deprecating terms. I had been so naive as to tell her all kinds of little things about my relations with Gino; and she used these confidences to wound me and to show me my present life and my future in a derisory light. Her friend, Riccardo, who seemed to make no distinction between Gisella and me, and looked on us both as easy girls unworthy of respect, lent himself willingly to Gisella's game and doubled the dose of her mockery and cruelty. But he did it good-naturedly and stupidly, because, as I have said, he was neither clever nor really bad. My engagement was only a joking matter for him, a pastime. But Gisella, who found my virtue a constant reproof, attacked me bitter and insistently, trying in every way she could to mortify and humiliate me.

She touched me chiefly on my weakest point: my clothes. "Really," she used to say, "I feel really ashamed to be seen with you today." Or else, "Riccardo would never let me go out in the kind of things you put on — would you, Riccardo? Love shows itself in these things, my dear!" I was ingenuous enough to rise immediately to the bait. I began to lose my temper. I stood up for Gino and, though with less conviction, for my clothes, and always came off the worst, red in the face, with my eyes full of tears.

One day Riccardo, moved to pity, said, "I'm going to give Adriana a present today. Come along, Adriana. I want to give you a purse." But Gisella opposed him violently, saying, "No, Riccardo!

No presents! She's got her Gino, let him give her presents." Riccardo, who had made the suggestion out of good nature, but
without imagining the pleasure his gift would have caused me,
yielded at once. And that very afternoon, out of pique, I went off to
buy myself a handbag with my own money. Next day I met the two
of them with my purse under my arm, and told them it was a present from Gino. This was the only victory I had in all the deplorable
squabbling. And it cost me very dear, because it was a nice purse
and I paid a great deal for it.

When Gisella imagined that by dint of sarcasm, humiliation,
and sermonizing she had worn me down sufficiently, she approached me and told me she had a suggestion to make. "But let
me tell you the whole story," she added. "Don't be your usual pig-
headed self before hearing what I've got to say."

"Go on," I said.

"You know I'm fond of you," she began. "You're like a sister to
me. With your good looks, you could have everything you want —
I hate seeing you go around so shamefully dressed that you look
like a beggar. Now, listen." She stopped and looked at me in all
solemnity. "There's a gentleman, a real gentleman, very distinguished, very decent, who has seen you and takes an interest in
you. He's married but his family lives in the provinces. He's a big
shot in the police," she added in an undertone, "and if you want to
get to know him, I can introduce you. Like I said, he's very elegant, very serious, and you can be quite sure no one will ever get
to know anything about it. He's very busy, anyway, and you'd only
see him two or three times a month, if that. He doesn't object to
your continuing with Gino if you like — doesn't mind your marrying him, but in exchange he'll see to it that you live an easier life
than you do now. What about it?"

"Thank him very much," I said frankly, "but I can't accept."

"Why not?" she asked. Her astonishment was sincere.

"Because I can't. I love Gino and if I accepted, I couldn't look
him in the face."

"Don't be silly! When I tell you Gino needn't know anything
about it!"

"That's just why."

"To think," she said, speaking as if to herself, "that if someone had put me onto anything like this. . . . What am I to say to him? That you'll think it over?"

"No, no — tell him I can't accept."

"You're a fool," said Gisella, disappointed, "that's giving good luck a kick in the pants."

She said many other things of the same nature, which I answered in the same way, and at last went away very dissatisfied.

I had refused the offer on an impulse, without thinking over what it implied. Then, when I was alone, I felt almost regretful: perhaps Gisella was right and that was the only way to obtain all the things I needed so desperately. But I drove the thought away at once, and clung even more closely to the idea of marriage and the regular if modest way of life I promised myself. The sacrifice I had apparently made now obliged me to get married at all costs, even more insistently than before.

But I could not repress a certain feeling of vanity and told Mother of Gisella's offer. I thought I would be giving her a two-fold pleasure — I knew she was proud of my looks and still clung to her theories — this offer flattered her pride and strengthened her convictions. But I was astonished at the state of agitation into which my tale threw her. Her eyes kindled with a greedy light, her whole face flushed with pleasure.

"Who is it?" she asked at last.

"A gentleman," I answered. I was ashamed to tell her it was someone in the police.

"Did you say he was very rich?"

"Yes. Apparently he earns a lot."

She did not dare to say what she was obviously thinking, that I had been wrong to turn down the offer.

"He's seen you and takes an interest in you? Why don't you let her introduce him to you?"

"What's the point, since I don't want him?"

"Pity he's already married."

"I wouldn't want to meet him if he wasn't."

"There are so many ways of going about things," said Mother. "He's rich, he likes you, one thing leads to another — he could help you, without asking for anything in return."

"No, no," I replied, "those people don't give anything for nothing."

"You never know."

"No, no," I repeated.

"It doesn't matter," said Mother, shaking her head. "Still, Gisella's a very nice girl and is really fond of you. Any other girl would be jealous and wouldn't have mentioned it to you. You can see she's a real friend."

After my refusal, Gisella did not talk of her gentleman friend anymore, and to my surprise she even stopped teasing me about my engagement. I continued to see her and Riccardo on the sly. But I mentioned her to Gino more than once in the hope they would make up, because I did not like these underhand dealings. But he never even allowed me to finish what I was saying, and only repeated his expressions of hatred, swearing that if ever he found out I was seeing her, everything would be over between us. He meant what he said, although I had an idea that he would not have been sorry for an excuse to break off the engagement. I told Mother of Gino's dislike for Gisella and she said, almost without spite, "He doesn't want you to see her because he's afraid you'll compare the rags you go about in with the clothes her fiancé gives her."

"No, he says it's because Gisella's bad news."

"He's bad news! I wish he'd find out you're seeing Gisella and really would break off the engagement."

I was terrified. "But Mother!" I exclaimed. "You'd never go and tell him!"

"No, no," she replied hastily, with a trace of bitterness. "It's your business, and I've got nothing to do with it."

"If you were to tell him," I said passionately, "it would be the last you'd ever see of me."

It was Indian summer and the days were mild and clear. One day Gisella told me she and Riccardo and a friend of his had planned an outing by car. They needed another woman to make up the foursome and had thought of me. I was delighted to accept because I was always on the lookout for any pleasure to lighten the misery of my days. I told Gino I had to pose for a few extra hours, and in the morning, fairly early, met the others by appointment on the other side of Ponte Milvio.

The car was already waiting and when I drew near, Gisella and Riccardo, who were sitting in front, kept their places, but Riccardo's friend jumped out and came to meet me. He was young, of medium height, bald, with a sallow face, large dark eyes, an aquiline nose, and a wide mouth whose corners turned up as if he were smiling. He was smartly but quietly dressed, quite differently from Riccardo, with a dark gray jacket and lighter gray trousers, a starched collar and black tie with a pearl tiepin. He had a kind voice and his eyes looked kind, too, but at the same time sad and disillusioned. He was very polite, even ceremonious. Gisella introduced him to me as Stefano Astarita, and I immediately felt sure that he must be the gentleman whose gallant suggestions she had conveyed to me. But I was not displeased at meeting him, because his suggestions had not really been offensive and from a certain point of view were even flattering. I gave him my hand, and he kissed it with a strange air of devotion, an almost painful intensity. Then I got into the car, he sat beside me, and we set off.

While the car sped along the bare, sunny road between parched fields, we hardly spoke. I was happy at being in a car, happy over the trip, happy at the fresh air that caressed my cheeks, and I never grew tired of looking at the country. It was only the second or third time in my life that I had been out for a real trip by car and I was almost afraid of missing something. I opened my eyes and tried to see as many things as possible — haystacks, farmhouses, trees, fields, hills, woods — thinking all the time that months, perhaps years, would pass before I could go on another such trip, and that I ought to get all the details by heart so that I would preserve a perfect memory of it. But Astarita, who was sitting stiffly beside me at a little distance, seemed to have eyes for me alone. His sad, longing gaze never left my face and figure, and his look had the effect on me of a hand touching me here and there. I do not say that this attention annoyed me, but it did embarrass me. Gradually I felt obliged to take some notice of him and talk to him. He sat with his hands on his knees and I could see that he was wearing a wedding ring and another ring with a diamond.

"What a lovely ring!" I exclaimed clumsily.

He lowered his eyes and looked at the ring, without moving his hand. "It was my father's. I took it from his finger when he died," he said.

"O!" I said, as if to apologize. And added, pointing to the wedding ring, "Are you married?"

"Indeed I am," he replied with grim complacency. "I've got a wife — children — everything."

"Is your wife beautiful?" I asked shyly.

"Not as beautiful as you," he replied without smiling, in a very low, emphatic voice, as if he were stating some important truth. And, with the hand on which he wore the ring, he tried to take my hand. But I pulled mine away at once.

"Do you live with her?" I asked at random.

"No," he answered. "She's living in —" and he mentioned a far-off provincial town, "and I'm living here — alone — I hope you'll come to visit me."

I pretended I had not heard the information he had given me in a tragic and almost convulsive fashion.

"Why? Don't you like living with your wife?" I asked.

"We are legally separated," he said, grimacing. "I was only a boy when I got married. The marriage was arranged by my mother. You know how they do these things — a girl of good family, with a handsome dowry. The parents fix everything up and it's the children who have to get married. Live with my wife? Would you live with a woman like this?" He took his wallet from his pocket, opened it, and handed me a photograph. I saw two dark, pale children, looking like twins, dressed in white. A little dark, pale woman, with close-set eyes like an owl's and a malicious expression, stood behind them placing her hands on their shoulders. I returned it to him. He put it away in his wallet.

"I'd like to live with you," he sighed,

"You don't know me at all," I said, disconcerted by his attitude of obsession.

"I know you very well, though! I've been following you for a month. I know all about you."

He was seated a little way off and he addressed me respectfully, but the whole time he was speaking, the depth of his feelings almost made his eyes roll.

"I'm engaged," I said.

"Gisella told me," he said in a strangled voice. "Don't let's talk about your fiancé. What does he matter?" He made a brief, jerky movement of feigned indifference with his hand.

"He matters a lot to me," I replied.

He looked at me. "I like you immensely."

"I noticed that."

"I like you immensely," he repeated. "Perhaps you don't realize how much."

He talked like someone out of his mind. But the fact that he sat apart from me and made no further attempt to take my hand reassured me. "There's no harm in your liking me," I said.

"Do you like me?"

"No."

"I'm rich," he said, contorting his features into a grimace. "I'm rich enough to make you happy — if you come to see me, you won't regret it."

"I don't need your money," I replied calmly, almost kindly.

He did not seem to have heard.

"You're very lovely," he said, looking at me.

"Thanks."

"Your eyes are beautiful."

"Do you think so?"

"Yes — so's your mouth — I want to kiss it."

"Why are you saying these things to me?"

"And I'd like to kiss your body, to . . . all of your body."

"Why are you talking to me like this?" I protested. "It isn't right. I'm engaged and going to be married in a couple of months."

"Please forgive me," he said. "But I get such pleasure out of saying these things — imagine I'm not speaking to you."

"Is Viterbo far now?" I asked in order to change the subject.

"We're nearly there. We'll have a meal at Viterbo. Promise you'll sit beside me at lunch."

I began to laugh because this obsessive intensity of his was very flattering to me. "All right," I said.

"Sit beside me as you are doing now," he continued. "Just to smell your body is enough for me."

"But I'm not wearing any perfume."

"I'll make you a present of some," he said.

We had reached Viterbo by now and the car slowed down as we entered the town. During the whole trip Gisella and Riccardo had not said a word. But as we began to thread our way slowly along the crowded main street, Gisella turned around.

"How are you two getting along? Do you think I didn't see you?" she asked.

Astarita said nothing. "You can't have seen anything. We were only talking," I protested.

"Right!" she said. I was utterly astonished by Gisella's behavior and also rather annoyed by Astarita's persistent silence.

"But if I tell you —" I began.

"Right!" she repeated. "Anyway, don't get so excited, we won't say anything to Gino."

Meanwhile we had reached the square, so we got out of the car and began to walk, in the mild and brilliant October sun, along the Corso among the crowd dressed up in their Sunday best. Astarita did not leave my side for one moment; he was still serious, indeed gloomy, carried his head stiffly above his high collar and kept one hand in his pocket, the other dangling at his side. He looked as though he were my keeper rather than my companion. Gisella, on the contrary, was laughing and joking with Riccardo and many people turned around to stare at us. We went into a café and had a vermouth standing at the bar. I suddenly noticed Astarita mumbling something threateningly and asked him what was the matter.

"There's an idiot over there by the door staring at you," he said heatedly.

I turned around and saw a slim, fair young man standing in the doorway of the café looking at me. "Why not?" I said cheerfully. "Suppose he does look at me?"

"It wouldn't take much to make me go over and hit him in the face."

"If you do, I'll never look at you again and I won't say a single word more to you," I said, feeling rather annoyed. "You've no right to interfere — you have nothing to do with me."

He said nothing and went over to the cash desk to pay for the drinks. We left the café and continued our walk along the Corso. The sun, the noise, and the movement of the crowd, all those healthy, rosy faces of the country people, cheered me up. When we reached an isolated little square at the end of one of the roads crossing the Corso, I suddenly said, "There, look! — if only I had a little house like that one over there, I'd be delighted to live there." And I pointed to a simple little two-storied house in front of a church.

"God forbid!" said Gisella. "Fancy living in the provinces — in Viterbo, what's more! I wouldn't, even if I was smothered in gold."

"You'd soon be fed up with it, Adriana," remarked Riccardo. "When you're used to living in a big town, you can't settle down in the provinces."

"You're wrong," I said. "I'd gladly live here with a man who loved me — four clean little rooms, an arbor, four windows — I wouldn't want anything more." I was quite sincere in what I said, because I imagined myself living in that little house in Viterbo with Gino. "What do you think?" I asked, turning to Astarita.

"I'd live here with you," he replied in an undertone, trying to avoid being overheard by the others.

"The trouble with you, Adriana," said Gisella, "is that you don't aim high enough. Those who ask too little of life get nothing."

"But I don't want anything," I objected.

"You want to marry Gino, though," said Riccardo.

"Yes, that I do want."

It was late by now, the Corso was emptying itself, and we entered the restaurant. The ground-floor room was packed, mostly with peasants in their Sunday best who had come to Viterbo for the market. Gisella turned up her nose, saying it stank enough to take your breath away, and asked the manager if we could go up to the second floor to eat. He said we could and led the way into a long, narrow room with only one window that gave onto the side street. He opened the shutters and closed the windows, then spread a cloth on the rustic table that filled most of the room. I remember the walls were covered with a faded wallpaper, torn in places, with a pattern of flowers and birds. Besides the table there was only a little glass-fronted sideboard full of dishes.

Meanwhile Gisella was walking around the room examining everything, even looking through the window that gave onto the side street. At last she pushed open a door that seemed to lead into another room and after having peeped in, she turned toward the proprietor and asked him in a tone of assumed carelessness what room it was.

"It's a bedroom" he said. "If any of you want to rest a bit after lunch —"

"We'll have a rest, won't we, Gisella?" said Riccardo with his silly giggle. But Gisella pretended she had not heard and after having peeped once more into the room, she carefully shut the door but did not quite close it all the way.

The cozy little dining room had cheered me up, and therefore I thought no more about the half-shut door or the glance of understanding that I imagined had passed between Gisella and Astarita. We sat down at the table and I had Astarita beside me as I had promised, but he did not seem to notice; he was so absorbed he could not even speak. After a while the proprietor came back with hors d'oeuvres and wine, and I was so hungry I flung myself on the food, and made the others laugh at me. Gisella took the opportunity to begin her usual teasing about my marriage.

"Go on, eat," she said. "You'll never get so much to eat with Gino, nor such good food."

"Why?" I asked. "Gino'll earn money."

"You bet, and you'll eat beans every day!"

"Beans are all right," laughed Riccardo. "In fact, I'm going to order some at once."

"You're a fool, Adriana," Gisella went on. "You need a man with something behind him, a decent man, who does things properly, who cares about you and doesn't oblige you to go without things, who makes it possible for you to set off your good looks. And instead of that you go and get mixed up with Gino."

I kept a stubborn silence, my head bent over my plate while I went on eating. Riccardo laughed. "In Adriana's place I wouldn't give up anything," he said, "neither Gino, since she likes him so much, nor the seriously intentioned fellow — I'd take both — and quite possibly Gino wouldn't have anything to say against the arrangement."

"He would," I said hastily. "If he even knew I'd gone on this trip with you today, he'd break off the engagement."

"Why?" asked Gisella, on her high horse.

"Because he doesn't want me to see anything of you."

"That dirty, ugly, dead-broke ignoramus!" said Gisella furiously. "I'd like to put him to the test — to go and say to him, 'Adriana is seeing me, she's been with me all day, so go ahead and break off the engagement!'"

"No, please!" I begged her, terrified. "Don't do it."

"It'd be the best thing that could happen to you."

"Maybe. But don't do it," I besought her again. "If you're fond of me, don't do it."

During this conversation, Astarita said nothing and ate hardly a mouthful. He still kept his eyes on me the whole time, with an exaggeratedly significant, desperate expression I found extremely embarrassing. I wanted to tell him not to stare at me like that, but I was afraid Gisella and Riccardo would make fun of me. For the same reason, I did not dare protest when Astarita seized the opportunity to squeeze my left hand, which I had placed on the bench where we were sitting, obliging me to go on eating with one hand only. I ought to have protested because Gisella suddenly burst out laughing. "She's quite true to Gino in what she says! But when it comes to deeds! Do you think I can't see you and Astarita holding hands under the table?"

I blushed awkwardly and tried to free my hand. But Astarita kept tight hold of it.

"Let them alone," said Riccardo. "What's the harm? It they hold hands, let's do the same."

"I was joking," said Gisella. "I don't mind, I'm glad."

When we had eaten our pasta, we were kept waiting for the next course. Gisella and Riccardo kept on laughing and joking and drinking, in the meantime, and made me drink too. It was good red wine, very strong, and soon went to my head. I liked the warm, sharp taste of it and, in my state of intoxication, did not feel at all drunk, but able to go on drinking indefinitely. Astarita, serious and absorbed, went on holding my hand and I now let him. I told myself that, after all, this was the least I could do. There was an oleograph stuck over the door, of a man and woman dressed in the fashion of fifty years earlier, who were embracing one another in an artificial, awkward way on a rose-covered balcony. Gisella noticed it and said she could not imagine how they could possibly kiss one another in that position. "Let's try," she said to Riccardo, "let's see if we can copy them."

Riccardo stood up, laughing, and assumed the attitude of the man in the oleograph, while Gisella, giggling too, leaned against the table in the same position as the woman in the picture against the rose-bedecked side of the balcony. With a tremendous effort they managed to bring their lips together, but almost at the very moment they lost their balance and toppled over together onto the table.

"Now, it's your turn!" said Gisella, excited by the fun.

"Why?" I asked, apprehensive. "What's it got to do with me?"

"Go on, try."

I felt Astarita put his arm around my waist and tried to free myself. "I don't want to," I said.

"Oh, what a spoilsport you are!" said Gisella. "It's only a joke."

"I don't want to."

Riccardo was laughing and urging on Astarita to make me kiss him. "If you don't kiss her, Astarita, I'll never look you in the face again." But Astarita was in earnest and almost frightened me: for him, this was obviously something more than a joke.

"Let me alone," I said, turning from him.

He looked at me, then glanced at Gisella with a query in his eyes as if he expected her to encourage him. "Go on, Astarita!" exclaimed Gisella. She seemed far more determined than he was, in a way I could vaguely sense was cruel and merciless.

Astarita held me still more tightly by the waist, pulling me toward him. Now it was no longer a joke and he wanted to kiss me at all costs. Without saying a word, I tried to free myself from his grasp, but he was very strong, and the more I pushed with my hands against his chest, the closer I could feel his face gradually approaching mine. But perhaps he would not have succeeded in kissing me, if Gisella had not come to his aid. Suddenly, with a triumphant squeal, she got up, ran behind me, grasped my arms, and pulled them backward. I did not see her but I felt her dogged determination in the way her nails buried themselves in my flesh and in her voice, which kept on repeating between bursts of laughter, in an excited, cruel and jerky way, "Quick, quick, Astarita! Now's your chance!" Astarita was now upon me. I did my best to turn my face away, the only movement I could make, but with one hand he took hold of my chin and forced my face toward his, then he kissed me hard and long on my mouth.

"Done!" said Gisella triumphantly, and went back to her place, delighted.

Astarita let go of me. "I'll never come out with the lot of you again," I said, feeling annoyed and hurt.

"Oh, Adriana!" said Riccardo, making fun of me. "And all for a single kiss!"

"Astarita's covered with lipstick!" exclaimed Gisella ecstatically. "What would Gino say if he came in now?"

Astarita's mouth really was covered with my lipstick, and even to me he looked ridiculous with a scarlet streak like that across his gloomy, sallow face. "Come on," said Gisella, "make up, you two — rub off his lipstick with your handkerchief. Whatever will the waiter think when he comes in, if you don't?"

I had to put a good face on the matter and, wetting a corner of my handkerchief with my tongue, I gradually wiped the lipstick off Astarita's sullen face. I was wrong, though, in showing how yielding I was, because immediately, as soon as I had put my handkerchief away, he put his arm around my waist. "Let go," I said.

"Come on, Adriana!"

"What difference does it make?" said Gisella. "If he likes it — and it doesn't do you any harm. He's kissed you anyway. Let him do as he likes."

So I yielded once again, and we stayed beside one another, his arm around my waist while I sat there stiffly and unwillingly. The waiter came in with the second course. While we were eating my bad mood passed, although Astarita held me close. The food was very good and, without noticing, I drank all the wine Gisella kept on pouring out for me. After the second course we had fruit and dessert. It was an excellent dessert, I wasn't used to things like that and therefore, when Astarita offered me his share I could not say no, and ate that too. Gisella, who had also drunk a great deal, began to coax Riccardo in all sorts of ways, putting little quarters of tangerines into his mouth and giving him a kiss with each one. I felt pleasantly tipsy, and Astarita's arm around my waist no longer troubled me. Gisella got up, more and more restless and excited every moment, and went to sit on Riccardo's knee. I could not help laughing when I heard Riccardo pretend to cry out in pain as if Gisella's weight were crushing him. All of a sudden, Astarita, who had not moved until then, content to have one arm around my waist, began to kiss me breathlessly on my neck, breasts, and cheeks. I did not protest this time, first because I was too tipsy to struggle and then because he seemed to be kissing another person, so little did I participate in his outburst, but kept as still and as stiff as a statue. In my state of intoxication I had the impression that I was standing outside myself, in some corner of the room, looking on indifferently, merely as a curious spectator, at Astarita's wild passion. But the others took my indifference for love and Gisella called out. "Good for you, Adriana — that's the way!"

I wanted to reply but changed my mind, I don't know why, and raising my glass full of wine I said clearly and resonantly, "I'm drunk!" and emptied it at one breath.

I believe the others clapped their hands. But Astarita stopped kissing me and, looking fixedly at me, said under his breath, "Let's go into the other room."

I followed his eyes and saw he was looking at the half-open door of the next room. I imagined he must be drunk, too, and nodded my refusal, but gently, almost flirtatiously.

"Let's go into the next room" he repeated, like a man in his sleep.

I noticed Gisella and Riccardo had stopped laughing and chatting and were watching us.

"Come on!" said Gisella. "Move it! What are you waiting for?"

I sobered up immediately. I was really drunk, but not so drunk as to be unaware of the danger threatening me. "I don't want to," I said. And I stood up.

Astarita got up, too, and seizing me by one arm tried to drag me toward the door. The other two began to egg him on again. "Go on, Astarita!" they urged.

Astarita half dragged me as far as the door, although I struggled. Then I freed myself with a sudden jerk and ran to the door that led out onto the stairway. But Gisella was quicker than I. "No, you don't, sweetie!" she cried. She leaped up from Riccardo's knees and ran over to lock the door, before I could get there, then took the key out.

"I don't want to," I repeated, terrified, standing beside the table.

"What harm can it do you?" asked Riccardo.

"Idiot!" said Gisella harshly, pushing me toward Astarita. "Such a fuss — go along, now."

I realized that despite her cruelty and insistence Gisella did not understand what she was doing. The plot she had laid for me must have seemed to her most delightfully clever and entertaining. I was also amazed at the gay indifference of Riccardo, whom I knew to be kindly and incapable of doing anything he thought malicious.

"I don't want to," I repeated again.

"Why not?" asked Riccardo. "What's wrong with it."

Gisella went on pushing me eagerly and excitedly.

"I didn't think you were so silly," she said. "Go on, Adriana, what are you waiting for?"

Up until now Astarita had not said a word; he stood motionless by the bedroom door, gazing at me. Then I saw him open his mouth as if to speak. "Come on," he said, speaking slowly and thickly, as though the words had a tricky consistency and he found it difficult to get them out. "Otherwise I'll tell Gino you came out with us today and let me make love to you."

I understood at once that he really would carry out his threat. You may well doubt words themselves, but there is often no mistaking the tone of voice in which they are uttered. He would certainly have told Gino, and that would have meant the end for me before I had really begun. Thinking it over today, I suppose I could have withstood him. If I had shouted, if I had struggled violently, I would have persuaded him that his blackmailing was as ineffective as his revenge. But perhaps it would have been no good, because his desire for me was stronger than my disgust. At the time, of course, I felt entirely overcome, and thought more of avoiding a scandal than of opposing him. I found myself plunged into this situation quite unprepared for it, with my mind full of plans for the future, which I desired to carry out at all costs. What happened to me at this time, in such a crude way, must, I think, happen to all those who have as simple, legitimate, innocent ambitions as I had. The world gets hold of us through our ambitions and sooner or later forces us to pay a high and painful price, and only outcasts and people who have renounced everything can ever hope to escape this payment

But at the very moment that I accepted my fate, I experienced a sharp and lucid sensation of pain. A flash of intuition seemed to light up the whole future path of my life, as a rule so dark and tortuous, and reveal it straight and clear before my eyes, showing me in that single moment what I would lose in exchange for Astarita's silence. My eyes filled with tears and I began to cry, putting my arm over my face. I realized I was weeping from utter resignation and not in rebellion, and that, in fact, my legs were carrying me toward Astarita in the midst of my tears. Gisella pushed me by the arm, repeating, "What are you crying for? Anyone would think it was the first time!" I heard Riccardo laugh; and I felt, without seeing him, that Astarita's eyes were upon me as I came slowly toward him in tears. Then I felt him put an arm around my waist and the door of the room closed behind me.

I did not want to see anything, even feeling seemed too much. And so I kept my arm obstinately across my eyes, although Astarita tried to draw it away. I suppose he wanted to behave like all lovers on such occasions, that is, to win me over gradually and almost unconsciously to his desires. But my obstinate refusal to take my arm away from my face obliged him to be more brutal and hurried than he wished. So, after he had made me sit on the edge of the bed and had tried in vain to coax me with caresses, he pushed me back against the cushions and threw himself on me. My whole body from the waist down was as heavy and inert as lead, and no embrace was ever accepted with greater submission and with less participation. But I stopped crying almost immediately, and as soon as he lay breathless on my breast, I removed my arm from my face and stared into the darkness.

I am convinced that at that moment Astarita loved me as much as a man can love a woman, and far more than Gino did. I remember that he could not stop running his hand again and again over my forehead and cheeks with a convulsive, passionate movement, trembling all over and murmuring words of love. But my eyes were dry and wide open, and my head, cleared now of the wine fumes, was filled with an icy, eddying clarity. I let Astarita caress me and talk to me while I followed my own thoughts. Once more I saw my own bedroom, as I had arranged it, with the new furniture I had not quite finished paying for, and felt a kind of bitter consolation. I told myself that now nothing could prevent my marrying and living the kind of life I wanted. But at the same time I felt my spirit was entirely changed and that a new certainty and decision had replaced my once fresh and ingenuous hopes. I suddenly felt much stronger, although it was a tragic strength, and shorn of love.

"It's time to go back into the other room," I said at last, speaking for the first time since we had entered the bedroom.

"Are you mad at me?" he immediately asked in a low voice.

"No."

"Do you hate me?"

"No."

"I love you so much," he murmured. And began once more tempestuously to cover my face and neck with rapid, passionate kisses. I let him have his way and then said, "Yes, but we must go."

"You're right," he answered. He broke away from me and began, as far as I could tell, to get dressed in the dark. I tidied myself as best I could, got up, and turned on the light over the bed. In that yellow light the room looked just as I had imagined from its stuffy, lavender-scented smell: the ceiling was low, the beams were whitewashed, the walls covered with French wallpaper, the furniture old and heavy. A marble-topped washstand stood in one corner and on it two jugs and basins with a green-and-pink flower pattern, and a large mirror in a gold frame. I walked over to the washstand, poured a little water into the basin and, dipping the end of the towel in it, I sponged my lips, which Astarita had bruised with his kisses, and my eyes, still red from crying. The mirror threw back from its scratched and coruscated surface a painful image of myself, and for a moment I looked at it spellbound, my heart filled with pity and wonder. Then I pulled myself together, tidied my hair with my hands to the best of my ability and turned toward Astarita. He was waiting for me by the door and as soon as he saw that I was ready, he opened it, avoiding my eyes and keeping his back turned to me. I switched off the light and followed him.

We were greeted cheerfully by Gisella and Riccardo, who had been carrying on in the same gay, careless manner as when we had left them. They had failed to understand how upset I had been before, and now were just as incapable of understanding my present serenity.

"Well you're quite the little innocent! You didn't want to, didn't want to, but as far as I can see you settled down to it very soon and very well," Gisella cried out. "Anyway, if you enjoyed it, good for you. . . . But it wasn't worth while making such a fuss about it."

I looked at her; it seemed to me extraordinarily unfair that she, who had urged me to yield and had even held my arms so that Astarita could kiss me more easily, should now be the one to reproach me for my complacency.

"You aren't very logical, Gisella," remarked Riccardo with his rough common sense. "First you persuade her and now you seem to be telling her she shouldn't have done it."

"Of course," replied Gisella harshly, "if she didn't want to, she's been very wrong. If I didn't want to myself, nothing, not even force, could make me. But she wanted to," she added, looking at me in a disgusted and dissatisfied way. "She wanted to. And how! I saw them in the car while we were coming to Viterbo. So she shouldn't have made such a fuss, that's all I'm saying."

I did not utter a word, being lost in admiration at the refinement of her pitiless and unwitting cruelty. Astarita came near and clumsily tried to take my hand, but I pushed him away and went to sit down at the end of the table. "Look at Astarita!" exclaimed Riccardo. "He looks as if he's just come away from a funeral!"

As a matter of fact, Astarita, with all his gloom and solemnity, seemed to understand me better than the others did. "You make a joke of everything," he said.

"Well, do you think we ought to burst into tears?" cried Gisella. "Now you two just sit and wait and be patient, like we did. It's our turn now. Come on, Riccardo!"

"Be careful," said Riccardo, getting up to follow her. He was obviously drunk and did not know himself what we had to be careful about.

"Come on, let's go!"

So they left the room, and Astarita and I were alone. I sat at one end of the table and he at the other. A ray of sunshine came in through the window and shone brightly on the untidy crockery, the fruit parings, half-empty glasses and dirty knives and forks. But Astarita's expression remained distressed and overcast, although the sun was shining full on his face. His desire had been appeased, but all the same the look of anguished intensity he had displayed at the beginning of our relationship was still present in his eyes. I felt sorry for him then, despite the harm he had done me. I realized he had been wretched before having me, and now, when it was over, he was no less wretched. He had suffered before because he had wanted me; he suffered now because I did not return his love. But pity is love's worst enemy; if I had hated him, he might have hoped that one day I would come to love him. But I did not hate him and since, as I have said, I felt sorry for him, I was sure I would never feel anything more toward him than an unwelcoming and frigid disgust.

We sat there a long time in the sunny room, waiting for Gisella and Riccardo to return. Astarita chain-smoked and he looked at me all the time through the clouds of smoke that enveloped him, with the eloquent gaze of a man who wants to say something but does not dare. I was sitting sideways at the table, with my legs crossed; the only desire in my heart was to get away. I did not feel tired, or ashamed of myself; if I wanted anything at all, it was to be alone and think over what had happened, at my leisure. This longing I had to be alone was side-tracked every now and again by silly things I noticed — the pearl in Astarita's tiepin, the pattern on the wallpaper, a fly walking around the edge of a glass, a little drop of tomato sauce that had splashed onto my blouse while I was eating, and I was annoyed with myself at being unable to think of anything more important. But this vacuity was of some use when Astarita, after a long silence, overcame his shyness and asked me, in a choking voice, "What are you thinking about?" I thought for a moment and then said simply, "One of my nails is broken and I can't think when or how I did it." It was true. But he looked at me bitterly and incredulously and from that moment definitely gave up any further attempt to talk to me.

At last, in God's good time, Gisella and Riccardo came back, looking a little worn out, but as cheerful and easygoing as before. They were surprised to find us so silent and solemn, but it was late now and lovemaking had made them calmer; it had quite a different effect upon them from what it had on Astarita. Gisella had even become affectionate to me, and no longer showed the cruelty and excitement she had before and after Astarita's blackmailing coup. I found myself almost believing his blackmail had contributed a new kind of sensual thrill to her relationship with Riccardo. She put her arm around my waist as we went downstairs. "Why are you making that face?" she murmured. "If you're worried about Gino, don't be — neither Riccardo nor I will talk to anyone about it."

"I'm tired," I lied. I was incapable of sulking, and her arm around my waist was enough to make my resentment fade.

"So am I," she answered. "I had the wind blowing in my face all the way here." A moment after, as we waited on the doorstep of the restaurant while the two men went toward the car, she spoke again.

"You aren't mad at me because of what happened?"

"Not at all," I answered. "What's it got to do with you?" Having got out of her little plot all the different kinds of satisfaction she could, she also wanted to be sure that I was not annoyed with her. I felt I understood her only too well. And for this reason, because I was afraid she might realize I understood her and be angry, I was anxious to dispel all her doubts and to make a show of affection toward her. I turned to her and kissed her on the cheek, saying, "Why should I be mad at you? You always said I ought to give up Gino and go with Astarita."

"That's it," she agreed emphatically. "I still think so. But I'm afraid you'll never forgive me."

She seemed anxious; and I, as if by some curious infection, was even more anxious than she was herself, for fear she might discover what I really felt.

"Obviously you don't really know me," I answered simply. "I know you want me to leave Gino because you're fond of me and you're sorry I don't do the best I can for myself. I might even say," I added, telling one more lie, "that perhaps you're right."

She was evidently satisfied and taking me by my arm said in conversational, but at the same time measured and confidential, tones, "You must understand what I mean. Astarita or anyone else would do — anyone but Gino! If you knew how it upsets me to see a beautiful girl like you throwing herself away! Ask Riccardo. I keep on at him all day long about you." She was chatting to me now without any embarrassment, as she usually did, and I was careful to agree with whatever she said. And so we reached the car. We took the places we had coming, and the car started up.

None of us spoke during the return journey. Astarita went on gazing at me, but with a look of humiliation rather than of desire. By now his gaze caused me no embarrassment and I felt no wish, as I had coming, to speak to him or to be pleasant. I breathed in the air that blew on my face from the open window and automatically counted the milestones that measured the distance from Rome. At a certain moment I felt Astarita's hand brush against mine and noticed he was trying to put something into it, a piece of paper, perhaps. I imagined that he had scribbled something to me because he did not dare to address me, but when I glanced down I saw that it was a banknote folded in four.

He looked at me fixedly while he tried to make me close my fingers over the note, and for a moment I was tempted to throw it in his face. But at the same time it occurred to me that such behavior would have been quite insincere, inspired by a spirit of imitation rather than by a deep impulse coming from the heart. The feeling I experienced at that moment bewildered me and, no matter how or when I have received money from men since, I have never again experienced it so clearly and so intensely. It was a feeling of complicity and sensual conspiracy such as none of Astarita's caresses in the restaurant bedroom had been able to rouse in me. It was a feeling of inevitable subjection that showed me in a flash an aspect of my own nature I had ignored until then. I knew, of course, that I ought to refuse the money, but at the same time I wanted to accept. And not so much from greed, as from the new kind of pleasure that this offering had afforded me.

Although I had decided to accept it, I made a movement as if my intention were to push back the note; I did this from instinct, with no shadow of calculation. Astarita insisted, still gazing into my eyes, and then I slipped the note from my right hand into my left. I felt strangely thrilled, my face was burning and my breathing labored. If

Astarita had been capable of guessing my feelings at that moment, he might have imagined I loved him. Nothing could have been further from the truth; it was only the money and the way it was earned and the way it was given me that filled my mind. I felt Astarita take my hand and I let him kiss it, then pulled it away. We did not look at one another again until we reached Rome.

Once back in town, we parted from each other almost as if we had been fugitives, as if each of us knew we had committed some crime and only wanted to get away and hide. As a matter of fact, something very like a crime had been committed that day, by all of us — by Riccardo through stupidity, by Gisella through envy, by Astarita through lust, and by me through inexperience. Gisella made a date with me for the following day to go and pose, Riccardo said good-night, Astarita could only press my hand silently, still as earnest and worried as ever. They took me as far as my own door. Despite my tiredness and remorse, I remember I could not help a feeling of satisfied vanity as I got out of the magnificent car at my own street door, under the very eyes of the family of the railwayman, our neighbors, who were looking out of their window.

I went and shut myself up in my own room, and the first thing I did was to look at the money. I found that there was not one, but three notes of a thousand lire each, and for a moment I felt almost happy as I sat on the edge of the bed. The money would not only pay the rest of the installments on the furniture, but would be enough for me to buy one or two other things I needed. I had never had so much money in my life before, and I could not stop fingering the notes and staring at them. My poverty made the sight of them not only delightful but almost incredible. I had to keep on looking longingly at these notes, as I had at my pieces of furniture, in order to convince myself that they really belonged to me.

5

MY LONG NIGHT'S DEEP SLEEP had obliterated, or so I thought, even the memory of my Viterbo adventure. Next day I awoke, my usual placid self, determined to persist in doing all I could to attain a normal family life. Gisella, whom I saw that morning, made no allusion to the trip, either out of remorse for what she had done or well-advised tact, and I was grateful to her for this. But I was becoming anxious about my next meeting with Gino. Although I was sure that I was not at all guilty, I knew that I would have to lie to him and I felt displeased at having to do this. I was not even sure whether I would be capable of doing it, because it would be the first time that I had not been absolutely straightforward with him. Of course, I had not told him that I had been seeing Gisella; my motives in this case had been so innocent that I had not even considered it a lie, but, rather, a resort to which I had been driven by his unreasonable dislike of her.

I was so worried that as soon as we met that day I found it difficult to prevent myself from bursting into tears, telling him everything and begging his forgiveness. The whole story of my trip to
Viterbo weighed heavily on me, and I longed to free myself by
talking about it. If Gino had been anyone else, and I had known
him to be less jealous, I would certainly have spoken of it, and
then, I thought, we would have loved one another more than ever,
and I would have felt cherished and bound to him by a tie stronger
than love itself. We were in the car as usual, in the usual suburban
avenue in the early morning. He noticed my uneasiness and asked
me what was the matter.

Now I'll tell him all about it — even if he kicks me out of the
car and I have to walk back into town, I thought. But I did not
have the courage and asked him instead whether he loved me.

"What a question!" he replied.

"Will you always love me?" I continued, my eyes brimming
over with tears.

"Always."

"Will we be married soon?"

He seemed irritated by my insistence.

"Really!" he exclaimed, "I might think you didn't trust me —
didn't we say we'd get married at Easter?"

"Yes, we did."

"Didn't I give you the money to set up house?"

"Yes."

"Well, then — am I the kind of man to keep my word, or not?
When I say a thing I do it. I bet it's your mother putting you up to
this."

"No, Mother's got nothing to do with it!" I denied, feeling
alarmed. "But tell me, will we live together?"

"Of course."

"And be happy?"

"It depends on us."

"Will we live together?" I repeated, unable to escape the recur-
rent thoughts my anxiety caused me.

"Oh, my God! You've already asked me, and I told you."

"I'm sorry," I said, "but sometimes it hardly seems possible."
Unable to control myself any longer, I began to cry. He was astonished at my tears, and also uneasy, but it was an uneasiness apparently filled with remorse, the reasons for which became clear to
me only much later on. "Come on, now!" he said. "What are you
crying for?"

I was crying really because of the bitterness and pain of being
unable to tell him what had happened and so freeing my conscience of the burden of regret. I was also crying because I felt humiliated at the thought that I was not good enough for anyone so
fine and perfect as he was. "You're right," I said at last with an effort, "I'm being stupid."

"I wouldn't say that — but I don't see what you've got to cry
about."

But that weight on my soul remained with me. That very afternoon, after I had left him, I went to church to make my confession. I had not been for nearly a year; I had known all along that I
could go at any time, and that had been enough for me. I had
given up going to confession when I kissed Gino for the first time.
I realized that, according to the church, my relations with Gino
were a sin, but since I knew we were going to get married, I did not
feel any remorse and meant to get absolution once and for all before my wedding.

I went to a little church in the heart of the city, the one with its
door between the entrance to a movie theater and the window of a
hosiery shop. It was almost pitch dark inside, except for the high
altar and a side chapel dedicated to the Madonna. It was a dirty,
neglected little church; the straw-bottomed chairs were pushed
here and there in the untidy way the congregation had left them
when they went out, and this made you think of some boring
meeting you'd heave a sigh of relief to get away from, rather than
of going to a Mass.

A feeble light falling from the apertures in the lantern of the
dome showed up the dust on the paved floor and the white cracks
in the yellow, mottled varnish of the imitation marble columns.
The numerous silver ex-voto tablets in the form of flaming hearts

that hung jostling each other on the walls created a gimcrack and melancholy impression. But a smell of stale incense in the air put heart into me. As a little girl, I had breathed in the same smell and the memories it awakened in me were all innocent and pleasurable. I seemed to be in a familiar spot, and although I had never been there before, I felt as if I had been frequenting that same church all my life.

But before confessing, I wanted to go into the side chapel where I had caught sight of a statue of the Virgin. I had been dedicated to the Virgin ever since the day of my birth. Mother even used to say that I looked like her, with my regular features and large, dark, gentle eyes. I had always loved the Madonna because she carried a baby in her arms and because her baby, who became a man, was killed; and she who bore him and loved him as any mother loves her son and suffered so when she saw him hanging on the cross. I often thought to myself that the Madonna, who had so many sorrows, was the only one who could understand my own sorrows, and as a child I used to pray to her alone, as the only one who could understand me. Besides, I liked the Madonna because she was so different from Mother, so serene and tranquil, richly clothed, with her eyes that looked on me so lovingly; it was as if she were my real mother instead of the mother who spent her time scolding me and was always worn out and badly dressed.

So I knelt down, and hiding my face in my hands, with my head bent, I said a long prayer to the Madonna in person, begging her to protect me, my mother, and Gino. Then I remembered it was my duty to bear no malice toward anyone and I called down the protection of the Madonna upon Gisella, and Riccardo, and in the end upon Astarita, too. I prayed longer for Astarita than for the others, just because I was full of resentment against him and I wanted to blot it out, to love him as I loved the others and forgive him and forget the harm he had done me. At length I felt so deeply moved that tears came to my eyes. I raised my eyes to the statue of the Madonna over the altar, and my tears were like a veil before me, so that the statue was misty and quivering as if seen through water, and the candles that glittered all round the statue made many little golden points, lovely to behold yet at the same time embittering, as are at certain times the stars we yearn to touch but know to be far beyond our reach. I remained for some time in contemplation of the Madonna, almost without seeing her; then the bitter tears began to trickle slowly from my eyes and roll down my face, tickling me, and I saw the Madonna looking at me, her baby in her arms, her face illuminated by the candle flames. She seemed to be looking at me with sympathy and compassion, and I thanked her in my heart. Then rising to my feet, my peace of mind restored, I went to confess.

The confessionals were all empty; but, while I was wandering around looking for a priest, I saw someone come out of a little door to the left of the high altar, pass in front of the altar, genuflect and cross himself, and make his way toward the other side. He was a monk, I did not know of what order, and summoning my courage I called out to him in a humble voice. He turned and came toward me at once. When he was nearby I saw that he was fairly young, tall and vigorous, with a rosy, fresh, and virile face framed by a sparse blond beard, blue eyes, and a high white forehead. I thought, almost involuntarily, that he was an extraordinarily good-looking man, of a kind rarely to be met with either in or out of church, and I was glad I was going to confess to him. I told him in an undertone what I wanted, then, making me a sign to follow him, he led the way to one of the confessionals.

He entered the box, and I went to kneel down in front of the grill. A small enameled plate nailed on to the confessional bore the name of Father Elia, and this name pleased and inspired faith in me. When I was on my knees, he said a short prayer and then asked me how long it was since I had last been to confession.

"Almost a year," I replied.

"That's a long time — too long. . . . Why?"

I noticed his Italian was not very good. He rolled his r's like the French do, and from one or two mistakes he made, adapting foreign words to Italian pronunciation, I realized he was French himself. I was glad that he was a foreigner, but I really could not have said why. Perhaps because when we are about to do anything we consider important, every unusual detail seems a sign of good omen.

I explained that the tale I was about to tell him would make it clear why I had gone so long without confession. After a short silence he asked me what I had to say. Then I began to tell him impulsively and trustingly of my relationship with Gino, my friendship with Gisella, the trip to Viterbo, Astarita's threat. Even while I was talking, I could not help wondering what impression my story would make on him. He was unlike most priests and his unusual appearance, as of a man of the world, set me thinking with curiosity what reasons could have led him to become one. It may seem strange that, after the extraordinary emotion my prayer to the Madonna had roused in me, I should be distracted to the point of asking myself questions about my confessor, but I do not think myself that there was any contradiction between my emotion and my curiosity. Both came from the bottom of my heart, where devotion and coquetry, sorrow and lust were inextricably mixed.

But, little by little, even while I was thinking about him in the way I have described, I experienced a feeling of relief and a comforting eagerness to tell him more, to confess everything. I felt uplifted and freed from the heavy sense of anguish that had weighed me down until then, as a flower wilting in the heat is revived at last by the first drops of rain. At first I spoke hesitantly and with difficulty; then my words began to flow more easily, and at last I spoke with emphatic sincerity and swelling hopes. I omitted nothing, not even the money Astarita had given me, the feelings the gift had awakened in me and the use I intended to make of it. He listened without comment and when I had finished said, "In order to avoid something you thought harmful, the breaking off of your engagement, you agreed to do yourself infinitely greater harm —"

"Yes, I know," I agreed, trembling, glad his sensitive fingers were probing my heart.

"As a matter of fact," he went on, as if talking to himself, "your engagement has nothing to do with it — when you gave way to this man, you yielded to a feeling of greed."

"Yes, yes!"

"Well, it was better for the marriage to be broken off than to do what you did."

"Yes, that's what I think now."

"That's not enough — you'll get married now, but at what cost to yourself? You'll no longer be able to be a good wife."

The inflexible harshness of his words struck me to the quick. "No, it isn't like that!" I exclaimed painfully. "For me, it's as though nothing had happened — I'm sure I'll be a good wife!"

He must have liked the sincerity of my reply. He was silent for some time and then went on more gently. "Are you sincerely penitent?"

"Yes, absolutely," I replied impetuously. It suddenly occurred to me that he might oblige me to give the money back to Astarita and although the idea of returning it was unpleasant in anticipation, nevertheless I would have obeyed him gladly, because the order came from someone I liked, who was able to dominate me in some strange way. But, without mentioning the money, he went on in his cold and distant voice to which the foreign accent added such a curiously warm overtone, "Now you must get married as soon as possible — you must put things straight — you must make your fiancé understand that you can't continue with him on the present terms."

"I have already told him that."

"What was his answer?"

I could not help smiling at the idea of him, so fair and handsome, asking me such a question from the shadows of the confessional.

"He says we'll get married at Easter," I replied with an effort.

"It would be better to get married at once. Easter's a long time yet," he replied after a moment's reflection, and this time he did not seem to be speaking as a priest but as a polite man of the world who was a little bored at having to busy himself with my affairs.

"We can't any earlier. I've got to make my trousseau, and he has to go home and tell his parents."

"Anyway," he continued, "he must marry you as soon as possible and until the wedding day you must give up all physical relations with your fiancé. This is a grave sin. Do you understand me?"

"Yes, I'll do it."

"You will?" he repeated doubtfully. "In any case, strengthen yourself against temptation through prayer — try to pray."

"Yes, I'll pray."

"As for the other man," he continued, "you mustn't see him for any reason whatsoever. This should not be difficult since you don't love him. If he insists, if he comes to see you, send him away."

I told him I would do that; and after much further advice pronounced in his cold and distant voice, which was nevertheless so charming to listen to, with its foreign pronunciation and the impression it gave of an education, he told me to say a number of prayers every day as a penance, and then gave me absolution. But before sending me away he made me say a Pater Noster with him. I gladly agreed because I was sorry to go away and hadn't yet heard enough of his voice.

"Our Father which art in Heaven," he said.

"Our Father which art in Heaven."

"Hallowed be thy name."

"Hallowed be thy name."

"Thy kingdom come."

"Thy kingdom come."

"Thy will be done on Earth, as it is in Heaven."

"Thy will be done on Earth, as it is in Heaven."

"Give us this day our daily bread."

"Give us this day our daily bread."

"And forgive us our trespasses as we forgive those who trespass against us."

"And forgive us our trespasses as we forgive those who trespass against us."

"And lead us not into temptation, but deliver us from evil."

"And lead us not into temptation, but deliver us from evil."

"Amen."

"Amen."

I have given the prayer in full in order to recapture my feelings when I said it after him. It was as if I were a tiny girl again and he was leading me by the hand from one phrase to the next. Meanwhile, however, I was thinking of the money Astarita had given me and felt almost disappointed that he had not told me to return it. I really would have liked him to order me to do so, because I wanted to give him concrete proof of my obedience and repentance, wanted to do something for him that would have been a real sacrifice. I got up when the prayer was at an end and he, too, came out of the confessional and started to leave, without looking at me and with only the very slightest nod in farewell. Then, without thinking what I was doing and almost despite myself, I pulled him by the sleeve. He stopped and looked at me with his clear, tranquil, inexpressive eyes.

He seemed even handsomer than ever to me and a thousand crazy ideas passed through my mind. I felt I could fall in love with him and wondered how I could manage to let him understand that I liked him. But at the same time my conscience warned me that I was in a church and he was a priest and my confessor. My mind was in turmoil with all these thoughts and images, which assailed me at one and the same time, so I was unable to speak for a moment.

"Is there anything else you want to tell me?" he asked, after waiting for as long as might reasonably be expected.

"I wanted to know whether I ought to give that man his money back," I said.

He glanced rapidly at me, a look that seemed to penetrate to the depths of my soul, it was so sharp and direct, then answered shortly, "Do you need it very much?"

"Yes."

"Well, then — you need not give it back — but in any case, do as your conscience tells you."

He said this in a particular tone, as if he meant to imply that our meeting was over, and I stammered my thanks without smiling, gazing into his eyes as I did so. I had really lost my head at the moment and almost hoped he would show me by some gesture or word that he was not indifferent to me. He certainly understood the meaning of my look, and a slight expression of amazement crossed his face. He made a little gesture of farewell and went away, turning his back on me, and leaving me standing by the confessional, confused and thoroughly upset.

I did not tell Mother anything about my confession, just as I had told her nothing of the Viterbo trip. I knew she had very set ideas about priests and religion; she said they were fine things, but the rich stayed rich and the poor stayed poor all the same. "The rich know how to pray better than we do, you can see that," she used to say. Her ideas on religion were like her ideas about family and marriage. She had once been religious herself and used to go to church, but everything had gone badly for her all the same, so she did not believe in it anymore. Once I told her our reward would come in the next world, and she became furious, telling me she wanted hers in this one, now, immediately, and if she didn't get it, that meant the whole thing was a pack of lies.

Next morning as I got into the car Gino told me his employers were going away and we would be able to meet at the villa for a few days. My first impulse was one of joy, because I liked lovemaking and liked it with Gino, as I believe I have already made clear.

But all at once I remembered my promise to the priest.

"I can't," I said.

"Why not?"

"Because it's impossible."

"All right, then," he said forebearingly, with a sigh, "tomorrow then."

"No, not even tomorrow — never again."

"Never!" he repeated in a low voice, pretending to amazed. "That's how it is now, is it? Never! You might at least explain why."

His face was full of jealous suspicion. "Gino," I said hurriedly. "I love you and haven't ever loved you so much as I do now — but just because I love you I've made up my mind that there shouldn't be anything like that between us again until we're married — I mean no lovemaking."

"Ah, now it all comes clear!" he said scornfully. "You're afraid I won't want to marry you."

"No, I'm sure you'll marry me. If I didn't think so, I wouldn't be making such preparations and wouldn't spend Mother's money that she's been saving all her life."

"What a big deal you make of your mother's money!" he said. He had become really unpleasant and I could hardly recognize him. "Why, then?"

"I went to confession, and the priest told me I mustn't make love with you anymore until we're married."

He made a gesture of disappointment and a word escaped him that sounded to me like an oath. "What business has that priest to stick his nose into our affairs?"

I preferred to remain silent.

"Why don't you say anything?" he insisted.

"I haven't anything more to say."

I must have seemed absolutely determined, because he suddenly changed his mind. "All right," he said, "anything you say. . . . Do you want me to take you back into town?"

"If you will."

I must say this was the only time he was unpleasant and unkind to me. By the following day he seemed resigned and was his usual affectionate self, full of polite attentions. So we continued to meet every day as before, except that we did not make love anymore but only talked to one another. Every now and again I gave him a kiss, although he had made it a point of honor not to ask me for one. I did not feel kissing him was really a sin, because, after all, we were engaged and soon to be married. When I think over that time nowadays, I imagine Gino was led to resign himself so quickly to his new part as a respectful fiancé by the hope of gradually diminishing the warmth of our relationship and bringing me, little by little, to a kind of rupture, almost without my being aware of the fact. A lot of girls, without realizing what is happening find themselves free once more after long and exhausting engagements, with no harm done except that the best part of their youth has passed. All unawares, when I told him of the priest's injunction, I had given him the excuse he was undoubtedly seeking to ease up our engagement. He certainly would never have had the courage by himself since he had a weak, selfish character, and the pleasure he derived from our relationship was greater than his desire to abandon me. The confessor's intervention gave him an opportunity to adopt a hypocritical and apparently disinterested solution.

After some time he began to meet me less often, only every other day. And I noticed that our trips in the car were briefer each time, and he was more and more absentminded when I talked of our plans for getting married. But although I vaguely sensed this change in his attitude, I suspected nothing, since these were only small things, trivialities, and he continued to behave in his usual kindly, affectionate way to me. One day he told me, with an apologetic look on his face, that for family reasons he would have to postpone the date of our marriage until after the summer.

"Are you awfully upset?" he added, seeing that I made no comment on what he had said, and only looked in front of me with a bitter, blank expression.

"No, no —" I said, pulling myself together, "— it doesn't matter — it can't be helped. It'll give me time to finish my trousseau."

"You're lying. You do mind a lot." It was odd how he wanted me to be upset at the postponement of our wedding.

"I don't."

"Then, if you aren't upset it means you don't really love me, and maybe actually you wouldn't mind if we never got married at all."

"Don't talk like that!" I exclaimed in alarm. "It would be terrible for me. I don't even want to think of it."

At that time I failed to understand the expression that passed across his face. Actually, he had wanted to test my affection and had realized to his dismay that it was still very strong.

Although the postponement of my marriage was not enough to rouse my own suspicions, it strengthened Mother's and Gisella's original convictions. Mother made no comment on the news at all, as was sometimes her way (and this was strange behavior on her part, given her violent and impulsive nature). But one evening while she was giving me my supper as usual, standing silently watchful for what I might need, I made some reference to the wedding.

"Do you know what they used to call a girl like you, in my day, a girl who keeps on waiting to get married and never does?"

I went pale and felt faint. "What?"

"A girl in the cooler," said Mother placidly. "He's keeping you in the cooler like leftover meat. But sometimes meat goes bad through being kept and then it gets thrown away."

I was enraged. "It isn't true!" I said. "It's the first time we've put it off, and only for a few months. The fact is you're furious with Gino because he's a chauffeur and not a gentleman."

"I'm not furious with anyone."

"Yes, you are — and because you had to spend money on the room for us, but you don't need to worry."

"Love's made you stupid, my girl!"

"Don't worry, I tell you — he'll pay back all the rest of the installments, and we'll give you every penny you've spent. Look." Carried away by passion I opened my bag and showed her the banknotes Astarita had given me. "That's money of his," I went on, and I was so infatuated that I almost believed my own lies. "He gave me this — and he'll give me more."

She gaped at the money and put on a sorry, disappointed look that filled me with remorse. I had not been so unkind to her for a long time now; and also I knew perfectly well that I had been lying and that Gino had not really given me the money at all. Without saying a word, she cleared the table, took up the plates, and went out of the room. After a moment's angry reflection, I got up and followed her. I saw her from the back, standing upright in front of the sink busy washing the plates, which she put down one by one on the marble drainboard, her head and shoulders slightly bowed, and I felt a rush of pity for her. Impulsively I threw my arms around her neck. "Forgive me for what I said," I pleaded. "I didn't really think it. But when you talk about Gino that way, you drive me out of my mind."

"Go on — leave me alone," she answered, pretending to struggle with me to free herself from my embrace.

"But you've got to understand!" I added passionately. "If Gino doesn't marry me, I'll either kill myself or go on the streets."

Gisella took the news that my marriage had been postponed in much the same way that Mother had done. We were in her furnished room when I told her. I was sitting fully clothed on the edge of the bed, and she was in her nightgown combing her hair in front of the dressing table. She let me get to the end without comment, then said with triumphant assurance, "You see, I was right."

"Why?"

"He doesn't want to marry you and won't ever marry you. Now it isn't going to be at Easter but at All Saints — then it'll be put off until Christmas — and then one day you'll get it in your head at last and you'll be the one to leave him."

Her words made me angry and unhappy. But I had already let myself go with Mother, so to speak, and anyway I knew that if I were to say what I thought, I would have to break off my friendship with Gisella. I did not want to do this, because she was, after all, my only friend. I ought to have said what I thought: that she did not want me to get married because she knew Riccardo would never marry her. This was the truth, but it was too spiteful a thing to say and I did not think it was fair to hurt Gisella just because she could not help giving way to her own feelings of envy and jealousy when she spoke of Gino.

I contented myself with saying, "Let's not talk about it any more, all right? It doesn't really matter to you whether I get married or not — and it hurts me to talk about it."

She suddenly left her place at the dressing table and came to sit beside me on the bed. "What do you mean — it doesn't matter to me?" she protested. "It matters a lot to me to see you being led by the nose like this," she added, putting her arm round my waist.

"But I'm not!" I said in a low voice.

"And I'd like to see you happy," she continued. She was silent for a moment. "By the way," she then said casually, "Astarita is always bothering me because he wants to see you again — he says he can't live without you — he's really in love with you! Do you want me to make a date for you with him?"

"Don't mention Astarita to me," I said.

"He realized he behaved badly on that trip we took to Viterbo," she continued, "but it was only because he loves you — he insists on seeing you, speaking to you. Why shouldn't you meet in a café, for instance, with me there, too?"

"No," I replied decisively. "I don't want to see him."

"You'll be sorry."

"You go out with Astarita!"

"I would like a shot, my dear! He's a generous man and he doesn't care what he spends — but he wants you; it's a fixation with him."

"Yes, I know, but I don't want him."

She continued arguing in Astarita's favor, but I would not let myself be persuaded. Just because I was afraid Gisella and Mother might be right and for some reason or other my marriage might come to nothing, I clung to the idea of marriage with an even greater and more tenacious hope.

6

EANWHILE, I HAD PAID OFF ALL the installments on the furniture and had begun to work even harder than ever to earn more money to pay for my trousseau. In the morning I posed in the studios, in the afternoon I shut myself in the living room with Mother and sewed until nightfall. She worked at the sewing machine, by the window, and I sat a little way off at the table, sewing by hand. Mother had taught me to be a seamstress, and I have always been very quick and good at it. There were always a number of buttonholes and eyelets to make and reinforce, and every shirt had to be initialed. I knew how to do initials particularly well, raised and firm, so that they seemed to stand out against the material. We specialized in men's wear, but sometimes we would make a blouse or chemise or a pair of women's underwear, but it was only cheap stuff because Mother did not know how to embroider and did not know any ladies who would give her orders.

While I was sewing, my mind wandered among thoughts of Gino, marriage, the Viterbo trip, Mother, my own life in fact, and the time passed quickly. What Mother used to think about I never knew, but she certainly thought about something, because when she was working the machine she always looked furious and if I spoke to her usually answered crossly. Toward evening, as soon as it began to get dark, I got up, shook off the ends of cotton and after I had put on my best clothes, I used to go out and meet Gisella, or, when he was off duty, Gino. I wonder today whether I was really happy. In a certain sense I was, because I was longing for something that I thought was near and attainable. Since then I have discovered that real unhappiness comes when all hope is gone, and then it is no use being well-off and in need of nothing.

More than once at this time, I noticed that I was being followed through the streets by Astarita. This used to happen very early in the morning when I was on my way to the studios. Astarita usually waited for me to come out, standing in a recess in the city wall on the opposite side of the road. He never crossed over, and while I walked hurriedly toward the square, skirting the houses, he contented himself with following me at a slower pace, hugging the walls. He was watching me, I suppose, and that was enough for him: behavior typical of a man so deeply in love. When I reached the square, he went and stood at the streetcar stop, just facing me. He continued to watch me, but I had only to look at him for him to grow embarrassed and pretend to be gazing up the road to see if the streetcar was coming. No woman can remain indifferent in the face of love of this nature; and even I, although I was determined never to speak to him, sometimes felt a flattered kind of pity for him. Then, depending on the day, either Gino or the streetcar would come along, and I would either get in with Gino or into the streetcar, and Astarita would be left where he stood, watching me as I vanished into the distance.

One evening when I reached home, I found Astarita standing hat in hand in the living room, leaning against the table and chatting with Mother. I forgot all pity and was filled with anger at seeing him in my house, especially when I thought what he might be saying to Mother to win her over to plead with me on his behalf.

"What are you doing here?" I asked.

He gazed at me and his face began to twitch convulsively, as it had in the car on the way to Viterbo when he told me he liked me. But this time he was unable even to speak. "This gentleman says he knows you," Mother began confidentially. "He wanted to see how you were." I realized from her tone that Astarita had talked to her exactly as I had thought he would, and probably had even given her money. "Do me a favor, get out of here," I said to her. She was alarmed, for my voice was almost savage, and went out into the kitchen without replying.

"What are you doing here? Go away!" I again said to Astarita. He looked at me and appeared to move his lips, but said nothing. His eyelids drooped right over his eyes, and I could almost see the whites; he looked to me as thought he might fall right down in a fit. "Go away," I repeated loudly, stamping on the floor, "otherwise I'll call out for help — I'll call a friend of ours who lives below."

I have often asked myself why Astarita did not try to blackmail me a second time by threatening to tell Gino what had happened at Viterbo if I did not yield to him. He could have blackmailed me with more likelihood of success this time, because he really had had me; there were witnesses and I could not deny it. I have come to the conclusion that the first time he only desired me and the second he loved me. Love longs to be reciprocated, and now that Astarita loved me, he must have felt how unsatisfactory his possession of me had been that day at Viterbo, when I lay dumb and inert like a corpse. But this time I was determined at all costs to let the truth come out; after all, if Gino loved me, he ought to understand me and forgive me. My determination must have convinced Astarita that a second attempt at blackmail would certainly be useless.

When I threatened to call for help, he said nothing, but, dragging his hat along the table, he went off toward the door. When he had reached the end of the table, he stopped and lowered his head, looking as though he were pulling himself together in order to speak to me. But when he raised his head once more and moved his lips, his courage seemed to fail him and he remained silent, staring at me. This second gaze seemed endless. Then with a nod he left me, shutting the door behind him.

I immediately went out to Mother in the kitchen.

"What did you tell that man?" I asked furiously.

"Nothing!" she replied in a fright. "He asked me what work we did; he told me he wanted me to make him some shirts."

"If you work for him I'll kill you!" I cried.

She looked at me in terror. "Who says I'm going to work for him? He can get someone else to make his shirts!" she replied.

"Didn't he speak about me?"

"He asked me when you were getting married."

"What did you tell him?"

"I said you were getting married in October."

"He didn't give you any money?"

"No, why?" She looked at me, feigning astonishment. "Should he have?"

I was sure from the tone of her voice that Astarita had given her money. I ran to her and seized her violently by the arm. "Tell me the truth . . . did he give you money?"

"No, he didn't give me anything."

Her hand was in her apron pocket. I seized her wrist violently and a banknote folded in two fell out of her open hand. Although I still had hold of her, she bent down and picked it up so greedily and so possessively that my fury subsided all at once. I remembered the agitation and delight Astarita's money had caused me the day we went to Viterbo, and I felt I had no right to condemn Mother because she had the same feelings and yielded to the same temptation. Now I wished I had not questioned her, had not seen the banknote. I contented myself with saying in a normal tone, "You see, he did give you something." And without waiting for her explanation, I left the kitchen. From some hints she let fall at dinner, I understood that she wanted to begin to talk again about Astarita and the money, but I changed the subject and she did not insist.

Next day Gisella came without Riccardo to the pastry shop where we used to meet.

"I have something very important to tell you today," she said without any preliminaries as soon as she sat down.

A kind of presentiment made me grow pale. "If it's bad news, please don't tell me," I said faintly.

"It's neither good nor bad," she said eagerly. "It's just a piece of news, that's all. I've already told you who Astarita is — "

"I don't want to hear anything about Astarita — "

"Now listen! Don't be such a child! Astarita's a very important person, as I told you before, one of the high-ups. He's a big shot in the political police."

I felt a little reassured, since after all I had nothing to do with politics. "It doesn't matter to me what Astarita is, even if he's a minister."

"Oh, you're so — " exclaimed Gisella. "Just listen, instead of butting in all the time. Astarita told me you simply must go to see him at the Ministry. He's got to talk to you — not about love," she added hurriedly, seeing I was about to protest. "He's got to tell you something very important — something that concerns you."

"Something that concerns me?"

"Yes. Something for your own good. At least, that's what he said."

What made me decide that this time I would accept Astarita's invitation, after so many refusals, I do not know myself. "Very well, I'll go," I said, feeling more dead than alive.

Gisella was rather disconcerted by my passivity. For the first time she noticed how pale and frightened I was.

"What's the matter?" she asked. "Is it because he's in the police? He's not after you! What are you scared of? He doesn't want to arrest you!"

I got up, although I felt dizzy. "All right," I said, "I'll go. Which Ministry is it?"

"Home Office. Just in front of the Supercinema. But listen — "

"At what time?"

"Any time in the morning. But listen — "

"Good-bye."

I slept very little that night. I could not understand what Astarita wanted of me, outside his own passion, but an intuition that seemed infallible to me told me it could not be anything good. The place he summoned me to led me to think it must be something to do with the police. I knew, on the other hand, as all poor people do, that when the police get going, it is never for your good, and after I had examined my own behavior in every detail, I came to the conclusion that Astarita wanted to blackmail me again by using some information he had obtained concerning Gino. I did not know anything about Gino's life, and it might be that he was politically compromised. I had never troubled myself with politics, but I was not so ignorant as not to know that there were a number of people who had no liking for the Fascist government, and that men like Astarita had the task of hunting out such enemies of the regime. My imagination depicted for me in vivid colors the dilemma Astarita would place me in: I would either have to give in to him again or let Gino go to prison. My anguish was caused by the fact that, while I did not at all want to satisfy Astarita, I did not want Gino to go to jail either. I felt no further pity for Astarita as I pondered over these matters, but only hatred. He seemed a low and vile creature to me, unfit to live, who deserved only merciless punishment. And it is true that among other projected solutions to my problem that night, I even contemplated murdering Astarita. But this was a morbid, half-waking fantasy rather than a solution; and, in fact, it kept me company until morning, like any fantasy that never properly develops into an objective and firm determination. I saw myself putting a sharp, pointed clasp knife with a sheath, which Mother used for peeling potatoes, into my purse, going to Astarita, hearing the invitation I feared, and then plunging the knife into his neck with all the strength of my muscular arm, just between his ear and white starched collar. I saw myself leaving the room, pretending to be absolutely calm and then running to hide at Gisella's or at some other friend's place. But although I went over these bloodthirsty scenes in my imagination, I knew all the time that I would never be capable of putting any one of them into action.

I dozed off toward dawn and slept a little, then day broke, I got up and went to my usual appointment with Gino.

"Tell me," I said as soon as we met in the suburban avenue after the usual greetings, trying to make my voice sound as casual as possible, "have you ever had anything to do with politics?"

"Politics? How do you mean?"

"I mean doing anything against the government."

He looked at me knowingly. "Tell me something," he said, "do I look like a fool to you?"

"No, but —"

"No, no — let's get this clear! Do I look like a fool?"

"No," I said, "you don't look like one, but —"

"All right, then," he said, "why the devil do you think I'd have anything to do with politics?"

"I don't know, but sometimes —"

"Forget it! You can tell whoever threw out any hints that Gino Molinari's not a damn fool."

At about eleven o'clock, after having wandered around the Ministry for more than an hour, unable to make up my mind to enter, I approached the porter and asked for Astarita. First I had to go up a wide marble staircase, then a smaller but still extremely wide one, then I was accompanied along a number of corridors into an anteroom with three doors leading into it. I had always associated the word "police" with the mean, filthy offices of the local branches, and was therefore astonished by the magnificence of the place where Astarita worked. The anteroom was vast, with a mosaic floor and old pictures such as you see in churches; leather chairs stood about against the walls and a huge table filled the center of the room.

Uneasy at such splendor, I could not help thinking that Gisella might be right — Astarita really must be someone important. His importance was impressed upon me by an unexpected occurrence. I had only just sat down, when one of the doors opened and a tall and beautiful, if no longer young, lady came out, dressed all in black, very smart, with a little veil over her face; she was followed by Astarita. I got up, thinking it was my turn. But after Astarita had made me a sign with his hand, as if to let me know that he had seen me, but that it was not quite my turn yet, he continued speaking to the lady in the doorway. Then, having accompanied her to the middle of the room, he bowed to her, kissed her hand, then left her, after making a sign to another person who was in the anteroom with me, an old man dressed in black with a little white beard and spectacles who looked like a professor. When Astarita beckoned, he rose immediately and hastened after him, humbly and eagerly. The two of them disappeared into the room, and I was left alone.

What had struck me most during Astarita's brief appearance had been the difference in his manner from what it had been on the Viterbo trip. Then I had see him looking awkward, convulsed, dumb, and half-crazed; now he seemed entirely master of himself, easy-mannered but precise, exuding an indefinable sense of discreet though authoritative superiority. Even his voice had changed. During the trip he had spoken in low, warm, strangled tones, but while he was speaking to the lady with the veil, his voice had sounded clear, cold, measured, calm. He was dressed as usual in dark gray, with a high white collar that gave his head a rigid look, but on this occasion his suit and collar, which I had noticed during the trip without giving them any special significance, seemed as perfectly matched as a uniform to the huge room with its severe, heavy furniture, and the silence and order that reigned there. Gisella was right, I thought, he really must be someone who counted for a great deal, and only love could explain his awkward manner and sense of inferiority with regard to me.

These reflections took my mind off my earlier feelings of agitation, so that when the door opened after a few minutes and the old man came out, I felt sufficiently in control of myself. But this time Astarita did not come to beckon me from the doorway. A bell rang, a servant went in to see what Astarita wanted and shut the door behind him, then returned, and, after having asked my name in a low voice, he said I could go in. I got up and went casually toward the room.

Astarita's office was a room not much smaller than the anteroom. It was empty except for a sofa and two leather armchairs in one corner, and in another a large table, at which Astarita was seated. Two white-curtained windows let in a cold, sunless light, so still and sad that it reminded me of Astarita's voice when he was talking to the lady with the veil. There was a huge soft carpet on the floor and two or three pictures hung on the walls. I can remember one of them: it was of an expanse of green fields bounded on the horizon by a chain of rocky mountains.

As I have said, Astarita was sitting behind a large table, and when I entered, he did not even look up from the papers he was reading or pretending to read. I say "pretending" because I felt sure that this was all a show intended to intimidate me and fill me with a sense of his authority and importance. In fact, when I drew near to the table, I saw that the paper he was studying so attentively contained only three or four lines with a scribbled signature below them. Besides, his agitation was revealed by the way the hand on which he was leaning his forehead, between two fingers of which he held a lighted cigarette, was visibly trembling. This trembling caused some of the ash to fall on the sheet of paper he was examining so closely and with such artificial attention.

I placed my hand on the edge of the table and said, "Here I am."

At these words, as if at a signal, he stopped reading, jumped to his feet and came around to greet me, taking my two hands in his. And all this, done in perfect silence, contrasted strangely with the authoritative and unconcerned attitude he was trying to maintain. As a matter of fact, as I soon learned, my voice alone had been enough to make him forget the part he had prepared himself to play; and his usual state of agitation had then irresistibly overwhelmed him. He kissed my hands, first one then the other, gazed at me while rolling his melancholy and lovelorn eyes, and made as if to speak, but his lips trembled and he was forced to remain silent.

"You've come," he said at last in the low, strangled voice I recognized as his.

Now I, perhaps by contrast with Astarita's attitude, felt full of self-assurance. "Yes, I've come," I said. "Actually, I shouldn't have — what have you got to tell me?"

"Come and sit down over here," he murmured. He had never let go of my hand and, still pressing it tightly, he led me to the sofa. I sat down, and all at once he knelt in front of me, put his two arms around my legs and pressed his forehead so hard against me that he hurt me, and after remaining for a long time like this, he lifted his bald head upward as though he wanted to lay it on my lap. I made a move as if to get up. "You had something important to tell me — say it, or I'll go away," I declared.

With an effort he got to his feet, sat beside me and took my hand.

"It's nothing," he murmured. "I wanted to see you again." I moved to get up once more, but he caught hold of me. "Yes," he added, "but I also wanted to tell you that you and I need to come to an understanding."

"In what way?"

"I love you," he said hurriedly. "I love you so much. . . . Come and live with me in my house, you can be mistress there . . . just as if you were my wife. . . . I'll buy clothes, jewels, anything you like, for you —"

He seemed crazed, the words poured confusedly out of his mouth while his lips remained almost motionless and twisted. "So that's why you made me come up here?" I asked coldly.

"Don't you want to?"

"I won't even discuss it."

Oddly enough, he said not a word to my reply. But he raised his hand and, almost hypnotizing me with his crazy, fixed stare, he stroked my face as if he wanted to memorize its shape. His fingers were light, and I could feel them trembling while the tips traced my face from the forehead to the cheek and back again. For a moment I was almost moved by compassion to say something less final and chilling to him, but he gave me no time. As soon as he had finished caressing me, he got up and spoke in halting and precise tones, a curious mixture of suppressed desire and some new and unknown sense of duty.

"Just a minute, though," he said. "I really have got something important to tell you." Meanwhile, he went back to the table and picked up a red folder.

It was my turn to become agitated when I saw him coming toward me with this red folder. "What is it?" I asked him faintly.

"It's — it's —" It was strange how the authoritative and official note in his voice became all mixed with his excitement "— it's some information about your fiancé."

"Oh!" I said, and for a moment, frightened to death, I shut my eyes. Astarita did not notice; he was turning over the pages and in his agitation was crumpling them.

"Gino Molinari, isn't he?"

"Yes."

"You're getting married in October, aren't you?"

"Yes."

"But Gino Molinari appears to be married already," he continued, "and, to be precise, to Antonietta Partini, the daughter of the late Emilio and Diomira Lavagna — for four years already. . . . They've got a child called Maria. . . . At the present time his wife is living in Orvieto with her mother."

I said nothing, but got up from the sofa and walked to the door. Astarita remained standing in the middle of the room, with the papers in his hand. I opened the door and went out.

I can remember that when I found myself in the street, among the crowds, on a fine and cloudy day of that mild winter, I felt with bitter certainty that my life, like a river that has been artificially turned from its course for a brief period, had begun once more to flow in its usual direction, without change or novelty, after an interruption caused by my hopes and the preparations for my marriage. Perhaps this sensation was due in part to the fact that in my bewilderment I was looking around me with a gaze shorn of its original bright hopefulness. The crowd, the shops, the streets, appeared to me, for the first time in many months, in a pitilessly objective light, neither beautiful nor ugly, neither interesting nor dull, but just as they were — as they must appear to a drunkard when his state of intoxication is past. But more probably it derived from my realization that the normal things of life were not, as I had supposed, my plans for happiness, but the exact opposite — I mean, all those things that are inimical to planning and programs are casual, faulty, and unforeseen agents of disillusionment and sorrow. If this were true, as I thought it must be, I had undoubtedly begun that morning to live again, after a state of intoxication lasting several months.

This was the only thought the discovery of Gino Molinari's deceit aroused in me. I did not dream of blaming him and did not really feel any deep sense of injury toward him. I had not been led astray without my own complicity. And the memory of the pleasure I had enjoyed in his arms was too recent for me not to try to find excuses, if not justification, for his lying. I supposed he had been weak rather than wicked, carried away as he was by desire, and that the fault, if fault there was, lay with my beauty, which made men lose their heads and forget all their scruples and obligations. In the long run Gino was no more to blame than Astarita, only he had used fraud whereas Astarita had used blackmail. Both of them loved me very much, and certainly would have preferred to possess me by legal means if they could, and would have secured for me that modest form of happiness that I had set my heart on. Fate, on the contrary, had led me, in my beauty, to meet the very men who could not obtain that kind of happiness for me. Unfortunately, even if there was no one to blame, there was most decidedly a victim, and that was myself.

This way of reasoning and arguing may seem feeble to some, after such a betrayal as Gino's. But every time I have been hurt, and I often have been, because of my poverty, innocence, and loneliness, I have always tried to find excuses for the wrongdoer and to forget the harm done me as quickly as possible. If the hurt changes me at all, I do not show it in my conduct and outward appearance, but far more deeply in my soul, which closes in upon itself like healthy flesh attempting as soon as possible to heal a wound. But scars remain and these almost unconscious wounds in the soul are always permanent.

With Gino the same thing happened. I bore him no grudge, not even for a moment, but within me I felt many things were shattered forever — my respect for him, my hopes of establishing a family, my desire not to admit that Gisella and Mother were right, my religious faith or at least the kind of belief I had held until then. I compared myself with a doll I had had when I was little — after I had beaten her and dragged her about all day long, I felt a kind of lump inside her, a sinister creaking, although her face was still as rosy and smiling as ever. I unscrewed her head, and little scraps of china, string, screws, and the works that made her talk and move her eyes about all tumbled out of her neck, together with odd pieces of wood and shreds of stuff whose function remained a mystery to me.

Stunned but calm, I returned home, and that afternoon went about my usual business, without telling Mother what had happened or the conclusions I had reached as a result. But I realized that I could not pretend to the extent of sewing my trousseau as I had done on other days. I picked up the things I had already made and those I still had to do and locked them away in the closet in my room. Mother could not help noticing I was unhappy, which was unusual, because I am nearly always gay and thoughtless. But I told her I was tired, as indeed I was. Toward evening, while Mother was sewing on her machine, I left my work, went into my room and stretched myself on the bed. I realized I was looking at the furniture, which I had finished paying for and was really mine now, thanks to Astarita's money, with very different feelings than before, without pleasure or hope. I did not feel unhappy but only tired and indifferent, as you do after some enormous but entirely useless effort you have made. I was physically tired, anyway, aching in all my limbs, with a deep longing for rest. Thinking in a confused way about my furniture and how impossible it would be to use it now as I had hoped, I fell asleep fully dressed on the bed. I slept soundly for about four hours, a deep, sorrowful sleep, woke up very late and called Mother out of the darkness that surrounded me. She ran in to me at once and told me she had been unwilling to wake me because she had seen me sleeping so peacefully and contentedly. "Supper's been ready for an hour," she added, standing there and looking at me. "What are you doing? Won't you come and have something to eat?"

"I don't want to get up," I answered, covering my dazzled eyes with one arm. "Why don't you bring it in to me?"

She went out and returned shortly after with a tray bearing my usual supper. She put the tray on the edge of the bed, and I pulled myself up and, leaning on one elbow, began to eat, without any appetite. But after the first few mouthfuls, I stopped eating and flung myself back on the pillows again. "What's the matter? Why aren't you eating anything?" Mother asked.

"I'm not hungry."

"Aren't you well?"

"I'm perfectly well."

"I'll take it away then," she grumbled. She lifted the tray off the bed and went to put it on the table near the window.

"Don't wake me tomorrow morning." I continued after a moment.

"Why?"

"Because I've made up my mind I'm not going to be a model anymore — you work too hard and earn too little."

"What'll you do?" she asked anxiously. "I can't keep you — you're not a child and you need a lot — and then there's so much to buy — your trousseau. . . ." She began to wail and moan.

"Don't bother me now," I said, slowly and wearily, without removing my arm from my face. "Don't worry, there'll always be enough money."

A lengthy silence followed. "Don't you want anything?" she asked at last, humiliated and anxious, like a maid who has been reprimanded for being too familiar and is hoping to be forgiven.

"Yes, please. Help me to undress. I'm so tired and I'm still so sleepy."

She obeyed and sitting on the bed took off my shoes and stockings, which she placed tidily on a chair at the foot of the bed. Then she took off my dress and helped me slip into my night-gown. I kept my eyes shut all the time, and as soon as I was under the covers, I curled up and hid my head in the sheet. Mother wished me good-night from the doorway when she had switched off the light, but I did not reply. I fell asleep again at once and slept all night, well into the morning.

Next morning I should have gone to my usual appointment with Gino, but when I woke up I realized I did not want to see him until the pain has passed and I was able to consider his treachery objectively, from a distance, like something that had happened to someone else, not to myself. Then, as always, I mistrusted things said and done under the stress of emotion, especially when the emotion as in my case, was not one of liking and affection. Certainly I did not love Gino any longer, but I did not want to hate him, exactly, because I thought that in doing so I would only burden my soul with a painful emotion, unworthy of me; and this in addition to the harm he had already done me through his betrayal.

In any case, I felt a kind of sensuous laziness that morning and was less unhappy than I had been the evening before. Mother had gone out early, and I knew she would not come back before midday. So I lingered in bed, and this was my first pleasure at the beginning of a new phase in my life from which I wished nothing but pleasure. Every day since childhood, I had got up in the early hours, and lying idly in bed without doing anything was a real luxury for me. I had never indulged myself, but now I made up my mind to lie in bed whenever I felt like it, and I planned to act in the same way about all the things I had rejected, up until now, on the grounds of my poverty and my dreams of a respectable family life. I thought how I enjoyed lovemaking and money and the things money can provide, and I told myself that, from now on, I would never refuse love or money or what money could bring, if I had the chance. Do not imagine that I thought these things heatedly, in resentment and a spirit of revenge. I was quite dispassionate as I lay there caressing the idea and enjoying it in anticipation. Every situation, no matter how unpleasant, has its reverse side. For the moment, I had lost marriage and all the modest advantages I had contemplated, but in return I had regained my freedom. My deepest hopes remained unchanged, certainly; but still, the easy life attracted me very much and its glittering prospect concealed from me all the sadness and resignation that lay behind my new resolve. Gisella's and Mother's sermons began to bear fruit. The whole time, although I had been living a virtuous life, I had known that my beauty was such as to be able to earn me anything I wanted, if I would only make up my mind. That morning was the first time I considered my body as a very convenient means for achieving the aims that hard work and honesty had not enabled me to attain.

These thoughts, or rather daydreams, made the morning pass like lightning, and I was astonished when I heard the church bells next door chiming midday and saw that a long ray of sunshine had come through the window and lay across the bed. The bells and the ray of sunshine, like my idleness that morning, seemed unusual, precious luxuries. The rich ladies who lived in villas, like Gino's mistress, must lie in their beds dreaming in just the same way at that very same moment, hearing the chimes and watching the ray of sunshine with astonished eyes. With a feeling that I was no longer the same busy, impoverished Adriana of yesterday, but quite a different being, I got out of bed at last and took off my nightgown in front of the closet mirror. I looked at myself naked in the mirror, and for the first time understood my mother's pride when she said to the artist, "Look at her breasts! Her legs — her hips." I thought of Astarita whose whole character, even his manner and voice, was changed by his desire for my breasts, my legs, my hips, and I told myself I would certainly find other men who would give me as much money and even more than he did, if they could have pleasure from me.

In my new character, I dressed lazily, drank some coffee, and went out. I went to a nearby bar and phoned Gino's villa. He had given me the number, telling me, with characteristic servility, to use it very sparingly because his employers did not like the phone to be used by the servants. I spoke first of all to a woman who must have been the parlormaid, and then Gino came almost immediately. He asked me at once whether I was feeling ill and I could not help smiling, since I recognized in his anxiety his old perfection of manner, which was perhaps not entirely assumed, and had done so much to deceive me. "I'm perfectly well," I replied. "I've never been so well in my life."

"When can I see you?"

"Whenever you want," I said, "but I'd like it to be like the first time — at the villa when your employers are away."

He realized what I meant at once. "They're going away in about ten days' time, for Christmas," he replied eagerly, "not earlier."

"All right, then," I replied carelessly, "I'll see you in ten days' time."

"What do you mean?" he asked in amazement.

"Before then, I'm busy."

"What's the matter?" he asked suspiciously. "Are you mad at me?"

"No," I replied. "If I were mad at you, I wouldn't want to see you at the villa, would I?" It had occurred to me that he might become jealous and pester me. So I added, "Don't be alarmed — I love you as I always did. Only I've got to help Mother with some extra work because of the holidays — and since I won't be able to get away from home until late and you're never free late at night, I'd rather wait until your employers go away."

"But what about the morning?"

"I'll be sleeping in the morning," I answered. "By the way — did you know I'm not a model anymore?"

"Why?"

"I got tired of it — you're glad, aren't you? I'll see you in ten days' time, then. I'll call you."

"All right."

He said "all right" without much conviction. But I knew him well enough to be sure that despite his suspicions he would not turn up before the ten days had passed. Rather, just because he was suspicious he would not turn up. The idea that I might have discovered his treachery must have filled him with terror and dismay. I hung up the receiver and realized I had spoken to Gino in a calm, good-natured, and even affectionate voice, and I congratulated myself. By and by my feelings for him would also become calm, good-natured, and affectionate, and I would be able to see him without any fear of plunging him, myself, and our relationship into the false and trying atmosphere of hatred.

7

*I*N THE AFTERNOON OF THAT very day, I went straight off to see Gisella in her furnished room. As was usual with her at that hour, she had only that moment got out of her bed, and was dressing for her date with Riccardo. I sat down on the unmade bed and, while she wandered about in the semidarkness of the untidy room full of clothes and knickknacks, I told her in the most matter-of-fact tone of voice how I had gone to call on Astarita and how he had told me that Gino had a wife and child. On hearing this news, Gisella exploded into an exclamation, I don't know whether of joy or surprise, came to sit on the bed facing me and, putting her two hands on my shoulders, gazed into my eyes.

"No, no — I can't believe it — a wife and daughter! Is it really true?"

"The daughter's called Maria."

Obviously she wanted to get to the bottom of the story and discuss it as fully as possible, and my peaceful attitude disappointed her.

"A wife and daughter — and the daughter's called Maria — can you talk about it like that?"

"How should I talk about it?"

"Aren't you upset?"

"Of course I'm upset."

"But how did he break the news? Did he say, 'Gino Molinari's got a wife and daughter,' just like that?"

"Yes."

"What did you say?"

"Nothing. What could I say?"

"But how did you feel? Didn't you burst into tears? After all, it's a disaster for you."

"No, it didn't occur to me to cry."

"Well, now you can't marry Gino," she exclaimed cheerfully after a moment's thought. "What a business, all the same! That man's got no conscience — a poor girl like you, who lived only for him, as you might say. Men are all scoundrels."

"Gino doesn't know yet that I know everything," I said.

"In your place, honey," she said eagerly, "I'd tell him what I think of him — and no one could keep me from slapping him a time or two."

"I've got a date with him in ten days," I answered. "I think we'll go on making love."

She drew back, staring straight at me. "But why? . . . Do you still like him! — after what he's done to you?"

"No," I answered, and I could not help lowering my voice, "I don't like him so much, but —" I hesitated, and then lied in a strained way "— slaps and shrieks aren't always the best way of getting even."

She looked at me a moment with half-shut eyes, standing back as painters do while scrutinizing their pictures.

"You're right —" she exclaimed. "I hadn't thought of that — but do you know what I'd do in your place? I'd let him stew in his own juice, calmly, sure of himself — and then one fine day — pow! — I'd ditch him."

I didn't say anything. She continued after a moment, in a less excited voice but just as lively and expressive. "Still, I can hardly

THE WOMAN OF ROME ❖ <i>123</i>

believe it — a wife and daughter — and he was so finicky about you! And he made you buy all that furniture and make a trousseau. It's a mess, a real mess!"

I remained silent. "But I knew all along!" she cried triumphantly. "I saw through him. You must admit that. What did I tell you? He doesn't mean what he says. Poor Adriana!" She threw her arms around my neck and kissed me. I let her kiss me.

"Yes, but the worst of it is, he's made Mother spend her money," I then said.

"Does your mother know?"

"Not yet."

"Don't be worried about the cash," she cried. "Astarita is so much in love with you — you only need to make up your mind and he'll give you all the money you want."

"I don't want to see anything more of Astarita," I answered. "Any man but Astarita."

I must say Gisella was no fool. She realized immediately that for the moment it was better not to mention Astarita, and she also knew what I meant by the phrase "any other man but Astarita." She pretended to think for a while.

"You're right, actually," Then she continued, "I see what you mean. I'd feel somewhat strange myself if I went out with Astarita after what happened — he wants things at all costs — and he told you about Gino to get even." She was silent again. "Leave it to me," she went on seriously. "Do you want to meet someone who will help you?"

"Yes."

"Leave it to me."

"But," I added, "I don't want to be tied up with anyone; I want to be free."

"Leave it to me," she repeated for the third time.

"Now I want to give Mother her money back," I continued, "and buy some things I need. And I don't want Mother to have to work anymore," I added.

Meanwhile, Gisella had got up and had seated herself at the dressing table. "You've always been too good, Adriana," she said as she hastily dabbed on some powder. "Now can you see what happens to people who are too good?"

"Did you know I didn't go to pose this morning?" I said. "I've made up my mind to give up being a model."

"You're right," she replied. "I only pose myself for —" and she named a certain artist — "just to do him a favor. But when he's finished, I'm through with it."

I felt very fond of Gisella, at that moment, and thoroughly comforted. The sound of her saying "Leave it to me" was reassuring, like a cordial and maternal promise to attend to my needs as soon as possible. I realized, of course, that Gisella was not inspired to help me by any affection she had for me, but rather by the almost unconscious desire, as in the Astarita affair, to see me reduced as quickly as possible to her own level. But no one ever does anything for nothing and, since in this case Gisella's envy coincided with my own convenience, I saw no reason to turn down her help merely because I knew it was given from selfish motives.

She was in a great hurry because she was already late for her date with her fiancé. We left the room and began to descend the steep, narrow staircase of the old house.

"You know, I'm beginning to think Riccardo wants to play me the same trick as Gino played you," she said on the way down, spurred on by her state of excitement and perhaps by the desire to soften the bitterness of my disillusionment, by showing me I was not the only unfortunate one.

"Is he married, too?" I asked innocently.

"No, but he tells me such stories — I think he's playing me for a fool. But I told him straight out, 'Look here, my dear, I don't need you, you can stay if you want, if not, clear out!'"

I said nothing, but I did not think there was much similarity between us or between my relationship with Gino and hers with Riccardo. In her heart, she had never had any illusions about Riccardo's intentions, and had not thought twice on occasion, as I well knew, about betraying him. I, on the contrary, had placed all the hopes of my inexpert heart on becoming Gino's wife and had always been faithful to him; certainly the favor Astarita had obliged me to do him at Viterbo by his blackmail could not really be called infidelity. But I thought she would probably be offended if I said this to her, so I did not speak. At the outer door she arranged to meet me on the following evening at a pastry shop, warning me to be punctual because she would probably have someone with her. Then she ran off.

I realized I ought to tell Mother what had happened but I did not dare. Mother really loved me; and being the opposite of Gisella, who saw in Gino's treachery only the triumph of her own theories and did not even try to conceal from me her cruel delight, Mother would feel more sorrow than joy at seeing how right she had been in the end. At heart she desired only my happiness and did not care how I achieved it; only she was sure Gino would not be able to give it to me. After much hesitation, I decided not to tell her anything. I knew that the following evening, deeds, not words, would open her eyes; and although I realized it was a brutal way of showing her the great change that had come about in my life, I liked the idea that by so doing I would avoid the many explanations, reflections, and comments Gisella had poured out so generously when I had told her the tale of Gino's deceit. To tell the truth, I felt a kind of disgust now for the whole institution of marriage and wanted to talk about it as little as possible and make others avoid the subject too.

The following day I pretended to have an appointment with Gino and stayed out all afternoon so that Mother, who was already suspicious, would not pester me all the time. I had had something new made for the wedding, a gray suitdress, which I had intended to wear immediately after the ceremony. It was my best dress and I hesitated a long time before putting it on. But then I thought that one day or another I would be obliged to wear it, and it would not be on any purer or happier day than today, and that, on the other hand, men judge by appearances and it would suit my purposes better to show myself at my best; and I laid my scruples aside. And so I put on, not without certain misgivings, my best dress that today, when I think of it, seems very plain and simple like all my clothes at the time, did my hair carefully, and painted my face, but no more than usual. And while on this subject, I must say that I have never understood why so many women in my profession plaster their faces so thickly and then go on the street looking as if they were wearing carnival masks. Perhaps it is because, with the life they lead, they would otherwise look too pale; or perhaps because they are afraid that if they did not paint themselves so crudely, they would not attract men's attention and so be able to show them that they are approachable. However tired I may be and however much I overdo it, I never lose my healthy, bronzed look, and I can say, without blushing, that my looks, without the aid of too much make-up, have always been enough to make men turn their heads to stare at me when I pass down the street. I don't attract men by using lipstick or mascara or peroxiding my hair, but by my majestic bearing (at least, that's what lots of them have told me), the sweet serenity of my expression, my perfect teeth when I laugh, and the girlish mass of my dark, wavy hair. Women who dye their hair and paint their faces probably do not realize that men, judging them for what they are from the very outset, feel a kind of disillusionment in anticipation. But I, being so natural and restrained, have always left them in doubt about my real character, and in this way have given them an illusion of adventure that, in the end, is what they want far more than the mere satisfaction of their senses.

When I was dressed and made up, I went to a movie and saw the same film through twice. I left the movie when night had fallen and went straight to the pastry shop where I had the appointment with Gisella. It was not one of the ordinary cheap places where we used to meet Riccardo on other occasions; it was an elegant place and I had never been there before. I realized that the choice of this place was meant specifically to provide a background worthy of me and to raise the price of my favors. Such attention to these and other details, which I will mention later, can lead a woman of my kind, if she is young and beautiful and knows how to use these gifts intelligently, to a steady, comfortable position in life, which is what we all aim at in our hearts. But not many do it; and I was never one of them who did. My humble origin has always made me look suspiciously at luxury. I have always felt ill at ease in restaurants, tearooms, and bourgeois cafés, ashamed to smile or make eyes at the men, as if, in all those glittering lights, I were running the gauntlet. I have always felt a deep and warm attraction for the city streets, with their palaces, churches, monuments, shops, and doorways, which make them more beautiful and welcoming than any restaurant or tearoom. It has always been a favorite habit of mine to go down into the street about the time of sunset and walk slowly along beside the lighted shop windows to watch the twilight gradually darken the sky above the roofs; I have always liked to wander among the crowds and to listen without turning around to the amorous suggestions that the most unexpected passersby, in a sudden exaltation of the senses, risk whispering on the spur of the moment.

I have always loved to pace up and down the same street again and again, feeling almost worn out at the end but as fresh and eager in my heart as at a fair, where the surprises are inexhaustible. The street has always been my restaurant, my drawing room, my café, and this is because I was born poor, and the poor are known to get their entertainment cheap by gazing at shop windows where they cannot afford to buy and at the facades of palaces where they cannot afford to live. For the same reason, I have always loved the churches, of which there are so many in Rome, a luxury within everyone's reach since they are always open, where the ancient, humble stench of poverty is often stronger than the smell of incense among the marble, the gold, and the precious ornaments. But a rich man, of course, does not walk through the streets or go to church; at most he crosses the city in his car, leaning back against the cushions and occasionally reading a newspaper. By preferring the street to any other spot, I immediately cut myself off from all those introductions that, according to Gisella, I should have sought out at the sacrifice of my own most deeply rooted tastes. I was never disposed to make such a sacrifice, and all the time I was Gisella's partner these tastes were a subject of heated discussion between us. Gisella did not like the street; churches meant nothing to her; and crowds only disgusted her and filled her with scorn. She aimed at the expensive restaurants, where attentive waiters anxiously watch their clients' slightest

gesture; fashionable dance halls, with a band in uniform and
dancers in evening dress; the smartest cafés and gambling halls. She
became quite a different person in such places, changed her gestures, carriage, and even the tone of her voice. In fact, she affected
the behavior of a real lady; and this was the ideal she aimed at, and
that later, as we shall see, she attained to some degree. But, in the
end, the most curious aspect of her success was that she met the
person fated to fulfill her ambitions not in a fashionable haunt, but
through me, in the street she loathed so heartily.

I found Gisella at the pastry shop with a middle-aged man, a
commercial traveler, whom she introduced as Giacinti. When
seated, he appeared to be of normal height, because his shoulders
were very broad, but when he stood up, he turned out to be almost
a dwarf, and his broad shoulders made him appear even shorter
than he was. His thick white hair, gleaming like silver, was brushed
straight up off his forehead, perhaps to make him seem taller,
and his face was red and healthy, with the regular and noble features of a statue; he had a handsome smooth forehead, large dark
eyes, a straight nose, and well-shaped mouth. But an unpleasing
expression of vanity, of conceit and false benevolence, made his
face, which at first sight seemed attractive and majestic, absolutely
repellent.

I felt rather shy and sat down without saying a word after the introductions were over. Giacinti, as though my arrival were only an
unimportant incident, whereas it was really the whole purpose of
the evening, went on with what he had been saying to Gisella.
"You can't complain of me, Gisella," he said, and placed a hand
on her knee, keeping it there all the time he was talking. "How
long did our — let's call it alliance — last? Six months? Well, can
you say, with your hand on your heart, that in all those six months
I sent you away dissatisfied?" His speech was clear, slow, accented,
emphatic, but he obviously spoke in that way not so much to make
himself understood as to listen to his own voice and enjoy every
word he uttered.

"No, no," said Gisella in bored tones, lowering her head.

"Get Gisella to tell you, Adriana," Giacinti went on in his

clear, emphatic voice. "Not only have I never stinted on money for her — shall we call them professional earnings? — but every time I came back from Milan I always brought her a present. Do you remember the time I brought you a bottle of French perfume, now? And the other time I gave you a silk and lace chemise? Women like to say men don't understand anything about lingerie — but I'm an exception to the rule!" He laughed, softly, showing perfect teeth but so curiously white that they seemed false.

"Give me a cigarette, do," said Gisella shortly.

"At once!" he replied with ironic courtesy. He offered me one, too, took one himself, and after he had lit it continued. "Do you remember the purse I brought you another time — a big leather one — that was something to write home about! Don't you use it anymore?"

"It's a morning bag," said Gisella.

"I like giving presents," he continued, turning to me, "not for sentimental reasons, you understand —" he shook his head, puffing smoke from his nostrils "— but for three clear reasons. One — I like to be thanked. Two — there's nothing like a present for getting yourself properly treated. In fact, anyone who has once had a present from you always hopes for another. Three — because women like an illusion and a present makes them feel there's some sentiment involved, even when there isn't."

"You're a deep one," said Gisella indifferently, without even looking at him.

He shook his head, showing all his teeth in a handsome smile. "No, I'm not deep — I'm simply a man with some experience of life who has been able to learn from his experience. . . . I know you have to do certain things with women, others with your clients, others with your servants, and so on. My mind's like an extremely tidy card index. For instance — a woman in the offing! . . . . I take down my notebook, look through it, find that certain measures obtained the desired effect, others didn't; I put the notebook back in its place and act accordingly. That's all there is to it." He stopped and smiled again.

Gisella was smoking with a bored look; I said nothing.

"And I find women are grateful to me," he continued, "because they realize at once that they won't have any disappointments with me. I know what they expect, their weaknesses, and their whims — just as I, myself, am grateful to a client who understands me at a glance, one who doesn't waste my time chatting, knows what he wants and what I want — I've got an ashtray on my desk in Milan with the words: 'Lord bless those who don't waste my time.'" He threw his cigarette down and looking at his watch added, "It's about time to go and have a meal."

"What's the time?"

"Eight. Excuse me a moment — I'll be right back."

He got up and went out at the end of the room. He really was very short, with his broad shoulders and thick white hair standing up on top of his head. Gisella crushed out her cigarette on the ashtray. "He's an awful bore and talks of nothing but himself," she said.

"I noticed that."

"Just let him talk, and say yes all the time," she went on. "You'll see, he'll tell you heaps of things — he thinks he's God knows what — but he's very free with his money and really does give you presents."

"Yes, but then he keeps on reminding you —"

She did not reply, but shook her head as if to say, "What can you do about it?" We were silent for a while, then Giacinti came back, paid, and we left the pastry shop.

"Gisella," said Giacinti, when we were in the street, "this evening is Adriana's — but would you like to come to supper with us?"

"No, no, thanks," Gisella replied hurriedly, "I've got a date." She said good-bye to Giacinti and went off.

"What a nice girl she is," I remarked to Giacinti as soon as she had gone.

He made a face. "Not bad," he said. "She's got a good figure."

"Don't you like her?"

"I don't require of anyone that they should be likable," he said, walking beside me and holding my arm tight, high up, almost under the armpit, "but that they should do well whatever they do — I don't ask a typist to be likable, for instance, but to be able to type quickly without making mistakes. And I don't ask a girl like Gisella to be pleasant, but to know how to do her job, that is, to give me a good time for the hour or two I spend with her. Now Gisella doesn't know how to do her job."

"Why?"

"Because she's always thinking about money — and she's always afraid she won't be paid or won't get enough. I don't expect her to love me, but it's part of her profession to behave as though she really did love me, and give me an illusion — that's what I pay her for. But Gisella makes it too obvious she's only doing it for her own interest — she doesn't even give you time to get your breath before she starts haggling. It's no good!"

We had reached the restaurant, a noisy place crowded with men of Giacinti's sort — commercial travelers, stockbrokers, shopkeepers, businessmen on their way through town. Giacinti entered first.

"Is my usual table free?" he asked as he gave the boy his hat and overcoat.

"Yes, Mr. Giacinti."

It was a table near the window. Giacinti sat down, rubbing his hands together.

"Got a good appetite?" he then asked me.

"I think so," I answered awkwardly.

"Good, I'm glad — I like people to eat when they're at the table. Gisella, for instance, never wanted to eat anything, said she was afraid of getting fat. . . . That's silly! There's a time for everything — when you sit down to the table you eat." He seemed full of resentment toward Gisella.

"But you really do get fat if you eat too much." I said timidly, "and some women don't want to put on weight."

"Are you one of those?"

"No, I'm not — but, as a matter of fact, they tell me I'm on the heavy side."

"Don't you listen to 'em — it's all envy. You're all right, as you are — I say so, and I know what I'm talking about." He patted my hand in a fatherly way as if to reassure me.

The waiter came. "First of all," said Giacinti, "take these flowers away, they're a nuisance to me. Then bring the usual — you know — double quick!"

The he turned to me. "He knows me and knows what I like. Leave it to him. You'll see you won't have anything to complain of."

And indeed I had nothing to complain of. All the courses that were served were delicious and plentiful, even if not the finest. Giacinti had a huge appetite and ate with concentration, his head lowered, his knife and fork firmly gripped; he did not look at me or talk, but acted as if he were by himself. He really was entirely engrossed in the act of eating and in his greed even lost his much-vaunted calm; his gestures were confused, as if he were afraid he would not be done in time and would have to go hungry. He pushed a piece of meat into his mouth; with his left hand hurriedly broke off a morsel of bread, bit it; with his other hand poured himself a glass of wine and began to drink before he had finished chewing. All the time he kept on smacking his lips, rolling his eyes, and shaking his head every now and again like a cat when it has got hold of too big a mouthful. Unlike my usual self, however, I was not at all hungry. For the first time in my life, I was going to make love to a man I didn't care for and didn't even know, and I looked him over carefully, noting my own feelings and trying to imagine how I would go through with it. After this first time, I used to pay no attention to the appearance of the men I went with; perhaps because, being driven by necessity, I quickly learned to pick out at first glance the one good or pleasing aspect in each man that would make intimacy bearable. But that evening I had not yet learned this trick of my profession, and I was seeking it instinctively, as you might say, without realizing what I was doing.

I have already said that Giacinti was not ugly; as long as he kept his mouth shut and did not reveal the consuming passion of his soul, he might even have been called handsome. This was saying a great deal, because, after all, love is very much a matter of physical contact; but it was not enough for me, because I have never been able to stand a man, let alone love him, only for his physical qualities. Now when supper was over and Giacinti, after a belch or two, had begun to talk again, once his ill-mannered greed was satisfied, I realized there was nothing in him, at least nothing I could discover, which would make him even tolerable. Not only did he talk about himself the whole time, as Gisella had said, but he did it in a most unpleasant, boring, and conceited way, telling me mostly things that did him no credit at all and only strengthened my first instinctive feeling of repulsion. There was absolutely nothing in him that I could like; and all the things he boasted of and enlarged upon as desirable qualities seemed dreadful faults to me.

Later I met other men, though not many, who were just as worthless, with nothing good in them at all to cling to that might make them likable; and I have always marveled at their existence and asked myself whether it was not perhaps my own fault if I was unable to discover at first sight the qualities they must undoubtedly possess. In time, however, I have become accustomed to such unpleasant companions, and I pretend to laugh, joke, and be what they believe I am and want me to be. But that first evening my discovery filled me with gloomy reflections. While Giacinti went on talking, fiddling at his teeth with a toothpick, I was telling myself I had taken up a very hard profession — the simulation of passionate love for men who actually roused the most contrary feelings in me — as in Giacinti's case. I told myself no money could repay such favors — that it was impossible, under such circumstances, not to behave like Gisella, who thought only of the money and showed it. It also occurred to me that that evening I would be taking this hateful Giacinti back to my poor little room, which I had intended to use so differently. And I thought how unfortunate I was and how fate had meant me to be under no illusions from the very beginning, by leading me to meet Giacinti and not some artless youth in search of adventure, or some ordinary, decent, unpretentious fellow, and that Giacinti's presence among my furniture would put the seal on my reunuciation of all the old dreams of a respectable, ordinary life.

He talked all the time, but still he was not so dull as not to notice that I was hardly listening to him and was not cheerful.

"Feeling glum, little girl?" he suddenly asked me.

"No, no," I replied, hurriedly pulling myself together, but half tempted by his deceptively affectionate tones to confide in him and talk a little about myself, since I had allowed him to talk of himself for so long.

"That's better!" he went on. "Because I don't like sadness. . . . And I didn't invite you here to be sad — you may have your reasons, I don't doubt it, but as long as you're with me leave your sorrow at home. I don't want to know anything about your affairs; I don't want to know who you are, what's happening to you, or anything else — I'm not interested. We've got a deal, you and I, even if it's not in writing. I guarantee to give you a certain sum of money and you in return guarantee to make me pass the evening pleasantly. Nothing else matters." He said these words seriously, perhaps a little irritated by the fact that I had not appeared to be listening to him attentively enough.

"But I'm not sad at all! Only it's so smoky in here — and noisy — I feel a little dizzy," I answered, without showing anything of the feelings that had stirred me.

"Shall we go?" he asked anxiously. I said yes. He called the waiter immediately, paid the bill, and we left.

"Shall we go to a hotel?" he asked me when we were out in the street.

"No, no," I answered quickly. I was frightened at the idea of having to show my papers; and anyway, I had already made up my mind in another direction. "Come to my place."

We got into a taxi and I gave my home address. As soon as the taxi started, he threw himself onto me, pawing me all over and kissing my neck. I could tell from his breath that he had had a lot to drink, and that he was drunk. He kept on calling me "baby," a term usually only used with little girls, and on his lips it irritated me, sounded ridiculous and slightly profane. I let him have his way for a while, then, pointing to the chauffeur's back, said, "Shouldn't we wait until we get there?"

He did not reply but fell heavily back against the cushions, red and congested in the face, as though suddenly attacked by an apoplectic fit. Angrily he muttered, "I pay him to take me where I want to go and not to busy himself with what's going on in his taxi." He was obsessed by the idea that money — and more especially his money — could shut anyone's mouth. I did not answer, and for the rest of the journey we sat stiffly beside one another without touching. The city lights flashed through the taxi windows, lit up our faces and hands for a moment, then were swallowed up again. It seemed strange to me to be beside that man whose very existence I had been unaware of a little time before and to be hurrying with such a man toward my own flat, to give myself to him as I would to my beloved. These reflections shortened the journey. I pulled myself together, amazed to see the taxi stop in the usual street before my door.

"Don't make a noise going in, because I live with my mother," I said to Giacinti in the dark on the way upstairs.

"Don't worry, baby," he answered.

When we reached the landing I unlocked the door. Giacinti followed me, I took his hand and, without switching on the light, led him across the hallway to the door of my room, which was the first on the left. I made him enter first, turned on the bedside lamp, and standing in the doorway gave a kind of farewell look around at my furniture. Giacinti, delighted at finding a new, clean room when he had probably been afraid he would find himself surrounded by filthy, ramshackle furniture, sighed with satisfaction and threw his overcoat down on a chair. I told him to wait for me and went out of the room.

I walked straight to the living room, where I found Mother sewing at the center table. When she saw me, she put down her work at once and started to get up, probably imagining she would have to fix my supper as on other evenings.

"Don't get up," I said. "I've already had my supper. I've got someone in the next room. Don't come in on any account."

"Someone there?" she asked in astonishment.

"Yes," I answered quickly. "Not Gino — a gentleman." Without waiting for her to question me further I left the living room.

I returned to my own room and locked the door. Giacinti, red in the face and impatient, came to me in the middle of the room and took me in his arms. He was much shorter than I, and bent me back against the end of the bed in order to reach my face with his lips. I tried not to let him kiss me on the mouth, and by turning my face away as if I were shy and then throwing my head back as if in ecstasy, I succeeded in my intention. Giacinti made love exactly as he ate, greedily, without discrimination, beginning in one place, then another, afraid he was missing something, blinded by my body as he had been by the food at the restaurant. After he had embraced me, he seemed to want to undress me as we were, still standing up. He uncovered one of my arms and a shoulder, and then began to kiss me again, as if the sight of my bare flesh had put his head in a whirl. I was afraid his clumsy gestures would tear my dress and at last I said, "Come on, get your clothes off," but without pushing him away.

He left me at once and began to undress, sitting on the edge of the bed. I did the same on the other side.

"Does your mother know?" he suddenly asked.

"Yes."

"What does she say about it?"

"Nothing."

"Does she disapprove?"

These details were obviously nothing more to him than an additional spice to his adventure. This trait is common to all men. Few can resist the temptation of mingling physical pleasure with some other kind of interest or even pity. "She neither approves nor disapproves," I said shortly, standing up and pulling my slip off over my head. "I'm free to do what I want." When I was naked I put my clothes neatly on a chair and then stretched myself on the bed, flat on my back, one arm under my head and the other across my breasts to cover them. I do not know why, but I remembered this was the position of the pagan goddess who resembled me in the colored print the stout painter had given Mother; and suddenly I felt resentfully angry at the thought of the great change in my life since that day. Giacinti must have been astonished at the firm, shapely beauty of my body, which was not apparent when I was fully dressed, for he stopped taking his clothes off and stared at me in amazement, his mouth half open and his eyes bursting out of his head.

"Hurry up," I said. "I'm cold."

He finished undressing and threw himself on me. I have mentioned his way of making love already, it was exactly like him, and I think I have described him adequately. I need only add that he was one of those men who become fearfully exacting at the thought of the money they have spent or are going to spend, as if they are afraid of being cheated if they don't take everything they think they have a right to. His aim, I soon realized, was to make our meeting last as long as he could and to get out of me all the enjoyment to which he thought he was entitled. With this in mind he labored over my body like someone over an instrument and urged me all the time to do the same with his. But although I obeyed him, I soon began to be bored and to watch him coldly, as if his obvious calculations had set a distance between us, and I were seeing not only him but also myself from a great way off, through a mirror of dislike and disgust. This was the very opposite of the feeling of affection I had tried instinctively to encourage at the beginning of the evening. Suddenly a wave of shameful remorse swept through me and I closed my eyes.

In the end he grew tired and we lay beside one another on the bed.

"You must admit," he said in self-satisfied tones, "that although I'm not so young as I was, I'm an exceptional lover."

"Yes, you are," I said indifferently.

"All the women say so," he went on, "and do you know what I think? Little bottles hold good wine — some men twice my size aren't up to anything!"

I began to feel cold and sitting up pulled a corner of the blanket over us both. He interpreted this as a sign of affection.

"Good girl," he said. "Now I'm going to have a little nap." Then he curled up against me and dropped off.

I kept still, lying on my back, his white head against my breast. The blanket covered us both to the waist and at first, as I looked at him, at his hairy chest with its flaccid folds of middle age, I felt once more that I was with an utter stranger. But he was asleep; and sleeping he no longer talked, looked, moved. Given his unlovable character, sleep revealed only the best of him; that is, he was just a man like any other, with no name or profession, no virtues or faults, simply a human being whose breast rose and fell as he breathed. It may seem odd, but as I looked at him and watched him trustfully sleeping beside me, I felt almost affectionate toward him, and this feeling was brought home to me by the care I took to avoid waking him by some movement. This was the impulse of sympathy I had been seeking in vain until that moment; the sight of his white head leaning heavily against my young breast aroused it in me. This sensation comforted me and almost made me feel less cold. For a moment, in fact, I experienced a kind of amorous exaltation that brought tears to my eyes. In reality my heart was full to the brim with affection — then as always — an affection that for lack of legitimate objects I poured out even on unworthy things and people, rather than leave it unused and unwanted.

After twenty minutes or so he woke up. "Did I sleep long?" he asked.

"No."

"I feel great." he said, getting out of bed and rubbing his hands together. "Really great! I feel at least twenty years younger!" He began to dress, exclaiming continually in his joy and relief. I dressed in silence.

"I'd like to see you again, baby," he said when he was ready. "What should I do?"

"Phone Gisella," I replied. "I see her every day."

"Are you always free?"

"Always."

"Long live freedom!"

Then, taking out his wallet, he asked me. "How much do you want?"

"You decide," I answered. "If you give me a lot you'll be doing a good deed; I need it," I added sincerely.

"If I give you a lot," he retorted, "it won't be to do a good deed — but because you're a beautiful girl and have given me a nice evening's entertainment."

"As you like," I said, shrugging my shoulders.

"Everything's got its own price and should be paid for according to its worth," he continued, taking the money from his wallet. "Good deeds don't exist. You've supplied me with certain things of a better quality than Gisella, for instance, would have supplied. And it's only fair that you should get more than Gisella. Good deeds have nothing to do with it. Here's a piece of advice — don't ever say, 'You decide.'. . . Leave that to the street vendors. If anyone says, 'You decide,' I'm always tempted to give them less than they deserve." He made an expressive face and held out the money.

As Gisella had said, he was generous, and the money was far more than I had expected. Once more as I took it I had the same powerful feeling of sensual complicity that Astarita's money had aroused in me during the Viterbo trip. I thought this must mean I had a vocation and was really born for my new profession even if I longed for something different in my heart of hearts. "Thanks," I said, and before realizing what I was doing, a grateful impulse made me kiss him on the cheek.

"Thanks to you," he replied, getting ready to go. I took his hand and led him in the dark through the hall to the front door. For a moment, when the bedroom door was shut and the front door not yet open, we were completely in the dark. And then some almost physical instinct told me that Mother must be hiding in a corner of the hall, in the dark where I was wandering with Giacinti. She must be squatting behind the door or in the other corner between the sideboard and the wall, and was waiting for Giacinti to leave. I remembered the other time, the night I returned late after being with Gino in his employers' villa; and I became very nervous at the idea that as soon as Giacinti had gone she might jump at me, seize me by the hair, drag me to the sofa, and start to beat me. I could feel she was there in the dark. I felt as if I could almost see her, and had a kind of shrinking sensation behind me, as if her hands were hovering over my head, ready to grip me by the hair. I had Giacinti by one hand and the money in the other. I decided that as soon as she sprang at me I would put the money in her hand. This would be a silent way of reminding her that she had been the one to urge me the whole time to earn money in this way; and it would also be an attempt to shut her mouth by appealing to the passionate love of money ever uppermost in her soul. Meantime I had opened the door.

"Bye-bye, then," said Giacinti. "I'll phone Gisella."

I watched him go downstairs, broad-shouldered, his white hair standing straight up on his head, waving his hand in farewell without turning around. And I shut the door. Immediately, as I had foreseen, Mother was upon me. She did not seize me by the hair as I had feared, but tried in a clumsy way I did not understand at first to embrace me. Faithful to my plan; I sought her hand and thrust the money into it. But she pushed it away and it fell to the ground. I found it on the floor next morning when I left my room. All this happened breathlessly, but without a word said on either side.

We went into the living room and I sat down sideways at the table. Mother sat in front of me and looked at me. She seemed worried and I felt awkward.

"Do you know, while you were in there, I suddenly felt scared for a moment?" she said unexpectedly.

"Scared of what?"

"I don't know," she replied. "First of all I felt lonely. I felt cold all over — not myself at all, everything was spinning around me, like when you've had too much to drink — everything seemed strange. I found myself thinking, That's the table, that's the chair, that's the sewing machine — but I couldn't really believe they were the table, the chair, the sewing machine. I didn't even seem to be myself. I said to myself, 'I'm an old seamstress, I've a daughter called Adriana.' . . . But I wasn't sure. I started to go over the past to convince myself, to think what I had been, when I was a girl, when I was your age, when I got married, when you were born. And I was afraid, because it all flashed past as a single day and I had suddenly grown old from being young as I was, and I hadn't noticed the change. . . . And when I'm dead, it'll all be as though I had never been born," she said with an effort, looking at me.

"Why are you thinking these things?" I said slowly. "You're still young. What's death got to do with it?"

She did not appear to have heard me and continued in her emphatic speech, which I found painful and artificial. "I tell you, I was afraid. And I thought, suppose someone didn't want to go on living, would they have to all the same? . . . I don't say you ought to kill yourself, you need courage to do that, but suppose you didn't want to live anymore, like you don't want to eat or walk, maybe. . . . Well, I swear by your dead father. . . . I don't want to go on living."

Her eyes were full of tears and her lips trembled. I felt like crying, too, and I got up and put my arms around her and went to sit on the sofa with her at the end of the room. We stayed there, holding one another close, both crying. I felt bewildered, because I was very tired and Mother's talk, with its disconnected and troubled logic, increased my bewilderment. But I was the first to pull myself together because, after all, I was only crying out of sympathy for her. I had given up crying about myself long since.

"Now, now," I said, patting her on the shoulder.

"Adriana, I mean it. . . . I don't want to go on living," she repeated through her tears. I patted her shoulder and let her cry to her heart's content without speaking. Meanwhile I could not help thinking that her tears were a sure sign of her remorse. She had always lectured me, saying I ought to follow Gisella's example and sell myself as best I could, that's true. But there is a great difference between saying and doing. And when she saw me bringing a man home, felt me put the money in her hand, it must have been a heavy blow to her. Now she saw the result of her lectures before her eyes, and she could not help being horrified. But at the same time she must have been incapable, somehow, of recognizing that she had been mistaken, and perhaps she felt a bitter kind of complacency at the uselessness now of any such recognition. And so, instead of telling me straight out, "You've done wrong — don't do it again," she preferred to talk to me of things that did not concern me, her life and her desire to die. I have noticed that many people, in the very instant when they perform some action they know to be wrong, try to cover themselves and restore their position by talking of higher things, which show them to themselves and to others in a disinterested, noble light that is in no way connected with what they are doing or allowing to be done. This is how it was in Mother's case — except that the majority act in this way quite consciously, while Mother, poor dear, did it all unawares, as her heart and circumstances taught her.

But her phrase about her wish to die rang true to me. I supposed that I, too, had not wanted to live after I had discovered Gino's deception. Only, my body went on living on its own, unconcerned with my will. My breasts, my legs, my hips, which gave men such pleasure, went on living; my hidden sex between my thighs went on living and made me desire love even when my will opposed it. It was no use stretching myself out on the bed determined to live no longer, not to wake in the morning — while I was asleep my body went on living, the blood flowed in my veins, my stomach and intestines went on digesting, the hair grew again under my arms where I had cut it, my nails grew, my skin was bathed in sweat, my strength renewed; and at a certain time in the morning my eyelids would open, without my conscious will, and my eyes would once more light upon the reality they hated, and I would realize that despite my desire to die I was still alive and had to go on living. So I might as well make the best of life and not think anymore about it, I concluded.

But I said nothing of all this to Mother because I realized such thoughts were just as sad as her own and would not have cheered her up at all. Instead, when she seemed to stop crying I left her side, saying, "I'm hungry." It was true, because in my nervousness I had hardly touched anything at the restaurant.

"There's your supper," said Mother, glad I was suggesting something commonplace and useful she could do. "I'll go and get it ready for you." She went out and I was left alone.

I sat down at the table in my usual place and waited for her to return. My head was empty and nothing was left of all that had happened except the sickly sweet odor of sex on my fingers and the salty streak of dry tears on my cheeks. I kept still and watched the shadows flung on the long bare walls of the living room by the hanging lamp. Then Mother returned with a plate of meat and vegetables.

"I haven't warmed up the soup, it wouldn't be good by now — and there wasn't much of it."

"It doesn't matter, this will do."

She poured me out a glass of wine full to the brim and stood as usual in front of me, motionless and attentive, while I ate.

"Is the steak all right?" she asked anxiously after a while.

"Yes, it's good."

"I told the butcher specially he was to give me a tender one." She seemed herself again and everything was exactly like it was on other evenings. I ate slowly and when I had finished I stretched my arms, yawning. I suddenly felt splendid, and this movement gave me a sense of pleasure because my body felt young, strong, satisfied.

"I'm very sleepy," I said.

"Wait, I'll go and make up the bed," said Mother eagerly, and started to go out. But I stopped her. "I'll do it myself," I said.

I got up and Mother picked up the empty plate. "Let me sleep, tomorrow morning," I said. "I'll wake myself."

She replied that she would do as I wanted, and when I had said good-night and kissed her, I went into my room. The bed was still as Giacinti and I had left it. I simply pulled the pillows and the blanket into place, then got undressed and slipped into bed. I lay there with my eyes wide open in the dark for a while, my mind a blank.

"I'm a whore," I said aloud at last, to see what effect the words would have on me. They did not seem to have any effect, so shutting my eyes I fell asleep almost immediately.

8

I SAW GIACINTI EVERY EVENING during the next few days. He phoned Gisella the next morning and, as soon as she met me in the afternoon, she gave me his message. Giacinti had to leave for Milan the evening before the day I had arranged to meet Gino and this was why I agreed to see him every evening. Otherwise I would have refused, because I had vowed to myself that I did not want ever again to have a settled relationship with any one man. I thought it was better, if I was taking up this profession, to do it in earnest, with a different lover each time, rather than deceive myself into thinking I was not taking it up by letting one man keep me; with the added danger of growing fond of him or he of me, and thereby losing not only my physical liberty but my emotional freedom as well.

In any case, my ideas about normal married life had remained unchanged; and I thought that if I were to marry, it would never be to a lover who had kept me and in the end had decided to make a business relationship legal, if not moral; but rather to a young man who would love me and whom I would love in return, someone of my own class, with similar tastes and ideas. What I wanted, in fact, was to keep the profession I had chosen completely separate from my earlier ambitions, without any contacts or compromises, since I felt I was equally well cut out to be a good wife and a good whore, but was quite incapable of maintaining a cautious and hypocritical middle way between the two. It was also true that there was probably more to be made out of the scruples of many men than out of the generosity of one man alone.

Every evening Giacinti took me to have supper in the same restaurant and then came home with me, remaining with me until late at night. By now Mother had given up any attempt to talk to me about my evenings, and contented herself with asking me whether I had slept well when she brought me my coffee on a tray late next morning. Before this, I used to go and sip my coffee in the kitchen, very early, without even sitting down, in front of the stove, feeling the biting cold of the water I had washed in still on my hands and face. Now instead Mother brought it to me and I drank it in bed, while she opened the shutters and began to tidy up the room. I never said anything to her that I had not already said in the past; but she had understood on her own that everything was changed in our life and she showed by her behavior that she realized perfectly well what the difference was.

She acted as if we had a tacit agreement, and seemed by her attentions to be begging me humbly to allow her to continue to serve me and make herself useful in our new way of life as she had always done before. And this habit of bringing me my coffee in bed must have reassured her to some extent, because many people, and Mother was one of them, endow habits with a positive worth even when they are not positive, as in the present case. With the same zeal she introduced many little changes of this kind into our daily life. For instance, she would prepare a great bowl of boiling water for me to wash in as soon as I got up, put flowers in a vase in my room, and so on.

Giacinti always gave me the same amount and, without talking about it to Mother, I used to put it in a drawer, in the box where she had placed her savings until now. I only kept a little small change for myself. I suppose she must have noticed the daily additions to our capital, but we never mentioned it to one another. I have noticed in the course of my life that even people who earn their livelihood by recognized means prefer not to speak about it, not only to strangers but even to friends. Probably money is linked with a sense of shame, or at least modesty, which prevents its being included in the list of ordinary topics of conversation and places it among those secret and inadmissible things that it is better not to mention; as if it were always disgracefully earned, no matter what its origin might be. But perhaps it is also true that no one likes to show the feeling money rouses in his soul, since it is a most powerful feeling and hardly ever disassociated from a sense of sin.

On one of those evenings Giacinti expressed a desire to sleep with me in my bedroom; but I sent him away on the pretext that the neighbors would see him in the morning when he left. In truth, since that first evening my intimacy with him had taken not a single step forward, surely through no fault of mine. But the way he had behaved the first evening was the way he continued to comport himself to the day of his departure. He was really a man of little or no worth, at least in his emotional relationships; and all the sentiment I could feel for him, I had felt that first day as he slept: a generic feeling that may have had nothing to do with him at all. The idea of sleeping with such a man was repugnant to me; and I was afraid I would be bored, as well, for I was sure he would keep me up half the night to confide in me and talk about himself. He was unaware, however, of both my boredom and aversion, and left me convinced that, in those few days, he had rendered himself absolutely lovable in my eyes.

The day of my appointment with Gino came at last, and so much had happened in those ten days that I felt as if a hundred years had passed since I used to see him on my way to the studios, and worked to save money and set up house, and considered myself an engaged girl soon to be married. He was there very punctually at the appointed time, and as I got into the car he seemed disturbed and very pale. No one likes to have a betrayal discovered, not even the boldest deceiver, and he must have thought a great deal and have had his suspicions during the ten days that had interrupted our usual meetings. But I showed no resentment and, as a matter of fact, I was not even pretending, because I felt perfectly serene; and when the bitterness of the first moment's disillusionment had passed, I felt a kind of indulgent and skeptical fondness for him. After all, I still liked Gino, as I knew from the first glance I gave him, and this was saying a lot.

"So your confessor's changed his mind?" he asked me after a while, as the car sped toward the villa. His tone was mocking but at the same time uncertain.

"No," I answered simply, "I've changed my mind."

"Have you finished all your work with your mother?"

"For the time being."

"Strange."

He did not know what he was saying, but he was obviously testing me to discover whether his suspicions were justified.

"Why is it strange?"

"I was just saying it for something to say."

"Don't you believe I've been busy?"

"I don't believe anything."

I had decided to shame him, but in my own way, by playing with him a little, like a cat with a mouse, without the brutal scenes Gisella had advised, which were not in harmony with my temperament.

"Are you jealous?" I asked him coyly.

"Me jealous? Good heavens!"

"Yes, you are — if you were sincere you'd admit it."

He took the bait I was offering. "Anyone in my place would be jealous," he said.

"Why?"

"Oh, come on! Did you think I would believe you? Such an important job that you couldn't spare five minutes to see me!"

"It's true, though," I said calmly, "I've worked very hard." And it was true — what else was it but work, and very tiring work, that I had been doing with Giacinti every evening? "And I've earned enough to pay off the rest of the installments and buy my trousseau," I added, making fun of myself. "So at last we'll be able to get married without any debts."

He said nothing; he was clearly trying to persuade himself of the truth of what I was saying, and was slowly abandoning his earlier suspicions. At that moment I made a gesture I had often made in the past. I flung my arms around his neck while he was driving and kissed him hard below the ear, whispering, "Why are you jealous? You know you're the only man in my life."

We reached the villa. Gino drove the car into the garden, shut the gate and went toward the tradesmen's entrance with me. It was twilight and the first lights were already gleaming in the windows of the houses round about, red in the bluish mist of the winter evening. It was nearly dark in the underground passage and there was a smell of slops and stuffiness. I stopped.

"I don't want to go to your room this evening," I said.

"Why not?"

"I want to make love in your mistress's room."

"You're out of your mind!" he exclaimed in scandalized horror. We had often gone into the upper rooms, but had always made love in his room in the basement.

"It's just a whim," I said. "What does it matter to you?"

"It matters a lot — something might get broken — you never know — and if they notice, what'll I do?"

"Oh what a tragedy!" I exclaimed lightly. "You'll get fired, that's all."

"And you can say it just like that?"

"How should I say it? If you really loved me you wouldn't think twice about it."

"I do love you, but I can't do this — let's not even talk about it. I don't want any trouble. I don't."

"We'll be careful. They won't notice."

"No."

I felt perfectly self-possessed. "I, who am your fiancée, ask you this one favor," I exclaimed, continuing to pretend what I did not really feel, "and you refuse because you're afraid I'll put my body where your mistress puts hers and lay my head where she lays hers — but what do you think? That she's better than I am?"

"No, but —"

"I'm worth a thousand of her!" I went on. "But so much the worse for you. You can make love to your mistress's pillows and sheets — I'm going!"

As I have already said, his respect and his subservience to his employers went very deep. He was nauseatingly proud of them, as if all their wealth were his, too. But seeing me speak in that way and turn away impetuously, with a determination he was not accustomed to find in me, he lost his head and ran after me.

"Wait a minute! Where are you going? I was just talking! Let's go upstairs, if you want to!"

I let him plead with me a little more, pretending to be offended. Then I agreed and we went to the upper floor, our arms around one another, and stopping on each step for a kiss, just like the first time, but with a change of heart — at least, speaking for myself. In his mistress's room I walked straight over to the bed and turned the covers down. He protested, once more mastered by fear. "You don't mean to get under the sheets?"

"Why not?" I replied calmly. "I don't want to get cold."

He said nothing, visibly upset. When I had prepared the bed I went in to the bathroom, lit the gas and turned on the hot-water faucet, just a trickle, so that the bath would not fill too rapidly. Gino, uneasy and dissatisfied, followed me and protested once more.

"Having a bath, too?"

"They have a bath after they've made love, don't they?"

"How should I know what they do?" he answered with a shrug. But I could see that in point of fact my boldness did not really displease him, he merely found it difficult to swallow. He was not a brave man and he liked to be on the right side of the law. But lawbreaking attracted him all the more since he hardly ever allowed himself to slip. "You're right, after all," he said with a smile after a moment's pause, wavering between temptation and reluctance, as he felt the mattress with his hand. "It's comfortable here — better than in my room."

"Didn't I say so?"

We sat down together on the edge of the bed. "Gino," I said, throwing my arms around his neck, "think how lovely it will be when we have a house of our own, just for the two of us. . . . It won't be like this — but it'll be our own."

I do not know why I said this. Probably because I knew for certain by now that all those things were out of the question and I liked to prick the place my soul was sorest.

"Yes, yes," he said, and kissed me.

"I know the kind of life I want," I continued, with the cruel feeling that I was describing something lost and gone forever, "not a fine place like this — two rooms and a kitchen would be enough for me. But everything would be my own and it would shine like a mirror — and we'd be peaceful. We'd go out on Sunday together, eat together, sleep together. Oh, Gino, just think how lovely it'll be!"

He said nothing. As a matter of fact, I remained quite unmoved as I said all this. I felt I was playing a part, like an actor on the stage. But this made it all the more bitter, because the cold, superficial part I was playing, which woke not the slightest echo of participation in my spirit, was what I had really been only ten days before. Meanwhile, while I was speaking, Gino undressed me impatiently. And I noticed once more, as I had when I got in the car, that I still liked him; perhaps my body, always ready to take pleasure from him, rather than my soul, which was by now estranged, made me so good-natured and quick to forgive. He caressed me and kissed me, and his caresses and kisses troubled my mind and the pleasure of my senses overcame the reluctance in my heart. "You make me die," I finally murmured, wholly meaning it, falling onto the bed.

Later on I put my legs under the sheets and so did he, and we lay together with the embroidered cover of the magnificent bed pulled up to our chins. Over our head was suspended a kind of canopy with a cloud of white, gossamer veils floating down over the head of the bed. The whole room was white, with long, soft curtains at the windows, beautiful low furniture against the walls, beveled mirrors, ornaments of glittering glass, marble, and silver. The exquisitely fine sheets were like a caress against my body; and, if I moved ever so slightly, the mattress yielded gently to my limbs and induced in me a deep desire for sleep and rest. Through the open door I could hear the quiet gurgling of the water flowing into the bath. I felt utterly content and not in the least resentful against Gino any longer. This seemed the best moment to tell him that I knew everything, because I was sure I would say it kindly, with no shadow of bitterness.

"So, Gino," I said in caressing tones after a long silence, "your wife's called Antonietta Partini."

Perhaps he was drowsing, because he jumped violently as if someone had tapped him unexpectedly on the shoulder. "What's that you said?"

"And your daughter's name is Maria, isn't it?"

He would have liked to protest again, but he looked into my eyes and realized it was useless. Our heads lay on the same pillow, our faces side by side, and I was speaking with my mouth almost on his. "Poor Gino," I said, "why did you tell me so many lies?"

"Because I loved you," he answered violently.

"If you really loved me, you ought to have thought how unhappy I'd be when I learned the truth, but you didn't think of that, Gino, did you?"

"I loved you," he interrupted me, "and I lost my head, and —"

"That's enough," I said. "I was very unhappy for a while — I didn't think you capable of such a thing — now it's over. Let's not mention it again. Now I'm going to have a bath." I pulled away the sheets, slipped out of bed and went into the bathroom. Gino stayed where he was.

The bath was full of hot water, a bluish color, lovely to see among all the white tiles and shining faucets. I stood in the bath and slowly let myself down into the steaming water. Lying in it, I shut my eyes. There was no sound from the next room; Gino must be thinking over what I had said and was trying to work out some plan whereby he could avoid losing me. I smiled at the thought of him in the big double bed, with my news still like a slap in the face. But my smile was not spiteful; it was the sort of smile caused by something amusing but completely impersonal, because, as I have said, I felt no resentment toward him but, knowing him for what he really was, only a kind of fondness for him. Then I heard him walking about, probably dressing. After a while he peeped in at the bathroom door and looked at me like a whipped dog, as if he did not dare to enter.

"So we won't be seeing anything more of each other," he said humbly, after a long silence.

I realized that he really loved me in his own way, although not enough to make lying to me and deceiving me utterly repulsive. I remembered Astarita and the thought that he, too, loved me in his own way. "Why shouldn't we?" I replied as I soaped one of my arms. "If I hadn't wanted to see you, I wouldn't have come today. We'll still meet, but no so often as before."

His courage seemed to return at these words. He came into the bathroom. "Shall I soap you?" he asked.

I could not help being reminded of Mother, who was also so full of attention and care for me each time she had renounced her parental authority.

"If you like," I said shortly. "Soap my back where I can't get at it." Gino picked up the soap and sponge; I stood up and he washed my back. I looked at myself in a long mirror opposite the bath and imagined I was the lady who owned all those lovely things. She, too, must stand up like that, and a maid, some poor girl like myself, had to bend over and soap her and wash her, taking care not to scratch her skin. I thought how lovely it must be to be waited on by somebody else and not do everything with your own hands; to keep still and limp while she bustles about full of respectful attention. I remembered the simple idea I had had the first time I went to the villa; without my shabby clothes, naked, I was the equal of Gino's mistress. But my fate, unfairly, was quite different.

"That'll do," I said to Gino in irritation.

He picked up the bathrobe and I got out of the bath; he then held it out behind me and I wrapped myself in it. He wanted to embrace me, perhaps to see whether I would repel him, and I let him kiss my neck as I stood there, motionless, wrapped in the bathrobe. Then he began to dry me all over, in silence, starting with my feet and going all the way to my breasts, eagerly and ably as if he had never done anything else in his life, and I shut my eyes and imagined once again that I was the mistress and he the maid. He took my passivity for acquiescence and I suddenly discovered that instead of drying me he was caressing me. At that I pushed him away, let the bathrobe fall, and went on tiptoe barefooted into the next room. Gino stayed in the bathroom to let the water out.

I dressed quickly and then walked around the room looking at the furniture. I stopped in front of the dressing table dotted with pieces of gold and tortoiseshell. Among the hairbrushes and perfume-bottles I noticed a gold powder compact. I picked it up and looked at it closely. It was heavy, apparently made of solid gold. It was square, of rolled gold in stripes, and a large ruby was set in the catch. I had a feeling of discovery, rather than of temptation — now I could do anything, even steal. I opened my bag and put the compact into it; being heavy it slipped right down into the bottom among my loose change and keys. In taking it, I felt a kind of sensual pleasure, not unlike the sensation accepting money from my lovers caused me. As a matter of fact, I did not have any use for such a valuable compact, it did not match my clothes or the kind of life I led. I was sure I would never use it. But in stealing it, I seemed to be obeying the logic that now governed the course of my life. I thought I might as well be hanged for a sheep as a lamb.

Gino returned and, with servile attention to detail, began to tidy up the bed and all the things he did not think were in their proper places. "Come on!" I said scornfully as I saw him looking around anxiously when he had finished, in order to make sure everything was in it usual place, "Come on! Your mistress won't notice a thing — you won't be fired this time!" I saw a flash of pain cross Gino's face at this and I was sorry I had said it, because it was spiteful and not even sincere.

We said nothing on the way downstairs or in the garden as we got into the car. Night had fallen some time since. And as soon as the car began to thread its way through the twisted streets of that fashionable district, I began to cry gently, as if I had been waiting only for that moment. I did not even know myself why I was crying, and yet I was filled with bitterness. I am not made to play disillusioned, angry parts, and the whole afternoon, although I had done my utmost to appear calm, disillusionment and anger had motivated many of my actions and words. Now for the first time, while I was still crying, I felt really resentful toward Gino, who, through his betrayal of me, had aroused emotions I found unpleasant and which did not suit my character. I thought how good and sweet I had always been and how perhaps I was not going to be so anymore from that moment, and the thought filled me with despair. I would have liked to ask Gino heartbrokenly, "Why did you do all this? How can I ever forget it and think no more about it?" But instead I said nothing, swallowed my tears and shook my head a little to make them run down my cheeks, as one shakes a branch to rid it of its ripest fruit. I hardly noticed that meanwhile we were driving right across the city. When the car stopped, I got out and held my hand out to Gino. "I'll phone you," I said, He looked at me with an expression of hope that changed to amazement when he saw my face bathed in tears. But he had not time to say a word, for I ran off with a wave of the hand and a forced smile.

9

*A*ND SO LIFE CONTINUED TO revolve for me, always in the same direction and with the same people, like the merry-go-rounds of Luna Park, where the flashing lights used to fill my heart with gaiety when I watched them from the windows of our apartment as a child.

Merry-go-rounds, too, have very few figures and they are always the same. The swan, the cat, the car, the horse, the throne, the dragon, and the egg swing around time and time again to the sound of a wailing, strident, clashing music, to be followed once again by the swan, the cat, the car, the horse, the throne, the dragon, and the egg, the whole night through. The figures of my lovers began to revolve for me in just the same way; no matter whether they were men I had already met or newcomers, they were all alike.

Giacinti returned from Milan with a pair of silk stockings as a gift, and I saw him every evening for some time. Then he went away again and I took up with Gino, seeing him once or twice a week. On other evenings I went with men I picked up in the street

or whom Gisella introduced to me. There were young men, older
men, and some quite old ones; some were charming and treated
me kindly, others were unpleasant and regarded me merely as an
object to be bought or sold; but, since I had made up my mind not
to become attached to any of them, it was always the same in the
end. We used to meet in the street or in a café, sometimes had
supper together, then hurried back to my place. There we shut ourselves up in my room, made love, chatted a little; and then the man
paid up and left, and I joined Mother in the room where she was
waiting for me. If I was hungry I had a meal, and then went to bed.

Very occasionally, if it was early, I slipped out again downtown
to find another man. But days and days passed when I saw no one
and stayed at home doing nothing. I had become very lazy; it was
a sad, voluptuous idleness, in which I indulged the desire for rest
and peace I shared with Mother and all the poor hardworking
people around me. Sometimes the mere sight of the empty savings box was enough to drive me out into the streets in the heart of
the city to seek company; but often my laziness triumphed and I
preferred to borrow money from Gisella or send Mother to do her
shopping on credit.

And yet I really cannot say I disliked this way of life. I soon realized that my passion for Gino had not been anything particularly unique and that in my heart of hearts I liked all men, for one
reason or another. I do not know whether this happens to all the
women who take up my profession or whether it means that I had
a special vocation for it; I only know that each time, I felt a thrill of
curiosity and expectation that was rarely disappointed. I liked the
long, slim, adolescent bodies of the young men, their clumsy gestures, their shyness, their sentimental glances, the coolness of their
hair and lips; I liked the muscular arms, the broad chests, the indefinable weight and power in the shoulders, bellies, and legs of
virile men in their prime; I even liked old men, because men are
different from women in that they are not limited by age, and even
in old age keep their charm or acquire a new one of a particular
kind. The fact that I changed my lover every time helped me to
notice qualities and defects at first sight, with that precise and

keen observation that can only be obtained by experience. The human body, besides, was an inexhaustible source of mysterious, insatiable delight; and I often found myself gazing at the limbs of my companions of a single night, or touching them with my finger tips as if I yearned to reach beyond the superficial relationship between us and discover the meaning of their physical beauty and explain to myself why I felt so deeply attracted. But I tried to hide my attraction as much as possible because these men in their perpetual vanity might have mistaken it for love; whereas, actually, love, at least as they understood it, had nothing to do with my feelings, which were more like the reverent trepidation I used to feel when I performed certain religious duties in church.

The money I earned in this way, however, was not as much as might be supposed. First of all, I was incapable of being as mercenary and greedy as Gisella. I wanted to be paid, of course, since I was not going with men for my own amusement; but my nature led me to give myself to them more out of physical exuberance than out of convenience and I did not think about the money until the time came to be paid, that is, when it it was too late. I always had a dim conviction that I was supplying men with goods that cost me nothing, something usually not paid for. I felt I received money as a gift rather than as dues. I felt love either should not be paid for or else could never be paid for enough; and between my modesty and my vanity I was unable to fix any price that did not seem purely arbitrary to me. Therefore, if they gave a lot, I thanked them too gratefully; if they gave me little, I could never persuade myself that I had been cheated and I did not protest. Only later, after much bitter experience, I decided to copy Gisella, who used to come to terms beforehand. But at first I always felt ashamed and could only mention payment in an undertone, so that often they failed to understand me and I had to repeat it.

There was another reason why my earnings were insufficient. This was the fact that, since I was far less careful about what I spent than I had been before, and had spread myself thin buying a few dresses, some perfume, toiletries, and other things that I needed professionally, the money my lovers gave me never went very far, much like the money I had earned as a model and by helping Mother with her sewing. I seemed no better off than before, despite the sacrifice of my honor. There were days when there was not a penny in the house, just as before and even oftener than before. I was tormented by my anxiety at having no settled future, just as before and to an even greater degree. I am rather carefree and phlegmatic by nature, and my anxiety never became an obsession as it would in someone not so well balanced and indifferent as I. But the thought was always at the back of my mind, like a worm in a piece of old furniture, and it was always warning me that I possessed nothing and that I could neither forget my condition and rest, nor improve it once and for all by means of my chosen profession.

Mother no longer felt at all anxious, or at least, if she did, she did not show it. I had told her right away that she need no longer ruin her sight by sewing all day long; and she immediately gave up most of her work, as if she had been waiting for this moment all her life — she kept only a few orders that she did when she felt like it, more as a pastime than a job. It was as if the effort she had made for so many years, beginning when she was a little girl, working as a maid in a clerk's family, had suddenly failed without leaving any trace or possibility of recuperation, like old houses that crumble in on themselves, and leave no outside wall standing but only a pile of rubble. For someone like Mother money meant chiefly eating and resting to her heart's content. She had more to eat than before and allowed herself all those little comforts that to the mind distinguish the rich from the poor, such as getting up late, sleeping after lunch, going out for a walk on occasion. I must say that the effect of these innovations was the most unpleasant part of my new life.

It is possible that people who are accustomed to slaving all their lives ought never to give it up; idleness and comfort ruin them even when their source is an accepted and legitimate one, as was not the case with us. As soon as our conditions improved, Mother began to put on weight, or rather, so rapidly did her anxious, breathless thinness vanish, she began to swell out unhealthily, in a way I felt was significant although I could not tell what it signified. Her bony hips put on flesh, her thin shoulders filled out, her cheeks, which had always seemed drawn in as though she were panting, became puffed and florid.

But the saddest result of Mother's weight gain was what happened to her eyes. In the past they had been large, wide open, with an ever alert and apprehensive expression; now they had become smaller and had an indefinable, ambiguous gleam. She had grown stouter, but was no handsomer or younger looking. She, rather than myself, seemed to bear the visible traces of our changed way of life in her face and figure, and I was unable to look at her without a painful feeling of remorse, pity, and disgust. She increased my embarrassment by letting herself go in manifestations of greedy, ecstatic satisfaction. The fact was, she could hardly believe she need no longer work her fingers to the bone, and her behavior was that of a person who has never eaten enough or slept enough in all her life.

Of course, I did not let her have any inkling of my feelings. I did not want to upset her, and in any case, I realized that before reproaching her with anything I ought to reproach myself. But every now and again some expression of annoyance escaped me, and I seemed to love her less, now that she was fat, swollen, and walked with a waddle, than I had when she had shouted at me, rushed up and down moaning and groaning all day, and was thin and distraught. "I wonder if Mother would have grown fat in the same way if I had come into money through a good marriage?" I often asked myself. I believe she would, now I think of it; and I attribute the disgust her obesity aroused in me to the way I could not help looking at her, full of remorse and complicity.

I did not conceal my new condition of life from Gino for very long. In fact I had to tell him almost immediately, the first time I saw him again, about ten days after we had made love at the villa.

One morning Mother came to wake me, "Do you know who's come and wants to speak to you?" she said in a hushed and conspiratorial voice. "Gino!"

"Let him in," I replied simply.

A little disappointed by the brevity of my reply, she opened the window, and went out. A moment later Gino entered and I saw at once that he was angry and worried. He said nothing in greeting, walked around the bed, and came to a standstill in front of me where I was lying sleepily watching him.

"Look here — you didn't pick up anything from my mistress's dressing table by mistake the other day, did you?" he asked.

Now it's coming! I thought. I noticed that I did not feel at all guilty. But Gino's servility impressed me in the usual painful way.

"Why?" I asked.

"An extremely valuable powder compact has disappeared. A gold one with a ruby. The mistress has turned the house upside-down. Since I was in charge of the villa I know they suspect me, although they haven't said anything. Luckily she only noticed it yesterday, a week after she got back, so it's possible one of the maids stole it. Otherwise they'd have fired me already, or charged me, had me arrested, or something —"

I was afraid some innocent person might have got into trouble through me. "They haven't done anything to the maids?" I asked.

"No," he replied nervously. "but a policeman came, and questioned us all. There's been no peace in the place for a couple of days."

I hesitated a moment, then I said, "I took it."

He stared at me, twisting his face into a disagreeable expression. "You took it! And that's how you tell me?"

"How should I tell you?"

"But that's what's called stealing."

"Yes."

He looked at me and suddenly became furious. Perhaps he feared the consequences of my action or perhaps he guessed in some dim fashion that I considered him ultimately responsible for the theft.

"So that's it! What's the matter with you?" he said. "So that's why you wanted to go into the mistress's bedroom! Now I get it! But I, my dear, don't want to have a thing to do with it. If you want to steal, do it anywhere you want, I don't give a damn, but not in the house where I work. . . . A thief! What a mess for me if I'd married you — I'd have married a thief. . . ."

I watched him closely while he let off steam. I was amazed now that I could have thought him perfect for so long. He was anything but perfect. At last, when I thought he had come to an end of all he could say in reproach, I said, "Why are you so angry, Gino? They aren't accusing you of having stolen it! They'll talk about it for a day or two more and then the whole thing will die down. And God knows how many powder compacts your mistress has."

"But why did you steal it?" he asked. Obviously he wanted to force me to say what he dimly guessed.

"Because," I answered simply.

"Because! That's not an answer."

"If you really want to know, then," I answered quietly, "I stole it, not because I wanted it or needed it, but because now I can even steal if I feel like it."

"What do you mean?" he began. But I did not let him continue. "At night now I go on the streets, I pick up a man, I bring him here, and afterward he pays me. If I do this I can steal, too, can't I?"

He understood and his reaction was typical of him. "So you do that, too . . . great . . . yes, I'd have been in big trouble if I'd married you!"

"I wouldn't have done it then," I said. "I've done it since I found out you've got a wife and child."

He had been waiting for this statement all along and answered promptly. "No, my dear — don't put the blame on me. No one has to be a whore and a thief if she doesn't want to."

"Obviously I was one without knowing it, then," I answered. "You gave me my chance to become it."

He realized from my lack of concern that there was nothing to be said, so he changed his tactics. "All right — what you are and what you do aren't my business. But I've got to have that compact back. Otherwise sooner or later I'll lose my job. You've got to give it back to me, and I'll pretend I've found it in the garden or somewhere."

I answered immediately. "Why didn't you say so before? If it's so you won't lose your job, take it. It's in the first drawer of the closet."

He hurried over to the closet at once in his relief, opened the drawer, took out the powder compact, and put it in his pocket. Then he looked at me with a different expression in his eyes, a hint of shame and a desire for reconciliation. But I really could not face the embarrassing scene his look promised.

"Have you got the car outside?" I asked.

"Yes."

"Well, it's late and you'd better not wait. We'll talk it all over the next time we meet."

"Are you mad at me?"

"No, I'm not mad at you."

"Yes, you are."

"No, I'm not."

He sighed, bent over the bed, and I let him kiss me.

"You'll phone me?" he asked as he reached the door

"Don't worry."

And in this way Gino learned of my new way of life. But the next time we met we did not mention the compact or my profession; they were like uninteresting, commonplace matters, whose only importance had been their novelty. He behaved more or less like Mother, in fact, except that he did not appear to feel even for one moment the shock Mother had felt the first time I took Giacinti home, and which, from time to time, I couldn't help seeing beneath her satisfaction and even in the unhealthy, puffy look she had. Gino's chief characteristic was a kind of dull and shortsighted cunning. I imagine that when he learned of the changes brought about in my life by his betrayal of me he simply shrugged his shoulders and said to himself, "Oh, well — two birds with one stone — this way, she can't reproach me and I can go on being her lover all the same." There are men who think themselves lucky if they can keep what they have, whether it is money or women or life itself, even at the expense of their own dignity. And Gino was one of them.

I continued to see him because, as I have said, I still liked him despite everything and there was no one I liked more. And also because, although I believed everything was over between us, I was not anxious for an abrupt, unpleasant break. I have never liked sharp breaks or sudden interruptions. I think things in life die as they are born, by themselves, through boredom, through indifference or even through habit, which is in itself a kind of steady and faithful boredom; and I like to be conscious of them dying in this way, naturally, without it being my fault or anyone else's, and slowly giving place to other things. After all, we never get clear, definite changes in life; and those who do make hurried changes risk seeing their old habits come to the fore once again, still alive and as deep-rooted as ever. I wanted to reach the stage where Gino's caresses would leave me as indifferent to him as did his words, and I was afraid that, if I did not let things take their own time, he would continually keep cropping up in my life and oblige me, despite myself, to renew our old relationship.

Another person who came back into my life at this period was Astarita. It was far simpler in his case than in Gino's. Gisella used to see him secretly and I suppose he made love to her just to be able to talk about me. Anyway, Gisella was on the lookout for an opportunity to mention him to me, and when she thought enough time had passed and I had recovered my good humor, she took me aside, and very cautiously told me that she had met Astarita and he had asked for news of me. "He didn't say anything exactly," she continued, "but I could see he's still in love with you. As a matter of fact, I felt sorry for him — he looks wretched. Of course, he didn't say anything to me — but I'm positive he'd like to see you again — and after all —"

"Listen, it's useless to go on talking this way!" I interrupted her.

"What way?"

"Beating around the bush like this! Why don't you say straight out that he sent you to me, that he wants to see me again, and you've promised to give him my reply?"

"Suppose I have?" she said, taken aback. "What then?"

"Then," I said, "you can tell him I've nothing against seeing him again — like I do the others, of course, from time to time, without committing myself."

She was completely astonished by my calm; she thought I hated Astarita and would never agree to meet him again. She did not understand that by now love and hatred had ceased to exist for me, and, as usual, thought that I had some hidden motive.

"You're right," she said, after a moment's reflection and with a certain shyness. "In your place I'd do the same. You have to over-look your dislikes in some cases. Astarita really loves you and might even have his marriage annulled and marry you. Still — you are a clever one! And I thought you were such an innocent!"

Gisella had never understood the least thing about me, and I knew by experience that I would be wasting my breath if I tried to explain to her. Therefore I agreed. "That's just how it is," I said, feigning nonchalance, and left her in a state of mingled admiration and envy.

She gave Astarita my reply and I met him at the same pastry shop where I had met Giacinti for the first time. As Gisella had said, he still loved me passionately and, in fact, as soon as he saw me he went as white as a sheet, lost his self-possession, and was unable to speak. His emotion must have been stronger than himself, and I believe some of the simple women of the people, like Mother, must be right when they say that some men have been bewitched by their lovers. I had cast a sort of enchantment over him, without any desire or intention on my part; and although he realized it and did all he could to break free he was quite inca-pable of doing so. Once and for all time I had rendered him infe-rior, dependent, subject to me; once and for all I had disarmed him, hypnotized him, and placed him at my mercy. He explained later that sometimes he used to rehearse to himself the cold, scornful part he would play, and even learned his phrases by heart; but as soon as he saw me, he grew pale, his breast was filled with anguish, his mind became a blank, and his tongue refused to speak. He even seemed unable to face me, he lost his head and felt driven irresistibly to throw himself on his knees before me and kiss my feet.

He really was different from all the others; I mean he was quite obsessed. The evening we met he begged me, as soon as we had had a meal at a restaurant in tense and nervous silence and had reached my place, to tell him every single detail of my life from the day we went to Viterbo until the day I broke up with Gino. "Why does it interest you so much?" I asked him in astonishment.

"There's no real reason," he replied, "but what difference does it make to you? Don't think about me, just talk."

"As far as I'm concerned," I said, shrugging my shoulders, "if it'll give you any pleasure —" So I told him precisely everything that had happened after the trip; how I had had a talk with Gino, had followed Gisella's advice, and had met Giacinti. The only thing I did not mention was the matter of the compact, perhaps because I did not want to embarrass him, given his profession as a policeman. He asked me a number of questions, especially about my meeting with Giacinti. He never seemed to tire of the details, it was as if he wanted to see and touch everything, take part in it, not only hear about it. I can't tell you how often he interrupted me with, "And what did he do?" or, "And what did you do?" When I had finished, he embraced me. "It was all my fault," he stammered.

"No, it wasn't," I said, rather bored by the discussion. "It wasn't anyone's fault."

"Yes, it was my fault. It was I who ruined you. If I hadn't behaved as I did at Viterbo, everything would have been different."

"You're absolutely wrong," I said quickly. "If it's anyone's fault, it's Gino's — it has nothing to do with you. You, my dear, wanted to have me by force and things taken by force don't count. If Gino hadn't deceived me, I'd have married him, then I'd have told him all about it and it would have been as if I had never met you."

"No, it was my fault . . . maybe it seemed like Gino was to blame . . . but in reality the fault was mine."

He seemed to cling to the idea that he was to blame, not because he was sorry, but because, on the contrary, it pleased him to think he had corrupted me and led me astray. But to say that it pleased him is too feeble an expression: I should say the idea excited him, and perhaps this was the chief cause of his passion for me. I understood this later on when I noticed that he often insisted on my telling him, when we met, all that had happened, in full detail, between me and my paying lovers. During these accounts, he had a troubled, tense, and attentive expression on his face that embarrassed me and filled me with shame. And immediately afterward he would throw himself onto me and while he was taking me, he would passionately repeat obscene, brutal, offensive words I won't mention, but which would be insulting to even the most depraved women. How he could reconcile this extraordinary attitude with his adoration of me I never could fathom; in my opinion it is impossible to love a woman and at the same time fail to respect her, but in Astarita love and cruelty were mixed, the one lent the other its own color and strength. I have sometimes thought that his strange excitement at imagining me degraded by his own fault had been suggested to him by his profession as a member of the political police; his function, as far as I could understand, was to find the weak point in the accused, and corrupt and humiliate them in such a way that they would be harmless ever afterward. He told me himself, I cannot remember in what connection, that every time he succeeded in persuading an accused man to confess or break down, he felt a peculiar kind of satisfaction, like the satisfaction of possession in love. "An accused man's like a woman," he used to say, "as long as she resists she can hold her head up. . . . But as soon as she's surrendered she's a rag and you can have her again how and when you like." But more probably his cruel, complacent character was natural to him and he had chosen his profession simply because that was his character, and not the other way around.

Astarita was not happy; in fact, his unhappiness seemed the most utter and incurable I had ever known, because it was not due to any external cause, but originated in some weakness or twist I never succeeded in fathoming. When he was not obliging me to tell him my professional adventures he usually knelt in front of me, put his head in my lap, and stayed like that, motionless, sometimes for an entire hour. I had only to stroke his head lightly every now and again, like mothers stroke their children. From time to time he uttered a moan, perhaps he was even crying. I never loved Astarita but at such moments he roused a feeling of immense pity in me, because I could see he was suffering and there was no way of alleviating his pain.

He used to talk very bitterly about his family: his wife, whom he hated; his little girls, whom he did not love; his parents, who had given him a difficult childhood and had forced him to make a disastrous marriage while he was still an inexperienced youth. He hardly ever referred to his profession. Only once he told me, with an expression of peculiar distaste, "there are lots of useful things in a house, even if they aren't all clean — I'm one of them — a garbage can for rubbish." But I formed the impression that on the whole he considered his profession an honorable one. He had a high sense of duty and was a model official — as far as I could judge from my visit to him at the Ministry and his way of talking — being zealous, secretive, sharpsighted, incorruptible, and inflexible. Although he formed part of the political police force, he declared he knew nothing about politics. "I'm a cog in a wheel," he said to me another time. "What they say, I do."

Astarita would have liked to meet me every evening, but in addition to the fact that I did not wish to be tied up to any one man, he bored me and his convulsive seriousness and strange ways made me feel uneasy, so that every time I left him I heaved a sigh of relief, although I pitied him. For this reason, I tried to avoid seeing him more than once a week. The rareness of our meetings certainly helped to keep his passion for me ever wakeful and burning. If I had agreed to live with him, on the other hand, as he continually suggested, he would gradually have become accustomed to my presence and in the end would have seen me for what I really am — a poor girl like dozens of others. He gave me the number of the phone on his desk at the Ministry. It was a secret number, known only to the chief of police, the head of the government, the minister, and a few other important people. When I phoned he used to reply at once, but as soon as he found it was me his voice, which had been clear and calm a moment before, became troubled, and he began to stutter. He really was completely submissive and under my thumb, like a slave. I remember that once I absentmindedly stroked his cheek, without having been asked. He immediately seized my hand and kissed it passionately. On other occasions he asked me to repeat my impulsive gesture; but caresses cannot be given to order.

Quite often I had no desire to go down into the streets to pick up men, so I stayed at home. I did not want to stay with Mother, because although we had a tacit agreement not to mention my profession, our conversation always came around to it, in awkward allusions, and I would almost have preferred to talk of it openly without concealment. Instead, I used to shut myself up in my room, warning Mother not to disturb me, and stretched myself out on the bed. My room looked onto the courtyard, through the closed window no noise reached me from outside. I used to doze for a while, then got up and wandered around the room, busy with some little task, tidying my things or dusting the furniture. These jobs were nothing more than a stimulus to set my mind working, an attempt to create an atmosphere of intense and secluded intimacy. I used to become more and more deeply immersed in my reflections, until in the end I hardly thought at all, and was content with feeling alive after so much wasted time and exhausting ways.

At a certain moment during the hours I spent in such seclusion a profound feeling of bewilderment always overcame me; I suddenly seemed to see the whole of my life and all of myself from all sides, with icy clearsightedness. The things I was doing split apart, lost the substance of their meaning, were reduced to mere incomprehensible, absurd externals. I used to say to myself, "I often bring home a man who has been waiting for me in the night, without knowing me. We struggle with one another on this bed, clutching each other like two sworn enemies. Then he gives me a piece of printed, colored paper. Next day I exchange this paper for food, clothes, and other articles." But these words were only the first step in a process of deeper bewilderment. They served to clear my mind of the censure, always lying in wait there, of my profession, and they showed me my work as a series of meaningless gestures, similar in every way to the routine motions of other professions. Immediately afterward a distant sound in the city or the creaking of some piece of furniture in the room gave me a ludicrous and almost delirious awareness of my existence. I said to myself, "Here I am and I might be elsewhere. I might exist a thousand years ago or in a thousand years' time. I might be black or old, blonde or short." I thought how I had come out of endless night and would soon go on into another endless darkness, and that my brief passing was marked only by absurd and trivial actions. I then understood that my anguish was caused, not by what I was doing, but more profoundly by the bare fact of being alive, which was neither good nor evil but only painful and without meaning.

This bewilderment used to make my flesh crawl with fear; I would shudder uncontrollably, feeling my hair stand on end, and suddenly the walls of my apartment, the city, and even the world seemed to vanish, leaving me suspended in dark, empty, endless space — suspended, what's more, in the same clothes, with the same memories, name, and profession. A girl called Adriana suspended in nothingness. This nothingness seemed to me something terrible, solemn, and incomprehensible, and the saddest aspect of the whole matter was my meeting this nothingness with the manners and outward appearance with which I met Gisella in the evening in the pastry shop where she waited for me. I found no consolation in the thought that other people also acted and moved in just as futile and inadequate a way under that nothingness, within that nothingness, surrounded by that nothingness. I was only amazed at their not noticing it, or not making their observations known, not referring more often to it, as usually happens when many people discover the same fact at once.

At these times I used to throw myself onto my knees and pray, perhaps more through a habit formed in childhood than from conscious will. But I did not use the words of the usual prayers, which seemed too long to my sudden mood. I used to throw myself onto my knees so violently that my legs hurt for some days afterward and pray aloud, "Christ have mercy on me," in a shrill and desperate voice. It was not really a prayer but a magic formula that I thought might dispel my anguish and bring me back to reality. After having cried out impulsively in this way, with all my strength, I remained for some time with my face in my hands, utterly absorbed. At last I would become aware that my mind was a blank, that I was bored, that I was the same Adriana as ever, that I was in my own room. I touched my body half astonished at finding it whole, and getting up from my knees I slipped into bed. I felt very tired and ached all over, as if I had fallen down a rocky slope, and I went to sleep immediately.

These states of mind, however, had no influence at all on my daily life. I went on being the same Adriana, with the same character, who took men home for money, went about with Gisella, and talked of unimportant things with my own mother and with everyone else. And I thought it was strange that I was so different alone, in my relationship with myself, from what I was in company and with other people. But I did not flatter myself that I was the only one to have such violent and desperate feelings. I imagined everyone, at least once a day, must feel his own life reduced to a single point of absurd, ineffable anguish — only their knowledge apparently produced no visible effect upon them either. They left their homes, as I did, and went around sincerely playing their insincere parts. This thought strengthened me in my belief that all men, without exception, deserve to be pitied, if only because they are alive.

PART II

I

*B*Y NOW GISELLA AND I were partners more than friends. We did not agree about the places to frequent, it is true, for Gisella preferred restaurants and fashionable haunts, while I preferred simple cafés and even the street; but we managed to come to an agreement even over this difference in taste: we used to go to the different places in turn. One evening, after we had dined in vain at a restaurant, we were on our way home when I became aware that a car was following us. I warned Gisella that we might have customers if we let them approach us. She was in an angry mood that evening, because she had had to pay for her supper without getting anything out of it and she had been extremely hard-up for some time. "You go," she replied rudely. "I'm going home to bed." Meanwhile the car had come up close to the curb and was keeping level with us at reduced speed. Gisella was near the wall and I was on the outside. I looked out of the corner of my eye and saw there were two men in the car.

"What shall we do?" I asked Gisella in a whisper. "If you don't come, I won't go either."

She in her turn cast a surreptitious glance at the car and, for a moment, she seemed to hesitate, still in a foul temper. "I'm not coming," she said finally. "You go. Are you scared?"

"No, but I'm not going unless you come, too."

She shook her head, glanced once more at the car, which was still keeping pace with us, and then, as if suddenly making up her mind, said, "All right. . . . But pretend nothing's up and we'll lead them on for a while. . . . I don't like picking them up here in the Corso."

We walked along for fifty yards or so, the car keeping alongside us the whole time. Then Gisella, reaching a corner, turned up into a dark and narrow side street with a narrow pavement running beside an old wall covered with posters. We heard the car turn on to the side street, too, and then the blinding white rays from the headlights fell on us. We felt as though the light stripped us naked and nailed us both against the damp wall, with its torn, faded advertisements; and we stood still. Gisella said to me in an irritable whisper, "What's this all about? Didn't they get a good enough look at us in the Corso? I've half a mind to go home —"

"No, no, don't!" I pleaded hastily. I did not know why myself, but I was extremely anxious to meet the two men in the car. "What does it matter? They all act this way."

She shrugged her shoulders and at the same time the headlights wavered and went out, and the car stopped by the pavement in front of us. The driver thrust a blond head and rosy face out the window.

"Good evening!" he said in a ringing voice.

"Good evening," replied Gisella, with great dignity.

"Where are you going to all on your lonesome?" he continued. "Can't we keep you company?"

He spoke in the ironical tones of a person who thinks he is being witty, but these were hackneyed phrases I had already heard hundreds of times before.

"That all depends —" replied Gisella, still very dignified. She, too, always made the same replies.

"Oh, come on, now!" insisted the man in the car. "Depends on what?"

"How much will you give us?" asked Gisella, going up to the car and putting her hand on the door.

"How much do you want?"

Gisella named a sum. "You're expensive!" he chirped. "Very expensive!" But he seemed inclined to accept. His friend, whose face was concealed, leaned forward and whispered something in his ear. But the fair young man shrugged his shoulders and then turning to us, said, "All right — get in."

His friend opened the door, got out and went to sit in the back of the car; he then opened the door on my side and invited me to get in beside him. Gisella sat with the blond young man. He turned to her. "Where shall we go?"

"To Adriana's," she answered and gave him the address.

"That's fine," said the blond. "Let's go to Adriana's"

Usually when I was with one of these men I did not know, in a car or elsewhere, I kept motionless and silent, waiting for them to speak or do something. I knew from experience that they are impatient to take the initiative and do not need any encouragement. That evening, too, I kept still and dumb while the car made its way through the city. All I could see of my neighbor, who was designated by the arrangement of places as my lover for the night, were his long, thin, white hands lying on his knees. He did not speak or move either, and his head was in shadow. I thought perhaps he was shy and suddenly felt attracted to him. I had been shy, too, and shyness always moved me, because it reminded me of what I had been like before I met Gino. Gisella was talking, though. She liked to talk politely of inconsequential matters as long as she could, just like a lady in the company of men who respect her.

"Is this your car?" I heard her ask.

"Yes," answered her companion. "I haven't pawned it yet . . . Do you like it?"

"It's very comfortable," said Gisella composedly, "but I prefer a Lancia — they're quicker and the springs are better. My fiancé has a Lancia."

This was true — Riccardo had a Lancia. Only he had never been Gisella's fiancé, and Gisella and he had not been meeting for some time now. The young man began to laugh. "Your fiancé's got a Lancia that goes on two wheels!" he said.

Gisella was very touchy and the slightest remark made her angry. "Look here," she said resentfully, "what do you take us for?"

"I don't know — tell me who you are," said the blond. "I don't want to make any false steps."

Another of Gisella's obsessions was to pass herself off as something she was not with her pick-up lovers — as a dancer, a typist, or a respectable lady. She did not realize that her claims were completely contradicted by the fact that she let herself be so easily approached and always mentioned the money part of the business immediately. "We're two dancers in the Caccini company," she said haughtily. "We're not in the habit of going out with the first man who turns up. But since the company isn't properly set up yet, we were just going for a little walk this evening. As a matter of fact, I didn't want to accept your offer — but my friend said you looked like distinguished people. If my fiancé got to know, I'd never hear the end of it."

The blond laughed again. "We're certainly two very distinguished people! But you're two whores off the street . . . so what's the problem?"

My neighbor spoke for the first time. "Shut up, Giancarlo," he said in an even voice.

I said nothing. I did not like being given that name, because of the malicious intention that prompted it, but after all, it was the truth.

"First of all, it isn't true," said Gisella, "and what's more, you're a creep."

The blond said nothing. But he slowed down at once and then brought the car to a standstill beside the curb. We were in a deserted and dimly lit side street with houses on either side. He turned to Gisella.

"What if I were to dump you out of the car?"

"Just try!" said Gisella, drawing back. She was very spirited and was not afraid of anyone.

At this, my neighbor leaned forward toward the front seat, and I saw his face. He was dark, with a shock of hair falling over his high forehead, large, dark, bulging eyes, a clear-cut nose, curving lips, and an ugly, receding chin. He was very thin, his Adam's apple showed above his collar. "Are you going to shut up or not?" he said to the blond, emphatically but patiently, and it seemed to me as if he were intervening in some affair that did not really concern him at all. His voice was neither deep nor very masculine; it sounded as though it might easily break into a falsetto.

"What's it got to do with you?" asked his friend, turning around. He said it in an odd kind of voice, however, as if he were ashamed already of his own coarseness and was not sorry his friend had intervened.

My neighbor continued. "What sort of behavior is this? We invited them — they trusted themselves with us — and now we're insulting them!" He turned toward Gisella. "Don't take any notice of him," he added kindly. "Perhaps he's had a drop too much to drink! I'm sure he didn't mean to offend you." The blond made a gesture of protest, but his companion stopped him by putting a hand on his arm and saying peremptorily, "You've had too much to drink, I tell you, and you didn't mean to insult her — now let's go."

"I didn't come here to be insulted," said Gisella quaveringly. She, too, seemed grateful to the dark man for his intervention.

"Of course! No one likes to be insulted — of course they don't!" he said.

The blond was gazing at them, with a stupid look on his red face, which seemed swollen and bruised in patches. He had round gray-blue eyes and his large red mouth looked greedy and uncontrolled. He gazed at his friend, who was patting Gisella's shoulder soothingly, and finally burst into sudden laughter. "Word of honor!" he exclaimed. "I don't understand a thing. Where are we? Why are we fighting? I can't even remember how it all began. Instead of having a good time, here we are quarreling — word of honor, it's enough to drive you crazy!" He was roaring with laughter and still laughing turned to Gisella. "Come on, beautiful," he said, "don't look at me like that — we were really made for each other."

"Actually, that's just what I was thinking," she said, forcing a smile.

"I'm the nicest guy in the world, aren't I, Giacomo?" he continued in a shrill voice, laughing uproariously. "I'm everything you could wish for. But you have to know how to take me, that's all. . . . Come on — give me a kiss now." He leaned forward and placed an arm around Gisella's waist. She pulled her face back a little and said, "Wait." She took a handkerchief out of her bag, wiped the lipstick off her mouth, then gave him a dry and demure kiss on the lips. While she was kissing him, he twisted his fingers convulsively, pretending to suffocate and turning it all to burlesque. They broke apart almost immediately and he started the car up again with emphatic gestures. "Here we go again! I swear I won't give you any further reason to complain of me. I'll be very serious, very well behaved, very distinguished. I'll authorize you to hit me on the head if I don't behave well." The car set off again.

He went on talking and laughing aloud, even taking his hands off the steering wheel to gesticulate, to our imminent danger, all the rest of the way. My neighbor, on the contrary, after his brief intervention, had relapsed into silence in his dark corner. I now felt extremely attracted to him and curiously keyed up. As I think back, I now see that this was the moment when I fell in love with him, or at least, began to associate him with all the things I liked that so far I had never had. Love, after all, needs to be complete and not a merely physical satisfaction; and I was still seeking the perfection I had once thought I could say I had found in Gino. Perhaps it was the first time, not only since I had become a prostitute, but in all my life, that I had met anyone like him, with his manner and voice. The stout painter I had posed for in the beginning was like him in a way, of course, but was older and more self-possessed, and in any case I would have fallen in love with him, too, if he had wanted me. His voice and manner aroused the same sensation I had felt the first time I had gone to the villa of Gino's employers, although in a different way.

Just as I had felt extraordinarily charmed by the orderliness, comfort, and cleanliness of the villa and had thought life did not seem worth living if you could not live in a house like that — so now, his voice and kindly gestures, and all they implied about his character, attracted me passionately. At the same time my physical desire was aroused, so that I longed to be caressed by his hands and kissed by his lips; and I realized that the intense and ineffable mingling of old aspirations and present desire, which is the essence of love and its inevitable accompaniment, was already working in me. But I was also very much afraid he might not notice what I was feeling and might escape me. Driven by my fear, I stretched out my hand toward his in the hope that he would press it. But his hands were indifferent to the clumsy touch of my fingers that tried to entwine themselves in his. I was dreadfully embarrassed, because I did not want to pull my hand away, but at the same time I felt I ought to, since he gave no sign of life. Then as the car turned a corner sharply, we were thrown against one another and I pretended I had lost my balance and let myself fall with my head on his knees. He shuddered but did not move. The motion of the car was a delight; I shut my eyes and thrust my face between his hands to separate them, as a dog does, and kissed them and tried to make him stroke my face in an affectionate caress I could have hoped was spontaneous. I realized I had lost my head and was dimly astonished that a few kindly words could have provoked such turmoil in me. But he did not grant me the caress I so humbly begged for, and after a while withdrew his hands. The car came to a standstill almost immediately.

The blond leaped out and assisted Gisella with mock courtesy. We, too, got out; I opened the front door and we entered the courtyard. The blond led the way upstairs with Gisella. He was short and stocky; he looked as though he would burst out of his clothes, but he was not fat. Gisella was taller than he. Halfway up, he dropped a step behind and taking hold of Gisella's dress by the hem he pulled it up, exposing her white thighs with the garters around them and her thin little buttocks. "The curtain's going up!" he exclaimed, in a burst of laughter. Gisella merely pulled her dress down again with one hand. I thought my companion must dislike such coarse behavior, and I wanted him to know that I disliked it, too.

"Your friend's very cheerful," I said.

"Yes," he replied shortly.

"Obviously things are going well for him."

We entered the house on tiptoe and I showed them straight into my room. Once the door was shut, we all four stood there for a moment, and since the room was small there seemed to be even more of us. The blond was the first to recover his self-possession. He sat down on the bed and began immediately to undress as if he were on his own. He was talking about hotel rooms and private rooms, and telling us of one of his recent adventures. "She says to me, 'I'm a respectable lady — and I don't want to go to a hotel.' So I told her the hotels were full of respectable ladies. 'But,' she says, "I don't want to have to give my name.' 'I'll say you're my wife,' I say. 'One more or less doesn't matter.' So we go to the hotel. I tell them she's my wife, we go up to our room — but when I really get down to things, she starts coming up with excuses, says she's changed her mind, doesn't want to, she really is a lady. . . . So I lose my patience and try to force her. I wish I hadn't! She opens the window, threatens she'll throw herself out. 'O.K.' I say, 'it's my fault for bringing you here.' Then she sits down on the bed and be-gins whimpering and telling a long, moving story, enough to break your heart. But if you wanted to know what it was all about, I couldn't tell you; I've forgotten it. I only know that in the end I felt so good that I went down on my knees to ask her forgiveness for having taken her for something she wasn't. 'Now, we understand each other,' I say, 'we won't do anything, we'll just lie down and sleep each on our own.' So that's that and I fall asleep at once. But halfway through the night I wake up and look over to her side. She's gone! Then I look at my clothes and see they're all rumpled, so I hunt through my pockets and find my wallet gone too. She was a real, respectable lady!" His burst of laughter was so infec-tious that it made Gisella laugh and me smile. He had taken off his suit, his shirt, shoes and socks, and now stood there in a pair of dove-colored woolen long johns, skintight from the ankles to his throat, which made him look like a tightrope walker or a ballet dancer. His comical aspect was emphasized still further by this garment, which is usually worn by older men, and at the sight I forgot his cruelty and almost felt attracted to him, because I have always been attracted to cheerful people and am more inclined to cheerfulness myself than to gloom. He began to strut, short and bouncing, about the room, as proud of his long johns as of a uniform. Then, from the corner where the chest of drawers stood, he suddenly leaped onto the bed, falling on top of Gisella, who squealed out in surprise, and threw her back as if to embrace her. But then, while still hovering on all fours over Gisella, he lifted his red, excited face with a comical gesture, as if struck by a thought, and looked back at the two of us, like a cat does before beginning to touch its food. "What are you two waiting for?" he asked. I looked at my companion. "Shall I take my clothes off?" I asked.

He was still wearing his coat collar turned up around his neck. "No, no," he answered with a shudder. "After them."

"Shall we go into the next room?"

"Yes."

"Go for a ride in the car," cried the blond, still hovering over Gisella. "The keys are still in it." But his friend pretended he had not heard him and we left the room.

We went into the anteroom. I motioned to him to wait for me and entered the living room, where Mother was sitting at the table in the middle, playing patience. As soon as she saw me, she got up and went out into the kitchen, without even waiting for me to speak. So I peeped through the door and told the young man he could come in.

I shut the door and went to sit down on the sofa in the corner by the window. I wanted him to sit down beside me and cuddle me; the others always did. But he did not even look toward the sofa and began to pace up and down the living room, all around the table, his hands in his pockets. I thought that perhaps he was bored by waiting. "I'm sorry," I said. "I've only got one bedroom I can use."

He stood still. "Did I say I wanted a room?" he asked me huffily but gently.

"No, but I thought —"

He took a few turns around the room. I could not control myself any longer. "Why don't you come and sit down here beside
me?" I asked, pointing to the sofa as I did so.

He looked at me, then appeared to make up his mind, and
came to sit down. "What's your name?" he asked.

"Adriana."

"I'm Giacomo," he said and took my hand. This was unusual
and again the idea flitted across my mind that he was shy. I let him
hold my hand and smiled at him to encourage him.

"So we're supposed to make love in a little while?" he said.

"Yes."

"And if I don't want to?"

"Then we won't," I replied lightly, thinking he was only joking.

"Very well," he replied emphatically. "I don't want to, I haven't
the slightest desire to."

"All right," I said. But actually his refusal was something so new
in my experience that I did not understand.

"You aren't offended? Women don't like to be turned down."

At last I understood what he meant and shook my head, incapable of saying a single word. So he didn't want me. I suddenly felt
desperate, on the point of bursting into tears. "I'm not offended at
all," I stammered. "If you don't want to — let's wait until your
friend's done and then you can go."

"I don't know," he protested. "I'm making you waste your time
— you could have earned something with another man."

I thought perhaps he could not, rather than would not. "If you
don't have the money," I said, "it doesn't matter. You can pay me
another time."

"You're a good girl," he said, "but I've got the money. In fact,
look — I'll pay you all the same, so it won't seem as though you
had wasted an evening." He put his hand into his jacket pocket,
took out a roll of notes that looked as though he had prepared
them beforehand, and went to put them down on the table, away
from me, with a clumsy yet strangely elegant and scornful gesture.

"No, no!" I protested. "Why should you? Don't even think
about it." But I said it weakly, because, actually, I was not at all

sorry to accept his money — it was at least some kind of link with
him, and by being in his debt I could always hope to pay him
back. He took my wavering refusal as an acceptance, which in fact
it was, and did not pick up the money that he had left on the table.
He came and sat down on the sofa again, and I put out my hand to
take his, although I felt it was an awkward, silly thing to do. We
looked at one another for a moment. Then he suddenly twisted
my little finger hard with his long, thin fingers. "Oh!" I said angrily. "What's the matter with you now?"

"I'm sorry," he replied. He looked so deeply embarrassed that I
was sorry I had reproached him so harshly.

"You hurt me, you know," I said.

"I'm sorry," he repeated. Seized by sudden agitation, he stood
up again and began to walk up and down. Then he came to a
standstill in front of me. "Shall we go out?" he asked. "This
waiting around here really gets on my nerves."

"Where shall we go?"

"I don't know — shall we go for a ride in the car?"

I remembered the times I had been out with Gino in a car and
replied hastily, "No, not in the car."

"Let's go to a café. There are some cafés around here, aren't
there?"

"Not around here, exactly — but I think there's a place just
outside the gates."

"Let's go there, then."

I got up and we left the living room. On our way down I tried to
joke with him. "Remember — that money you gave me gives you
the right to come and see me any time you like . . . do you understand me?"

"I understand you."

It was a mild, dark, damp winter night. It had been raining all
day and the paved road was covered with large black puddles in
which the unwavering lights of the rare street lamps were reflected. The sky was cloudless above the walls, but there was no
moon and only a few stars shone dimly through the mist. From
time to time, unseen streetcars passed behind the walls, scattering

vivid flashes from the electric lines, which for a brief moment lit up the sky, the ruined towers and the buttresses covered with greenery. When I was out in the street, I remembered I had not been in the direction of the amusement park for months. I usually turned right toward the square where Gino used to meet me. I had not gone in the direction of Luna Park, I remembered, since I was a young girl and used to go out for walks with Mother, when we climbed the wide road below the walls and went to enjoy the lights and the music, without daring to enter because we had no money. On that side, on the main road, stood the villa with the little tower through whose open windows I had had a glimpse of the family seated around the table; the villa that had first made me dream of marriage, a house, and a family life of my own. I felt drawn to talk to my companion about that time, my youth, my hopes, not only from a sentimental impulse, but also, I must confess, for interested motives. I did not want him to judge me from appearances. I wanted him to see me in a better light, which I believed to be a truer one. Some people put on their best clothes and fling open the finest rooms in their house in order to welcome honored visitors; the equivalent for me of those best clothes and guest rooms were the girl I had been, my dreams and ambitions. And I counted on my memories, although they were so poor and uninteresting, to make him change his mind and bring him nearer to me.

"No one ever walks on this part of the road," I said as we walked along. "But in the summer everyone in the neighborhood goes for walks here. I used to — a long time ago now. It took you to bring me here again."

He had taken my arm and was helping me along the flooded roadway.

"Who did you go with?" he asked.

"With my mother."

He began to laugh so unpleasantly that I was astonished.

"Mother," he repeated, dwelling on the *m* sound. "*Mama* . . . There's always a *mama* . . . a *mama*. . . . What will *Mama* say? What will *Mama* do? *Mama, mama*."

I thought that perhaps he had some hidden reason for feeling resentful toward his own mother. "Did your mother do anything to hurt you?" I asked.

"No, she didn't do anything," he replied. "Mothers never do anything. Who hasn't got a mother? Do you love your mother?"

"Of course — why?"

"Oh, nothing," he replied hastily. "Don't pay any attention to me. . . . Go on. . . . So, you used to go out with your mother —"

The tone of his voice was neither reassuring nor inviting. But still I felt impelled to continue my reminiscences, partly out of liking for him, partly out of self-interest.

"Yes, we used to go out together, especially in the summer, because our apartment is stifling then. . . . Look — you see that little villa over there?"

He stood still and looked. But the windows of the villa were shut; it looked quite uninhabited. It seemed smaller than I remembered it and rather ugly and forbidding, cramped between the long, low railwaymen's houses. "Well, what about it?"

I felt almost ashamed now of what I was about to say.

"I used to pass by that villa every evening," I continued with an effort, "and the windows were open because it was summer, as I said. I used to watch a family sitting down to a meal, then —" I stopped, feeling suddenly embarrassed.

"And?"

"You aren't interested in all this," I said, and felt I was being both sincere and cunning in my shamefacedness.

"Why? Everything interests me."

"Well, then," I went on hurriedly, "I got the idea firmly fixed in my head that one day I would have a little house like that and would do just the things I used to see that family doing."

"Oh, I see!" he exclaimed. "A little house like that — you didn't aim very high."

"It's not so bad in comparison with the house we live in now," I said, "and, you know, at that age you get so many ideas in your head."

He pulled me toward the villa by one arm. "Let's go and see if that family still lives there."

"What's the matter with you?" I said. "Of course, they're still there."

"All right, let's see."

We were just outside the villa. The narrow, overgrown garden was dark, the windows, the little tower, all dark. He went up to the gate. "There's even a mailbox," he said. "Let's ring and see if anyone's in. Still — this little house of yours looks empty."

"No, don't!" I said laughing. "Don't do anything. What's got into you?"

"Let's try." He lifted his hand and pressed the doorbell.

I felt like running away, afraid someone might turn up. "Let's go, let's go!" I begged him. "Now they'll look out the window, and what kind of fools will they take us for?"

"What will *Mama* say, eh?" he repeated like a refrain, letting me tug him away. "What will *Mama do?*"

"You sure have something against mothers!" I said, walking fast.

We had reached the amusement park. Last time I had gone there I remembered there had been a huge crowd of people jostling one another, festoons of colored lamps, stalls with their acetylene lights, decorations in the booths, music, and noise. I was a little disappointed at finding nothing of all this. The fence appeared to surround a dark, deserted dumping ground for building materials, rather than an amusement park. The arches of the switchbacks, with an occasional seat still suspended here and there, appeared over the top of the fence, looking like gross-bellied insects whose flight had been suspended by a sudden paralysis. The low, pointed roofs of the rain-soaked, unlighted booths gave an impression of sleep. Everything seemed dead, as was right, since it was winter. The open space in front of the amusement park was deserted and covered with puddles. One single street-lamp shed a faint light.

"This is Luna Park in summer," I said. "There's always a huge crowd. But it isn't open in winter. Where shall we go?"

"What about that café over there?"

"It's a tavern, really."

"Let's go to the tavern, then."

We passed beneath the city gate and saw an illuminated glass door facing us on the ground floor of a row of little houses. I only realized when I was inside that it was the café where I had had a meal with Mother and Gino, and Gino had told the insolent drunk to mind his own business. There were only two or three people seated, eating food out of newspaper on the marble-topped tables, and drinking the host's wine. It was colder inside than out; the air smelled of rain, wine, and sawdust and the stoves appeared to have gone out. We sat in a corner and he ordered a liter of wine.

"Who's going to drink a liter?" I asked.

"Why? Don't you drink?"

"Only a little."

He poured himself a full glass and tossed it down in one gulp, but with an effort and no pleasure. This gesture confirmed in me what I had already noticed about him — he did everything as an act of will, from the outside, without taking any part in what he was doing, as if he were acting. We remained silent for a while; he kept staring at me with his bright, intense gaze, and I looked around the room. The memory of that distant evening in the tavern with Mother and Gino returned to me, and I was uncertain whether what I was feeling was regret or irritation. I had been very happy then, certainly; but how deluded! At last I came to the conclusion inside myself that it was exactly like opening a drawer left untouched for years, and instead of finding in it all the lovely things you had hoped for, you find only a few rags, moths, and dust. Everything had come to an end, not only my love for Gino, but youth itself and all its disappointed dreams. The truth of this was clearly shown by the fact that I had been able to make use of my memories, knowingly and calculatingly, in order to move my companion.

"At first I didn't like that friend of yours who was with us," I said, apropos of nothing, "but now I'm almost fond of him — he's so cheerful."

"First, he's not a friend of mine," he answered abruptly, "and then — he's not at all likable."

I was astonished at the violence of his tone. "Don't you think so?" I asked mildly.

He took a drink and continued. "You ought to avoid witty people like the plague — there's usually nothing underneath all their wit. You ought to see him in his office! He's not witty there."

"What sort of office?"

"I don't know — a patent office —"

"Does he make a lot of money?"

"A lot."

"Lucky fellow!"

He poured out some wine for me. "Why do you go around with him if you dislike him so much?" I asked.

"He's a childhood friend," he said, making a face. "We went to school together — all childhood friends are like that."

He drank again and added, "Still, he's better than me in some ways."

"Why?"

"When he does anything he does it in earnest, but in my case, first I want to do it and then —" his voice broke off suddenly into a falsetto and I started, amazed "— when it comes to the point I don't do it. This evening, for instance. . . . He phoned me and asked me if I wanted to, you know, go after women. . . . I agreed, and when we met you, I really wanted to make love to you. But then, when we got back to your place, all my desire vanished —"

"Vanished —" I repeated, looking at him.

"Yes. You no longer seemed to be a woman in my eyes — you seemed an object, a thing — you remember when I twisted your finger and hurt you?"

"Yes."

"Well, I did it to find out if you really existed — like that — even by making you feel pain."

"Yes, I existed all right," I said smiling. "You hurt me a lot." Now I began to understand, and it was a relief, that it was not because he disliked me that he had not wanted me. But in any case, there is never anything strange about people. As soon as you try to understand them, you find that their behavior, however unusual, is always due to some perfectly plausible motive. "So you didn't like me?"

He shook his head. "Not really — you or any other girl would have been just the same thing."

"Look here," I asked after a moment's hesitation, "you aren't impotent, by any chance?"

"Good God, no!"

I now felt a pressing desire to be intimate with him, to bridge the gap between us, to love him and be loved by him. I had denied that his refusal had offended me, but actually, if not offended, I was indeed hurt and wounded in my pride. I knew I was beautiful and attractive and I did not believe he had any valid reason for not desiring me.

"Listen," I said simply, "let's finish our wine and then go home and make love."

"No, it's out of the question."

"Then you mean I didn't attract you even when you saw me in the street the first time."

"It isn't that — but do try to understand."

I knew no man can resist certain arguments. "Obviously I don't attract you," I repeated simply, feigning bitterness, and at the same time I stretched out my hand and caressed his face with my palm. My hands are long, large, and warm; and if it is true that a person's character can be seen in her hand, there can be nothing vulgar about mine, as there is in Gisella's, whose hands are red, rough, and shapeless. I began to stroke his cheek, his temples, his forehead beneath his hair, looking at him all the time with an insistent, yearning sweetness. I remembered Astarita had done this to me at the Ministry, and I realized once more that I was truly in love. At first he remained still and unmoved by my caresses; then his chin began to tremble, a sign in him, as I noticed later, that he was excited, and an extremely youthful expression of distress, just like a boy's, was stamped on his face; I was filled with pity for him and was glad of this pity because it meant I was getting in touch with him.

"What are you doing?" he murmured. "We're in public."

"What do I care?" I answered unconcernedly.

My cheeks were burning despite the cold in the tavern, and I was surprised at seeing a little cloud of steam issue from our mouths at every breath. "Give me your hand," I said. Unwillingly he let me take it and I lifted it to my face, saying, "Feel how my cheeks are burning?"

He made no reply, only looked at me, his chin quivering. Someone came in, making the glass doors rattle, and I withdrew my hand. He sighed with relief and poured himself some wine. But as soon as the intruder had passed us, I stretched out my hand again and slipping it between the edges of his jacket I unbuttoned his shirt and touched his bare chest near his heart. "I want to warm my hand," I said, "and I want to feel your heart beating." I turned my hand over, touched him with the back of it, and then with the palm again.

"Your hand's cold," he said, looking at me.

"It'll get warm now," I smiled. I stretched out my arm and slowly passed my hand over his chest and thin ribs. I felt profoundly happy because I knew he was near me, and I was filled with love for him, so much love of my own that I had no need of his. "It won't be long before I kiss you," I warned him jokingly as I gazed at him.

"No, no!" he objected, trying to laugh, too, but really alarmed. "Try to control yourself!"

"Let's leave here, then."

"All right, let's go, if you want to."

He paid for the liter of wine he had not finished drinking and left the tavern with me. He now seemed aroused in his own way, but not through love, as I was, but rather through some strange ferment that the events of the evening had stirred up in his mind. Later, when I knew him better, I discovered that the same excitement always overtook him whenever, for some reason or other, he came across some hitherto unknown aspect of his character or was strengthened in his knowledge of it. For he was very self-centered — though in a lovable way — or rather, he was self-absorbed.

"It's always like this with me," he began, as if talking to himself, while I took him home almost at a running pace. "I have a great longing to do something, am filled with enthusiasm, everything seems flawless; I feel sure I'll act as I mean to and then, when I really have to act, everything collapses and I cease to exist — I become cold, idle, cruel — like I was when I twisted your finger."

He was talking absentmindedly in a kind of monologue, possibly with a kind of bitter complacency. But I was not listening to him because I was so full of joy, and I sped across the puddles on winged feet. "You've already told me all this," I said gaily, "but I haven't told you what I feel. . . . I want to hug you close, to warm you against my body, to feel you beside me and make you do what you don't want to do. . . . I won't be happy until you have."

He said nothing. He did not even seem to hear what I was saying, he was so deeply absorbed in thinking over what he had said himself. Suddenly I slipped my arm around his waist. "Put your arm around my waist, won't you?" I said.

He appeared not to have heard me, so I took his arm and, managing as best I could, as one does when slipping on a coat, I put his arm around my waist. We went on walking awkwardly because we were both wearing heavy winter coats and our arms could hardly reach around each others' waists.

When we were below the tower of the little villa I stood still. "Give me a kiss," I said.

"Later," he replied.

"Give me a kiss."

He turned and I kissed him violently, placing my two arms around his neck. His lips were closed but I thrust my tongue between them and then between his teeth, which he finally unclenched. I was not sure he was returning my kiss, but I did not mind. Then we drew apart and I saw a great crooked red patch of lipstick around his mouth that made his serious face look oddly funny. I burst into happy laughter.

"Why are you laughing?" he murmured.

I hesitated, then decided not to tell him the truth, because I enjoyed seeing him hurrying along beside me so earnestly, quite unaware of that patch on his face.

"Oh, nothing," I said. "Because I'm happy — don't think about me." And I gave him another rapid kiss on the mouth, feeling on top of the world.

But when we reached the front door, the car had gone.

"Now Giancarlo's left," he said irritably. "I'll have to walk miles to get home."

I did not let myself be annoyed by his unkindly tone of voice, because by now nothing could offend me. His faults appeared to me in a special light that rendered them lovable, as always happens when one is in love.

"There's night service on the streetcars — and if you like you can stay and sleep with me," I said, with a shrug.

"No, no, not that," he replied hastily.

We entered and climbed the stairs. When we reached the hall, I pushed him into my room and peered rapidly into the living room. It was dark, except for the window where a ray of light from a streetlamp lit up the sewing machine and chair. Mother must have gone to bed, and I wondered whether she had seen Gisella and Giancarlo and spoken to them. I closed the door again and went into my own room. He was walking about restlessly between the bed and the chest of drawers.

"Listen," he said. "It'd be better if I went."

I pretended I had not heard him, took off my coat, and hung it up. I felt so pleased that I could not help saying with all the vanity of a housewife, "How do you like this room? Don't you think it's cozy?"

He looked around him at last and made a grimace I did not understand. I took his hand and made him sit on the bed. "Now leave it all to me," I said. He looked at me as he sat there with his coat collar still turned up, his hands in his pockets. I removed his coat, slipping it off carefully, then his jacket, and hung it with the coat on a hanger. In no hurry, I undid his tie and then took off tie and shirt together and hung them over a chair. Then I knelt down and taking his foot onto my lap, like a shoemaker, I pulled off his shoes and socks and kissed his feet. I had begun slowly and methodically, but, little by little, as I removed his clothes, a kind of frenzy of humility and adoration grew upon me. Perhaps it was the same feeling I had when I knelt down in church, but this was the first time I had ever felt it for a man and I was happy, because I was sure that this was pure love, far removed from all sensuality and vice.

When he was naked, I knelt down between his thighs and took his sex, like a dark flower, between the palms of my hands, and for a moment pressed it hard against my cheek and hair, with my eyes shut. He let me do whatever I wanted, and I enjoyed the bewildered expression on his face. Then I got up, went behind the bed, and quickly undressed, letting all my clothes fall on the floor and trampled them. He was still seated on the edge of the bed, shivering, with downcast eyes. I came up behind him and, possessed by some gay fit of violence, I seized him and pushed him over, his head on the pillows. He had a long, slim, white body; bodies, like faces, have their own expressions, and his was chaste and young. I stretched myself beside him, my own body running the length of his, and felt how ardent and strong and dark and fleshy my body was in comparison with his thinness, slightness, coldness, and whiteness. I clung to him violently and pressed my body against his hips and threw my arms across his chest, my face on his with my lips to his ear. I felt as though I wanted, not so much to make love to him, as to wrap myself around him like a warm blanket and infuse him with my own ardor. He lay on his back with his head slightly raised, his eyes open, as if he wanted to watch everything I was doing. His keen glance swept down my spine and gave me a strange feeling of uneasy discomfort; however, for a while I paid no heed to it, being led on by my first impulse.

"Don't you feel better now?" I murmured suddenly.

"Yes," he replied in a distant, neutral tone.

"Wait," I said.

But at the very instant when I was about to embrace him with renewed passion. I felt his cold, steady gaze once more taut upon my back, like a piece of wet wire, and I suddenly felt ashamed and bewildered. My ecstasy died down; slowly I slipped from him and let myself fall on my back, separate from him. I had made a great effort of love. I had put into it the whole impulse of an innocent and primitive despair. The sudden realization that my effort was useless filled my eyes with tears, and I put my arm across my face to hide from him the fact that I was crying. Apparently I had been mistaken; I could not love him or be loved by him, and I also thought that he must be judging me, without any illusions, for what I really was. Now, I knew I was living in a kind of fog I had created in order to avoid mirroring myself in my own conscience. But he, on the contrary, had dispersed the fog with his glances and had placed the mirror once more before my eyes. And I saw myself as I really was, or rather, as I must have been for him.

"Go away," I said at last.

"Why?" He raised himself on one elbow and looked at me in embarrassment. "What's the matter?"

"You'd better go," I said, keeping my arm over my face. "Don't think I'm angry with you, but I can see that you don't feel anything for me so —" I did not finish but shook my head.

He did not answer, but I felt him move and leave my side; he was dressing. I then felt a stabbing pain, as though someone had wounded me deeply and was now twisting a thin, sharp knife into the heart of the wound. I was in pain as I listened to him dressing, in pain at the thought that in a few moments he would be gone forever and I would never see him again, in pain at my suffering.

He dressed slowly; perhaps he expected me to call him back. I remember hoping at one moment to hold him there by exciting his desire for me. I had lain down beside him with the coverlet drawn over me. Now, with a coquettishness I knew to be desolate and despairing, I moved my leg so as to make the cover slip off my body. I had never offered myself in this way and for a while, as I lay there naked, with my legs apart and my arm over my eyes, I had the almost physical illusion that his hands were on my shoulders and his mouth on mine. But then, almost immediately, I heard the door close.

I stayed as I was, motionless on my back. I believe I passed from sorrow to a kind of drowsiness and then fell asleep without being aware of having done so. But when the night was well advanced, I awoke and realized for the first time that I was alone. During my first sleep the sense of his presence had remained with me despite the bitterness of his departure. Somehow, I fell asleep again.

2

THE FOLLOWING DAY I WAS surprised to find myself feeling as languid, melancholy, and indifferent as if I were just recovering from a month's illness. I have a cheerful nature and my cheerfulness, which is due to my physical health and vigor, has always been stronger than any misfortune that has befallen me, so much so that on occasion I have been irritated at feeling cheerful despite myself, even when circumstances did not really warrant it. On most days, for instance, as soon as I got up I felt an impulse to sing or say something amusing to Mother. But that morning my involuntary lightheartedness was entirely lacking; I felt aching, dull, quite without the usual impetuous appetite for the coming twelve hours of life the day had to offer. I told Mother, who noticed my unusual mood at once, that I had had a bad night.

This was true; except that I gave as a cause only one of the many effects of profound humiliation inflicted on my spirit by Giacomo's rejection. As I said before, I no longer minded being what I was; I could see no reason, in my own eyes, why I should not be that. But I had hoped to love and be loved; and Giacomo's refusal, despite the complicated reasons he had given me for it, were, I thought, all due to my profession, which suddenly became hateful and intolerable to me on this account.

Self-love is a strange beast that may lie dormant under the cruelest blows and then awaken and be mortally wounded at the slightest scratch. One memory above all others stung me and filled me with bitterness and shame, the memory of a phrase I had uttered the evening before while I was hanging up my coat, "How do you like this room?" I had said. "Don't you think it's cozy?"

I remembered he had not answered, but had looked around him, making a grimace I had not understood at the time. Now I realized it was an expression of disgust. Certainly he had been thinking to himself: a streetwalker's room. As I thought it over, I writhed at having said it with such ingenuous pride. I ought to have realized that to anyone like him, so civilized and sensitive, my room must have seemed a sordid hovel, made even uglier by the extremely modern furniture and the use to which I put it.

I wished I had never uttered that miserable phrase! But now it was out and there was no more to be done about it. This phrase seemed like a prison from which I could never escape on any terms. To forget it or pretend to myself that I had never said it would be like forgetting myself or pretending to myself that I did not exist.

These reflections had the effect on me of a slow poison making its harmful way through the most precious blood in my veins. Although in the morning I usually tried to prolong my state of idleness, the moment always came when the sheets revolted me, and my body, as if moved by a will of its own, threw them off and leaped out of bed. But the opposite happened on that day; the whole morning passed, it was lunchtime, and although I tried to urge myself to get up, I could not stir. I felt tied down, inert, powerless, torpid, and at the same time I was aching all over as if my immobility had been won at the expense of some enormous, desperate effort. I felt as though I was one of those rotten old boats sometimes seen anchored in a marshy inlet, their holds full of black, stinking water. If anyone boards one of them, the decaying planks give way instantly and the boat, which has been there perhaps for years, sinks in a flash. I do not know how long I stayed there that way, uncomfortably wrapped up in the blankets, staring into the void, the sheets drawn up to my nose. I heard the bells chime midday, then strike one, two, three, four o'clock. I had locked the door and every now and again Mother came and knocked anxiously. I told her I would get up soon and that she was not to disturb me.

When the light began to fade, I summoned up my courage and, with what seemed to be a superhuman effort, I threw off the blankets and got out of bed.

My limbs were heavy with inertia and disgust; and I dragged myself about the room rather than walked as I washed and dressed. My mind was a blank; I only knew, with the whole of my body rather than my mind, that for that day at least I had not the slightest desire to go out and pick up a lover. As soon as I was dressed, I went and told Mother we were going to spend the evening together. We would go out for a stroll in the town and later we would have a vermouth in a café.

Mother's delight at an invitation of this kind, which she was not accustomed to, irritated me, I did not know why myself; and once again I noticed without any tenderness what flabby, swollen cheeks she had and what tiny eyes, filled with a wavering and uncertain light. But I restrained the impulse to make some sharp remark to her that might have destroyed her happiness, and sat down at the table in the dimly lit room, waiting for her to dress. The white light shed through the curtainless windows by the streetlamp shone on the sewing machine, lit up one of the walls. I lowered my eyes to the table and in the half-light I glimpsed the rows of gaily figured patience cards with which Mother used to relieve the boredom of her long evenings alone. At this I suddenly felt a strange sensation: I felt as if I were Mother, Mother herself in flesh and blood, waiting for her daughter Adriana in the next room to have done with one of her johns. This sensation can probably be attributed to the fact that I was seated in her chair, at her table, in front of her cards. Places do occasionally conjure up feelings in this way; and many people when they visit a prison, for example, imagine they feel the same chill, despair, and sense of isolation experienced by the prisoner who once languished there. But the living room was not a prison and Mother's sufferings were neither so weighty nor so easily imaginable. She was only living as, I suppose, she had always lived. Nevertheless, perhaps because a moment earlier I had felt a hostile impulse toward her, the intuitive sense of the life she lived was enough to produce in me a kind of reincarnation. When good people want to excuse a blameworthy deed they sometimes say, "Put yourself in her place." Well, at that moment I put myself in Mother's place to such an extent that I persuaded myself I was Mother.

I was Mother, but with a consciousness of being her, which she certainly did not have; otherwise she would have rebelled in some way. I suddenly felt shriveled, wrinkled, crippled, and realized what old age was, in that it not only changes the body but makes it weak and powerless. What was Mother like? I had seen her sometimes when she was undressing and, without reflecting, I had noticed her shrunken, flabby, grayish breasts, her yellow, relaxed belly. I now felt in my own person those breasts that had given me milk, that belly that had given me birth. I could touch them, and I seemed to experience the same regret and helpless anguish that the sight of her changed body must have caused in her. Youth and beauty make life beautiful and even gay. But when they are gone? I shuddered with terror and shaking off the nightmare for a moment, congratulated myself on being, in reality, Adriana, who was both young and beautiful and had nothing in common with Mother, who was neither young nor beautiful nor ever would be again.

At the same time, slowly, like some mechanism that has run down and gradually begins to pick up speed again, my mind began to formulate thoughts that must have come to her while, alone in the room, she waited for my return. It is not at all difficult to imagine what a person like Mother must have thought in similar circumstances; only in most people such thoughts are necessarily the product of reproach and scorn; and actually they do not so much imagine, as fashion for themselves a kind of dummy on which to vent all their hostility. But since I loved Mother and was putting myself in her place through affection, I knew that her thoughts at such moments were not selfish, fearful, or shameful, but were, in fact, unrelated in any way to what I did and was. I knew, rather, that her thoughts were incidental and insignificant — the kind a poor, ignorant old woman would have — since she had never been able to believe or think the same thing for two days running, without being sharply contradicted by necessity. Great thoughts and emotions, even when they are sad and negative, need shelter and a period of growth; they are delicate plants that require time to give them strength and firm rooting. But Mother had never been able to cultivate anything in her mind and heart other than the short-lived weeds of day-to-day reflections, resentments, and worries. And so I was able, as in fact I did, to sell myself for money in my own room; but Mother, as she sat in the living room before her patience cards, went on revolving in her mind the usual nonsense, if the things she had lived for throughout her life may justly so be called — the price of food, the gossip of the neighborhood, the household chores, the fear of accidents, the work she had to sew, and other such trivialities. At most, perhaps, day in day out, she listened for the clock to strike in the neighboring belfry and, without attaching much importance to them, had such vague thoughts as: Adriana's being longer than usual this time! Or, on hearing me open the door and saying a word or two in the hall: Adriana's finished. What else? Now, through this power of imagination, I was wholly my mother, body and soul; and, because I was able to put myself so truly and nakedly in Mother's place, I felt I loved her again even more than before.

The noise of the door being opened awoke me from my kind of daydream. Mother was lighting the lamp. "What are you doing in the dark?" she asked me, and I leaped to my feet, dazzled, and looked at her. She had put on brand-new clothes: I took that in at first glance. She had not put on a hat, because she never wore one, but was wearing an elaborately cut black dress. On her arm she was carrying a large, black leather bag with a yellow metal clasp, and had a short cat fur around her neck. She had damped her gray hair and combed it carefully, pulling it tightly piled on top of her head into a little knot stuck through with hairpins. She had even dabbed some pink powder on her once dry and withered but now too florid cheeks. I could hardly help smiling when I saw her so dressed up and serious; and, in my usual affectionate way, I said, "We'd better be going."

I knew Mother enjoyed ambling slowly along, when the traffic was at its height, through the main streets where the best shops in town are to be found. So we took a streetcar and got off at the top of Via Nazionale. When I was a little girl, Mother used to take me for walks along this street. She used to begin from Piazza dell'Esedra, on the right-hand sidewalk, and proceed slowly, looking attentively into every shop window until we reached Piazza Venezia. Then she would cross over and return to Piazza dell'Esedra, still looking at every single thing in the windows and dragging me along by the hand. Then, without having bought even a pin or having dared to enter one of the numerous cafés, she used to take me home, tired and sleepy. I remember I did not enjoy these walks myself because, unlike Mother, who seemed content to feed her appetite on detailed and delighted window shopping, I had wanted to enter the shops, to buy and take home some of the many lovely new things offered for sale in so much light behind the gleaming windows. But I realized very young that we were poor and I never expressed my feelings in any way. Only once I made a scene, I cannot remember why. We rushed along the crowded street, Mother dragging me by one arm while I tugged against her with all my might, shouting and crying. Until at last Mother lost her patience and boxed my ears instead of giving me the object I craved; and, at each successive blow, I forgot the pain of not being allowed to have what I wanted.

Here I was, then, once more at the far end of the sidewalk opposite the Piazza dell'Esedra, on Mother's arm, as if all the years had made no difference. Here the pavements were swarming with feet wearing shoes, boots, high boots, shoes with heels and shoes without, and some in sandals, which, to look at them, made one's head go round; here the people were strolling up and down in couples, or in groups of men, women and children, or alone: some slow, some in a hurry, all alike, perhaps just because they all wanted to be different, with the same clothes, the same hair, the same faces, eyes, and mouths. Here were the furriers, bootmakers, stationers, jewelers, watchmakers, booksellers, florists, drapers, toyshops, hardware stores, milliners, hosiers, glove shops, cafés, theaters, banks; here were the lighted windows of the buildings with people walking up and down or working at desks; the electric signs, always the same; on the street corners stood the newspaper kiosks, the chestnut sellers, the unemployed selling *ruban de Bruges* and rubber rings for umbrellas. Here were the beggars, a blind man with black spectacles, cap in hand at the top of the street, his head thrown back against the wall, lower down an elderly woman suckling a child at her shrunken breast, and lower still an idiot with a shiny yellow stump like a knee-joint where his hand should have been. As I found myself once more in that street, among such familiar things, I had a funereal impression of immobility, which made me shudder profoundly and feel momentarily naked, as if the icy breath of fear had passed between my body and my clothes. The clamorous, impassioned voice of a woman singing came from the radio of a nearby café. She was singing *Faccetta nera* — it was the year of the Abyssinian war.

Mother naturally had no inkling of what I was feeling; and, of course, I did not show it. As I have already said, I look good-natured, docile, even-tempered, and other people cannot easily guess what is going on inside my head. But at one moment I felt moved despite myself — the woman's voice had now started on a sentimental song — my lips trembled and I spoke to Mother. "Do you remember when you used to take me up and down this street to look in the shop windows?"

"Yes," she replied, "but everything cost less in those days — that bag, for instance — you'd have got it for thirty lira then."

We passed on from the leather shop to the jeweler's. Mother stopped to look at the jewelry. "Look!" she exclaimed ecstatically, "just look at that ring! Heaven knows what it would cost — and that heavy gold bracelet! I'm not keen on rings and bracelets myself — but I do like a nice necklace. I had a coral necklace once — but then I had to sell it."

"When?"

"Oh, years ago now."

I do not know why, but I was reminded that so far, with all my professional earnings, I had never yet been able to buy myself even the simplest ring. "You know," I said to Mother, "I've made up my mind not to bring men home anymore. It's over."

This was the first time I had mentioned my profession to Mother in so many words. She had a look on her face that I failed to understand at the time. "I've told you time and again," she said, "do what you like. If you're happy, I'm happy."

But she did not seem happy. "We'll have to take up the life we were living before. . . . You'll have to start cutting out and sewing shirts again," I continued.

"I did it for years," she said.

"We won't have so much money as we have now," I insisted rather cruelly. "We've been spoiled lately. . . . I don't know what I'll do myself."

"What do you think you'll do?" Mother asked hopefully.

"I don't know," I answered. "Be a model, perhaps — or help you with your work."

"What help will you be to me!" she said discouragingly.

"Or else," I went on, "I can be a maid — what is there to do?"

Mother's face now looked sad and bitter, as if she had in a moment shed the accumulated fat of recent times, as trees shed their dead leaves at the first chill of autumn. "You must do what you want," she repeated, but this time with conviction. "As long as you're happy, that's all I say."

I realized that two opposing passions were struggling within her: her love for me and her attachment to an easy way of life. I was sorry for her and I would have preferred her to have had the courage to give up one or the other of these two emotions for good and all, and either be all love or all calculation. But this happens very rarely and we spend our lives canceling the effects of our virtues with those of our vices. "I wasn't happy before," I said, "and I won't be happy now — only I can't go on anymore that way."

After this we said nothing more. Mother's face was all gray and collapsed, and her old drawn look of thinness seemed to become visible once more beneath her current florid appearance. She looked at the shop windows just as zealously and with as much concentration as before; but mechanically now, with no delight or curiosity, as if her mind were engrossed with something else. Perhaps her eyes were unseeing even while she gazed; or rather, she saw not the goods exposed in the windows, but her sewing machine with its tireless treadle, the needle thrusting madly up and down, the heaps of unfinished shirts lying on the table, and the black cloth she used to wrap around the completed work before taking it across town to her clients. But there were no such visions between my eyes and the shop windows. I saw them perfectly and my thoughts were crystal clear. I could make out all the objects behind the glass windows, with their price tags, one by one. I told myself I might not want to continue in my profession, did not want to, in fact, but there was actually nothing else I could do. I might now, within certain limits, have purchased most of the objects I was contemplating, but the very day I returned to being a model or any similar employment, I would have to give those things up forever, and the usual mean, comfortless life of repressed desires, useless sacrifice, and profitless saving would begin all over again for Mother and me. I might even aspire to owning some jewelry now, if I could find someone to give it to me. But if I returned to my old way of life, jewels would be as far out of my reach as the stars in heaven.

A rush of disgust for the old life, so stupidly harsh and hopeless, overwhelmed me and at the same time I had a vivid sense of the absurdity of my reasons for wishing to change my profession. Just because a student over whom I had lost my head had refused to have anything to do with me! Because I had persuaded myself that he despised me! Because I would have liked to be something different from what I was. I told myself it was only pride and that I could not, out of mere pride, plunge myself, and Mother in particular, back into the old, wretched conditions. I suddenly envisioned Giacomo's life, which for a brief moment had drawn near to mine and mingled with it, running off in another direction while my own continued along the path I was already treading. If I found someone who loved me and wanted to marry me, I'd change, even if he were poor, I thought, but it wouldn't be worthwhile for a whim. At this thought, my heart was filled with the sweet calm of liberation. I have often had the same feeling since, not only every time I have not refused what fate seemed to offer me in life, but when I have even gone out to meet it. I was what I was, and I had to be that and nothing else. I might be either a good wife, although this may seem odd, or a woman who sells herself for money, but I could not be a poor woman struggling and scrimping all her life long, with no other aim than the satisfaction of her own pride. Having made peace with myself, I smiled.

We were standing in front of a women's clothing shop that displayed silks and woolens. "Look what a lovely scarf!" Mother said. "That's just what I want."

Feeling composed and serene once more, I raised my eyes and looked at the scarf she meant. It really was lovely, in black and white, with a pattern of birds and branches. The shop door was open, with the counter in full view, and on the counter stood a case divided into little sections all filled with similar scarves, heaped untidily together. "Do you like it?" I asked Mother.

"Yes, why?"

"You shall have it. But first give me your purse and you take mine."

She did not understand and gaped at me. I said nothing but took her large black leather bag and put my smaller one into her hands. I undid the clasp of her bag and keeping it open with my fingers I slowly entered the shop, like someone intending to make a purchase. Mother, who still did not understand but dared not question me, followed me in.

"We want to see some scarves," I said to the clerk, as I walked up to the showcase.

"These are silk, these cashmere, these wool, these cotton —" she said, tumbling the scarves out before me.

I walked right up to the counter, and holding the purse level with my stomach, I began to examine the scarves with one hand, opening them and holding them up to the light to see the patterns and colors better. There were at least a dozen black-and-white ones, exactly alike. I let one slip onto the edge of the case, with an end hanging over the counter.

"I really wanted something brighter," I said to the girl.

"There's a better-quality article," said the clerk, "but it's more expensive."

"Let me see it."

She turned to lift down a case from the shelves. I was ready and drawing away from the counter a little, I opened the bag. It only took a moment to pull the scarf down by one end and then press myself up against the counter again.

Meanwhile the clerk had lifted the case down from the shelf. She put it on the counter and showed me some larger and finer scarves. I examined them at my leisure, commenting on the colors and patterns, and even showing them to Mother with little exclamations of approval that she, having seen everything and looking more dead than alive, answered by nods.

"How much are they?" I asked at last.

The clerk told me the price. "You were right," I said regretfully. "They're too expensive, for us, anyway — but thanks all the same."

We left the shop, and I walked quickly toward a nearby church, since I was afraid the clerk might notice the theft and run after us through the crowd. Mother, hanging on to my arm, looked about her with a suspicious and bewildered air, like someone who has been drinking and is none too certain that the things he sees wavering and shifting before his eyes are not drunk, instead. I could not help laughing at her bewilderment. I did not know why I had stolen the scarf; it was not important in itself because I had already stolen the compact from the house of Gino's employer, and in such matters what counts most is the first step. But the sensual pleasure of the first time came back to me; and I felt I understood now why so many people steal. A few steps brought us to the church on a side street.

"Shall we go in for a moment?" I asked Mother.

"If you like," she answered submissively.

We entered the little white church, circular in shape, which resembled a dance hall, with its double ring of columns encircling the floor. A dull light poured down from the windows in the dome onto the two rows of pews, polished by use. I raised my eyes and saw that the dome was frescoed all over with figures of angels with outspread wings, and I felt certain that those splendid, handsome angels would protect me, and that the clerk would not notice the theft before evening. The silence, the smell of incense, the shadow and sense of absorbed prayer in the church, all helped to reassure me after the confusion and excessively strong light in the street. I had entered the church hastily, almost knocking into Mother, but I grew calmer at once and my fear subsided. Mother made as if to fumble inside my bag, which she was still holding. I held her own out to her. "Put your scarf on," I whispered to her.

She opened the bag and arranged the stolen scarf on her head. We dipped our fingers in the holy-water stoup and went to sit down in the first row of pews facing the high altar. I knelt down and Mother remained seated, her hands in her lap, her face shadowed by the scarf, which was too large for her. I realized she was distressed; and I could not help comparing my own calm with her agitation. I felt in a sweet and conciliatory frame of mind, and although I knew I had done something forbidden by religion, I felt no remorse and was far nearer a religious state than I was when I had done nothing wrong and had worked my fingers to the bone to eke out a living. I remembered the shudder of bewilderment I had experienced a moment earlier while looking at the crowded street, and I was comforted by the idea that there was a God who could see clearly into me and saw there was nothing bad, and that the mere fact of being alive rendered me innocent, as, in fact, all men are. I knew this God was not there to judge and condemn me, but to justify my existence, which could only be good since it descended directly from Him. While I mechanically repeated the words of the prayer, I was looking at the altar, where the dark image in a picture dimly visible behind the candle flames appeared to be the Madonna, and I realized that between the Madonna and myself the question was not whether I should behave in a particular way, but more essentially whether I should feel encouraged to continue living at all. The encouragement I was seeking suddenly seemed to me to be pouring out toward me from the dark figure behind the altar candles, in the form of a sudden sensation of heat that flooded my whole being. Yes, I was encouraged to go on living, although I knew nothing about life or why I was alive.

Mother sat there, sullen and bewildered. Turning around to look at her, I could not help smiling affectionately at her. "Say a little prayer — it'll do you good," I whispered. She shivered, hesitated and then unwillingly knelt down, her hands joined. I knew she did not want to believe any longer in religion; it seemed to her a kind of false consolation whose aim was to make her be good and forget the harshness of life. Nevertheless I saw her lips moving mechanically and the expression of suspicious ill humor on her face made me smile again. I wanted to reassure her, tell her that I had changed my mind and she had nothing to worry about, she would not be obliged to work as she had in the past. There was something ingenuous about Mother's bad temper; she was like a child when it is refused a sweet it has been promised, and this seemed to be the most important aspect of her behavior to me. Otherwise I might have thought she counted on my profession to enable her to enjoy all her little comforts; and I knew in my heart that this was not true.

Having said her prayers, she crossed herself angrily and rapidly, as if to show clearly that she had done it only to please me. I got up and motioned to her to come out. On the doorstep she took off the scarf, folded it carefully and replaced it in her bag. We returned to Via Nazionale and I walked toward a pastry shop. "Now, we're going to have a vermouth," I said.

"No! Why should we? We don't need one," protested Mother, in a voice that sounded both pleased and apprehensive. She was always like that, afraid from old habit that I would spend too much. "What'll it cost?" I said. "One vermouth!" She was silent and followed me into the shop.

It was an old-fashioned place, with a counter and wainscot of polished mahogany and a number of showcases filled with handsome boxes of sweets. We sat down in a corner and I ordered two vermouths. The waiter made Mother feel embarrassed, and while I was ordering she sat there stockstill and awkward, her eyes cast down. When he had brought our drinks she picked up the little glass, sipped the wine, put it down again, then said seriously, "It's good."

The waiter had brought a metal and glass cake stand with some cakes in it. I opened it. "Have one," I said to Mother.

"No — please!"

"Go on — have one!"

"It'll spoil my appetite."

"One cake!" I looked at the cakes and chose a millefeuilles and gave it to her. "Eat this one," I said. "It's not heavy."

She took it and ate it in little mouthfuls, remorsefully looking at each bite she had taken. "It's really good," she said at last.

"Have another one," I said. This time she did not need pressing and accepted another cake. When she had finished the vermouth, we sat on without speaking, watching the customers coming and going in the shop. I could see that Mother was glad to be sitting in a corner with two cakes and a vermouth inside her, that she was interested and amused by the incessant movement of the people, and that she had nothing to say to me. This was probably the first time she had ever been in such a place and the novelty of the experience impeded any thoughts she might have on the subject.

A young lady entered, holding the hand of a little girl who was wearing a large white fur neckpiece, a short dress and white cotton gloves and stockings. The mother chose a cake from the stand on the counter and gave it to her.

"When I was a little girl, you never took me into the pastry shops," I said.

"How could I have afforded it?" she asked,

"And now it's I who take you," I said in even tones.

She was silent for a moment, then said sulkily, "Now you're throwing it in my face because you brought me here — I didn't want to come."

I put my hand on hers. "I'm not throwing anything in your face," I said. "I'm glad I brought you here. Did grandmother ever take you to pastry shops?"

She shook her head. "I never went outside our own district until I was eighteen."

"You see," I said, "you need someone in a family who will do certain things for the first time sooner or later. You didn't do them, nor your mother, nor probably your mother's mother. So I'm doing them. You can't go on like that for ever!"

She did not answer and we stayed there for another quarter of an hour watching the people. Then I opened my purse, took out my cigarette case and lit a cigarette. Women like me often smoke in public places in order to attract men. But I was not thinking of picking anyone up just then. On the contrary, I had decided for that evening at least to have nothing to do with them. I simply wanted to smoke. I put the cigarette to my lips, drew in the smoke, then blew it out of my mouth and nostrils, holding the cigarette between two fingers and watching the people.

But there must have been something provocative in the gesture, because I immediately noticed someone near the counter about to sip a cup of coffee he held in one hand, who stopped with the cup halfway to his lips and began to stare at me. He was about forty years old, short, with thick, curly hair, bulging eyes, and a heavy jaw. He was so stocky that he seemed to have no neck. He stood there staring at me, like a bull that has seen a red rag and stands motionless before lowering its head to attack. He was well, though not fashionably, dressed, with a close-fitting overcoat that accentuated the breadth of his shoulders. I lowered my eyes, and for a moment started to consider what there was for and against such a man. I knew his character was such that one glance from me would be enough to make the veins in his neck stand out and his face grow purple, but I was not at all sure that I liked him. Then I realized that the desire to attract him had set my whole body on edge, like hidden sap bursting out of the rugged bark of some tree in a number of tender shoots, forcing me to relinquish my reserved manner. And this was only one hour after I had decided to change my profession. I said to myself that there was nothing to be done about it, it was stronger than I was. But my thoughts were quite cheerful; for since I had left the church I had become reconciled to my fate, whatever it was, and I felt that my acceptance of it was worth more to me than any noble rejection. So after a moment's consideration, I raised my eyes and looked at him. He was still there, like a wild beast, his cup in his thick, hairy hand, his bovine eyes fixed on me. At that I made up my mind on the moment and threw him a lengthy, caressing glance, with all the skill I could summon. He received it full in the face and grew purple as I had foreseen he would. He sipped his coffee, put the cup down, and strutted in his close-fitting overcoat, with stiff little steps, to the cash desk, and paid. He turned in the doorway and made me a definite, imperious signal of understanding. I looked my acceptance in return.

"I'm going to leave you now," I said to Mother. "You stay here, though, in any case we couldn't go out together."

She was enjoying the sights in the pastry shop and started in alarm. "Where are you going? Why?"

"There's someone waiting for me outside," I said as I got to my feet. "Here's the money — pay for everything and go home. I'll be there before you, but I won't be alone."

She looked at me in dismay and with a kind of remorse, I thought. But she did not say anything. I nodded good-bye and went out. The man was waiting in the street. I was hardly out of the place when he was on me, grasping my arm firmly. "Where shall we go?"

"To my place."

So, after a few hours of anguish I gave up the unequal struggle against what appeared to be my fate. Indeed, I welcomed it with greater love, as one embraces a foe one cannot defeat; and I felt liberated. Some people may think it very easy to accept an ignoble but profitable fate rather than renounce it. But I have often wondered why misery and anger dwell in the hearts of those people who try to live according to certain precepts and to conform to certain ideals, when those who accept their own lives — which are, after all, emptiness, darkness and weakness — are so often gay and carefree. In such cases the individual does not obey any precepts but his own temperament, which then takes shape as his true and unique destiny. My temperament, as I have already said, was to be gay, kindly, serene, at all costs; and I accepted it.

3

I GAVE UP GIACOMO ALTOGETHER, deciding to think no more about him. I felt I loved him and if he were to return I would be happy and would love him more than ever. But I also knew I would never let myself be humiliated by him again. If he came back, I would stand there before him, enclosed in my own life as in a fortress, which would really be impregnable and unshaken until I left it of my own accord. "I'm a whore off the streets," I would say to him, "nothing more — if you want me, you have to accept me for what I am." I had realized that my strength lay not in my desire to be something I was not, but in my acceptance of what I was. My strength lay in my poverty, my profession, Mother, my ugly house, my simple clothes, my humble origin, my misfortunes, and more profoundly in the feeling that made me able to accept all these things, a feeling as deeply embedded in my soul as a precious stone in the bowels of the earth. But I was quite sure I would never see him again, and this certainty made me love him in a melancholy, helpless way quite new in my experience, which had its own sweetness; as we love the dead who never will return.

At this time, I broke off my relationship with Gino once and for all. As I have already said, I dislike sudden breaks and I prefer things to live their own lives and die their own deaths. My relations with Gino were a good example of this desire of mine. They ceased because the life in them ceased, not through my fault and not even, in a certain sense, through Gino's. They ceased in such a way as to leave me no regrets.

I had continued to see him every now and again, two or three times a month. I did still like him, although I no longer respected him. One day he rang up and asked me to meet him at a café, and I told him I would be there.

The café was in my own neighborhood. Gino was waiting for me in the inner room, a windowless little place, the walls covered with majolica tiles. As I entered, I saw he was not alone. Someone was sitting beside him with his back toward me. I could see only that he was wearing a green raincoat and was blond, with a crew cut. I went up to them and Gino got to his feet, but his companion remained seated. "Let me introduce my friend Sonzogno," said Gino. Then he stood up, too, and I held out my hand. But when he took it, I felt as though he were gripping me in a vise and a little cry of pain escaped me. He let go at once and I sat down smiling. "Do you know you hurt me?" I said. "Is that what you always do?"

He did not reply, did not even smile. His face was paper-white, his forehead hard and bulging, his eyes tiny and sky-blue in color; he was flat-nosed and had a mouth like a slit. His hair was bristly and colorless, cut short, his temples squashed in. But the lower part of his face was broad, his jaw heavy and ugly. He seemed always to be grinding his teeth, as though he were chewing something, and it looked as if one of the nerves under the skin of his cheek was twitching and trembling all the time. Gino's attitude to him was one of admiring and respectful friendship.

"That's nothing!" he said. "If you knew how strong he is! He's got a killer's punch."

I thought Sonzogno regarded him with hostility.

"That's a lie," he said in a flat voice. "I haven't got a killer's punch. . . . I might have."

"What's a killer's punch?" I asked.

"When you can kill a man with a single blow — then you're forbidden to use your fists — it's like using a gun."

"Feel how strong he is!" insisted Gino excitedly, as if eager to ingratiate himself with Sonzogno. "Just feel. Let her touch your arm."

I hesitated, but Gino was insistent and his friend also seemed to expect it. So I stretched my hand out, limply, to pinch his arm. He bent his forearm to flex his muscles, seriously, almost grimly. And then I felt beneath my fingers, through his sleeve, something that was like a bundle of iron cords, and I had a shock of surprise because he looked so slight. I withdrew my hand with an exclamation of mingled disgust and wonder. Sonzogno looked at me complacently, a slight smile playing on his lips.

"He's an old friend of mine," said Gino. "We've known each other quite a while, haven't we, Primo? We're almost brothers, you might say." He patted Sonzogno on the shoulder, saying, "Good old Primo!"

Sonzogno shrugged his shoulders as if to shake Gino's hand off. "We're neither friends nor brothers," he said. "We used to work together in the same garage, that's all."

Gino was not at all disconcerted. "Oh, I know you don't want to be anyone's friend — you're always alone, on your own — no women, and no men."

Sonzogno looked at him. He had a fixed stare, incredibly insistent and unblinking; Gino was obliged to turn his eyes away. "Who told you that crap?" asked Sonzogno. "I hang out with anyone I like — men or women."

"I was only talking." Gino's cocksure air had vanished. "I've never seen you with anyone, that's all."

"You've never known anything about my affairs."

"Well, I used to see you morning and evening every day —"

"What if you did see me every day?"

"Well," said Gino disconcerted, "I've always seen you by yourself, and I thought you never hung out with anyone — if a man has a girl or a friend, you always get to know it."

"Don't be a moron," said Sonzogno brutally.

"Now you're even calling me a moron," said Gino flushing, and feigning his usual bad temper. But he was obviously scared.

"Yes," repeated Sonzogno. "Don't be a moron or I'll break your face."

I suddenly realized he was not only quite capable of doing it, but that he actually intended to do it. Placing one hand on his arm, I intervened. "If you want to fight it out, please do it when I'm not here — I can't stand violence."

"Here I am, introducing a young lady, a friend of mine, to you," said Gino sulkily, "and you frighten her, the way you act! She'll think we're enemies!"

Sonzogno turned to me and smiled for the first time. When he smiled he screwed up his eyes, wrinkled his forehead, and showed not only his little bad teeth but even his gums. "The young lady isn't frightened, are you?" he asked.

"I'm not frightened at all," I answered dryly, "but I don't like violence, as I've told you."

A long silence ensued. Sonzogno remained motionless, his hands in the pockets of his raincoat, the nerves in his jaw twitching as he stared at nothing; Gino was still smoking, with bent head, and the smoke crept up his face and ears that were still crimson. Then Sonzogno got up. "Well — I'm off," he said.

Gino leaped eagerly to his feet. "No hard feelings, then, eh, Primo?" he said as he held out his hand.

"No hard feelings," repeated Sonzogno through clenched teeth. He shook my hand, but without hurting me this time, and went away. He was slight and short; and it was really impossible to see where all his strength came from.

"You may be friends and even brothers — but the way he talked to you!" I said jokingly to Gino as soon as he had gone.

Gino had recovered by now. "He's made that way," he said, shaking his head. "But he's not bad. It suits me to stay on the right side of him. He's useful to me sometimes."

"In what way?"

I noticed Gino was excited, trembling from the desire to tell me something. His face had suddenly become wildly excited and eager.

"You remember my mistress's compact?"

"Yes — well?"

Gino's eyes shone with delight. "Well, I thought it over and didn't give it back," he said lowering his voice.

"You didn't give it back?"

"No. After all, I thought, she's rich and one compact more or less won't make any difference to her — especially since the deed was already done," he added with characteristic reserve, "and, after all, I wasn't the thief."

"I was the thief," I said quietly.

He pretended not to have heard me. "Still, later on, there was the problem of selling it," he continued. "It was a showy thing, easy to identify, and I didn't dare. So I kept it in my pocket for a good while until at last I met Sonzogno, told him the whole story —"

"Did you even tell him about me?" I interrupted.

"No, not about you — I told him a girlfriend had given it to me, without mentioning any names, and he . . . Just think, in three days he sold it and brought me the cash — of course, he kept his share, like we agreed." He was trembling with joy and after having looked around him, he pulled a bundle of notes out of his pocket.

I do not know why but at that moment I felt a deep aversion to him. It was not that I criticized what he had done — I had no right to do that at all — but his gloating irritated me. Besides, I guessed he was keeping something back and what he had not told me was certainly far worse. "You were right," I said shortly.

"Here," he said, undoing the roll of banknotes, "these are for you — I've counted them."

"No," I replied immediately, "I want nothing, absolutely nothing."

"Why not?"

"I don't want anything."

"You're trying to insult me," he said. A shade of doubt and distress flitted across his face, and I was afraid I really had offended him. I placed my hand on his. "If you hadn't offered it to me," I said with an effort, "I'd have been — well, not offended, perhaps, but surprised — but now it's done it's all right as it is. I don't want it, because it's over as far as I'm concerned, that's all. I'm glad you've got it, though."

He looked at me doubtfully, not understanding what I was saying, scrutinizing me as though he wanted to discover the hidden motive behind my words. I have realized since, when I have thought about him, that he was incapable of understanding me because he lived in a different world from mine, with different ideas and emotions. I do not know whether it was a worse world or a better one; I only know that some words did not have the same meaning for him as they did for me, and that most of the actions I criticized in him seemed to him both lawful and proper. He seemed to ascribe the utmost importance to intelligence, by which he meant cleverness. And in dividing humankind into two groups — those who were clever and those who were not — he always tried to place himself in the first category. But I am not at all clever myself, perhaps not even intelligent, and I have never been able to understand how a bad deed can be explained away, let alone admired, merely because it was cleverly done.

The doubt that was tormenting him suddenly seemed to dissolve. "I know what it is!" he exclaimed. "You don't want to take the money because you're afraid — you're afraid the theft might be discovered. But you don't have to worry. Everything's come out all right."

I was not afraid, but I did not trouble to deny it because I had not understood the second part of his sentence.

"What do you mean?" I asked. "Everything's come out all right."

"Yes," he replied. "Everything's all right — you remember! I told you they suspected one of the maids, didn't I?"

"Yes."

"Well — I'd had it with that maid because she gossiped about me behind my back. . . . A few days after the theft I could see things were looking bad for me — the police officer had been back twice, I thought I was under surveillance. Remember, they hadn't searched the house yet. . . . So I got the idea of a second theft that would provoke a search, so that the blame for both thefts would fall on her."

I remained silent, and after having glanced at me with wide-open, glittering eyes, as if to see whether I was admiring his cunning, he continued. "The mistress had some dollars in a drawer. I took them and hid them in the maid's room in an old suitcase. When they did search the house, of course the dollars were found and she was arrested. She swears she's innocent, naturally, but who'd believe it? They found the dollars in her bedroom."

"Where is this woman now?"

"In prison, and she won't confess. But do you know what the police officer told the mistress? 'Don't worry, ma'am,' he said, 'by hook or by crook, she'll confess in the end.' Know what they mean? By hook or by crook? They'll beat her up."

I looked at him and, seeing him so excited and proud of himself, I felt all chilled and confused. "What's her name?" I asked casually.

"Luisa Fellini — she's not so young, and she's very stuck-up — to hear her talk, she's a maid by mistake and no one is as honest as she is!" He smiled, highly amused.

I made an effort, like someone trying to take a deep breath. "Do you know you're contemptible?" I said.

"What? Why?" he asked me in amazement.

Now that I had told him he was contemptible, I felt freer and more determined. My nostrils quivered with rage. "And you wanted me to take that money!" I continued. "But I could feel it was money I shouldn't take."

"What's all the fuss?" he said, trying to regain his composure. "She won't confess — and then they'll let her go."

"But you've just said yourself that they'll keep her in prison and beat her up!"

"I was just talking."

"It doesn't matter. You've sent an innocent woman to jail — and then you have the gall to come and tell me about it! You're contemptible."

He suddenly grew furious, the blood left his face. He gripped my hand. "You just stop calling me contemptible."

"Why? I think you're contemptible and I'll say so."

He lost his head and made a curiously violent gesture. He twisted my hand in his as if he wanted to crush it and then suddenly bent his head and bit my hand hard. I freed myself with a jerk and stood up. "Are you crazy?" I exclaimed. "What's got into you now? Biting? It's no good — you're scum and you'll always be scum." He did not reply but sunk his head on his hands as if he wanted to tear his hair out.

I called the waiter and paid for all the drinks, mine, his, and Sonzogno's. "I'm going," I said. "And I'm telling you — everything's over between us. Don't show up again, don't look for me, don't come — I don't know you anymore." He said nothing, but kept his head lowered. I left.

The café was at the top of the main road not far from the house where I lived. I began to walk slowly along on the side opposite the city walls. It was night, the sky was covered with clouds and a fine rain was falling like watery dust through the mild, unstirring air. The walls were in darkness as usual, except for an occasional rarely spaced streetlamp. But I immediately noticed a man slip away from one of the streetlamps as I left the café and begin to follow along the walls at my pace in the direction I was going. I recognized Sonzogno, with his raincoat nipped in at the waist and his blond, shaven head. He looked small there beneath the walls, disappeared every now and again in the shadows, then reappeared in the gleam of a streetlamp. For the first time I felt sick of men, all men, always after my skirt, like a bunch of dogs following a bitch. I was still trembling with rage; and as I thought of the woman Gino had sent to jail I could not help being filled with remorse, because, after all, I had been the one to steal the compact. But perhaps what I felt were revolt and irritation rather than remorse. Although I rebelled against injustice and hated Gino, yet I hated hating him and knowing injustice had been done. I am not really made for such things; I felt terribly distressed and not at all myself. I walked hurriedly, wanting to reach home before Sonzogno approached me, as he apparently intended doing. Then I heard Gino's voice calling me desperately from behind. "Adriana! Adriana!"

I pretended I had not heard and hastened on. He took me by the arm. "Adriana! We've always been together — we can't leave each other like this —"

I freed myself with a jerk and went on walking. The clear-cut little figure of Sonzogno shot out of the darkness into the circle of light shed by a streetlamp on the other side of the road beneath the walls. "But I love you, Adriana," Gino continued as he hurried along beside me.

I felt both pity and hatred for him, and this mixture of emotions was indescribably distasteful to me. I tried to think about something else. I suddenly had a kind of illumination, I don't know why. I remembered Astarita and how he had always offered me his assistance, and I thought he would almost certainly be able to have the poor woman released. This idea revived my spirits immediately; my heart was freed of its load and I even felt as if I did not hate Gino anymore and was only sorry for him. I stood still and addressed him calmly. "Gino," I said, "why don't you go away?"

"But I love you."

"I loved you, too — but it's all over. Go away now, it'll be better for both of us."

We were standing in a dark stretch of the road where there were no shops or streetlamps. He took hold of me around the waist and tried to kiss me. I could have broken free easily enough because I am very strong and no one can kiss a woman if she doesn't want it. But some malicious whim put it into my head to call Sonzogno, who was standing motionless on the other side of the road under the walls, watching us, his hands in the pockets of his raincoat. I suppose I called him because now that I had discovered a way of remedying the harm Gino's action had done, my curiosity and coquetry were aroused once more. "Sonzogno! Sonzogno!" I cried out twice, and he immediately crossed the road. Gino was disconcerted and let me go.

"Tell him he's got to let me alone," I said to Sonzogno calmly as soon as he came up. "I don't want him anymore. He won't believe me; maybe he'll believe you since you're a friend of his."

"Did you hear what the young lady said?" asked Sonzogno.

"But I —" began Gino.

I supposed that they would continue arguing for some time, as usually happens; and that at last Gino would become resigned and go away. But instead I suddenly saw Sonzogno make a gesture I did not understand; Gino stared at him for a moment in amazement, then collapsed wordlessly on the ground, rolling off the pavement into the gutter. Or perhaps all I saw was Gino falling and guessed from that what Sonzogno's gesture had been. The movement was so swift and silent that I thought I had imagined it. I shook my head and took another look. Sonzogno stood in front of me, his legs wide apart, and was looking at his clenched fist; Gino, who was lying on the ground with his back to us, had come to again and had slowly lifted his head as he leaned on one elbow in the gutter. But he did not look as though he wanted to get to his feet; rather, it seemed as if he preferred to keep on staring at a small scrap of white paper that could be clearly seen glimmering against the mud in the ditch.

"Let's go," said Sonzogno at last, and I went as in a dream toward my own place with him.

He walked in silence, holding me by the arm. He was shorter than I, and his hand gripping my arm was exactly like an iron press.

"You shouldn't have hit Gino like that," I said after a while. "He'd have gone away all the same without being hit."

"He won't bother you anymore this way," he replied.

"But how did you do it?" I asked. "I didn't even see what you did — I just saw Gino fall."

"It's a matter of practice," he said.

I longed now to squeeze his arm and feel his hard, taut muscles again beneath my fingers. He aroused more curiosity than attraction in me, but chiefly fear. Still fear can be a pleasant and exciting feeling in a way, until the cause of it is known.

"What have you got here inside your arm?" I asked. "I still can't believe it!"

"But I let you touch it," he said with such earnest vanity that it sounded sinister.

"Not properly — Gino was there — let me feel it again."

He stood still and flexed his arm, looking sideways at me with a serious and, in a certain way, ingenuous air. But there was nothing childlike about his ingenuousness. I stretched out my hand and slowly felt his muscles, running my hand all the way down his arm from the shoulder. The sensation of feeling them, so alive and as hard as iron, was extraordinary. "You're really very strong," I said in a ghost of a voice.

"Yes, I'm strong," he affirmed grimly. And we began walking again.

I was sorry I had called him, now. I did not like him. Besides, his seriousness and his behavior frightened me. We reached my house without speaking. I took out my key. "Thanks for seeing me home," I said and held out my hand.

"I'm coming up," he said and drew near.

I wanted to say no. But his way of staring into my eyes fixedly and with incredible insistence, overwhelmed and troubled me. "If you like," I said. And I did not realize until after I had spoken to him that I had used the intimate form of speech with him.

"Don't be scared," he said, interpreting my distress in his own way. "I've got some money. I'll give you twice what the others give you."

"What's that got to do with it?" I said. "It's not because of the money —" But I saw a strange gleam flit across his face, as if a threatening suspicion had struck him. Meanwhile I had opened the door. "I was only feeling a little tired," I added.

Once in my room, he undressed with the precise movements of an orderly man. He wore a scarf around his neck, and he carefully unrolled it, then folded it up and put it into the pocket of his raincoat. He hung his jacket over the back of a chair and arranged his trousers so as not to spoil the creases. He put both his shoes under the chair with his socks tucked into them. I noticed that all his clothes were new, from head to foot, not deluxe but good, solid quality. He did all this in silence, neither slowly nor hurriedly, with systematic, thoughtful regularity, and he took no notice of me. I had undressed meantime and was lying naked on the bed. If he desired me he certainly did not show it, unless the ceaseless twitching of his jaw muscles just under the skin meant he was in a state of excitement; but that could not be so, because he had had it before, when he did not seem even to be thinking about me.

I have already said that I like order and cleanliness very much, since they seem to indicate corresponding spiritual qualities. But Sonzogno's order and cleanliness aroused very different sensations in me that evening, something between horror and fear. That was the way surgeons got ready in a hospital, I could not help thinking, when they had to perform some bloody operation. Or worse, slaughterers, under the very eyes of the lambs they are about to kill. Lying there on the bed, I felt as helpless and powerless as an unconscious body about to undergo an experiment. His silence and indifference left me in doubt as to what he intended to do to me as soon as he had finished undressing. So when he came up to the head of the bed, stark naked, and, strangely, placed his two hands on my shoulders as if to hold me still, I could not prevent a shudder of fear. He noticed it. "What's wrong?" he asked me through his clenched teeth.

"Nothing," I answered. "Your hands are freezing."

"You don't like me, do you?" he said, still gripping my shoulders as he stood by the head of the bed. "You prefer the people who pay you, don't you?" As he spoke he stared at me, and the look was unbearable.

"Why?" I said. "You're a man like all the rest. Besides, you said yourself you'd pay double."

"I know what I'm talking about," he said. "You and your kind make love to the rich folk, the upper crust. I'm just someone like you, and all you whores only make love to gentlemen."

I recognized in his voice the same sinister, inflexible desire to stir up a quarrel that had made him insult Gino on the slightest pretext only a short while before. I had supposed at the time that he had his own reasons for bearing Gino a grudge. But I now realized that his grim, incalculable touchiness was always on the alert, and when he was possessed by such a devil, you would be in the wrong no matter how you dealt with him.

"Why do you want to insult me?" I asked, rather heatedly. "I've already told you all men are the same to me."

"If you were telling the truth, you wouldn't be making that face. You don't like me, do you?"

"But I've already told you!"

"You don't like me," he continued, "but I regret to tell you, you have to like me."

"Oh, leave me alone!" I said in sudden irritation.

"As long as I was useful in getting rid of your lover," he went on, "you wanted me. Then afterward you'd rather have sent me away. But I came up instead. You *don't* like me, do you?"

I was really frightened now. His urgent words, his calm, pitiless voice, the fixed stare in his eyes that seemed to have changed from blue to red, everything seemed to be carrying him on toward some fearful goal. I realized too late that any attempt to stop him on his path would be as hopeless a task as keeping a rock from rolling down a steep slope. I merely shrugged my shoulders violently.

"You don't like me, eh?" he went on. "You look disgusted when I touch you — but I'll change your look for you, honey!" He raised his hand as if to slap me. I was expecting something of the sort and tried to protect myself with my arm. But he managed to strike me all the same, shockingly hard, first on one cheek and then, as I tried to turn my face away, on the other. This was the first time in all my life that anything of this kind had happened to me; and despite the sting of the blows I was more surprised than hurt at first. I uncovered my face. "Do you know what you are?" I said. "You're a bastard."

He seemed struck by this phrase. He sat on the edge of the bed and rocked himself back and forth, gripping the mattress with both hands. "We're all bastards," he said, without looking at me.

"It takes real courage to hit a woman!" I said. But all at once I was unable to continue, for my eyes filled with tears, caused not so much by the blows I had received as by the nervous tension of the whole evening, with all its many unpleasant and disgusting episodes. I remembered Gino lying flat in the mud, remembered how indifferent I had been and how I had gone off cheerfully with

Sonzogno, thinking only of testing the exceptional strength of his muscles. I was overcome by remorse, pity for Gino, and disgust at myself, and I realized I had been punished for my insensitivity and stupidity by the same hand that had struck Gino down. I had delighted in violence and now that same violence had been turned against me. I looked at Sonzogno through my tears. He was sitting on the edge of the bed stark naked, white and hairless, his shoulders bowed, his arms that gave no hint of their strength hanging loosely. I felt an unexpected desire to lessen the distance between us.

"But won't you tell me why you hit me, at least?" I said with an effort.

"There was a look on your face," he said reflectively, the nerve in his jaw twitching.

I realized that if I wanted to get nearer to him, I would have to tell him all I was thinking, hiding nothing from him.

"You thought I didn't like you. Well, you were wrong," I answered.

"Maybe."

"You were wrong. As a matter of fact, you frighten me, I don't know why. That's why I had that look on my face."

He turned around sharply at these words, looked at me suspiciously. But he calmed down at once and asked, with a hint of vanity, "So I frightened you, did I?"

"Yes."

"And do I still frighten you?"

"No, you can kill me if you want, now — I don't care anymore." This was the truth; I really wanted him to kill me just then, because I had suddenly lost all desire to go on living. But he grew angry.

"Who said anything about killing you?" he said. "Why were you afraid of me?"

"How do I know? You frightened me. You can't explain these things."

"Did Gino frighten you?"

"Why should he frighten me?"

"But why do I frighten you?" All his vanity had gone by now; there was a hint of fury in his voice once more.

"Well," I said to soothe him, "you frighten me because it's plain to see you're capable of anything."

He said nothing and sat there pensively for a moment. Then he turned around. "Does all this mean you want me to get dressed and get out?" he asked me threateningly.

I looked at him and realized he was once more in a fit of rage. If I refused him, I would be exposing myself to further, and possibly even worse, violence. I would have to accept him. But I remembered his pale eyes and was filled with disgust at the idea that they would be fixed on mine during the act of love.

"No, you can stay if you like," I said feebly, "but turn off the light first."

He stood up, small, white, but extremely well proportioned except for his short neck, and went on tiptoe to switch the light off by the door. I realized immediately that getting him to put the light out had not been a good idea; for as soon as the room was plunged into darkness, the fear I thought had left me returned again, uncontrollably. It was as though there were in the room with me, not a man, but a leopard or some other wild beast, which might crouch down in a corner or leap on me and tear me to pieces. Perhaps he was slow finding his way among the chairs and other furniture in the dark; or perhaps fear made his absence seem longer. I certainly had the sensation that ages had passed before he reached the bed, and when I felt his hands on me, I could not repress another convulsive shudder. I hoped he had not noticed it, but his instincts were as delicate as an animal's and I immediately heard his voice, close beside me. "Are you still afraid?" he asked.

My guardian angel must have been there in the darkness. Some nuance in his voice told me he had raised his arm and was waiting to strike me according to whether I answered yes or no. I realized he knew he was terrifying, and wanted to be otherwise and to be loved like all other men. But he knew no other means of achieving this end than by rousing a deeper fear. I lifted my hand and, under the pretense of caressing his neck and right shoulder, I discovered that his arm was indeed raised as I had supposed, ready to fall and strike me in the face. I spoke with an effort, trying to give my voice its usual calm and gentle intonation. "No," I said, "it's the cold this time, really — let's get under the covers."

"All right, then!" he said. This "all right," in which remained the echo of a threat, only deepened my fear, if anything. As he embraced and caressed me under the covers, while all around us was darkness, I experienced a moment of acute, anguish, one of the worst in my life. Fear stiffened my limbs, which drew back and shuddered uncontrollably at the contact of his peculiarly smooth, sinuous, writhing body; but at the same time I told myself it was ridiculous to be afraid of him at such a time, and I tried with all the strength of my mind to overcome my fear and give myself to him fearlessly like a cherished lover. My fear lay not so much in my limbs, which still did as I bid them no matter how reluctantly, but more intimately in the depths of my womb, which seemed to close and reject his touch with horror. At last he took me and I felt a pleasure made black and atrocious by fear. I could not restrain a long, wailing cry in the dark, as if the final embrace had been the embrace of death, not of love, and that cry the cry of my life departing from me, leaving behind a tortured, spent body.

We lay there silent in the dark afterward. I was exhausted and fell asleep almost at once. I soon felt the sensation of a terrific weight on my chest, as if Sonzogno were squatting upon me, huddled up naked as he was, gripping his knees between his arms, his face leaning on his knees. He was seated on my chest, his bare, hard buttocks pressed against my neck, his feet were on my stomach; as I continued to sleep his weight increased, and although I was asleep, I tossed restlessly about trying to rid myself of him, or at least shift him. At last I felt as if I was suffocating and I tried to cry out. My voice remained imprisoned in my breast, as I cried out soundlessly for what seemed to me an endless period of time; at last I managed to force it out and woke up, moaning loudly.

The light was lit on the night table and Sonzogno was leaning his head on one arm and looking at me. "Did I sleep long?" I asked.

"Half an hour," he said through his teeth.

I threw him a glance that must still have been filled with terror of the nightmare I had had, because he asked me with a curious note in his voice, as if he wanted to resume the conversation, "Are you still afraid?"

"I don't know."

"If you knew who I was," he said, "you'd be more afraid than ever."

All men feel inclined to talk about themselves and confide in a woman after they have made love. Apparently, Sonzogno was no exception to the rule. His voice was unusually casual, lazy, affectionate even, with a touch of vanity and complacency. But I felt terribly afraid once again and my heart began to pound in my breast as if it were going to burst.

"Why?" I asked. "Who are you?"

He looked at me, not so much hesitating as savoring the effect of his words on me. "I'm the man of Via Palestro," he said slowly at last. "That's who I am."

He did not think it was necessary to explain what had happened at Via Palestro and this time his vanity was right. Quite recently a horrible crime had been committed in a house in that street, all the papers had been filled with it, and all the people who get worked up over this kind of thing had discussed it. Mother, who spent a great part of the day spelling out the crime news in the papers, had been the first to mention it to me. A young jeweler had been murdered in his flat where he lived alone. Apparently the weapon used by Sonzogno — for I was sure now that he was the murderer — was a heavy bronze paperweight. The police had found no helpful clues. Apparently the jeweler was also a receiver of stolen goods and the police imagined, rightly, as it turned out, that he had been killed during some illegal transaction.

I have often noticed that when a piece of news fills us with amazement or horror, our minds become blank and we fix our attention on the first thing our eyes fall upon, but in a particular way, as if we wanted to pass through its surface and reach some undefined secret hidden within. This was what happened to me after Sonzogno had told me who he was. My eyes were wide open, my mind a complete blank, like a receptacle containing liquid or fine powder that suddenly begins to leak — except that my mind, although blank, was ready and waiting to receive some other matter, and the sensation was painful because I longed to fill the void and could not. Meanwhile I was staring at the wrist of Sonzogno, who was stretched out beside me, leaning on one elbow. His arm was white, smooth, hairless, full, giving no hint of his exceptional muscles. His wrist was also round and he wore a leather strap, like a watch strap without a watch, the only object he had kept on in his nakedness. The black, glossy color of this strap seemed to give some significance, not only to his arm, but to the whole of his white, naked body, and I tried to define this significance in my mind but was unable to do so. It had a sinister connotation; it conjured up the idea of a ring in a convict's chain. But there was something both beautiful and cruel about this leather strap; it was like an ornament that emphasized the unexpected and feline character of Sonzogno's brutality. My blank state of mind lasted only a moment. Then my head was suddenly filled with a host of tumultuous thoughts beating about like birds in a crowded cage. I remembered I had been afraid of Sonzogno from the very first moment; I remembered I had made love to him; and I realized that by yielding to his embraces in that darkness I had learned everything that he had concealed from me through my horrified body, even before my ignorant mind had been aware of it, and that was why I had cried out as I had.

Finally I said the first thing that came into my mind: "Why did you do it?"

His lips hardly moved as he answered me. "I had something valuable to sell. . . . I knew he was a swine, but he was the only dealer I knew. . . . He offered me a ridiculous price — I already hated him because he had tried to swindle me before this. . . . I told him I wanted the object back and also told him he was a cheat. . . . He said something to me that made me lose my patience."

"What did he say?" I asked. I now noticed with astonishment that as Sonzogno told me the story my fear began to diminish and despite myself a feeling of complicity thrilled me. In asking him what the jeweler had said, I realized I was hoping it had been something so outrageous that the crime was excusable, if not completely justifiable.

"He said he would turn me over to the police if I didn't go, so I thought: I've had enough — and when he turned away —" He did not finish the sentence but stared at me.

"What was he like?" I asked, and at the time my curiosity seemed purposeless and idle.

"Bald — rather short — a sly face like a hare's —" he answered precisely. But he spoke with an expression of unemotional dislike that brought the man before me and made me hate him, too — this receiver of stolen goods, with a face like a hare's, who had been deceitful and suspicious as he reckoned up the worth of the object Sonzogno had brought him. I was no longer afraid of anything. Sonzogno seemed to have transferred to me his hatred of his victim and I was not even sure that I condemned him. I actually seemed to understand what had happened so well that I felt I, too, might have been capable of the same crime. How well I understood his phrase: "He said something to me that made me lose my patience!" He had already lost patience with Gino once and then again with me, and it was only by a lucky chance that Gino and I were still alive. I understood him so well, I had penetrated into him so thoroughly, that not only did I no longer fear him, but I even felt a kind of horrified attraction for him — the very attraction I had been unable to feel so long as I knew nothing of the crime and considered him as just one of my many lovers.

"Aren't you sorry?" I asked. "Don't you regret it?"

"It's done now," he replied.

I looked at him intently and was surprised to find myself nodding my head in approval at his reply. Then I remembered that Gino, too, in Sonzogno's words, was a swine, and yet he was also a man and had loved me and I had loved him. I thought that if I reasoned in this way, I might even find myself approving of Gino's murder in the near future. After all, the jeweler was no better and no worse than Gino, the only difference being that I did not know him, and I found his murder justifiable merely because I had heard someone say in a certain tone of voice that he had a face like a hare's. Remorse and horror filled me — not for Sonzogno, who was made that way and had to be understood before he was judged, but for myself, who was not like Sonzogno, but nevertheless had let myself be infected by the contagion of hatred and blood. Overcome by agitation, I sprang up on the bed. "Oh, my God!" I repeated, "My God! Why did you do it? And why did you tell me about it?"

"You were so frightened of me," he answered simply, "yet you didn't know anything. I thought that was strange, so I told you. Luckily," he added, amused by his own idea, "luckily the rest aren't all like you, otherwise, I'd have been caught by now."

"You'd better go and leave me alone," I said. "Go on."

"What's the matter with you now?" he asked.

I could tell from his tone that he was growing angry. But I thought I could also discern a kind of pain at finding himself alone, condemned even by me, when only a moment before I had given myself to him.

"Don't think I'm afraid of you," I added hastily. "I'm not afraid at all. But I've got to get used to the idea. I've got to think it over. Then you can come back and you'll find me changed."

"What is there to think over?" he said. "You aren't going to turn me in to the police, are you?"

These words gave me exactly the same sensation I had had when Gino told me of his treachery toward the maid: as if we were living in different worlds. I made an effort to control myself. "But I'm telling you, you can come back!" I said. "Do you know what any other woman would have said? She'd have said she didn't want to have anything more to do with you, or ever see you again."

"But meanwhile you're telling me to get out."

"I thought you wanted to go. . . . One minute more or less. . . . But if you want to stay, stay. Do you want to sleep here? If you like you can sleep with me and go away tomorrow morning. Is that what you want?" It is true that I made these suggestions in a dull, sad, puzzled voice, and there must have been a lost look in my eyes. Nevertheless, I made them and I felt I was glad to do so. Perhaps I was mistaken, but I thought I saw a gleam of gratitude in the look he gave me.

"No, I was just talking," he said as he shook his head. "I've got to go." He stood up and went over to the chair where he had left his clothes.

"As you like," I replied, "but if you want to stay, you know you can. And if you need somewhere to sleep one of these nights," I added with an effort, "you can come here."

He said nothing, he was dressing. I got up, too, and put on a dressing gown. I felt crazy as I walked about, as if the room were full of voices whispering mad, impassioned words in my ear. Perhaps it was this sensation of being crazed that made me do what I did then. While I was wandering about the room, moving slowly, although I felt frenzied, I saw him bend down to tie his shoelaces. I immediately knelt down in front of him. "Let me do it," I said. He seemed amazed but did not protest. I took his right foot, rested it on my lap and tied his shoe with a double knot. Then I did the same with his left foot. He did not thank me and said nothing; probably neither of us understood why I had done such a thing. He slipped on his jacket. Then he took out his wallet and started to hand me some money.

"No, no," I said with an involuntary catch of the voice, "don't give me anything — it doesn't matter."

"Why? Isn't my money as good as another man's?" he asked in a voice already altered by anger. I thought it was strange that he did not understand my instinctive disgust for that money, probably taken from the still warm pockets of the dead man. Or perhaps he did understand it, but wanted to compromise me by making me a kind of accomplice, and at the same time wanted to discover what my feelings for him really were.

"No," I said, "it's not that. But I wasn't thinking about money when I called out to you. It doesn't matter."

He was pacified. "All right," he said, "but I'd like to leave you a souvenir." He pulled something out of his pocket and put it on the marble top of the night table.

I looked at it without picking it up and saw it was the compact I had stolen some months earlier from Gino's employer. "What is it?" I stammered.

"Gino gave it to me, it's the thing I had to sell. . . . He wanted to get it for nothing, but I think it's quite valuable, really, it's gold —"

"Thanks," I said, controlling myself.

"Not at all," he replied. He put on his raincoat and fastened the belt. "So long, then," he said from the doorway. Shortly afterward I heard the front door close.

When I was alone, I walked over to the night table and picked up the compact. I felt bewildered and at the same time darkly amazed. The compact glittered in my hand and the ruby set in the catch suddenly seemed to grow, to become a round, red drop that spread until it covered the gold. In the palm of my hand lay a round, glowing, bloody stain that weighed as much as the compact itself. I shook my head and the red stain disappeared, and once more all I saw was the gold compact with the ruby clasp. Then I placed the compact on the night table once more, lay on the bed wrapped in my dressing gown, switched off the light, and began to consider.

I supposed that if anyone had told me the tale of the compact I would have been as highly entertained as if I were being told of some almost incredible chain of circumstances. It was one of those tales that provoke the exclamation, "What a coincidence!" Women like Mother would work out lottery numbers based on it — this number standing for the dead man, another for the gold, another for the thief. But this time it had happened to me, and to my astonishment I became aware of the difference between being on the inside of an event and being only an outsider. In fact, the way it had happened to me, it was as if someone had planted a seed and then forgotten it — on rediscovering it, he finds it has grown into a flourishing plant, covered with leaves and buds ready to burst into flower. Only — what a seed, what a plant, what buds.

I let my mind wander backward from one thing to another, but I could not find the starting point. I had given myself to Gino because I hoped he would marry me, but he had betrayed me and out of pique I had stolen the compact. When I had told him of the theft, he had become frightened, and, to prevent his being dismissed, I had returned the compact to him so that he could restore it to its owner. But instead of returning it, he had kept it, and, being afraid of being accused of the theft, he had inculpated the maid who had been sent to prison. The maid was innocent and in prison they beat her. Meanwhile Gino had given the compact to Sonzogno to sell; Sonzogno had gone to the jeweler; the jeweler had offended Sonzogno; Sonzogno in a fit of rage had killed him; the jeweler was dead and Sonzogno was a murderer. I realized I could not trace the blame back to myself; otherwise I would have had to come to the conclusion that my desire to get married and have a family was the prime cause of this chain of misfortunes. All the same I could not rid myself of a feeling of remorse and consternation. At last I was driven to conclude after much thinking that the whole fault was due to my legs, my hips, my breasts, all that beauty of which my mother was so proud, a quality in itself entirely innocent, like everything else given us by nature. But such thoughts were caused by my irritation and despair, as we allow one absurd thought to drive out others a hundred times as absurd. I knew in my heart that no one was really to blame and everything was as it had to be, although it was all intolerable, and if guilt and innocence really must be attributed, then each individual was equally guilty and equally innocent.

Meanwhile darkness gradually invaded me, like floodwater rising from the ground floor to the upper stories of a house. My faculty of judgment was the first to be submerged. But my imagination, on the other hand, dallied until the last with the fascination of Sonzogno's crime. The crime, however, was detached from any association of reproach or horror, like an event both inexplicable and, in its way, strangely delicious. I imagined Sonzogno walking along Via Palestro, his hands in his raincoat pockets, then entering the house, standing in the jeweler's parlor awaiting him. I seemed to see the jeweler come in and shake Sonzogno's hand. He was behind his desk, Sonzogno held out the compact, the jeweler examined it and shook his head, feigning scorn for the object. Then he raised his harelike face and made a ridiculous offer. Sonzogno looked at him fixedly, his eyes full of rage, and jerked the compact violently out of his hand. He then accused the jeweler of wanting to cheat him. The jeweler retaliated by threatening to denounce him to the police and warned him to get out. Then, as if to put an end to the discussion, he turned away or bent his head. Sonzogno picked up the bronze paperweight and hit him once on the head. The jeweler tried to escape and then Sonzogno leaped on him and struck him repeatedly until he was quite sure he was dead. Then Sonzogno pushed him down onto the floor, searched the drawers, took what money he could find, and made his escape. But before leaving, as I had read in the papers, he ground the dead man in the face with the heel of his shoe in a renewal of rage.

I lingered in fascination over all the details of the crime. I followed Sonzogno, caressing his gestures almost lovingly. I was the hand that held out the compact, picked up the paperweight, and struck the jeweler. I was the foot that crushed the dead man's face in fury when it was all over. There was no horror or blame in my fancied visions, but neither was there any approval. If anything, I experienced the same sensation of strange delight we feel when we are children listening to the tales our mothers tell; it is warm, huddled up near our mother, and we follow with rapt attention the adventures of those legendary heroes. Only my tale was grim and bloody, its hero was Sonzogno and a helpless and astonished sorrow mingled with my delight. Seeking to discover the hidden significance of the tale, I began to run through it again, to recapitulate all the stages of the crime. I experienced once more that same obscure pleasure and was faced again with the mystery. And then, like someone falling headlong into the gap between two precipices through a miscalculation of the distance, I fell asleep between two episodes in my mental wanderings.

I slept for about a couple of hours and then awoke. Or rather, I began to wake up physically, while mentally I was still in a state of stupor. My hands were the first to wake; I stretched them out before me like a blind man in the dark, without knowing where I was. I had fallen asleep lying at full-length on my bed; now I found myself standing upright in a narrow space between smooth, vertical, unbroken walls. It immediately suggested the idea of a prison cell to me, and at the same time I remembered the maid Gino had had arrested. I was the maid, and in my heart I felt all the anguish she was suffering for the injustice done to her. From this pain came the physical sensation that I was no longer myself, but the maid; and her sorrow altered me, imprisoned me in her body, gave me her face, forced her gestures upon me. I put my hands to my face and wept, and imagined myself wrongly imprisoned in a cell from which I could never escape. But at the same time I knew I was Adriana, who had suffered no injustice, who had never been imprisoned, and I knew that one single gesture would free me and I would no longer be the maid. But I could not imagine what this gesture might be — although I suffered indescribably through my desire to escape from my prison of pity and anguish. Suddenly Astarita's name flashed through my mind, shot through by the same spasmodic light and shade that dazzle the eyes of someone who has received a violent blow. I'll go and see Astarita and get her freed, I thought; I stretched out my hands once more and discovered a narrow slit in the vertical walls of my cell — I could escape. I took a few steps in the dark, felt the switch under my fingers, turned it on with hysterical speed. The room leaped into light. I was standing near the door, naked, panting, my face and body dripping with cold sweat. The cell I had been imprisoned in was only the angle between the closet, the corner of the room, and the chest of drawers — a narrow space closed almost entirely by the walls and furniture. In my sleep I must have got up, walked forward, and forced myself into it.

I switched the light off once more, and, counting my steps, went back to bed. Before falling asleep, the thought came to me that although I certainly could not bring the jeweler back to life, I could save, or try to save, the maid, and this was the only thing that mattered. It was all the more my duty now that I had discovered I was not as good as I had always believed myself to be. Or at least my goodness did not exclude a taste for blood, admiration of violence, and delight in crime.

4

THE FOLLOWING MORNING I dressed carefully, put the compact into my purse, and went out to telephone Astarita. I felt strangely lighthearted; the anguish Sonzogno's revelations had caused me the evening before had entirely vanished. I have many times in my life since noticed that vanity is the worst enemy of charity and moral reproof. What I now felt, instead of fear and horror, was a kind of vanity at the thought that I was the only one in town who knew how the crime had been committed and who had done it. I said to myself, "I know who killed the jeweler" and seemed to look at people and things with different eyes from the day before. I imagined there must even be some change in my features, and I was almost afraid that Sonzogno's secret could be read in the expression of my face. At the same time, I felt a mild, pleasant, irresistible longing to tell someone what I knew. The secret overflowed from my heart like too much water from a small vessel, and I was tempted to pour it out to someone else. I suppose this is the chief reason why so many criminals tell their sweethearts or wives about the crimes they have committed; then the women tell it to their best friend and the best friend tells someone else, until it reaches the ears of the police and brings about the ruin of all of them. But I think, too, that in speaking of their crimes the criminals are trying to free themselves of an intolerable burden by making others share it. Just as if guilt were something that could be parceled out and borne by many until it becomes slight and unimportant, and not, as it really is, a load that cannot be transferred, whose weight is never lessened by being shared by others, but on the contrary increases with the number of those who bear it.

As I walked through the streets in search of a public telephone, I bought a couple of newspapers and looked for further details of the crime in Via Palestro. But some days had already passed; I could only find a few disappointing lines under the subhead NO CLUES IN JEWELER'S DEATH. I realized that unless he made some clumsy mistake, Sonzogno would never be discovered. The illegal character of the victim's business made police inquiries extremely difficult. As the papers said, the jeweler had secret and inadmissible contacts with people of all classes and conditions; the murderer might have been someone he had never seen before, who had killed him on an impulse. This explanation was nearest to the truth. But for the very reason that this was perfectly true, the police had obviously given up any hope of discovering the murderer.

I found a public telephone in a little restaurant and dialed Astarita's number. I had not phoned him for at least six weeks and I must have surprised him because at first he did not recognize my voice and spoke to me in the businesslike tones he used in the office. For a moment I even had an idea that he did not want to have anything more to do with me; and to tell the truth, my heart missed a beat at the thought of the maid in prison and the bad luck of Astarita's ceasing to love me just when his intervention was necessary in order to save the poor woman. My dismay, however, was mixed with pleasure, because, by restoring to me my lost sense of goodness, it made me see that the woman's release really mattered to me and that, despite my intimacy with the murderer Sonzogno, I was still the same gentle, compassionate Adriana I had always been.

Frightened, I gave Astarita my name and was relieved to hear the tone of his voice change on the instant; it became troubled and eager, and he stumbled over his words. I must admit that I almost felt an impulse of affection for him then, because a love of that kind, which is always flattering to a woman, reassured me and filled me with momentary gratitude. I made an appointment in caressing tones; he promised to come without fail, and I left the restaurant.

It had been raining hard all night as I suffered from my nightmares; often in my sleep I had heard the hiss of rain mingling with the howling wind to form a kind of wall of bad weather around the house, increasing the solitude and intimacy of the darkness in which I struggled. But the rain had stopped toward morning and the last gusts of wind had found strength to sweep away the clouds, leaving a limpid sky and the air clean and still. After phoning Astarita, I began to walk along an avenue of plane trees in the early morning sun. A slight dizziness was all that remained of my disturbed night and it soon passed in the cool air. I gloried in the lovely day and everything I saw had a quality of charm about it that delighted and attracted me. I admired the trunks of the plane trees, with their bark of overlapping white, green, yellow, and brown scales that seemed gold from a distance; I admired the rings of dampness that remained around the edges of the dry paving stones; I admired the houses which bore traces of the night's downpour in great patches of damp on their facades; I admired the passersby, men hurrying to their work, maids carrying shopping bags, boys and girls with books and satchels holding their parents' or elder brothers' hands. I stopped to give alms to an old beggar and while I was hunting for some money in my bag, I realized I was gazing fondly at his old military cloak and delighting in the patches at the elbows and around the collar. There were gray, brown, yellow, and faded green patches, and I loved observing the colors and seeing how well sewn they were, with big stitches in black cotton. I surprised myself imagining how he must have worked one of these mornings, cutting away the worn parts with a pair of scissors, contriving a patch from some old rag, fitting it over

the hole, sewing it lovingly. Those patches gave me as much pleasure as the sight of newly baked bread gives a hungry man, and as
I left him, I could not help looking back at them again and again.
I suddenly thought how wonderful it would be to live a life as
limpid, clear, and lovely as that morning was. A life that had been
washed clean of all its muddy aspects, where even the humblest
thing might be looked at fondly. My desire, so long dormant and
unexpressed, for a normal family life, with just one man and a
new, clean, neat, shining house, was revived by the thought. I realized I did not like my work, although by a strange contradiction
I was designed for it by nature. It did not seem to me to be clean;
my body, my fingers, my bed, seemed to have a perpetual aura of
sweat, sperm, impure warmth, sticky emanations about them, no
matter how much I washed myself and straightened up my room.
And the very fact of dressing and undressing almost every day
under the eyes of different men prevented me from looking upon
my own body with the sense of pleasure and intimacy I would
have enjoyed, which I remembered feeling as a young girl when I
looked at myself in the mirror or in the bath. It is lovely to be able
to look at your own body as at something new and unknown,
which grows, becomes stronger and more beautiful of its own accord. In order to give my lovers this impression of novelty each
time, I had deprived myself of it forever.

In the light of these reflections, Sonzogno's crime, Gino's
wickedness, the maid's misfortunes and all the other intrigues I was
involved in appeared to be the consequences of my own disorderly
life. Consequences, however, without any particular meaning,
which burdened me with no sense of sin and could be set aside as
soon as I was able to satisfy my old aspirations for a regular life. I experienced an overwhelming desire to straighten out my life in
every way, and to come to terms with morality, which condemned
a profession like mine; with nature, which intended a woman of
my age to bear children; with material desire, which dictated a life
lived among beautiful things, lovely new clothes and light, clean,
comfortable houses. The problem was that one thing excluded the
other; if I chose to align myself with morality, I could not at the

same time follow the dictates of nature; and material desire contradicted both morality and nature. The usual lifelong irritation filled me at knowing myself to be in debt to necessity and incapable of satisfying its demands except by sacrificing my highest aims. But I realized once again that I had not yet accepted my fate entirely and this gave me some hope, since I thought that as soon as I had an opportunity of changing my life, I would not let myself by taken unawares, and I could take advantage of it consciously and decisively.

I had made the appointment with Astarita for midday as soon as he left the office. I had an hour or two to wait, so having nothing to do I decided to go and see Gisella. I had not seen her for some time and I imagined someone must have taken the place in her life that had previously been filled by Riccardo, someone halfway between a fiancé and a lover. Gisella, too, hoped to straighten out her life one day. I suppose this hope is common to all women of my kind. But I was inclined to it by nature, whereas in Gisella, who thought worldly considerations of supreme importance, it was above all a matter of social decorum. She was ashamed for other people to take her for what she really was, although her vocation for her profession was far deeper than mine. I was not at all ashamed; I only felt an occasional sense of servitude and betrayal of my own nature.

When I reached Gisella's house, I started to go upstairs. But the concierge called out to me, "Are you going up to see Signorina Gisella? She doesn't live here now."

"Where's she gone?"

"Number seven, Via Casablanca." This was a new street in one of the new districts. "A blond man with a car came and they took her stuff and went away."

I realized immediately that this was just what I had been expecting to hear — that she had left with a man. I do not know why, but suddenly I felt tired, my legs were trembling and I had to lean against the doorpost to keep from falling. But I recovered and decided after a moment's thought to go and call on Gisella at her new address. I hailed a taxi and told the driver to take me to Via Casablanca.

As the taxi sped along, we left the center of the town and its rows of old houses crowded close together in the narrow streets. The streets grew wider, branched off, converged in open squares, became wider and wider. The houses were new and here and there I caught a glimpse of the green countryside between them. I felt that my journey had some hidden, extremely painful meaning, and I became sadder with every passing moment. I suddenly remembered the efforts Gisella had made to deprive me of my innocence and make me like herself; and I began to cry as instinctively as a wound bleeds.

When I got out of the taxi at the end of the journey, my eyes were shining, my cheeks wet. "You shouldn't cry, miss," the driver said. I only shook my head and went toward the entrance of Gisella's house.

It was a little white building, in modern style, and had evidently been erected quite recently; barrels, tools, and beams were piled up in the barren little garden and splashes of whitewash showed on the bars of the gate. I entered a bare white hall and saw a white stairway with opalescent windows through which filtered a peaceful light. The porter, a redheaded youth in workmen's overalls, quite different from the usual old and dirty porters one sees, showed me into the elevator. I pressed the switch and the elevator began to ascend; it smelled pleasantly of new, highly polished wood. There seemed to be something new in the very hum of the machinery; it was like a mechanism that had been functioning for only a short time. The elevator rose to the top floor and as it went up, the light increased. It was as though there was no ceiling and the elevator was going right up into the sky. Then it stopped, I got out and found myself on a dazzling white landing in brilliant light, standing in front of a handsome door with polished brass handles. I rang: a thin, dark little maid with a sweet face, dressed in a white lace cap and embroidered apron came and opened the door.

"Is Signorina de Santis in?" I asked. "Please tell her it's Adriana."

She left me and went along the passage to a door with opalescent panes of glass like those on the staircase. The passage was all white and bare, too, like the rest of the house. I judged it to be a small apartment, not more than four rooms. It was heated and the warmth from the radiators brought out the pungent smell of the new white-wash and paint. Then the glass-fronted door at the end of the hall opened and the maid returned to tell me I could go through.

I saw nothing when I first entered because the winter sun was blinding as it flooded the room through a wide window that took up the whole of the wall facing the door. The flat was on the top floor and the only thing visible through those windows was blue sky glowing with the light of the sun. For a moment I forgot the purpose of my visit and experienced a feeling of well-being as I shut my eyes in the sunshine, as warm and golden as an old liqueur. But Gisella's voice made me start. She was seated in front of the window, and facing her across a low table covered with bot-tles was a little gray-haired woman, her manicurist.

"Oh, Adriana!" she said, with assumed nonchalance. "Do sit down. I won't be a moment."

I sat down near the door and looked around me. It was a long, narrow room. There really was not much furniture, only a table, a sideboard, and a few chairs in some light-colored wood, but every-thing was new and shining in the sun. The sun was really luxu-rious; sunshine like that was only to be had in wealthy houses, I could not help thinking. Again I shut my eyes deliberately in order to enjoy the delicious sensation, and thought of nothing. Then I felt something soft and heavy fall onto my lap; I opened my eyes and saw a huge cat, a kind I had never seen before, long-haired, soft as silk, grayish-blue in color, with a sulky, haughty expression I didn't like. The cat began to rub against me, mewing raucously and lifting the tip of its tail. Then it curled up on my lap and began to purr. "What a lovely cat!" I said. "What kind is it?"

"A Persian," said Gisella proudly. "It's very valuable. A cat like that costs anything up to a thousand lire."

"I've never seen one before," I said as I stroked it.

"Do you know who's got one just like it?" said the manicurist. "Signora Radaelli. You should see how well she treats it! Better than a human being. The other day she even sprayed perfume all over it. Shall I just touch up your toenails, miss?"

"It doesn't matter, Marta," said Gisella. "That'll do for today."
The manicurist put her tools and little bottles away in a suitcase,
said good-bye, and left.

When we were alone, we looked at one another. Gisella
seemed all new, like the house. She was wearing a pretty red an-
gora sweater and a brown skirt I had not seen her in before. She
had put on weight, her bosom was fuller, her hips filled her skirt
out more. I noticed her eyelids were rather swollen, like a person
who eats well, sleeps well, and has no worries. It was her eyelids
that gave her a rather sulky look.

"Well — what do you think? Do you like my place?" she asked
me as she examined her fingernails.

I am not at all envious by nature. But at that moment I felt the
sting of envy for the first time in my life; and I was amazed that
there could be people in the world who nourished such a feeling
in their hearts their whole life through, for I found it extremely
painful and unpleasant. My face was drawn, as though I had suddenly gone thin, and this made it impossible for me to smile at
Gisella and say something complimentary as I would have
wished. For Gisella herself I experienced a keen feeling of repulsion. I wanted to hurt her, say something spiteful to her, insult her,
humiliate her, poison her happiness, in fact. What's come over
me? I thought in bewilderment, while still continuing to stroke
the cat. Am I no longer myself? Luckily this feeling did not last
long. From the depths of my spirit all the goodness of which I was
capable was already stirring and laying siege to envy. I reminded
myself that Gisella was my friend and her good fortune was therefore mine, and that I ought to be glad for her sake. I pictured
Gisella entering her new house for the first time and clapping her
hands with joy; and at that the icy paralysis of envy vanished from
my face and I once more felt the warmth of the sun, but in a more
intimate fashion, as though it had penetrated into my heart.

"How can you ask?" I said. "Such a gay, lovely place! How did
it happen?"

I thought I sounded sincere as I said these words and I smiled,
more as a reward to myself than at Gisella.

"Do you remember Giancarlo?" she replied with self-assurance and a confidential air. "That blond I quarreled with right away that first evening? Well, he came to see me again. . . . He wasn't nearly as bad as he seemed at first sight. Then we met again, a lot of times. A few days ago he said, 'Come on, I've got a surprise for you.' I thought he wanted to give me a purse, a bottle of perfume, or some other little present, you know. Instead he brought me here in the car and showed me in. The house was all empty; I thought it must be his own place. Then he asked me if I liked it, so I said yes, but without dreaming what he meant, of course! Then he said, 'I've rented this apartment for you.' You can just imagine how I felt!"

She smiled with dignified complacency as she looked around her. I got up impulsively, went over to her. "I'm delighted," I said as I kissed her, "absolutely delighted, I really am."

This gesture dispelled all hostile feelings from my heart. I went up to the window and looked out. The house stood on a kind of rise with a vast landscape beneath it. It was a cultivated plain, traversed by a winding river, with woods, farms, clumps of rocks here and there. Nothing could be seen of the town but a few high buildings, the last blocks in a suburb, over in one corner of the view. A line of blue mountains stood out clearly on the horizon, against the background of the luminous sky.

"It's a magnificent view," I said turning to Gisella.

"Isn't it?" she answered. She walked over to the sideboard, took out two small glasses and a squat decanter, and put them on the table. "Will you have a liqueur?" she asked carelessly. Obviously all her gestures as mistress of a house of her own filled her with satisfaction.

We sat down at the table and sipped our liqueur in silence. I could see that Gisella was embarrassed and I wanted to do something to relieve her. "Still, it wasn't very nice of you," I said gently. "You ought to have let me know."

"I didn't have time," she answered hurriedly. "You know what moving is, and then I've had so much to do buying the things I needed most — furniture, linen, dishes — I haven't had a moment to breathe. It's a big job, setting up house." She pinched her lips together like a proper lady as she spoke.

"I see what you mean," I said, without a trace of spite or bitterness, as if the whole matter had nothing to do with me. "Now that you have a place of your own and are better off, it bothers you to see me. You're ashamed of me."

"I'm not at all ashamed," she replied with a touch of annoyance, apparently more irritated by my reasonable tone of voice than by my words. "If you think that, you're really stupid. Only we won't be able to see each other now the way we did before. I mean — go out together and all that. If he found out, I'd be in real trouble."

"Don't worry," I replied gently. "You won't see anything more of me. I just came over today to find out what had happened to you."

She pretended she had not heard and this strengthened me in my belief. A short silence ensued.

"What about you?" she asked with false solicitude.

Immediately, so spontaneously that it frightened me, I thought of Giacomo. "Me?" I replied in a choked voice. "Nothing. Everything's the same."

"What about Astarita?"

"I've seen him from time to time."

"And Gino?"

"I'm through with him."

The memory of Giacomo wrung my heart. But Gisella interpreted the deep mortification she read in my face in her own way. She probably thought I was embittered by her own good luck and scornful manner.

"Still, no one will ever get it out of my head that Astarita would set you up in a place of your own if you wanted him to," she said, feigning an interest after a moment's reflection.

"But I don't want him to," I said calmly. "Neither Astarita nor anyone else."

She appeared disconcerted by my reply. "Why not? Wouldn't you like to have a place like this?"

"The house is beautiful," I said, "but I want above all to be free!"

"I'm free!" she replied resentfully. "I'm freer than you are. I've got the whole day to myself."

"That's not the kind of freedom I meant."

"What did you mean then?"

I realized I had offended her, if only by not showing enough admiration for the house she was so proud of. But she would have been even more deeply offended if I had explained to her that I didn't despise it and that actually I did not want to tie myself to any man I did not love. I preferred to change the subject.

"Show me around the house," I said hurriedly. "How many rooms are there?"

"What do you care about the house?" she said with childish disappointment. "You said yourself you didn't want a place like this."

"That's not what I said," I replied calmly. "It's a lovely house — I wish I had one like it."

She said nothing. She was gazing downward with a sulky expression. "So," I went on weakly after a moment, "you don't want to show me around?"

She raised her eyes and I saw to my amazement that they were full of tears. "You aren't the friend I thought you were!" she exclaimed. "You're — you're bursting with envy and so you're trying to run the place down just to upset me." She was speaking to the air, her face bathed with tears. They were tears of rage and she was the one who was envious this time, a pointless envy that was sharpened unconsciously by my hopeless love for Giacomo and the bitter sense of separation it gave me. But although I understood her so well, indeed, just because of this, I was sorry for her. I got up, went over to her, put my hand on her shoulder.

"Why say that?" I said. "I'm not envious. I'd like other things — that's all. But I'm glad you're happy. So, come on, show me the other rooms," I said, hugging her.

She blew her nose and yielding to my persuasion said, "There are four rooms, in all — and they're practically empty."

"Come on, show me."

She got up, led the way into the hall, and opening one door after another showed me a bedroom with only a bed and an armchair at the foot of it, an empty room where she intended to put another bed for "guests," a little cubbyhole for the maid, with hardly room to swing a cat in. She showed me these rooms with a kind of annoyance, opening the doors and explaining what they were to be used for without any pleasure in them. But her bad mood gave way to vanity when she showed me the bathroom and the kitchen, both tiled in majolica, with their new electric machines and shining faucets. She explained how the machines worked, how much better they were than gas, how clean they were and how little they consumed, and although I was really not at all interested, I pretended this time to be enthusiastic and exclaimed in admiration and surprise. She was so delighted with my attitude that when we had seen the whole apartment she said, "Let's go and have another liqueur."

"No, no," I said, "I've got to go."

"What's the hurry? Stay a while."

"I can't."

We were in the hallway. She hesitated a moment, then said, "But you must come again . . . do you know what we could do? He often goes out of Rome — I'll let you know and you bring along two friends of yours and we'll have some fun."

"Suppose he finds out?"

"Why should he?"

"All right, then," I said. I hesitated in turn, then took courage. "By the way," I said, "has he ever mentioned that friend of his who was with him that evening?"

"The student? Why? Did you like him?"

"No, I only wondered."

"We saw him yesterday evening."

I could not conceal my agitation. "Listen," I said uncertainly, "if you see him tell him to come see me. But you know — casually, without insisting."

"All right, I'll tell him," she answered. But she was looking at me suspiciously and her glance embarrassed me, because I felt that my love for Giacomo was written in large letters on my face. I understood from the tone of her voice that she would not pass on the message. In despair, I opened the door, said good-bye to her, and hurried downstairs without turning back. On the second landing I stopped and leaned against the wall, looking up. Why did I tell her? I thought. What came over me? I went on down the stairs with bowed head.

I had made the appointment with Astarita at my own place; when I got there, I was worn out. I was no longer accustomed to going out in the morning and the sun and exercise had tired me. I did not even feel unhappy, I had already paid for my visit to Gisella when I had cried in the taxi on my way to her new apartment. Mother came and opened the door and told me someone had been waiting for me in my room for an hour. I went straight in and sat down on the bed, taking no notice of Astarita who was standing before the window, apparently staring down into the courtyard. I kept still for a moment, pressing my hand to my heart and panting because I had come upstairs so quickly. My back was turned to Astarita, I was gazing absently at the door. He had greeted me, but I had not answered. Then he came and sat down beside me and put his arm around my waist, looking earnestly at me.

In all my worries I had forgotten his crazy desire that was always kindled and alert. An acute revulsion came over me. "Tell me, do you always want it?" I said, in a slow, disagreeable voice as I drew back from him.

He said nothing but took my hand and raised it to his lips, looking upward at me. I thought I would go crazy and pulled my hand away. "You're always ready, aren't you?" I went on. "Even in the morning? After you've been working all morning? Before you've had your lunch? On an empty stomach? You know, you're really amazing!"

I saw his lips tremble and his eyes go wide. "But I love you!"

"But there's a time for making love and a time for other things. I made an appointment with you for one o'clock just so you'd know it wasn't to make love and you — really you're amazing! Aren't you ashamed of yourself?"

He stared at me in silence. Suddenly I felt I understood him all too well. He was in love with me and had been waiting for this appointment for days. While I had been struggling with so many difficulties, he had been thinking of nothing else but my legs, my breasts, my hips, my mouth. "So," I said, a little less angrily, "if I were to get undressed now —"

He nodded in agreement. I burst out laughing, not unkindly but bitterly. "It wouldn't occur to you that I might be unhappy or just not feel like it — that I might be hungry or tired or have some other worries — that wouldn't ever cross your mind, would it?"

He looked at me, then suddenly threw himself upon me and, hugging me closely, buried his face in the hollow between my neck and shoulder. He did not kiss me, he only pressed his face against me as if to feel the warmth of my flesh. He was breathing heavily and sighed from time to time. I was no longer irritated by him, his gestures roused my usual anxious pity. I only felt unhappy. When I thought he had had his fill of sighs, I pushed him off.

"I asked you here on a serious matter," I said.

He looked at me, then took my hand and began to stroke it. He was tenacious and for him, really, nothing existed but his desire.

"You're in the police, aren't you?"

"Yes."

"Well, then — have me arrested, send me to prison." I said this quite firmly. At the time, I really wanted him to do it.

"Why? What's happened?"

"I'm a thief," I said loudly. "I've committed a theft and an innocent woman has been arrested in my place. So — arrest me. I'm quite willing to go to jail. That's what I want."

He did not seem surprised, only annoyed.

"Slow down!" he said with a grimace. "What happened? Tell me about it."

"I've told you, I'm a thief." In a few words I told him about the theft and how the maid had been arrested instead of me. I told him of Gino's trick, but I did not mention his name. I referred to him only as a servant. But I felt violently tempted to tell him about Sonzogno and his crime and I could hardly keep it back. At last I said, "Now you choose . . . either you get that woman out of prison or I'll go and give myself up."

"Slow down," he repeated, raising his hand. "What's the hurry? For the time being she's in jail — but she hasn't been sentenced yet. Let's wait."

"No, I can't wait! She's in jail and they say she's been beaten up. . . . I can't wait. You've got to make up your mind now."

He realized from my voice that I was speaking in earnest. He got up with a disconcerted look on his face and began to walk about the room. Then, as if speaking to himself, he continued. "There's the question of the dollars."

"But she's been denying that all along! The dollars were found again. We could say it was revenge on the part of someone who hated her."

"Have you got the compact?"

"It's here," I said, taking it from my bag and handing it to him.

But he refused to touch it. "No, no, you mustn't give it to me," he said. "I could have that woman released," he went on after a moment's hesitation, "but at the same time the police would have to have the proof that she was innocent — this compact, to be exact."

"Take it, then, and give it back to its owner."

He laughed disagreeably. "Obviously you know nothing about these matters! If I accept this compact from you, I'm morally bound to have you arrested. Otherwise they'd say, 'How did Astarita get hold of the stolen object? who gave it to him? how did he get it? and so on. . . . No, you'll have to find some way of getting the compact to the police, but without giving yourself away, of course."

"I could mail it."

"No, you can't mail it."

He paced about the room then came and sat down beside me. "This is what you'll have to do," he said. "Do you know any priest?"

I remembered the French monk I had confessed to when I came back from Viterbo. "Yes, my confessor," I said.

"Do you still go to confession?"

"I used to."

"Well — go to your confessor and tell him the whole story. Just as you told me. And beg him to take the compact and give it to the police on your behalf. No confessor could refuse to do this. He's not obliged to give any information to the police because he is bound by the seal of the confessional. A day or two later I'll call you . . . I'll . . . Anyway, your maid will be released."

I was overcome by joy and could not help flinging my arms around his neck and kissing him. He continued in a voice already trembling with desire. "But you mustn't do these things, you know. . . . When you need money, just ask me and I . . ."

"Can I go and see the confessor today?"

"Of course."

I stood there motionless for some time, staring fixedly in front of me, with the compact in one hand. I experienced a feeling of profound relief, as if I were that maid, and as I imagined her relief, so much greater than my own, at being released, I really felt as if I were her. I was no longer unhappy, tired, or disgusted. Meanwhile Astarita was stroking my wrist with his fingers and trying to insert them into my sleeve to touch my arm. I turned and spoke caressingly, gazing sweetly at him.

"Is it really so important to you?" I asked.

He nodded, incapable of speech.

"Aren't you tired?" I continued tenderly and cruelly. "Don't you think it's getting late — that it would be better to put it off until another day?"

He shook his head.

"Do you love me so much?" I asked.

"You know I love you," he said in a low voice. He came forward to embrace me, but I avoided him. "Wait," I said.

He calmed down at once, because he knew I had assented. I got up, went slowly to the door and locked it. Then I walked over to the window, opened it, drew the shutters together and closed the window again. I could feel his eyes on me the whole time as I walked about the room with slow, lazy, stately movements, and I could well imagine how wonderful my unexpected acquiescence must seem to him. When I had closed the shutters, I began to

hum softly in a gay, intimate voice, and still humming I opened
the closet, took off my coat, and hung it up. Then, still humming
I looked at myself in the mirror. It seemed to me I had never been
so beautiful — my eyes were sparkling, deeply and sweetly, my
nostrils quivered, my mouth was half open, showing my white,
even teeth. I realized I was beautiful because I was pleased with
myself, and felt myself to be good. I raised my voice a little as I
sang, and at the same time began to unbutton my bodice from
the bottom up. I was singing a silly song that was popular at the
time. It ran: *I'm singing the ditty I like so much that goes du-du,
du-du, du-du.* The silly refrain seemed to me to be like life itself,
obviously absurd, but at moments sweet and fascinating. Suddenly, when I had already bared my breasts, someone knocked at
the door.

"I can't," I said composedly. "Later —"

"It's urgent," said Mother's voice.

A suspicion crossed my mind. I went to the door and unlocked
it, then peered out.

Mother beckoned to me to come out and shut the door.

"There's a man who wants to speak to you urgently," she whispered in the dark outer room.

"Who is it?"

"I don't know. A dark young man."

I opened the door of the living room very quietly and peeped
in. Then I saw a man leaning against the table with his back to
me. I recognized Giacomo immediately and shut the door again
quickly.

"Tell him I'm just coming," I said to Mother. "And don't let
him leave that room."

She told me she would and I returned to my room. Astarita was
still sitting on the bed, as I had left him.

"Quick," I said. "Quick . . . I'm sorry — but you have to go."

He became distressed and began to stammer some protest. But
I cut him short. "My aunt's been taken ill in the street," I said. "I've
got to go to the hospital with my mother as quickly as possible." It
was a fairly transparent lie, but I could not think of anything else at

the moment. He looked at me stupidly, as if he could not believe his own bad luck. I saw that he had removed his shoes, and his feet in their striped socks were resting on the floor.

"Come on! What are you staring at me for? You've got to go!" I said in exasperation.

"All right — I'll go," he replied, and bent down to put his shoes on again. I stood in front of him to hand him his coat. But I knew I would have to promise him something if I wanted him to intervene in the maid's favor. "Listen," I said, as I helped him on with his coat, "I'm awfully sorry about this — but come back tomorrow evening after supper. We won't be interrupted then. I'd have had to send you away again almost immediately today, anyway. It's actually better this way."

He said nothing and I accompanied him to the door, leading him by the hand as if it were his first visit to the house. I was so afraid he might go into the living room and see Giacomo.

"Remember — I'm going right to that confessor today," I said at the door. He replied with a nod, as if to imply that he understood. His face looked disgusted and frozen. I was so impatient I could not wait for his farewell and almost slammed the door in his face.

5

WHEN MY FINGERS WERE on the handle of the living room door, it struck me with sudden force that short of a miracle I was bound to establish between Giacomo and myself the same unhappy relations I had with Astarita. I now saw that the mixture of subjection, fear, and blind desire that Astarita felt for me was exactly what I felt for Giacomo; and although I knew that I ought to behave differently if I wanted to be loved, nevertheless I felt irresistibly drawn to place myself on a lower, dependent plane of anxious uncertainty with him. I could not have explained the reasons for my state of inferiority — if I could have done so, it would no longer exist. I only knew instinctively that we were made of different stuff. I was harder than Astarita but more fragile than Giacomo; and just as there was something that prevented me from loving Astarita, so something prevented Giacomo from loving me. My love for Giacomo, like Astarita's for me, had started badly and would end worse. My heart was pounding and I felt breathless even before seeing him and speaking to him; I was terribly afraid I would make some false step, show him my eagerness and desire to please him, and so lose him again once and for all. This is surely the worst curse of love — that it is never requited, and when you love you are not loved in return, and when you are loved you do not love. Two lovers never meet on the same level of emotion and desire, although this is the ideal for which each human being strives. I knew, without any shadow of doubt, that just because I had fallen in love with Giacomo, he had not fallen in love with me. And I also knew, although I did not want to acknowledge it to myself, that no matter what effort I might make, I would never succeed in forcing him to fall in love with me. All this flashed through my mind while I stood hesitating outside the door, in a state of ghastly agitation. I felt dizzy, on the point of doing the most ridiculous things, and this irritated me extremely. At last I took courage and entered the room.

He was still standing as he had been when I had peered at him through the crack of the door, that is leaning against the table, with his back to me. But when he heard me come in, he turned around. "I was just passing by," he said, looking at me with critical, calculating attention. "So I thought I'd drop in — perhaps I shouldn't have." I noticed he was speaking slowly, as if he wanted to have a good look at me before committing himself to speech; and I could not help feeling anxious, wondering what I seemed like to him, perhaps different and less attractive than his memory of me that had led him to visit me after such a lapse of time. But I felt reassured as I remembered how beautiful I had looked when I had gazed at myself in the mirror a little earlier.

"Not at all," I said, a little breathlessly. "You were right to come — I was just going out to lunch. We could eat together."

"Do you mean you recognize me?" he asked, perhaps ironically. "Do you know who I am?"

"Of course, I know you!" I said foolishly. And before my self-control could influence my actions, I had taken his hand and raised it to my lips, with a glance full of love. His confusion delighted me.

"Why didn't you call, you naughty boy?" I asked, in an anxious and tender voice.

He shook his head. "I've been very busy," he said.

I had quite lost my head. After kissing his hand, I placed it on my heart below my breast. "Feel how my heart is beating!" I said. But at the same time I told myself I was a fool because I knew I ought not to have done and said that. He made a certain embarrassed face, so I added, quickly, "I'm just going to put my coat on. I'll be right back. Wait for me."

I felt so completely bewildered and so afraid of losing him that when I was in the outer room I turned the key violently in the lock and removed it from the keyhole. In this way, if he tried to leave while I was dressing, he would be unable to. I went into my bedroom, crossed over to the closet mirror and removed all the makeup from my eyes and mouth with the corner of my handkerchief. Then I took my lipstick and touched up my lips again, but just barely. I went over to the coatrack, looked for my coat, could not find it, felt lost, then remembered I had hung it up in the closet, pulled it out, and put it on. I looked at myself in the mirror once more and decided my hairstyle was too showy. I combed out my hair in a great hurry and rearranged it as I used to wear it when I was engaged to Gino. Meanwhile, as I did my hair, I swore to myself solemnly that from that moment on I would repress all the unconsidered impulses of my passion and would exercise a strict control over my words and gestures. At last I was quite ready. I went into the outer room and looked in at the door of the living room to call Giacomo.

But as we were about to leave, the house door, which in my turmoil, I had forgotten to unlock, gave me away.

"You were afraid I'd run away," he murmured while, very confused, I hunted for the key in my bag. He took the key from my hand and unlocked the door himself, looking at me and shaking his head with a kind of fond severity. My heart was filled with joy and I ran downstairs after him.

"You aren't annoyed, are you?" I asked him breathlessly as I took his arm. He did not answer.

We walked along arm in arm in the sunshine, past the house doors and shops down in the street. I was so happy walking beside him that I completely forgot my good resolutions; and when we passed the little villa with the tower, it was as though someone had taken my hand and inspired me to squeeze his. At the same time I realized I was leaning forward, so as to have a better view of his face.

"Do you know that I'm awfully glad to see you?" I said.

He made his usual embarrassed face. "I'm glad, too," he said, but the tone of his voice was not exactly glad, I thought.

I bit my lips until they bled and disentangled my fingers from his. He did not seem to notice; he was looking around and seemed distracted. But when we reached the gateway in the walls, he hesitated, stopped, and spoke.

"Listen," he said in a reticent way, "I have to tell you something."

"Tell me then."

"I only came to see you by chance — and by the same chance I haven't a penny on me. So it'll be better for us to part." As he said this he held out his hand.

My first reaction was one of terror. He's leaving me, I thought, and in my bewilderment I saw no other remedy but to cling hard to his neck, beseeching him not to go, and weeping. But on second thought the very excuse that he had given for leaving me showed me an easy way out, and my feelings changed. It occurred to me that I would be able to pay for his lunch, and the idea of paying for him, as so many had paid for me, delighted me. I have already mentioned the sensual pleasure I felt every time I received money for my services. Now I discovered that paying money out is no less thrilling a pleasure. And the mingling of love with money, whether the money is given or received, is not only a matter of profit. "Don't even think about it!" I exclaimed impetuously. "I'll pay. Look — I've got some money." And I opened my purse to show him some bills I had put into it the evening before.

"It isn't done," he protested, with a trace of disappointment.

"What does that matter? You've come back; it's only right that I should celebrate your return."

"No," he said. "Better not." He tried again to shake hands and leave me. This time I took his arm.

"Let's not talk about it anymore." And I started toward the restaurant.

We sat at the same table as before and everything was just as it had been, except for a ray of wintry sunlight that shone through the glass-fronted door and lit up the tables and the wall. The proprietor brought the menu and I gave my order in a firm, protective voice, just as my lovers did for me. He said nothing while I was ordering, his eyes were downcast. I had forgotten the wine because I don't drink; then I remembered he had had some wine last time we were together so I asked for a liter.

As soon as the proprietor had gone, I opened my bag, took out a hundred-lira note, folded it in four and, after a rapid glance around, held it out to Giacomo under the table.

He looked at me questioningly.

"The money," I said in a low voice. "Then you can pay afterward."

"Oh, the money," he said slowly. He took the bill, opened it out on the table, looked at it, then folded it again, opened my purse and put it back — all this in ironical seriousness.

"Do you want me to pay?" I asked him, feeling disconcerted.

"No, I'll pay," he said.

"Then why did you say you hadn't any money?"

He hesitated for a moment. "I didn't come to see you by chance," he replied with bitter sincerity. "The fact is — I've been thinking of coming for a month now. But every time I found myself outside your place, I felt impelled to go away again. . . . So I thought I'd say I didn't have any money, in the hope that you'd send me to the devil." He smiled and passed his hand over his chin. "Apparently I was mistaken."

So he had tried out a kind of experiment on me. He did not want to have anything to do with me. Or rather, his heart was torn in two between the attraction I had for him and the equally potent aversion he had for me. Later I was to discover that his capacity for feigning a part he did not feel sincerely was an essential part of his character. But at that time I felt utterly confused. I did not know whether I ought to be cheerful or to feel upset by his deceit and his defeat.

"But why did you want to go away?" I asked mechanically.

"Because I realized I felt nothing for you. Or rather, all I felt was the kind of desire my friend felt for your girlfriend that evening."

"Did you know they're living together?" I asked.

"Yes," he replied scornfully, "they're made for one another."

"You felt nothing for me," I said, "and you didn't want to come see me — and yet you came!" His lack of logic was something of a consolation in the disillusionment I had foreseen my love would cause me.

"Yes," he replied, "because I'm what's usually called a weak character."

"Still, you came, and that's enough for me," I said cruelly. I stretched my hand out under the table and placed it on his knees. Meanwhile I was watching him and saw that my touch troubled him, his chin began to quiver. I was delighted at seeing him so moved; and I realized that although he wanted me very much as he had confessed when he said he had been thinking about coming to see me for a whole month, there was a part of him that was hostile to me. I would have to do everything that lay in my power to humiliate and destroy that part. I remembered his keen, cutting gaze at my naked back the first time we were together, and I told myself I had been wrong to let myself be frozen by such a look, and that if I had persisted in my efforts to seduce him, the look would have faded, just as the convulsive dignity in his face was now breaking up and fading.

Leaning against the table, as if I wanted to speak to him confidentially, I went on caressing him and at the same time saw with gay satisfaction the effects of my caresses as they were reflected in his face. He was looking at me with an offended, questioning air out of his large, dark, shining eyes with their long, feminine eyelashes.

"If it's enough for you to please me this way, go ahead," he said at last.

I straightened myself immediately. And at that moment the proprietor put the knives and forks and plates on the table. We began to eat in silence; neither of us had any appetite.

"If I were you, I'd try to make me drink," he said.

"Why?"

"Because I do what other people want me to more easily when I'm drunk."

His phrase, "If it's enough for you to please me this way, go ahead," had already offended me. What he said about drinking was enough to convince me that my efforts were useless.

"I only want you to do what you feel like doing," I said in despair. "If you want to go, go — there's the door."

"I'd have to be sure that that was what I wanted, if I were to go away," he said teasingly.

"Do you want me to go?"

We looked at one another. In my misery, I was quite determined. And my determination seemed to trouble him as much as my caresses had done a moment earlier. "No," he said with an effort, "stay here."

We continued to eat in silence. Then I saw him pour out a large glass of wine and empty it at a gulp. "You see," he said, "I'm drinking."

"I can see that."

"I'll soon be drunk and then I might even make you a declaration of love."

His words pierced me to the heart. I really could not continue to suffer in this way. "Stop it," I said humbly, "stop torturing me."

"Am I torturing you?"

"Yes, you're making fun of me. . . . Now the only thing I ask of you is not to bother with me. . . . I've got a crush on you — it'll pass — but meanwhile, leave me alone."

He said nothing and drank off a second glass of wine. I was afraid I had offended him. "What's the matter?" I asked. "Are you mad at me?"

"Mad at you? Not at all."

"If you like making fun of me, it's all right. I was just talking."

"But I'm not making fun of you."

"And if you like saying cruel things to me," I insisted, driven by I knew not what desire to humble myself before him, without calculation or cunning, to the point of abjection, "say them. I'll love you all the same — even more. Even if you hit me, I'd kiss the hand that did it."

He was examining me attentively. He seemed extremely embarrassed, obviously he found my passion disconcerting. "Let's go, all right?" he then said.

"Where?"

"To your place."

I was so hopeless that I had almost forgotten the cause of my hopelessness; and his invitation, so unexpected, when we had only just finished the first course and half the wine was left in the carafe, astonished more than delighted me. I supposed rightly that not love, but his embarrassment at what I was saying, made him want to interrupt his meal.

"You can't wait to be done with me, can you?" I said.

"How did you guess?" he asked, but his reply, too cruel to be true, inexplicably encouraged me.

"Some things go without saying," I said, lowering my eyes. "Let's finish our meal, though — then we'll go."

"As you like. But I'll get drunk."

"Get drunk, then, as far as I'm concerned."

"But I'll get so drunk, I'll be ill, and then instead of having a lover to love, you'll have a sick man to nurse."

I was simple enough to show my anxiety and stretched out my hand toward the carafe. "Don't drink, then!" I said. He burst into laughter. "You fell for it!" he said.

"Fell for what?"

"Don't worry. I don't get sick as easily as all that."

"I was thinking of you," I said, feeling humiliated.

"Of me — oh, oh!"

He continued to tease me. But his innate kindness underlay all his teasing and so I did not mind very much.

"Why don't you drink, though?" he added.

"I don't like it. Besides, a glass is enough to make me drunk."

"What does that matter? We'll be drunk together."

"Women are ugly when they're drunk. I don't want you to see me drunk."

"Why? What's ugly about it?"

"I don't know. It's awful to see a woman stagger around, talk rubbish, make coarse gestures. It's sad. I'm a disgraced woman, I know, and I know that's how you think of me. But if I were to drink and you saw me drunk, you'd never look me in the face again."

"Suppose I ordered you to drink?"

"You really want to see me humiliated," I said pensively. "The only good thing about me is that I'm not clumsy. Do you really want me to lose that quality, too?"

"Yes, that's just what I want," he said emphatically.

"I don't know what sort of a kick you get out of it, but if it gives you one, pour me some wine." And I held out my glass.

He looked at the glass, at me, then burst into laughter again. "I was only joking," he said.

"You're always joking."

"So you're not clumsy?" he went on after a moment, looking at me attentively.

"That's what they say, anyway."

"Do you think I agree?"

"How do I know what you think?"

"Let's see. What do you suppose I think and feel about you?"

"I don't know," I said slowly and fearfully. "Certainly you don't love me as I love you. . . . Perhaps I please you, as a woman can please a man if she's not really ugly."

"Oh, so you think you aren't really ugly!"

"Yes," I said proudly. "In fact, I know I'm beautiful; but what use have my looks been to me so far?"

"Beauty isn't meant to be of any use."

Meanwhile we had finished our meal and had nearly emptied two carafes. "You see," he said, "I've been drinking, but I'm not drunk." But his shining eyes and trembling hands seemed to contradict him. I looked at him with a glimmer of hope. "You want to go home, eh?" he added. "Venus in her entirety encircling her prey."

"What's that?"

"Nothing. Only a line of verse I translated to fit the occasion. Innkeeper!"

He was still speaking emphatically but farcically. And farcically he asked the proprietor how much the bill was and thrust the money under his nose, adding an exaggerated tip, as he said, "This is for you." Then he swallowed the rest of the wine and joined me outside the restaurant.

As soon as I was in the street, I felt frantic to reach home. I knew he had come to see me against his will and I knew he hated and despised the feeling that had driven him to seek me out. But I had a great faith in my beauty and my love for him, and was impatient to overcome his hostility with these weapons. A gay, aggressive will inspired me once more, and I felt sure my love would prove to be stronger than his aversion, and that at last, in the ardor of my own fire, the harsh, unyielding mettle in him would be melted and he would reciprocate my love.

"Still," I said as I walked along beside him in the street, empty at that early hour in the afternoon, "you've got to promise you won't try to get away once we're home."

"I promise."

"And you've got to promise something else."

"What?"

I hesitated before answering. "The other time," I said, "everything would have gone all right if you hadn't looked at me in a certain way that made me feel ashamed. You've got to promise me you won't look at me like that again."

"Like what?"

"I don't know — a nasty look."

"You can't control the way you look at things," he replied after a moment. "But if you want, I won't look at you at all. I'll shut my eyes. . . . That'll be all right."

"No, it won't," I protested obstinately.

"How do you want me to look at you, then?"

"The way I look at you," I answered. I took hold of him by the chin while we were still walking and showed him how he ought to look at me. "Like this, meltingly —"

"Oh, I see, meltingly —"

When we were on the squalid and filthy staircase that led to my apartment I could not help remembering the place Gisella lived in, so clean, white, and shining. "If I didn't live in an ugly old house like this," I said, as if speaking to myself, "and weren't disgraced as I am, you'd like me a lot more."

Quite unexpectedly he stood still and took hold of me by the waist with both hands. "If that's what you think," he said earnestly, "you can be sure you're mistaken." Something very like affection seemed to gleam in his eyes. At the same time he bent down and sought my mouth. His breath smelled strongly of wine. I never could stand the stink of wine; but in his mouth at that moment it seemed innocent and charming, touching almost, as touching as it would have been in the mouth of an inexperienced boy. I also realized that my words had unintentionally touched him on his most sensitive spot. I imagined I had awakened in his heart a spark of affection. Afterward I recognized it was, if anything, an impulse of self-love and in embracing me he was submitting to a kind of moral blackmail rather than yielding to an amorous impulse. Subsequently I blackmailed him in the same way quite often: by accusing him of despising me because of my poverty and my profession. And I always achieved the desired results, although as my understanding of him grew, this was peculiarly humiliating and disappointing.

But I did not know him so well then as I came to later on. And his kiss filled me with joy, as if I had won a decisive victory. I merely touched his lips with mine, content with the gesture alone, and taking him by the hand I pulled him up the last flight of stairs gaily and ardently, saying, "Come on, come on, let's run up!" He let himself be dragged up without a word.

I entered my room almost at a run — knocking him against the walls of the entrance as though he were a puppet. I entered with violence and, rather than joining him, I flung him on the bed. Then I noticed for the first time that he was not only drunk, as I had foreseen, but was so drunk that he was on the point of vomiting. He was extremely pale, kept passing his hand across his forehead with a bewildered expression, had a dazed and wandering look in his eye. I noticed all this in a flash; and immediately I began to be afraid he might really be sick, and for the second time our meeting would go up in smoke. I was filled with remorse as I walked about the room undressing, because I had not prevented his drinking. I was almost in despair. But notably, it never even crossed my mind to give up on his love, for which I so yearned. I hoped for one thing only — that he would not feel so sick as to be unable to make love to me, and that if he really were so sick, the effects of it would not make themselves felt until after my desire had been satisfied. I was truly in love with him, but I was so afraid of losing him that my love was unable to go beyond the limits of selfishness.

So I pretended I did not notice his drunkenness and after removing my clothes I sat down on the bed beside him. He was still wearing his overcoat, just as when he had entered the room. I began to help him to get undressed and as I helped him, I kept on talking to distract his attention and prevent its occurring to him to get up and leave me.

"You haven't told me how old you are, yet," I said. Meanwhile I was pulling off his overcoat and he was holding up his arms passively to make it easier for me.

"I'm nineteen," he said after a moment.

"You're two years younger than I am."

"Are you twenty-one?"

"Yes, nearly twenty-two, in fact."

My fingers fumbled clumsily with the knot in his tie. Slowly, with difficulty, he pushed me away and undid the knot. Then he let his arms fall, and I slipped the tie off. "This tie's all worn," I said, "I'll buy you one — what's your favorite color?"

He began to laugh and I loved him then because he had such a charming way of laughing. "You really mean to keep me!" he said. "First you want to pay for my meal, and now you want to give me a tie."

"Silly!" I said with intense affection. "What does it matter? It would please me to give you a tie, why would you object?" Meanwhile I had taken off his jacket and vest and he was sitting on the edge of the bed in his shirt.

"Can you tell I'm nineteen?" he asked. He always liked talking about himself. It didn't take me long to discover this.

"Yes and no," I said, hesitating in a way I knew he would find flattering. "Your hair gives you away, mostly," I added, stroking his head. "A man's hair isn't alive. I couldn't tell from your face."

"How old would you say I am?"

"Twenty-five."

He was silent and I saw him shut his eyes as if overcome by his drunkenness. I was seized once more by the fear that he might be sick, so I hurried to take off his shirt. "Tell me more about yourself," I added. "Are you a student?"

"Yes."

"What are you studying?"

"Law."

"Do you live with your family?"

"No, they're in the country at S —"

"Do you live in a boardinghouse?"

"No, a furnished room," he replied mechanically with his eyes shut. "Apartment eight, 20 Via Cola di Rienzo, at Mrs. Amalia Medolaghi's — she's a widow."

His chest was bare now. I could not help running my hand amorously over his chest and neck. "Why are you just sitting there? Aren't you cold?" I asked.

He raised his head and looked at me. "What do you think — that I haven't noticed?" he laughed, his voice rather sharp.

"Noticed what?"

"That without seeming to, you've been undressing me — I may be drunk but I'm not as drunk as all that."

"Well," I said, disconcerted, "what if I have — what's the matter with that? You should have done it yourself — since you didn't, I've been helping you."

Apparently he did not hear what I was saying. "I'm drunk," he said, shaking his head, "but I know perfectly well what I'm doing and why I'm here. . . . No, I don't need any help, thank you."

He suddenly unfastened his belt violently, with arms whose thinness made them look like a puppet's, and flung off his trousers

and everything else he was wearing. "And I know what you expect
from me, too," he added as he gripped my hips with both hands.
His strong, nervous hands squeezed me and the drunken look in
his eyes seemed to have been replaced by a kind of malicious en-
ergy. I was to encounter this same malice later, even in the moments when he seemed to most abandon himself. It was a clear
sign of the lucid consciousness he kept in reserve, whatever he was
doing and which, as I was to discover later to my sorrow, prevented
him from really loving or communicating with anyone.

"This is what you want, isn't it?" he added, as he clutched me
and dug his nails into my flesh. "This, and this, and this." Each
time he said "this" he made a gesture of love, kissing me, biting
me, pinching me where I least expected it. I was laughing and
wriggling and struggling, too happy at his sudden reawakening to
notice how forced and lacking in spontaneity his behavior was. He
really hurt me, as though my body was an object of hatred for him
and not of love. And more rage than desire gleamed in his eyes.
Then, his frenzy ceased as suddenly as it had begun. In a curious,
inexplicable fashion, as though overcome once more by his feeling
of drunkenness, he fell back full-length on the bed and shut his
eyes, and I found myself beside him with the strange sensation
that he had never moved or spoken, had never touched me or embraced me. As if it all had yet to begin.

I remained there utterly still for some time, kneeling on the
bed in front of him, my hair hanging over my eyes, looking at him
and touching his long, thin, beautiful, pure body with timid fingertips. His skin was white and his bones stuck out, his shoulders
were broad and thin, his hips narrow, his legs long, and he was
hairless except for a few hairs on his chest. His belly was flattened
because of the way he was lying, so that his sex appeared raised
and offered. I do not like violence in love, and this was why I felt
as if nothing had happened between us and everything was still to
begin. So I waited for peace and silence to be restored between us
after that forced, ironical moment of tumult, and when I felt once
more my usual serene and impassioned self, I let myself down beside him, as if I were slowly slipping into the lovely waters of a mo-

tionless sea on a blazing day, and I twisted my legs around his and wrapped my arms around his neck and clung to him. This time he neither moved nor spoke to the end. I called him by the sweetest names, panted in his face and wrapped him in the hot, tight mesh of my embraces, while he lay as motionless and supine as if he were dead. I learned afterward that this detached passivity was the highest proof of love he could give.

Much later in the night I raised up on my elbow and gazed at him intensely, in a way which is still, after so long, a precise and painful memory. He was sleeping with his head buried sideways in the pillow; his usual air of wavering dignity, which he tried to maintain at all times and at all costs, had abandoned him; and nothing remained in his features, which sleep revealed in all their sincerity, except his youthfulness, more like an indefinable freshness and innocence than an expression mirroring some special quality or tendency in his soul. But I remembered that I had seen him alternately spiteful, hostile, indifferent, cruel, and full of desire, and I felt a melancholy and anxious discontent, for I knew that his spite, his hostility, his indifference, his desire, all these things that differentiated him from me and everyone else, had their origin in some deep center that was still secret and unknown to me. I did not want him to explain his attitudes by taking them down and examining them in words, as the parts of a machine can be taken down and examined; I wanted instead to have known them, down to their most delicate roots, through the act of love alone, and unfortunately I had failed in this. The little of him that escaped me was all himself, and the greater part that did not escape me was unimportant and useless to me. Gino, Astarita, and even Sonzogno, had been nearer to me and better known. I looked at him and felt anguished because the most profound parts of our beings had not been able to meet and join, as our bodies had done only a little while before. My deepest part was widowed and was weeping bitterly, mourning the chance that had been lost. Perhaps there had been a moment while we were loving one another when he had let down his defenses, and by a gesture or a word I might have entered him and he would have been mine forever. But I had not recognized the right moment and now it was too late; he was sleeping, and had gone away from me once more.

While I continued gazing at him, he opened his eyes, but kept quite still, with his head still buried sideways in the pillow. "Have you been asleep, too?" he asked.

There was a different note in his voice, I thought. It was more intimate and trusting. I was filled with a sudden hope that during his sleep our intimacy had grown in some mysterious way. "No, I've been watching you," I said.

He was silent a moment. "I want to ask you a favor —" he continued "— but can I rely on you?"

"What a question."

"Will you do me the favor of keeping a parcel I'll give you for a few days? Then I'll come and collect it and perhaps bring you another."

At any other time I would have shown some curiosity over this matter of the parcels. But just then the only thing that mattered to me was Giacomo and our relationship. I thought it would give me another opportunity for seeing him; that I ought to do all I could to please him; and that if I were to question him, he might regret his suggestion and withdraw it. "If that's all," I said lightly.

He was silent again for a long time, as if he were meditating. "So you agree?" he said then.

"I've already told you so!"

"And don't you want to know what's inside the parcels?"

"If you don't want to tell me," I answered, doing my utmost to appear detached, "it means you have your reasons: I don't ask you what they are."

"But it might be something dangerous. . . . What do you know?"

"I'll have to risk it."

"It might," he continued, lying flat on his back while his eyes gleamed with an ingenuous amusement, "it might be stolen goods — I might be a thief."

I remembered Sonzogno, who was not only a thief but a murderer, and my own thefts of the compact and the scarf; and I thought what a curious coincidence it was for him to pass himself off as a thief to me, when I really was a thief, living among thieves. "No, you're not a thief, I'm sure!" I said gently as I caressed him.

His face clouded over; his pride was always alert and the strangest and most unexpected things offended him. "Why not? I might be."

"You don't have the face for it — of course, anything's possible — but really, you don't look like one."

"Why? What do I look like?"

"What you are. A young man of good family, a student —"

"I told you I was a student. But I might be something else, too, as in fact, I am."

I was no longer listening to him. I was thinking that I did not have a thief's face either; and yet I was one; and I longed to tell him so. This temptation was partly due to his own curious attitude. I had always thought stealing was something blameworthy; yet here was a someone who not only did not disapprove of such an act, but seemed to find in it some positive aspect totally mysterious to me.

"You're right," I said, after a moment's hesitation. "I don't think you're a thief, because I'm convinced you aren't one; but as to what you look like — you might even be one — people don't always look like what they are. Do I look like a thief, for instance?"

"No," he replied without looking at me.

"And yet I am one," I said composedly.

"You are?"

"Yes."

"What did you steal?"

I had put my purse down on the night table. I picked it up, took out the compact, and showed it to him. "This, in a house where I happened to be a while ago, and a silk scarf in a shop the other day, which I gave to my mother."

It would be wrong to think I told him all this out of vanity. Actually I was led to do it by a desire for intimacy and emotional complicity. For lack of anything better, even the confession of a crime can draw people together and arouse love. I saw him become serious and look at me pensively. I was suddenly afraid he might think badly of me and might decide not to see me again. "But don't think I'm glad I stole them," I said hastily. "I've decided to give the compact back; today, in fact. I can't give the scarf back, but I'm sorry and I've made up my mind not to ever do it again."

His usual malice sparkled in his eyes as I was speaking. He looked at me and suddenly burst into laughter. Then he gripped me by the shoulders, threw me onto the bed, and began to squeeze and pinch slyly, as he had before, repeating, "Thief! You're a thief, you're a thief, a great big thief, a sweet little thief, an adorable thief," with a kind of sarcastic affection that left me in doubt as to whether I ought to be offended or flattered. But his impetuousness excited and pleased me in a way. It was better than his former deathly passivity, in any case. So I laughed and wriggled all over because I am very ticklish and he, perversely, was tickling me under the arms. But all the time I was twisting and laughing to the point of tears, I could see that his face, bending over me so pitilessly, remained closed and withdrawn. Then he stopped, as suddenly as he had begun, and threw himself back upon the bed. "I'm not a thief, though — I'm really not — and there aren't any stolen goods in those parcels."

I could see that he was bursting to tell me what the parcels contained and that the whole thing was a matter of vanity for him more than anything else — a vanity not vastly different from Sonzogno's, when he told me of his crime. Men have many things in common, despite all their differences; and when they are with a woman they love, or with whom they have at least made love, they always tend to show off their virility by boasting of the dangerous, energetic things they have done or are going to do.

"You're dying to tell me what's in the parcels," I said gently.

He was offended. "You're a fool. I don't care at all. But I ought to tell you what's in them so that you can decide whether you're going to do me the favor or not. So — they contain propaganda."

"What do you mean?"

"I belong to a group of people," he said slowly, "who don't love, let us say, the present government: they hate it in fact, and want to get rid of it as soon as possible. The parcels contain a lot of pamphlets printed secretly, in which we explain to people why it isn't a good government and how it can be gotten rid of."

I had never had anything to do with politics. Matters of government did not touch me, or many other people, I believe. But I remembered Astarita and his occasional references to politics.

"But it's forbidden! It's dangerous!" I exclaimed in alarm.

He looked at me with evident satisfaction. At last I had said something he liked and that flattered his ego. "Yes," he agreed with extreme and slightly emphatic gravity, "in fact it is dangerous. Now it's up to you to decide whether you'll do me the favor or not."

"I wasn't speaking for myself," I retorted hotly. "I was thinking of you. As far as I'm concerned, I'll do it."

"I warn you," he said again, "it's really dangerous. If they find them, you'll end up in jail."

I looked at him and a flood of uncontrollable emotion swept over me. I do not know whether it was for him or for something else I could not define. My eyes filled with tears. "Don't you understand it doesn't matter to me at all?" I stammered. "I'd go to prison — so what?" I shook my head and the tears ran down my cheeks.

"And now what are you crying for?" he asked in astonishment.

"I'm sorry," I said. "I'm being stupid — I don't know why myself, maybe because I wish you'd realize how much I love you and how ready I am to do anything for you."

I had not yet learned that I must not mention my love to him. At my words, he did what I was to see so often in the future, his face filled with an expression of vague, distant embarrassment and he averted his eyes. "All right," he said hurriedly, "I'll bring you the parcel in a couple of days. We're agreed, then. And now I've got to go, it's getting late." As he spoke, he leaped from the bed and began to dress quickly. I stayed where I was, on the bed, with my emotion and tears, naked and a little ashamed, either because I was naked or because I had been crying.

He picked his clothes up off the floor where they had fallen and put them on. He went over to the coatrack, got his overcoat, slipped into it and came over to me. "Feel here," he said, with that charming, ingenuous smile I found so attractive.

I looked and saw he was pointing to one of the pockets of his overcoat. He had come near to the bed so that I could stretch out my hand without any effort. I felt something hard through the material of the pocket. "What is it?" I asked, without understanding.

He smiled in satisfaction, put his hand into his pocket and slowly drew a large, black pistol half out of it, staring at me fixedly all the while. "A pistol!" I exclaimed. "What are you going to do with it?"

"You never know," he said. "It may come in useful one day."

I did not know what to think, but he did not even give me time. He replaced the weapon in his pocket, bent down, brushed my lips with his as he said, "All right, then — I'll be back in two days." Before I could recover from my surprise, he was gone.

Since then I have often thought over our first assignation and have reproached myself bitterly for not having foreseen the danger his passion for politics exposed him to. I know I never had any influence over him; but at least, if I had known many of the things I have learned since, I would have been able to advise him and when advice was useless, I would have been at his side, fully conscious and decisive. The fault was certainly mine, or rather, was the fault of my ignorance, which, however, I could not help, as it was due to my condition. As I have already said, I had never given any thought to political things, of which I understood nothing and which I felt to be extraneous to my destiny, as if they were not unfolding around me but on another planet altogether. When I read a newspaper I always skipped the first page with its political news, which didn't interest me, and went on to glance through the reports of criminal cases, where certain incidents and crimes gave my mind something to feed on, at least. My condition was actually very like that of those transparent little creatures that live, they say, in the depths of the sea, in the dark almost, knowing nothing of what is happening on the surface in the sunlight. Politics, like many other things that men seem to think so important, reached me from a higher and unknown world, they were even weaker and more incomprehensible to me than the light of day to those simple creatures in the depths of the sea.

But the fault lay not only in myself and my ignorance. In his vanity and lightness, he was at fault, too. If I had sensed anything else but vanity in him, as, in fact, there was, perhaps I would have acted differently and would have forced myself to understand and get to know all the things I was ignorant of: I cannot say with what success. And at this stage I would like to point out something else, which certainly contributed to my nonchalance, this was the fact that he always seemed to be acting a part in a farce rather than behaving seriously. He seemed to have built up an ideal character, piece by piece, but was able to believe in it only up to a certain point, and was striving all the time, almost mechanically, to adapt his actions to this ideal character. This ceaseless comedy created the impression that he was taking part in a game he had, in a certain sense, mastered perfectly; but, as happens in games, it also made what he was doing seem far less serious. At the same time it suggested that for him nothing was irreparable, that at the last moment, even if he were defeated, his opponent would return his losses to him and would shake his hand. Now perhaps he really was playing, like boys whose irrepressible instincts lead them to make a game of everything. But his opponent was in earnest as was evident later. So when the game was up, he found himself unarmed and helpless, outside all games, caught in a mortal strait.

All these things, and others far sadder and no less reasonable, occurred to me later on when I thought over what had happened. But at the time the idea that his business of the parcels might influence our relationship in any way did not even cross my mind. I was glad he had returned to me, glad I could do him a favor and at the same time have an opportunity of seeing him again. I did not look beyond this double source of happiness. I remember that when I happened to think vaguely and dreamily about the odd favor he had asked me I shook my head as if to say, "Schoolboy tricks!" and turned my mind to other things. In any case, I was so happy that even if I had wanted to, I would not have been capable of directing my thoughts to any troubling topic.

6

*E*VERYTHING SEEMED TO BE improving: Giacomo had
come back and at the same time I had found the way to have
the maid who had been unjustly accused released from jail,
without being obliged to take her place. After Giacomo left that
day, I spent at least a couple of hours delighting in my own happiness, as one might delight in a jewel or other precious object
newly possessed, that is, in a puzzled, astonished, dazed way that
did not, however, exclude profound enjoyment. The bells ringing
for vespers roused me from this voluptuous contemplation. I remembered Astarita's advice, the urgent need to help the wretched
woman who was in jail. I dressed hurriedly and went out.

It is sweet, in winter, when the days are short and the whole
morning and the early hours of the afternoon have been passed at
home alone in thought, to go out and walk the streets in the heart
of the city, where the traffic is thickest, the crowds fullest, the
shops most brilliantly lit. In the pure, cool air, amid the noise,
movement, and glitter of city life, the brain clears and the heart

lightens, fills with a joyous excitement and gay intoxication, as if all our difficulties had suddenly been solved and nothing was left but to wander lightheartedly and thoughtlessly among the crowd, content to follow any fleeting sensation suggested to an idle mind by the pageant of the streets. It really seems at such times as if for a few moments all our trespasses had been forgiven, as the Christian prayer says, without any merit on our part and without retribution, merely by virtue of some mysterious and general benevolence. Naturally, this requires a happy or at least contented frame of mind, since otherwise city life provokes an anguished sense of absurd, aimless motion. But as I said, I was happy that day, and I was most aware of this when I began to walk the sidewalks in the center of town, among the crowds of people.

I knew I had to go to church to make my confession. But probably just because I knew that this was my purpose and was glad I had resolved to do it, I was in no hurry and did not even think about it. I walked slowly from one street to another, stopping from time to time to look at the goods on display in the shop windows. If anyone who knew me had seen me then, they would certainly have thought I was intent on picking up some man. But, truly, nothing could have been further from my thoughts. I might have let some man I liked the look of stop me, but not for money, only out of an impulse of gaiety, an exuberance for life. But the few men who came up to me with the usual phrases and offers of company, when they saw me standing still and looking in at the shop windows, had nothing that attracted me about them. So I made no reply, did not even look at them, and continued to walk along the pavement with my usual lazy, majestic gait as if they did not even exist.

The sight of the church where I had been to confession before, after the trip to Viterbo, caught me unaware, in this gay and absent mood. The baroque facade of the church, standing there as it did between the movie posters and the hosier's window, which were both brilliantly lit, sunk in darkness and set like a folding screen in an indentation of the street, its high pediment topped by two trumpeting angels and streaked with violet reflections from the luminous sign on a neighboring house, seemed to me like the dark, wrinkled face of an old woman beckoning to me confidentially from the shadow of an old shawl, among the other, lighted faces of the other passersby. I remembered the handsome French confessor, Father Elia, and how I had been attracted by him, and I thought no one could perform the task of returning the compact better than he, for he was young, intelligent, and a man of the world, different in every way from other priests. Besides, Father Elia already knew me, in a way, and so I would find it easier to confess to him the many terrible, shameful things that weighed so heavily upon my soul.

I climbed the steps, pushed aside the heavy covering over the door, and entered, putting a handkerchief on my head. While I dipped my fingers in the holy water stoup, I was struck by a scene carved around the edge of the stoup — it showed a naked woman, her hair streaming in the wind, her arms raised as she fled, pursued by a foul dragon, with a parrot's beak, that was standing upright on its hind legs like a man. I seemed to recognize myself in that woman and thought how I, too, was fleeing just such a dragon, that the course of my flight was circular, like hers, but that as I ran around in circles, I sometimes found I was not fleeing but was following a desire and gaily pursuing the ugly beast. I turned from the holy water stoup to the church as I crossed myself, and it seemed to me to have remained in the same darkness, squalor, and disorder I had noticed the last time I had seen it. Everything lay in darkness, as then, except the high altar with all its candles burning closely around the crucifix in a confused glitter of brass candlesticks and silver vases. The chapel dedicated to the Madonna, where I had prayed so fervently and uselessly, was also illuminated. Two vergers were standing on ladders fixing gold-fringed red hangings to the architrave. I found that Father Elia's confessional was engaged, so I went and knelt down in front of the high altar on one of the displaced straw-bottomed chairs. I was not at all moved, but merely impatient to settle the matter of the compact. My impatience had something peculiar about it, it was gay, impetuous, self-congratulatory and rather vain, the kind you feel when you are on the point of doing some good deed you have been contemplating for a long time. I have often noticed that this kind of impatience, which springs from the heart and is deaf to the counsel of intelligence, usually ends by compromising the good deed and often doing greater harm than would more calculated behavior.

As soon as I saw the person who was confessing get up and go away, I went straight to the confessional, knelt down, and began to speak quickly, without waiting for the confessor to address me. "Father Elia," I said, "I have not come to make my confession in the usual sense. I have come to speak to you of a very serious matter and to ask you a favor I am sure you will not refuse."

The confessor's low voice on the other side of the grill invited me to proceed. I was so sure Father Elia was on the other side that I almost imagined I could see his calm, handsome face outlined against the dark grill pierced with little holes. Then, for the first time since I had entered the church, an impulse of devout and trusting emotion swept over me. It was as though my soul felt impelled to free itself from my body and kneel down naked on the steps before the grill, with all its stains exposed. I felt for a moment as if I were a disembodied spirit, free, formed of light and air, as they say we are after death. And I imagined, too, that Father Elia, whose spirit was so much more luminous than mine, had broken free of the prison of the flesh and had caused the grill, the walls, and the darkness of the confessional to vanish and stood there in person before me, dazzling and comforting. Perhaps this is the emotion we ought to feel every time we kneel down to confess. But I had never felt it so intensely before.

I began to speak with my eyes closed, leaning my head against the grill. And I told him everything. I told him of my profession, of Gino, Astarita, Sonzogno, of the theft and the murder. I told him my name, Gino's, Astarita's, and Sonzogno's. I told him where the theft and the murder had taken place, told him where I lived. I even described what the different people looked like. I do not know what impulse swept me along. Perhaps it was the same impulse that a housewife feels when she finally decides to clean up her house after a long period of neglect and is unable to rest until she has swept away the last speck of dust, the last bit of fluff under the furniture or in the corners. And, in fact, as I went on telling my tale in all its particulars, I felt as if I were unburdening my heart and soul and felt lighter and cleaner.

I spoke in the same quiet, reasonable voice the whole time. The confessor listened to me without interruption to the very end. When I stopped a moment's silence ensued. Then I heard a dreadful, slow, unctuous, dragging voice address me. "You have told me of terrible, fearful things, my child, the mind finds them hardly credible. But you did well to come to confession — I will do everything that lies in my power for you."

A long time had passed since my first and only confession in that church. And in the pleasant turmoil of my self-complacent goodness I had almost forgotten Father Elia's most pleasing characteristic — his French pronunciation. The priest who was addressing me had no special accent, but he was undoubtedly Italian and had the peculiarly oily voice you hear in the mouths of so many priests. I suddenly realized the mistake I had made and an icy shudder ran through me — as if my fingertips had encountered the cold, quivering scales of a serpent when I had confidently stretched out my hand to pluck a lovely flower. The unpleasant surprise of being faced with a confessor I had not expected was enhanced by the sense of horror his dark, insinuating voice aroused in me.

"Are you really Father Elia?" I stammered with an effort.

"Himself in person," replied the unknown priest. "Why? Have you been here before?"

"Once before."

The priest was silent for a moment. "Everything you have told me should really be reconsidered point by point. You have told me not one, but many things, some of which concern yourself, and some other people. As far as you are concerned — do you understand that you have sinned grievously?"

"Yes, I know," I murmured.

"And do you repent?"

"I believe I do."

"If you are sincere in your repentance," he began, speaking in a confiding, paternal undertone, "you may certainly hope for absolution. Unfortunately you are not the only one. . . . There are

the others, the crimes and faults of the others. You have come to
know a terrible criminal: a man has been murdered in the most
hideous way! Do you feel no impulse in your conscience to reveal
the criminal's name and bring him to justice?"

In this way he suggested that I should denounce Sonzogno. I do
not say he was wrong, as a priest. But the proposal, made in that insinuating voice and at just that time, only increased my doubts and
fears. "If I say who did it," I stammered, "I'll be put in jail myself."

His reply was immediate. "Men, like God himself, will be capable of appreciating your sacrifice and repentance. The law both
punishes and forgives. But in exchange for a little suffering, so
slight when compared to the agonies of the victim, you would
have helped to reestablish justice, which has been so foully offended. Oh, do you not hear the voice of the victim vainly beseeching his murderer for mercy?"

He continued to exhort me, choosing his words carefully and
complacently from the conventional phrases proper to his office.
But my only desire now was to get away, I felt almost hysterical.

"I need to think about denouncing him," I said hurriedly. "I'll
come back tomorrow and tell you what I've decided. Will I find
you here tomorrow?"

"Certainly, at any time."

"All right," I said dazedly. "All I ask of you for the time being is
to hand over this object." I stopped speaking, and after a short
prayer he asked me once more if I had really repented and determined to change my way of life, then he gave me absolution. I
crossed myself and left the confessional. At the same time he
opened his door and stood before me. All the fears his voice had
inspired in me were confirmed immediately at the sight of him.
He was short, with a huge head that hung sideways as if he had a
perpetual stiff neck. I did not have time to examine him thoroughly, I was in such a hurry to escape and he filled me with such
horror. I glimpsed a brownish yellow face, a pale, high forehead,
eyes sunk deep in their orbits, a flattened nose with wide nostrils,
and a large shapeless mouth with purplish, sinuous lips. He was
probably not old, he was simply ageless. Clasping his hands on his

breast and shaking his head he addressed me in heartfelt tones. "But why, my dear child, did you not come to me sooner? Why? How many terrible things you would have been spared."

I wanted to tell him what I was thinking: that God would never have wanted me to come like this, but I restrained myself, and taking the compact from my purse I gave it to him. "Please be as quick as you can," I said earnestly. "I can't tell you how the thought of that poor woman in jail on my account torments me."

"I'll go this very day," he replied, as he clasped the compact to his breast and shook his head with a deprecatory and aggrieved air.

I thanked him in a low voice, and having nodded to him I left the church as quickly as I could. He remained standing where he was beside the confessional, clasping his hands to his breast and shaking his head.

Out on the street, I tried to think more coolly about what had happened. Now that I had shaken off my first confused terrors, I realized that what I was most afraid of was that the priest would not respect the seal of the confessional, and I tried to clarify to myself what grounds I might have for my fears. I knew, like everybody else, that confession is a sacrament and is therefore inviolable. I also knew it was impossible for any priest, no matter how corrupt he might be, to violate it. But his advice to me to denounce Sonzogno to the police made me fear he might take it upon himself, since I had not done so, to reveal the name of the perpetrator of the crime in Via Palestro. His voice and appearance, however, caused me the gravest fears. I am emotional rather than reflective and I have an instinct for danger, like some animals. All the reasons my mind marshaled to reassure me were nothing in comparison with my unreasoned presentiment. It's true that the seal of the confessional is inviolable, I thought, but only a miracle can prevent that priest from denouncing Sonzogno, me, and all the others.

Something else helped to give me the sensation of some mysterious and impending disaster: the substitution of the second confessor for the first. Obviously the French monk was not Father Elia, although he had listened to me in the confessional that bore that name. Who was he then? I was sorry I had not asked the real

Father Elia for news of him. But I was half afraid the ugly priest would tell me he knew nothing of him, confirming the apparitional aspect the figure of the young monk was assuming in my mind. There really was something of the phantom about him, both because he was so utterly different from other priests and because of the way he had appeared in my life and had then vanished. I actually began to doubt whether I had ever seen him, or, rather, whether I had ever seen him in the flesh, and I imagined for a moment that I might have had an hallucination. Because I now discovered in him an undeniable resemblance to Christ himself, as he is usually portrayed in sacred paintings. But if this were true, if Christ himself had appeared to me in my hour of sorrow and had heard my confession, his substitution by the sordid, repellent priest I had just seen clearly boded ill. It meant, if nothing else, that religion had abandoned me at the moment of my greatest spiritual anguish. It was like opening a safe containing a treasure of gold coins, in order to meet the most urgent need, and finding instead only dust, cobwebs, and the excrement of mice.

I returned home with this presentiment that some misfortune would surely result from my confession and went straight to bed, without supper, convinced that this would be my last night at home before being arrested. But I must say that I was not at all afraid now and had no desire to avoid my fate. My initial terror, born of a nervous weakness common to nearly all women, had yielded to something more than mere resignation, a determined desire to accept the destiny that threatened me. I felt a kind of voluptuous delight, in fact, in letting myself sink to the depths of what I imagined must be the last stage of despair. I felt protected, in a sense, by the excess of my misfortune; and I found a certain pleasure in the thought that nothing worse could happen to me except death, which I no longer feared.

But next day I waited in vain for the expected visit from the police. That whole day and the next passed without anything occurring to justify my apprehension. During this whole time I never left the house, or even my room, and I soon tired of thinking over the consequences of my rashness. I began to think about Giacomo again and realized I was longing to see him at least once more, before the priest's denunciation, which I now considered inevitable, took effect. Toward evening on the third day I got up, dressed carefully, and left the house.

I knew Giacomo's address and it took me twenty minutes to reach his house. But just as I was about to enter the main door I remembered I had not warned him I was coming, and I suddenly felt shy. I was afraid he might be annoyed at seeing me or even send me away. My impatient step slowed down, and I stopped outside a shop, with my heart full of sadness, wondering whether it would not be better to turn back and wait for him to make up his mind to call on me. I realized that at the beginning of our relationship, in particular, I ought to be very wary and subtle and never let him know that I was in love with him and could not live without him. On the other hand, turning back seemed very bitter to me, since I was uneasy on account of the confession and I needed to see him, if only to take my mind off my worries. My eye fell on the window of the shop in front of me. It was full of shirts and ties and I suddenly remembered I had promised to buy him a new tie to replace his threadbare one. When people are in love, their minds never work properly; I told myself I could make the gift of a tie an excuse for my visit, without realizing that the gift itself would emphasize the submissive, anxious nature of my feeling toward him. I went into the shop and after spending a long time over my choice I bought a gray tie with red stripes, the handsomest and most expensive of them all. The man behind the counter asked me, with the somewhat indiscreet courtesy of salesmen who think they can influence their customers in their choice, whether the tie was for a fair or a dark man. "He's dark," I replied slowly and, realizing I had pronounced the word "dark" in a caressing tone, I blushed at the thought that the salesman might have noticed it.

The widow Medolaghi lived on the fourth floor of a gloomy old palace whose windows looked out onto the Tiber embankment. I walked up eight flights of stairs and rang the bell of a door hidden in the shadows, without even waiting to recover my breath.

The door opened almost immediately and Giacomo appeared on the threshold. "Oh, it's you!" he exclaimed in surprise. He was obviously expecting someone.

"May I come in?"

"Yes . . . yes. . . . Come this way."

He led me from the dim hall into the sitting room. It was dark here, too, because the windows had little, round, red, leaded panes, like ones in a church. I glimpsed a quantity of black furniture inlaid with mother-of-pearl. A round table with a blue crystal decanter of an old-fashioned shape stood in the middle. There were many carpets and a very worn white bearskin. Everything was old, but clean and neat and as if preserved within the deep silence that had apparently reigned in the house since time immemorial. I went and sat down on a sofa at the other end of the room.

"Were you expecting anybody?" I asked.

"No. But why have you come?" The words were not actually very welcoming. But he did not seem angry, only surprised.

"I've just come to say hello," I smiled. "Because I think this will be the last time we'll see one another."

"Why?"

"I'm positive that tomorrow at the latest they'll come for me and take me to jail."

"To jail? What the devil do you mean?"

His voice and expression changed and I realized that he was afraid on his own account; perhaps he thought I had denounced him or compromised him in some way by talking to someone about his political activities. "Don't worry," I smiled again. "It's nothing to do with you, not even remotely."

"No, no," he replied hurriedly, "but I can't understand, that's all. Why should you go to jail?"

"Shut the door and sit down here," I said, pointing to the sofa beside me.

He shut the door and then sat down beside me. Then I told him the whole story of the compact, very calmly, including my confession. He listened with his head bowed, without looking at me, biting his nails, which was always a sign that he was interested. "So I'm sure that that priest will play a dirty trick on me. What do you think?" I concluded.

He shook his head and spoke, not looking at me but at the leaded panes in the windows. "He shouldn't, in fact, I don't think he will. It's not enough for a priest to be ugly. . . ."

"But you should have seen him!" I interrupted eagerly.

"He'd have to be monstrous to do such a thing! But, of course, anything can happen," he added hurriedly, with a laugh.

"So you think I shouldn't be afraid."

"Yes. All the more so, since you can't do anything — it doesn't depend on you."

"That's a nice way to talk! People feel afraid because they're afraid! It's stronger than us."

He suddenly made a fond gesture typical of him. He put one hand on my neck and laughed as he gave it a little shake. "You aren't afraid, though, are you?" he said.

"But I tell you I am!"

"You aren't afraid, you're a brave woman!"

"I tell you I was terrified! I even went to bed and didn't get up for two days."

"Yes, but then you came to see me and tell me everything with the utmost composure. You don't know what it is to be afraid."

"What should I have done?" I asked, smiling despite myself. "I can't exactly scream for fear!"

"You aren't afraid."

A moment's silence followed. Then he asked me in an odd tone of voice that surprised me, "What about this friend of yours — let's call him your friend — Sonzogno? What sort of a man is he?"

"Like a lot of others," I answered vaguely. I could not think of anything in particular to say about Sonzogno at that moment.

"But what's he like? Describe him."

"Why? Do you want to have him arrested?" I asked, laughing. "If you do, I'll be put into jail, too, remember! He's a little blond." I added, "short, broad-shouldered, with a pale face, blue eyes, nothing special, in fact. The only outstanding thing about him is that he's terrifically strong."

"Strong?"

"You wouldn't think it to look at him. But if you touch his arm, it's like iron." Seeing that he was interested, I told him the story of the incident between Sonzogno and Gino. He made no comment, but asked when I had finished, "So you think Sonzogno's crime was premeditated? I mean — that he thought it all out and then did it in cold blood?"

"Not at all," I answered. "He never plans anything. A moment before laying out Gino flat on the ground with that punch, he probably wasn't even dreaming of such a thing . . . and the same with the jeweler."

"Then why did he do it?"

"Because . . . Because it's stronger than he is — like a tiger. One moment it's calm, the next it hits out at you with its paw, and no one knows why." Then I told him the whole story of my relationship with Sonzogno, how he had struck me and threatened to murder me in the dark. "He never thinks," I concluded. "At a certain moment a force stronger than his will takes hold of him — it's best to keep your distance at such times. I'm sure he went to the jeweler's to sell him the compact, then the jeweler insulted him, and he murdered him."

"He's kind of a brute, then."

"Call him what you like. It must be an impulse," I added, trying to define in my own mind the feeling Sonzogno's homicidal mania inspired in me, "like the one that drives me to love you. Why do I love you? God only knows. Why does Sonzogno at certain moments feel an impulse to murder? God only knows this, too. I don't think there's any explanation for these things."

He reflected. Then he raised his head. "And what sort of impulse do you think I feel toward you?" he asked. "Do you think I feel the impulse to love you?"

I was terrified that I might hear him say he did not love me. So I covered his mouth with my hand. "Please," I begged him, "don't tell me anything about what you feel for me."

"Why not?"

"Because I don't need to know. . . . I don't know what you feel for me and don't want to know. . . . It's enough for me to love you, myself."

He shook his head. "It's a bad thing for you to love me," he said. "You ought to love a man like Sonzogno."

I was really amazed. "What are you saying? A criminal?"

"Suppose he is a criminal? Still, he has the impulses you mentioned. Just as Sonzogno has the impulse to kill, I'm sure he'd have the impulse to love, quite simply, without any complication. But I on the other hand —"

I did not let him continue. "You can't compare yourself with Sonzogno," I protested. "You are what you are. He's a criminal, a monster. And anyway, it isn't true that he might have the impulse to love — a man like that can't love. It's nothing more than a satisfaction of the senses for him. . . . It's all the same to him whether it's me or any other woman."

He did not seem convinced, but he said nothing. I took advantage of his silence and slipped my fingers under his cuff, along his wrist, trying to reach up his arm. "Mino," I said.

I saw him start. "Why are you calling me Mino?"

"It's short for Giacomo. Can't I?"

"No, no, it doesn't matter, of course you can. Only it's what they call me at home, that's all."

"Is that what your mother calls you?" I asked, letting go of his wrist and slipping my hand under his tie, stroking his bare chest between the edges of his shirt with my fingertips.

"Yes, it's what my mother calls me," he said impatiently. "It's not the only thing you say that my mother says too," he continued after a moment, in a voice that was partly sarcastic and partly scornful. "Basically, you share the same opinions about everything."

"What, for instance?" I asked. I was excited and hardly heard what he was saying. I had unbuttoned his shirt and was trying to reach his thin and graceful boyish shoulder with my hand.

"This, for instance," he replied. "When I told you I was involved with politics, you immediately exclaimed in a frightened voice, 'But it's illegal! It's dangerous!' Well, that's exactly what my mother would have said, in the exact same tone of voice."

I was flattered by the idea that I resembled his mother, first of all because she was his mother and then because I knew she was a lady. "Silly boy!" I said tenderly. "What's the harm in that? It means your mother loves you as I do. It's very true that it's dangerous to have anything to do with politics. A young man I knew was arrested and he's been in jail two years now. And for what? They're stronger, anyway, and as soon as you do anything they put you in prison. . . . I think it's possible to live very well without politics."

"My mother, my mother!" he exclaimed, jubilant and sarcastic. "That's exactly what my mother would say."

"I don't know what your mother says," I replied, "but I'm sure that whatever it is, it's for your own good. You ought to leave politics alone. It's not like it's your profession. You're a student. A student's job is to study."

"Study, get a degree, and make a position for yourself," he murmured, as if speaking to himself.

I did not answer, but putting my face up to his I offered him my lips. We kissed and then drew apart. He seemed sorry he had kissed me and looked at me with a hostile and mortified expression. I was afraid I had annoyed him by interrupting his political outburst with my kiss. "But anyway," I added hastily, "do what you like. I've nothing to do with your affairs. As a matter of fact, since I'm here you might as well give me that parcel, and I'll hide it for you, as we arranged."

"No, no," he replied with intensity, "Good God, it wouldn't work now — not with your friendship with Astarita — suppose he found out!"

"Why? Is Astarita so dangerous?"

"He's one of the worst," he replied earnestly.

I felt an inexplicable, mischievous impulse to wound him in his pride. But not spitefully, affectionately. "As a matter of fact." I said gently, "you never really meant to give me that parcel."

"Then why did I mention it to you?"

"Because — well, don't be offended, now — I think you mentioned it to look good to me — to show me you really did dangerous, illegal things."

He grew irritated and I realized I had struck home. "What non-sense!" he said. "You really are stupid. But what makes you think so?" he asked awkwardly, suddenly calm once more.

"I don't know," I answered with a smile. "It's your whole way of doing things. Perhaps you aren't aware of it, but you never give the impression that you're serious about what you do."

He made a burlesque-like gesture, as if revolting against himself. "And yet it's an extremely serious matter," he said. He stood up and, stretching out his thin arms, began to recite emphatically in a falsetto voice:

> "My sword, give me my sword!
> I alone will fight, alone will fall."

He was so funny, waving his arms and legs about, he looked rather like a marionette.

"What does that mean?" I asked.

"Nothing," he replied. "It's a line out of a poem." His excitement suddenly gave way to a strangely depressed and reflective mood. He sat down again and continued earnestly, "And yet, look, I'm so much in earnest about everything I do that I actually hope I'll be arrested . . . and then I'll show everyone whether I'm serious or not."

I said nothing, but took his face between the palms of my hands and began to stroke it. "Your eyes are so beautiful," I said. It was true, his eyes were exceptionally beautiful, large and gentle, with an intense and innocent expression. He became disturbed again, his chin began to tremble. "Why don't we go into your bedroom?" I murmured.

"Don't even think about it — it's next to the widow's room — and she's there the whole day long, with the door open, watching the passage."

"Let's go home to my place then."

"It's too late. . . . You live too far away. I'm expecting some friends before long."

"Here, then."

"You're crazy!"

"You're scared, you mean," I insisted. "You aren't afraid to go in for political propaganda — at least, that's what you say — but you're afraid of being caught in this sitting room with the woman who loves you. What could happen, anyway? The widow might send you away, and then you'd have to find another room."

I knew that if I made it a matter of pride, I could get anything out of him. And indeed he seemed to be persuaded. Actually, his desire must have been at least as strong as mine. "You're crazy," he repeated. "It might be more of a bother to be sent away from here than to be arrested. Besides, where can we lie?"

"On the floor," I said, softly and with intense affection. "Come on — I'll show you how to do it." He now seemed to be in such a state that he could not speak. I got up from the sofa and slowly lay down on the floor. The floor was covered with rugs and in the middle of the room stood the table with the carafe. I stretched myself out on the rugs, my head and breasts under the table; then I pulled Mino down by one arm, forcing him to lie reluctantly on top of me. I threw my head back, shutting my eyes, and the ancient smell of dust and fluff in the carpet seemed as sweet and intoxicating as if I were lying in a field in springtime and the smell was the scent of flowers and grass, not dirty wool. Mino lay on me and his weight made me feel the delightful hardness of the floor, and I was happy because he did not feel it and my body was his bed. Then I felt him kissing my neck and my cheeks and I was filled with a great joy, because he never did this. I opened my eyes; my face was turned toward my shoulder, one cheek against the rough wool of the carpet, and I could see, beyond the carpet, a wide stretch of wax-polished mosaic and the lower part of the double folding doors beyond that. I heaved a deep sigh and closed my eyes again.

Mino was the first to get back up. I stayed for a long moment as he had left me, flat on my back with one arm over my face, my dress disordered, my legs apart. I felt happy, and blank in my happiness, and I thought I could have stayed there for hours, with the pleasant hardness of the floor under me, and the smell of dust and fluff in my nostrils. Perhaps I even dropped off into a light, rapid sleep for a second, for I seemed to be dreaming that I really was in a flowery meadow, stretched out on the grass with the sunny sky over me instead of the table. Mino must have thought I was feeling ill, because I suddenly felt him shake me. "What's the matter?" he said under his breath. "What are you doing? Get up, quick!"

With an effort I removed my arm from my face, slowly came out from under the table and stood up. I felt happy and I was smiling. Mino looked at me in silence, his back against the sideboard, bent over and still panting, his expression hostile and bewildered. "I never want to see you again," he said at last. At the same time his bowed body gave a strange, involuntary shudder as though he were a puppet and a spring had suddenly gone in him.

I smiled. "Why?" I said. "We love one another — we'll see each other again." And going up to him, I caressed him. But he turned his white, contorted face away from me.

"I never want to see you again," he repeated.

I knew his hostility was chiefly due to his remorse at having yielded to me. He never resigned himself to making love to me without a feeling of reluctance and deep regret. He was like a man who decides to do something he does not want to do and knows he ought not to do. But I was sure his bad mood would be short-lived and that his desire for me, however he might struggle against it and hate it, would always be stronger in the end than his singular longing for chastity. So I took no notice of his words, and, remembering the tie I had bought for him, I went over to the shelf where I had put my gloves and purse.

"Come on, now," I said. "Don't be so angry! I won't come here again. Will that do?"

He made no reply. At that moment the door was flung open and an elderly parlormaid showed two men into the room. "Hello, Giacomo," said the first, in a deep, thick voice.

I realized these must be his political comrades and looked at them curiously. The one who had spoken was a giant — he was taller than Mino, broad-shouldered, and looked like a professional boxer. He had blond ruffled hair, blue eyes, a flattened nose, and a red, shapeless mouth. But his expression was open and pleasant, with a mixture of shyness and simplicity I found attractive. Although it was winter, he wore no overcoat, only a white turtleneck sweater underneath his jacket, which emphasized his sportsman-like appearance. His red hands, with their thick wrists, which stuck out of the rolled cuffs of the sweater, struck me at once. He must have been very young, about Giacomo's age, probably. The other man was about forty, and, in contrast to his companion, who was evidently a workingman or a peasant, looked and dressed like a man of the middle class. He was short and looked tiny beside his friend. He was a very dark little man and his face was eclipsed by a huge pair of tortoiseshell glasses. A snub nose peered out from beneath them, and below this nose he opened a very wide mouth, really a slit stretching from ear to ear. His thin, unshaven cheeks with their black stubble, his threadbare collar, his creased and spotted suit, in which his wretched little body floated loosely, everything about him gave an impression of deliberate, aggressive negligence, of complacent poverty. To tell the truth, I was astonished at the appearance of these two men, because Mino always dressed with a kind of careless elegance and gave many indications that he belonged to a different social class from theirs. If I had not seen them greet Mino, and Mino return their greeting, I would never have imagined they were friends of his. I instinctively liked the tall one and disliked the short one.

"Perhaps we've come too early?" the tall one asked, with an embarrassed smile.

"No, no," said Mino, pulling himself together. He was dazed and seemed to find some difficulty in recovering himself. "You're right on time."

"Punctuality is the courtesy of kings," said the little man, rubbing his hands together. Suddenly, as if he found his phrase extremely funny, he burst into a fit of unexpected laughter. Then, just as he had laughed, with the same disagreeable suddenness, he grew serious once more, so serious that I almost doubted whether he had ever laughed.

"Adriana," said Mino with an effort, "let me introduce two friends of mine — Tullio," and he pointed to the little one, "and Tommaso."

I noticed he did not mention surnames and I thought the names he gave were probably false. I held out my hand, with a smile. The big man gave it a squeeze that hurt my fingers; but the little one wetted them with the sweat that bathed his palm. "Delighted," said the little one, with a heartiness that seemed to me burlesque. "Pleased to meet you," said the big one simply, as if he liked me, I thought. I noticed he had a slight dialectic intonation in his voice.

We looked at one another in silence for a moment "We can go away, Giacomo, if you like," said the big man. "If you're busy now we can come back tomorrow."

I saw Mino start and look at him, and I could see he was about to tell them to stay and ask me to leave. I knew him well enough by now to understand that he could not have done otherwise. I remembered that I had given myself to him only a few minutes before — the sensation of his lips kissing me was still warm on my neck and the feeling of his hands clinging to me was in my flesh. It was my body, not my soul — which was always ready to yield and be resigned — which rebelled as if against treatment unworthy of its beauty and of the gift it had made. I took a step forward. "Yes, you'd better go," I said violently, "you can see each other tomorrow. I've still got a lot of things to say to Mino."

Mino objected with an air of startled displeasure.

"But I've got to talk to them."

"You can talk to them tomorrow."

"Well," said Tommaso good-naturedly, "make up your mind — if you want us to stay, say so. If you want us to go . . ."

"We ask nothing better," intervened Tullio, with his usual laugh.

Mino still hesitated. My body, despite myself, made another aggressive thrust. "Listen," I said, raising my voice, "a few minutes ago Giacomo and I were making love, here, on the floor, on this carpet. What would you do in his place? Would you send me away?"

I believe Mino blushed. He certainly became confused, turned his back peevishly, and went over to the window. Tommaso gave me a sidelong look and then said, without smiling, "I see — we'll go. Good-bye, Giacomo — we'll see you tomorrow at the same time."

But my words seemed to have upset little Tullio. He gaped at me, his eyes wide open behind his thick lenses. Certainly he had never heard a woman speak so frankly, and at that moment a thousand dirty thoughts must have crossed his mind. But the big man called to him from the doorway. "Let's go, Tullio," he said, and he, without taking his lustful, astonished eyes off me, walked backward to the door and left.

I waited for them to leave and then walked over to Mino, who was still standing by the window, his back to the room, and put an arm around his neck.

"Now I bet you can't stand me."

He turned slowly and looked at me. His eyes were full of anger; but at the sight of my face, which must have been loving, gentle, and in its way, innocent, his look changed and he spoke in a reasonable, almost sad, voice. "Are you happy, now? You got what you wanted."

"Yes, I'm happy," I said, hugging him hard. He let me, then asked, "What was it you wanted to say to me?"

"Nothing," I replied. "I wanted to spend the evening with you."

"But I'm going in to eat soon," he said. "And I eat here — with the widow Medolaghi."

"So, invite me to dinner."

He looked at me and smiled slightly at my boldness. "All right," he said resignedly, "I'll go warn them. How do you want me to introduce you?"

"As you like — as a relation."

"No, I'll introduce you as my fiancée — will that do?"

I did not dare to let him see how delighted I was at his suggestion. "It's all the same to me," I said, pretending to be indifferent, "as long as we can be together — as fiancés or anything else."

"Wait here, I'll be right back."

He went out and I walked over to a corner of the sitting room, pulled up my dress, and hastily buttoned my underwear, which had remained disarranged from the confusion of lovemaking and the unexpected arrival of his friends. A mirror on the wall facing me showed me my long, perfect leg, sheathed in silk, and it made a curious impression on me among all that old furniture, in that silent, secluded atmosphere. I remembered the time when I had made love to Gino in his mistress's villa and had stolen the compact, and I could not help comparing that distant moment in my life with the present one. At that time I had felt a sense of emptiness, bitterness, and a desire to revenge myself, if not upon Gino directly, at least upon the world, which by means of Gino had hurt me so cruelly. Now, instead, I felt happy, free, light. Once more I realized I really loved Mino and it did not matter much that he did not return my love.

I smoothed my dress, went over to the mirror, and tidied my hair. The door opened behind me and Mino returned.

I hoped he would come up to me and kiss me from behind while I was looking at myself in the mirror. But instead he went to sit down on the sofa at the end of the sitting room. "That's done," he said, as he lit a cigarette. "They've set another place — we'll go in to dinner soon."

I left the mirror and came to sit beside him, putting my arm through his and pressing against him. "Those two were your political friends, weren't they?" I said at random.

"Yes."

"They can't be very rich."

"Why not?"

"Judging by the way they dress, anyway."

"Tommaso is our bailiff's son," he said, "and the other one's a schoolteacher."

"I don't like him."

"Who?"

"The schoolteacher. He's dirty-minded and gave me such a look when I said I had been making love to you."

"He must have liked you, obviously."

We were silent for some time.

Then I said, "You're ashamed to introduce me as your fiancée. If you want, I'll go."

I knew this was the only way to wring an affectionate gesture out of him: by blackmailing him with the accusation that he was ashamed of me. And, as I had expected, he immediately put his arm around my waist.

"I suggested it," he said. "Why should I be ashamed of you?"

"I don't know. I can see you're in a bad mood."

"I'm not in a bad mood. I'm dazed," he answered, in a tone of voice that was almost scientific. "And that's because we've made love. Give me time to get over it."

I noticed he was still very pale and was smoking with disgust.

"You're right," I said. "I'm sorry. But you're always so cold and withdrawn that you make me lose my head. If you were different, I wouldn't have insisted on staying a while ago."

He threw his cigarette down.

"I'm not cold and withdrawn," he said.

"And yet —"

"I like you a lot," he continued, looking at me attentively, "and in fact I didn't resist you a little while ago as I meant to." This phrase delighted me and I lowered my eyes without speaking. "Still, I suppose you're right, really . . . this can't be called love."

My heart hurt me and I could not help murmuring, "What do you mean by love, then?"

"If I loved you," he replied, "I wouldn't have wanted to send you away a moment ago. And then I wouldn't have been angry when you wanted to stay."

"Were you angry?"

"Yes — and now I'd be chatting to you, I'd be cheerful, gay, witty, amusing, I'd be caressing you, complimenting you, kissing you, making plans for the future — isn't that how love is?"

"Yes," I said softly. "At least, these are the effects of love."

He was silent for a long time and then said, without any pleasure, but with a dry humility: "I do everything in the same way; without loving what I'm doing or feeling it in my heart —

knowing intellectually how to do it and occasionally even doing it, but always coldly and from the outside. That's how I am and apparently I can't be otherwise."

I made a great effort to control myself.

"I like you as you are," I said. "Don't worry." And I embraced him with intense affection. Almost at the same instant, the door opened and the old servant looked in to tell us dinner was ready.

We left the sitting room and went along a passage to the dining room. I remember all the details of that room and the people in it perfectly, because I was as sensitive to impressions at that time as a photographic plate. I felt I was not so much acting as watching myself act, with wide, melancholy eyes. Perhaps this is an effect of the feeling of rebellion we experience when faced with a reality that causes us to suffer and that we wish were otherwise.

I don't know why, but Signora Medolaghi, the widow, seemed to me to resemble closely the black ebony furniture with the white mother-of-pearl inlays in her parlor. She was a middle-aged woman, imposingly tall, with a voluminous bosom and massive hips. She was dressed entirely in black silk, had a broad, flabby face, whose pallor was just like mother-of-pearl, framed in black hair that looked dyed, and she had huge, dark shadows under her eyes. She was standing in front of a flowered soup tureen and was serving the soup with a kind of disdain. The weighted lamp that had been pulled down over the table lit up her bosom — which was very like a large, black, shiny parcel — and left her face in shadow. In that shade her white face with its black-ringed eyes reminded me of the little silk masks worn during carnival. The table was small and four places were laid, one on each side. The widow's daughter was already seated in her place and did not get up when we entered.

"The young lady can sit here," said the widow Medolaghi. "What's the young lady's name?"

"Adriana."

"Just like my daughter," said the woman, without thinking what she was saying. "We've got two Adrianas." She spoke self-consciously, without looking at us, and obviously she did not welcome my presence there at all. As I have already said, I used hardly any makeup, never dyed my hair and, in fact, gave no hint of any kind of my profession. But anyone could see that I was a simple, uneducated girl of the people, and I took no trouble to conceal it. What sort of people you bring to my house! the lady must have been thinking at that moment. A common girl.

I sat down and looked at the girl who shared my name. In everything she was precisely the half of me — her head, her bosom, her hips. She was thin, with scanty hair and a refined, oval face with huge dull eyes whose expression was terrified. I looked at her and saw that under my gaze, she lowered her eyes and forehead. I thought she might be shy. "Do you know," I said, to break the ice, "it seems curious to me that someone else should have the same name as I do and yet be so different?"

I had spoken at random, to start the conversation flowing, and it was a silly remark. But to my surprise I received no reply. The girl looked at me with wide-open eyes and then bent her head over her plate and began to eat in silence. Suddenly the truth dawned upon me; she was not shy but terrified. And I was the cause of her terror. She was terrified by my beauty, which exploded in the dusty, spent air of her house like a rose in a cobweb; by my exuberance, which could not pass unnoticed even when I was silent and motionless; but above all by the fact that I was a common girl. A rich man surely bears no love toward a poor man, but neither does he fear him, and he knows how to keep him at a distance through his own pride and conceit; but a poor man who by education or by origin has the soul of a rich man is absolutely terrified by a real poor man, like someone who feels predisposed to catch a certain illness from those who are already infected. The two Medolaghi women were certainly not rich, otherwise they would not have let rooms. Since they were conscious of their poverty but unwilling to admit it, my presence as a poor girl wearing no mask struck them as both dangerous and insulting. Who can say what passed through the girl's mind when I spoke to her? . . . This girl here is talking to me, she wants to become my friend, I won't be able to get rid of her. . . . I realized all these things in a flash and decided not to utter another word until the end of the meal.

But her mother, who was more uninhibited and possibly more curious, did not want to renounce all conversation. "I didn't know you were engaged," she said to Mino. "How long have you been?"

Her voice was affected and she spoke from behind the mass of her bosom as if from behind a protective trench.

"About a month," said Mino. This was true, we had known one another for only a month.

"Is the young lady a Roman?"

"Indeed she is, seven generations back."

"And when is the wedding to be?"

"Soon — as soon as the house we're going to live in is free."

"Oh, you've already got a house?"

"Yes, a little villa with a garden — and a little tower. It's charming."

This was how he described, in his sardonic tone of voice, the little villa I had pointed out to him on the main road near my apartment.

"If we wait for that house," I said, with an effort, "I am afraid we'll never get married."

"Nonsense," said Mino cheerfully. He seemed completely recovered and even had more color in his cheeks. "You know it will be free on the day we fixed."

I don't like playacting so I said nothing. The maid changed the plates. "Villas, Signor Diodati," said Signora Medolaghi, "are all very well but they aren't convenient. You need a lot of servants."

"Why?" said Mino. "That won't be necessary. Adriana will be cook, maid, housekeeper . . . won't you, Adriana?"

Signora Medolaghi sized me up with a glance. "Really," she said, "a lady has other things to do beside thinking of cooking and sweeping and making beds. But if the young lady Adriana is accustomed to it, in that case —" She did not finish her sentence and turned her attention to the plate the parlormaid was offering me. "We didn't know you were coming; we could only add another egg or two."

I was angry with Mino and with the woman and was almost tempted to reply, "No, I'm accustomed to walking the streets." But

Mino, who was bubbling over with a crazy kind of gaiety, poured himself out a generous glassful of wine, poured some for me — Signora Medolaghi's eyes followed the bottle uneasily — and continued. "Oh, but Adriana's not a lady! And she never will be — Adriana's always made beds and swept floors. Adriana's a girl of the people."

Signora Medolaghi looked at me as if she were seeing me for the first time. "Exactly as I was saying — if she's accustomed —" she repeated, with insulting politeness. Her daughter bowed her head over her plate.

"Yes, she is," went on Mino, "and I'm certainly not going to be the one to make her give up such useful habits. Adriana's a shirt-maker's daughter and a shirtmaker herself — aren't you, Adriana?" He stretched his arm across the table, seized my hand, and turned it over, palm upward. "She paints her nails, I know, but it's the hand of a working girl — big, strong, unaffected — like her hair, curly but rebellious, coarse at the roots." He let my hand fall and pulled my hair hard, like an animal's. "Adriana, in fact, is in every way a worthy representative of our fine, healthy, and vigorous people."

There was a kind of sarcastic challenge in his voice; but no one took it up. The daughter looked through me, as if I were transparent and she were looking at some object behind me. The mother ordered the maid to change the plates, then, turning to Mino, asked him in an entirely unexpected fashion, "So, Signor Diodati, did you go to see that play?"

I almost burst into laughter at her clumsy way of changing the subject. Mino, however, remained unruffled. "Don't mention it!" he exclaimed. "It was awful."

"We're going tomorrow. They do say the actors are excellent."

Mino replied that the actors were not actually as good as the papers said; the lady was astonished that the papers should lie. Mino replied calmly that the papers were one lie from beginning to end; and from that moment the conversation dealt with similar matters. As soon as one of these themes of conversation was exhausted, Signora Medolaghi started on another, with poorly concealed haste. Mino, who seemed highly amused, went along with the game and replied readily. They talked about actors, night life in Rome, cafés, movies, theaters, hotels, and so on. They were like two pingpong players, intent on returning the ball to one another without letting it drop. But while Mino did it out of that habitual spirit of comedy, which was so highly developed in him, Signora Medolaghi did it out of fear and disgust at me and anything connected with me. She seemed to imply by her extremely formal, completely conventional talk, "This is my way of telling you how indecent it is to marry a common girl, and in any case how indecent it is to bring her to the house of the widow of the civil servant Medolaghi." The daughter hardly breathed; terrified, she seemed to be longing openly for the meal to come to an end and for me to be gone as quickly as possible.

For a while I found some amusement in following this conversational skirmish, but I soon got tired of it and let the sorrow that was eating at my heart invade me completely. I realized that Mino did not love me, and the knowledge was bitter. Besides, I had noted that Mino had made use of my confidences to improvise on our make-believe engagement, and I could not quite understand whether he had wanted to make a fool of me, of the two women, or of himself. Perhaps of all of us, but chiefly of himself. It was as if he, too, had nourished in his heart the same aspirations toward a normal, decent life as I had, and, for reasons different from mine, had given up all hope of being able to fulfill them. On the other hand, I understood that his praise of me as a girl of the people in no way flattered me or the common people — it had been nothing more than a means of making himself unpleasant to the two women. These observations brought home to me the truth of what he had been saying shortly before — that he was incapable of loving with his heart. Never had I understood so well as at that moment that everything is love, and that everything depends on love. And this love either was or was not. If there was love, then one loved not only one's own lover but all people and all things, as I did; but if there was no love, one loved nobody and nothing, as in his case. And the absence of love, in the end, caused incapacity and impotence.

The table had been cleared by now and in the circle of light shed by the chandelier onto the tablecloth sprinkled with crumbs stood four coffee cups, a tulip-shaped terracotta ashtray, and a large, white, mottled hand, adorned with several cheap rings, which held a burning cigarette: Signora Medolaghi's hand. My bosom suddenly swelled with impatience and I rose to my feet. "I'm sorry, Mino," I said, deliberately exaggerating my Roman accent, "but I'm busy. . . . I've got to go."

He crushed out his cigarette in the ashtray and got up as well. I said good evening in ringing, common tones, made a slight bow that Signora Medolaghi returned stiffly and the daughter ignored, and then I left. In the entrance I spoke to Mino. "I'm afraid Signora Medolaghi will ask you to find another room after this evening."

He shrugged his shoulders. "I don't think so. I pay her well, and very punctually."

"I'm going," I said. "This meal has made me unhappy."

"Why?"

"Because I'm truly convinced that you're incapable of love."

I said this sadly, without looking at him. Then I raised my eyes, and I thought he looked grieved, but perhaps it was the shadow in the hall on his pale face. I suddenly felt full of remorse. "Are you offended?" I asked.

"No," he said with an effort, "it's the truth, after all."

My heart overflowed with affection for him, I embraced him impulsively and said, "It isn't true . . . I only said it out of spite. And anyway, I love you so much all the same. . . . Look — I brought you this tie," I opened my purse, took out the tie, and offered it to him. He looked at it.

"Did you steal it?" he asked.

It was a joke and, as I thought later, probably revealed more fondness for me than the warmest thanks could have done. But at that moment it pierced me to the heart. My eyes filled with tears. "No, I bought it — in a shop just down below," I stammered.

He realized my humiliation and hugged me. "Silly," he said. "I was only joking. But anyway, I'd like it even if you had stolen it — maybe even more."

"Wait, I'll put it on for you," I said, feeling slightly consoled. He lifted his chin and I undid his old tie, turned back his collar, and knotted the new one for him.

"I'm going to take this ugly worn-out tie away," I said. "You mustn't ever wear it again." What I really wanted was to have some keepsake from him, something he had worn.

"I'll see you soon, then," he said.

"When?"

"Tomorrow, after supper."

"All right." I took his hand to kiss it. He pulled it away, but was not in time to prevent me brushing it with my lips. Without looking back, I rushed away down the stairs.

7

*A*FTER THAT DAY, I WENT ON leading my usual life. I really loved Mino, and more than once I felt tempted to give up my profession, so complete a contrast to real love. But despite the fact that I had fallen in love, my condition remained unaltered, I was still at the same point: that is to say, I had no money and no possibility of earning any except in that way. I did not want to accept money from Mino; and in any case he had only a limited amount, since his family sent him barely enough to pay for his upkeep in town. Actually, I must admit at this point that I always felt an irresistible desire to pay the bill myself in all the places, cafés or restaurants, we frequented. He always refused my offers and every time I was disappointed and embittered. When he had no money, he took me to the public parks and we sat together on a bench talking and watching the passersby, like two poor people.

"But if you don't have any money," I said to him one day, "let's got to a café anyway. I'll pay . . . what difference does it make?"

"It's out of the question."

"Why? I want to go to a café and have a drink."

"Go by yourself, then."

In fact, what mattered to me was not so much going to a café as paying for him. I had a deep, obstinate, and painful desire to do so; and even more than paying for him, I would have liked to have handed all the money I earned straight over to him, as soon as I received it from my lovers. I thought that only in this way could I show him my love; but I also thought that by keeping him I would bind him to me with a bond stronger than that of simple affection. "I'd be so pleased to give you some money," I said to him another time. "And I'm sure it would give you some pleasure to have it!"

He began to laugh. "Our relationship, at least as far as I'm concerned, isn't based on pleasure!"

"On what, then?"

He hesitated. "On your desire to love me," he then replied, "and on my weakness in the face of this desire; but that doesn't mean my weakness has no limits."

"How do you mean?"

"It's very simple," he said coolly, "and I've explained it to you over and over again — we're together because you wanted it this way. I, on the contrary, did not want it, and even now, in theory at least, I would rather not —"

"Stop, enough!" I interrupted, "let's not talk about our love. I shouldn't have mentioned it."

Often since then, thinking about his character, I have come to the painful conclusion that he did not love me at all, and that I was only the object of some mysterious experiment of his. In reality, he was interested only in himself; but within these limits his character revealed itself to be extremely complicated. He was the son of a well-to-do provincial family, as I believe I have already said, delicate, intelligent, cultured, educated, serious. His family, as far as I could make out from the little he told me, for he was not fond of talking about it, was one of those families that I, in my unfulfilled dreams of normalcy, would have liked to have been born in to. It was a traditional family: his father was a doctor and landowner, his mother was still young and stayed at home most of the time, thinking only of her husband and children; there were three younger sisters and an older brother. The father, it's true, was a busybody and local authority, his mother extremely bigoted, his sisters rather frivolous, and his older brother absolutely dissolute, like his friend Giancarlo. But after all, these faults were all very tolerable and for me, who had been born among people whose way of life was so different in every way, they did not even seem to be defects. It was a closely united family, too, and all of them, parents and children alike, were devoted to Mino.

My own feeling was that he was very lucky in having been born into such a family. But he, on the contrary, felt an aversion, a dislike and disgust for them that I found quite incomprehensible. And he seemed to feel the same aversion, dislike, and disgust for himself, for what he was and what he did. But this self-hatred appeared to be only a reflection of his hatred for his whole family. In other words, he seemed to hate in himself all that part of him that had remained attached to his family or had in any way come under the influence of the family circle. I have said he was educated, cultured, intelligent, delicate, serious. But he despised his intelligence, manners, culture, delicacy, seriousness, merely because he suspected that he owed them to the milieu and the family into which he had been born and where he had grown up. "But really," I said to him once, "What would you like to be? These are all fine qualities — you ought to thank your lucky stars that you have them."

"Right," he said, scarcely moving his lips. "A lot of good they do me — If I'd had my way, I'd rather have been like Sonzogno."

He had been deeply impressed by the story of Sonzogno; I don't know why. "What a horror!" I exclaimed. "He's a monster, and you want to be like a monster!"

"Obviously I wouldn't want to be like Sonzogno in every respect," he explained. "I mentioned Sonzogno merely to make my meaning clear. Sonzogno is fit to live in this world, and I'm not."

"Do you want to know what I would like to have been?" I then asked him.

"Let's hear it."

"I would have liked," I said slowly, savoring the words in each of which one of my most cherished dreams seemed to be embodied, "to have been just what you are and what you are so unhappy at being. I would have liked to have been born into a family as rich as yours, which would have given me a good education. I would have liked to have lived in a lovely, clean house like yours. I would have liked to have had good teachers and foreign governesses, as you had. I would have liked to have spent the summer at the seaside or in the mountains, and to have had good clothes, and to be invited out and to receive guests. And then I would have liked to marry someone who loved me, a decent person who worked and was well-to-do, too, and I would have liked to live with him and bear his children."

We were lying on the bed as we talked. Suddenly he leaped upon me, as was his way, clutching me and shaking me as he repeated, "Hurray, hurray, hurray! In fact, you'd have liked to have been like Signora Lobianco."

"Who's Signora Lobianco?" I asked, disconcerted and a little offended.

"A terrible harpy who often invites me to her parties in the hope that I'll fall in love with one of her horrible daughters and marry her, because I'm what's called, in wordly jargon, a good match."

"But I wouldn't like to be at all like Signora Lobianco!"

"But that's what you'd certainly be if you had all the things you mentioned. Signora Lobianco, too, was born into a wealthy family who gave her an excellent education, with good teachers and foreign governesses, sent her to school and even to the university, I believe. She, too, grew up in a lovely, clean house; she, too, went to the seaside or the mountains every summer; she, too, had beautiful clothes and was invited out and gave parties — lots of invitations and lots of parties; she, too, married a decent man, Lobianco the engineer, who works and brings a great deal of money into the house. And she has had a number of children by this husband of hers — to whom I even believe she has been faithful — three daughters and a son to be exact, but despite all this, as I said, she's a terrible harpy."

"She must be a harpy quite independently of her surroundings!"

"No, she's one like her friends and the friends of her friends."

"Maybe," I said, trying to break away from his sarcastic embrace, "but everyone's got their own character. Maybe Signora Lobianco's a harpy, but I'm sure that under those conditions I'd have turned out far better than I am."

"You'd have turned out no less horrible than Signora Lobianco."

"Why?"

"Because."

"But, look, do you think your family's horrible, too?"

"Of course, loathsome."

"And you're horrible too?"

"Yes, in all the parts of me that come from my family."

"But why? Tell me why."

"Because."

"That's not an answer."

"It's the same answer Signora Lobianco would give you if you asked her certain questions," he replied.

"What questions?"

"We needn't mention them," he said lightly. "Embarrassing questions — a 'because' said with conviction shuts the mouth of even the most curious person — 'because,' for no reason — 'because' —"

"I don't understand you."

"What does it matter if we don't understand each other, as long as we love each other — which is true?" he concluded, embracing me in his ironical and loveless way. And so the discussion ended. For just as he never gave himself up completely, emotionally speaking, and always seemed to keep something back, perhaps the most important part, so that his rare outbursts of affection were actually worthless, in exactly the same way he never revealed the whole of what he was thinking. Every time I believed I had reached the very core of his intelligence, he repelled me with some joke or burlesque gesture, to distract my attention. He really was elusive, in every sense. And he seemed to me to be like an inferior person, almost like a kind of object of study and experiment.

But perhaps it was for this very reason that I loved him so much, so helplessly and submissively.

Sometimes, too, he seemed to hate not only his own family and his own milieu, but all humankind. One day he remarked — I cannot remember in what connection, "The rich are appalling, but the poor certainly aren't any better, if for different reasons."

"It would be easier if you just confessed frankly that you hate all mankind without exception."

He began to laugh. "In the abstract," he replied, "when I'm not among them I don't hate them; on the contrary, I hate them so little that I believe in their progress. If I didn't believe this, I wouldn't trouble myself with politics. But when I'm among them they horrify me. Really," he added sadly, "people are worthless."

"*We're* people," I said, "so we're worthless, too, and therefore we have no right to judge."

He laughed again. "I don't judge them," he replied. "I smell them — or rather, I sniff them out — like a dog sniffs the scent of a partridge or a hare. But does the dog judge them? I sniff them and I find they're malicious, stupid, selfish, petty, vulgar, deceitful, shameful, full of filth. I sniff them out. It's a feeling; can you abolish a feeling?"

I did not know what to reply and limited myself to saying, "I haven't got that feeling."

Another time he said, "Men may be good, or bad, I don't know, but they're certainly useless, superfluous —"

"What do you mean?"

"I mean it would be wonderful if the whole of humanity were wiped out. It's only an ugly excrescence on the face of the Earth, a wart. The world would be far more beautiful without people, their cities, their streets, their ports, all their little arrangements. Think how beautiful it would be if there were nothing but sky, sea, trees, earth, animals."

I could not help laughing. "What strange ideas you have!" I exclaimed.

"Humanity," he continued, "is a thing without head nor tail . . . decidedly negative, though. The history of humankind is nothing but one long yawn of sheer boredom. What need is there of it? Speaking for myself — I could have done very well without it."

"But you're part of this humanity yourself," I objected. "Could you have done without yourself, then?"

"Especially without myself."

Chastity was another of his obsessions, all the more singular in that he did not try to practice it and the idea served only to spoil his pleasure. He sang its praises continually, especially just after we had made love, as if out of pique. He used to say lovemaking was only the silliest and easiest way of freeing oneself from all questions, by forcing them out below, secretly, without anyone noticing, like embarrassing guests shown out by the back door. "Then, when the operation has been performed, you go out for a stroll with your accomplice — wife or mistress — wondrously disposed to accept the world as it is — even the worst of all possible worlds."

"I don't understand you," I said.

"And yet you ought to understand this, at least," he said. "Isn't it your speciality?"

I felt offended. "My specialty, as you call it," I said, "is to love you. But if you like, we won't make love anymore — I'll love you all the same."

He laughed. "Are you quite sure?" he asked; and that day we argued no more. But he came back to the same things repeatedly; so that in the end I took no further notice, but accepted this as I did so many other traits in his paradoxical character.

He never talked to me about politics though, except for an occasional reference. Even today I have no idea what he was aiming at, what his ideas were, what party he belonged to. My ignorance is partly due to his secretiveness over this aspect of his life, and partly to the fact that I myself understood nothing about politics and my shyness and indifference prevented my asking him for all the explanations that might have enlightened me. I was wrong; and God knows I regretted it later on. But at the time I thought it was very convenient not to be involved in things I believed were no concern of mine, and to think only of love. I behaved, in fact, like so many other women, wives and mistressses, who sometimes do not even know how their men earn the money they bring home. Quite often I met his two companions, whom he used to see almost every day. But they did not mention politics in my presence; they either joked or talked of unimportant matters.

And yet I was unable to shake off a constant feeling of apprehension because I could not forget that plotting against the government was dangerous. What I feared most was that Mino might be drawn into some act of violence; in my ignorance I was unable to separate the idea of a plot from that of weapons and blood. In this connection I remember something that shows to what extent I felt, however obscurely, that it was my duty to intervene in order to ward off the dangers that threatened him. I knew that the carrying of arms was illegal; and that a man might be sentenced to jail merely for carrying a weapon without a permit. Aside from this, it is extremely easy to lose one's head at certain moments, and the use of arms has so often compromised people who otherwise would have been saved. For all these reasons I thought that the pistol Mino was so proud of was not only unnecessary, but positively dangerous, for he might be obliged to use it or it might simply be discovered on him. But I did not dare to mention it to him, since I realized it would have been useless. In the end I decided to act secretly. On one occasion he had explained to me how the weapon worked. One day while he was asleep, I took the pistol out of his trousers pocket, pulled out the cylinder, and removed the bullets. Then I put the pistol together again and replaced it in his pocket. I hid the bullets in a drawer underneath my lingerie. I did all this in an instant and then went to sleep again beside him. Two days later I put the bullets into my purse and went to throw them into the Tiber.

One day Astarita came to see me. I had almost forgotten him; and as far as the matter of the maid went, I believed I had done my duty and I did not want to think anymore about it. Astarita told me the priest had delivered the compact to the police and that the owner, on the advice of the police themselves, had withdrawn her accusation, and the maid had been declared innocent and set free. I must admit that this news delighted me, especially since it dispelled the feeling of foreboding I had had ever since my last confession. I thought not of the maid, who was by now free, but of Mino, and told myself that now, since there was no further danger of the denunciation I had been so afraid of, I had nothing more to fear for either of us. In my delight I could not help embracing Astarita.

"Was it so important to you to get that woman out of jail, then?" he asked me with a doubtful expression.

"It may seem strange to you," I lied, "who lightheartedly send who knows how many innocent people to jail every day, but it was real agony to me."

"I don't send anyone to jail," he stammered. "I only do my duty."

"Did you see the priest yourself?" I asked him.

"No, I didn't see him, I phoned. They told me the compact had, in fact, been given up by a priest, who had received it under the seal of the confessional. So then I recommended her release."

I remained pensive, I did not know why myself.

"Do you really love me?" I asked him then.

This question put him into turmoil immediately and he embraced me tightly. "Why do you ask me that?" he stammered. "You ought to know by now."

He wanted to kiss me but I avoided him. "I asked you," I said, "because I want to know if you'll always help me — every time I ask you — like you helped me this time."

"Always," he replied, trembling all over. "But you'll be kind to me?" he asked, putting his face up to mine.

Now I had firmly decided, after Mino had returned to me, that I would not have anything more to do with Astarita. He was different from my usual paying lovers; and although I did not love him and indeed felt a positive aversion for him at times, perhaps for this very reason I felt that giving myself to him would be like betraying Mino. I was tempted to tell him the truth, "No, I shall never be kind to you again," but then I suddenly changed my mind and controlled myself. I remembered what power he had, how Giacomo might be arrested at any time, and that if I wanted Astarita to intervene to free him it was unwise to offend him. I resigned myself and said quickly. "Yes, I'll be kind to you."

"Tell me," he insisted, feeling emboldened, "tell me — do you love me a little?"

"No, I don't love you," I said firmly, "and you know it — I've already told you that so many times."

"Won't you ever love me?"

"I don't think so."

"But why?"

"There isn't any reason."

"You love someone else."

"That's no business of yours."

"But I need your love," he said in despair, looking at me with his bilious eyes. "Why, why won't you love me a little?"

That day I allowed him to remain with me until late into the night. He was inconsolable because of my inability to love him and seemed unconvinced of the truth of what I said. "But I'm no worse than other men," he protested. "Why couldn't you love me instead of someone else?" Really, I felt sorry for him; and since he insisted on questioning me about my feelings for him and on trying to find some fuel for his hopes in my replies, I felt almost tempted to lie to him, if only to give him the illusion he so longed for. I noticed that he was more mournful and sickened that night than he usually was. It was as though he wanted his gestures and attitudes to awaken in me, from without, the love my heart denied him.

I remember that at a certain moment he asked me to sit naked in an armchair. He knelt down in front of me and put his head in my lap, crushing his face against my belly and remaining motionless like this for a long time. Meanwhile I had to stroke his head again and again with a light, incessant caress. This was not the first time he had obliged me to perform a kind of mimicry of love; but he seemed more desperate that day than usual. He pressed his head violently into my lap as if he wanted to enter into me and be swallowed up, and he groaned occasionally. In those moments he no longer seemed like a lover, but a child seeking the warmth and darkness of his mother's womb. And I thought that many men would like never to have been born; and that this gesture of his, perhaps unconsciously, expressed that dim longing to be engulfed once more in the shadowy womb from which he had been painfully expelled into the light.

That night he remained kneeling so long that I became drowsy and fell asleep, with my head flung back against the chair, my hand resting on his head. I do not know how long I slept. At a certain moment I seemed to wake up and glimpse Astarita, no longer kneeling at my feet but seated in front of me, already dressed, gazing at me with his mournful, bilious eyes. But perhaps it was only a dream, or a hallucination. The fact is that I suddenly really woke up and found that Astarita had gone, leaving the usual sum of money in my lap where he had lain his face.

About a fortnight passed, and these were among the happiest days in my life. I saw Mino almost every day and although there was no change in our relationship I contented myself with the kind of habit we had established, in which we seemed to have found by now some common ground. It was silently taken for granted between us that he did not love me, that he would never love me, and that in any case he preferred chastity to love. It was equally taken for granted that I loved him, that I always would love him despite his indifference to me, and that in any case I preferred a love like that, incomplete and wavering though it might be, to no love at all. I am not made like Astarita; and having once resigned myself to the fact that I was not loved, I found much pleasure all the same in loving. I cannot swear that at the bottom of my heart I did not nurse a hope that my submissiveness, patience, and affection might one day make him love me. But I did nothing to encourage this hope; and it was, more than anything else, the slightly bitter spice to his uncertain, grudging caresses.

But I certainly did all I could to enter unobtrusively into his life, and since I could not do so by the main door, I exercised my ingenuity in trying to enter by the back door. Despite his explicit and I believe genuine hatred of people, some curious contradiction gave him an irresistible impulse to preach and act in support of what he thought was for the good of humankind. And although this impulse was almost always checked by sudden regrets and sarcastic disgust, it was sincere.

At that time he appeared to become passionately interested in what he ironically referred to as my education. As I have said, I tried to bind him to me and so I favored this inclination of his. This experiment ended almost immediately, however, in a way worth mentioning. He came to see me for several evenings running and brought some books of his with him. After he had explained briefly what the subject was, he began to read a passage here and there. He read well, with a great variety of expression in his voice according to the subject matter, and with a passion that made him flush and gave his features an unusual animation. But I was usually unable to understand what he read however hard I tried; and I soon gave up listening to him and contented myself with watching the different expressions that flitted across his face while he was reading, a pleasure I never tired of.

During these readings he really abandoned himself completely, without any fear or irony, like someone in his own element who is no longer afraid of showing his sincerity. This fact struck me, because until then I had always thought that love, not literature, was the most favorable condition in which the human soul could blossom. Apparently in Mino's case the opposite was true; certainly I never, not even in his rare moments of affection, saw such enthusiasm and candor in his face as there was when, raising his voice in curiously hollow tones or lowering it in a conversational way, he read me passages from his favorite authors. At such times he entirely lost his air of theatrical, burlesque artificiality, which never left him completely even in his most serious moments, and gave the impression that he was always acting a superficial, premeditated part. Quite often I even saw his eyes fill with tears. Then he would shut the book. "Did you like it?" he would ask me abruptly.

I usually answered that I had liked it, without saying why. I could not be more specific because, from the very outset, as I have said, I gave up all effort to grasp the meaning of such obscure stuff. But one day he insisted. "Tell me why you liked it," he said. "Explain why."

"To tell you the truth," I replied after a moment's hesitation, "I can't explain anything because I didn't understand anything."

"Why didn't you tell me?"

"I didn't understand anything — or only a very little — of what you were reading."

"And you let me go on reading without warning me!"

"I saw you enjoyed reading and I didn't want to spoil your pleasure — anyway, I'm never bored — you're very amusing to watch while you're reading."

He leaped to his feet in a rage. "What the devil! You're a fool, a cretin — and here I am, wasting my breath — you're an idiot!" He pulled back the book as though he were going to fling it at my head, but controlled himself in time and continued to insult me this way for a while.

I allowed him to let off steam for some time and then spoke. "You say you want to educate me," I said, "but the first condition for my education would be to do something so I wouldn't have to earn my living in the way you know I do — I certainly don't need to read poetry or reflections on morality to pick up men. I could even not know how to read or write and they'd pay me just the same."

"You'd like to have a beautiful house, a husband, children, clothes, a car, wouldn't you?" he replied sarcastically. "The trouble is that not even the Lobianco women read — for different reasons from yours, but no less justifiable, from their point of view."

"I don't know what I'd like," I said, a little irritated, "but these books don't suit my way of life. It's like giving a beggar a priceless hat and expecting her to wear it with her usual rags."

"That may be," he said, "but this is the last time I'll ever read you a line."

I have mentioned this slight quarrel because it is so characteristic of his way of thinking and behaving. But I doubt whether he would have continued in his efforts to educate me, even if I had not confessed my inability to understand him. It was not so much his inconsistency that made me think this as his singular inability, which I would call physical, to persist in any effort that demanded sincere, sustained enthusiasm. He never spoke of it in so many words, but I realized that the burlesque quality of his words often corresponded in fact to a spiritual condition. He would get worked up, as it were, over any purpose and as long as the fire of this enthusiasm lasted he would see that purpose as something concrete and attainable. Then suddenly the fire would die out and he would feel only boredom, disgust, and above all, a sensation of utter absurdity. Then he would either abandon himself to a kind of dull, inert indifference, or act in a conventional and superficial way, as if the fire had never died out — in a word, pretend. I find it difficult to explain what happened to him at such times — it was probably a sharp interruption in his vitality, as if the very warmth of his blood had suddenly withdrawn from his mind, leaving only an arid void. It was an immediate interruption, unforeseeable and total, comparable to the interruption of an electric current, which plunges into sudden darkness a house only a moment before brilliantly illuminated; or to a motor when wheel after wheel, it ceases to move and stands still, when the power is cut off. This constant ebb and flow of his deepest vitality was first revealed to me by the frequent alternation in him of states of ardor and enthusiasm with others of apathy and inertia; but in the end it was shown to me fully by a curious incident to which I attributed little importance at the time, but which later appeared highly significant.

"Would you like to do something for us?" he asked me one day, quite unexpectedly.

"Us who?"

"For our group. Help us distribute our leaflets, for instance?"

I was always on the alert for anything that might bring me nearer to him and strengthen our connection.

"Of course," I replied eagerly, "tell me what I have to do and I'll do it."

"Aren't you afraid?"

"Why should I be? If you do it —"

"Yes, but first I have to explain what it's about," he said. "First you have to understand the ideas for which you run such risks."

"Explain them, then."

"But you won't be interested."

"Why? First of all, they'll surely interest me, besides, everything you do interests me, if only because you do it."

He looked at me and suddenly his eyes sparkled and his cheeks grew unexpectedly flushed. "All right," he said hurriedly, "it's too late today — but I'll explain everything tomorrow — myself, since books bore you. But remember, it'll take a long time, and you'll have to listen and follow me — even if you think you don't understand sometimes."

"I'll try to understand," I said.

"You ought to," he replied, as if speaking to himself. And he left me.

Next day I waited for him but he did not come. Two days later he arrived and as soon as he was in my room he sat down on the armchair at the foot of the bed without saying a word.

"Well," I said gaily, "I'm ready — I'm listening."

I had noticed his downcast expression, his opaque eyes, and his wilted, exhausted manner, but I did not want to remark on it.

"It's no good listening," he said at last, "because you won't hear anything."

"Why?"

"Because."

"Tell me the truth," I protested. "You think I'm too stupid or too ignorant to understand certain things, don't you? Thanks."

"No, you're wrong," he said seriously.

"Why, then?"

We continued like this for some time, with me insisting on knowing why and him refusing to explain. "Do you want to know why?" he said at last. "Because I wouldn't know how to express those ideas to you myself today."

"Why not? — since you think about them all the time."

"I do think about them the whole time, I know. But since yesterday, and for who knows how much longer, those ideas aren't clear to me anymore, in fact I don't understand a thing."

"You can't mean it."

"Try to understand me," he said. "Two days ago, when I suggested that you should work for us, I'm sure that if I had explained our ideas to you, I'd not only have done it vigorously, clearly, and persuasively, but you'd have understood them perfectly. Today I might move my tongue and lips to utter certain words, but it would be something mechanical, in which I participated not at all. Today," he repeated, emphasizing each syllable as he spoke, "I don't understand a thing."

"You don't understand a thing?"

"No, I don't understand a thing. Ideas, concepts, facts, memories, convictions, everything has been transformed into a kind of mush, a mush that fills my head —" he tapped his forehead with his finger "— my whole head — and disgusts me as if it were excrement."

I looked at him in puzzled suspense. A quiver of exasperation seemed to run through him at this.

"Try to understand me," he cried, "today everything seems incomprehensible. Not only ideas, but everything ever written or said or thought — it all seems absurd. For instance, do you know the Lord's Prayer?"

"Yes."

"Say it, then."

"Our Father, which art in Heaven," I began.

"That's enough," he interrupted. "Now just think for a moment how many ways this prayer has been said over the centuries, with how many different emotions! Well, I don't understand it at all, not at all. You might as well say it backward, it'd be all the same to me."

He was silent for a moment. "It isn't only words that have this effect on me," he continued, "but things, too — people. There are you sitting on the arm of this chair beside me, and maybe you think I see you. But I don't see you because I can't understand you — I can even touch you and still not understand you. I will touch you, in fact —" as he spoke he jerked aside my dressing gown and uncovered my breast, as if seized by a sudden frenzy. "I'm touching your breast — I can feel its shape, warmth, form, I see its color, its outline . . . but I don't understand what it is. I say to myself: here's a round, warm, soft, white, swelling object, with a little round, dark knob in the middle, which gives milk and gives pleasure if it is caressed. But I don't understand a thing. I tell myself it's beautiful, that it ought to fill me with desire, but I still don't understand a thing. Do you see what I mean, now?" he repeated furiously, grabbing my breast so hard that I could not repress a cry of pain. He let go of me at once. "Probably," he observed reflectively after a moment, "it's just this kind of incomprehension that makes so many people cruel. They are trying to rediscover contact with reality through other people's pain."

There was a moment of silence. Then I spoke. "If this is true, how do you manage when you have to do certain things?"

"What, for instance?"

"I don't know — you tell me that you distribute leaflets, and that you write them yourself. But if you don't believe in them, how can you write them and distribute them?"

He burst into a fit of sarcastic laughter. "I behave as if I believed in them."

"But that's impossible."

"Why impossible? Almost everyone does it, except in the case of eating, drinking, sleeping, and making love. Almost everyone does things as if they believed in them. Hadn't you noticed that?" He laughed nervously.

"I don't," I replied.

"You don't," he replied, almost insultingly, "exactly because you limit yourself to eating, drinking, sleeping, and making love whenever you feel like it. It isn't necessary to pretend in these things, it seems — which is a lot. But at the same time, it's not much." He laughed, suddenly slapped me hard on the thigh, and then took me into his arms, squeezing me and shaking me as he usually did. "Don't you know this is the world of 'as if'?" He began to repeat, "don't you know that everyone, from the king to the beggar, behaves 'as if' — it's the world of 'as if, as if, as if' . . ."

I let him have his way because I knew that at such moments it was better not to be offended or to protest, but to wait for him to get it all out. But at last I said firmly, "I love you — that's the only thing I know and it's enough for me."

"You're right," he said simply, suddenly growing calm again. The evening finished in the usual way, without our speaking any further about politics or his incapacity to discuss them.

When I was alone again, I concluded after much reflection that perhaps things were as he said; but that it was far more likely that he was unwilling to talk to me about politics because he thought I would not understand and also, perhaps, because he was afraid I might compromise him through some indiscretion. Not that I thought he was lying, but I knew from experience that everyone can have a day when the world seems to fall to pieces, or, as he said, when you do not understand a thing, not even the Lord's Prayer. I, too, when I was ill, or in a bad mood for some reason, had experienced more or less the same sensations of boredom, disgust, and dullness. Evidently there was some other motive behind his refusal to let me share his most secret life; mistrust, as I have said, either of my intelligence or of my discretion. I realized afterward, when it was too late, that I had been mistaken, and that in his case, either through his youthful inexperience or weakness of character, those morbid states of mind assumed a special gravity.

But at the time I thought it would be wiser to retreat and not disturb him with my curiosity; and I did so.

8

I DON'T KNOW WHY, BUT I remember perfectly even the weather we were having at that time. February had come and gone, cold and rainy, and with March began the first milder days. A close network of white gossamer clouds veiled the whole sky and dazzled the eyes as soon as one stepped from the darkness of the house into the street. The air was sweet but still numb from the rigors of winter. I walked along in that thin, anaesthetized, and somnolent light with stupefied pleasure, and every now and again slackened my pace and closed my eyes; or stood still in amazement to gaze at the most insignificant things: a black-and-white cat licking itself on a doorstep, a hanging branch of oleander snapped off by the wind but which perhaps would flower all the same, a tuft of green grass springing up between the slabs of a sidewalk. The moss that the rain of the past months had sprinkled along the base of the houses filled me with a deep sense of peace and trust: I thought that if such lovely emerald velvet could flourish in the sparse soil between the jagged edges of bricks and cobblestones, then my life, whose roots were no deeper than those of moss and which also throve on the most meager nourishment and was really nothing more than a kind of mold growing at the foot of a building, had perhaps some likelihood of continuing and flourishing. I was convinced that all the unpleasant matters of the immediate past were now settled once and for all; that I would never see Sonzogno again or hear his crime mentioned; and that from now on I could peacefully enjoy my relationship with Mino. And with these thoughts, I seemed to taste to the full the real savor of life for the first time, composed as it was of mild boredom, opportunity, and hope.

I even began to consider the possibility of changing my way of life. My love for Mino made me indifferent toward other men, and so I no longer had even the incentives of curiosity and sensuality in my casual encounters. But I also thought that one way of life was as good as another, and that it was not worthwhile making much of an effort to change. I thought I would do so only if I acquired new habits, affections, and interests and became completely different than what I had been so far, without shocks or interruptions, through force of circumstance and independently of my own will. I saw no other way of changing my life; for the time being I was not at all ambitious for material success and progress, nor did I not think that by changing my way of life I would be able to better myself in any way.

One day I imparted these ideas to Mino. "I think you're contradicting yourself, aren't you?" he said, after listening to me attentively. "Aren't you always saying you'd like to be rich, have a beautiful house, and a husband and children? These are good things, and you may still have them some day — but you never will if you go on thinking that way."

"I didn't say I'd like them," I replied, "but that I would have liked them — that is, if I could have chosen before I was born, I certainly wouldn't have chosen to be what I am. But I was born in this house, with this mother, in these conditions, and after all, I am what I am."

"And that is?"

"That is, it seems absurd to me to long to be someone else. I'd only want to be someone else if I could continue to be myself at the same time; or if I could really enjoy the change, but it isn't worthwhile turning into a different person just to do it."

"It's always worthwhile," he said under his breath, "if not for yourself, then for other people."

"And then," I continued, without heeding his interruption, "the facts are what matter most. Do you think I couldn't have found a rich lover like Gisella? Or even have gotten married? If I haven't, it means that really, despite all my talk, I didn't truly want to."

"I'll marry you," he joked, hugging me playfully, "I'm rich. . . . When my grandmother dies, which won't be long now, I'll inherit acres and acres of land, not to mention a villa in the country and an apartment in town. We'll set up house properly, you'll receive the ladies of the district on appointed days. We'll have a cook, a parlormaid, a one-horse carriage or a car. One day we might even, with a little effort, discover that we're of noble birth and we'll be called count and countess or marquis and marquise."

"It's impossible to have a serious conversation with you," I said, pushing him away. "You make a joke of everything."

One afternoon I went to the movies with Mino. On our way back we got into a very crowded streetcar. Mino was to come home with me and we were to dine together at the tavern near the walls. He took the tickets and made his way ahead through the crowd that packed the middle of the tram. I tried to keep close to him, but lost sight of him when the crowd lurched forward. While I was standing crushed against one of the seats looking for him, I felt someone touch my hand. I lowered my eyes and there, seated right below me, was Sonzogno.

I gasped, felt myself grow pale and my expression change. He was staring at me with his usual intolerable intensity. Then, half-rising in his seat, he said to me between clenched teeth, "Do you want to sit down?"

"Thanks," I stammered. "I'm getting off soon."

"Sit down."

"Thanks," I repeated and sat down. If I had not, I might have fainted.

He remained standing beside me, as if he were keeping guard over me, holding on to the back of my seat and the one in front with both hands. He had not changed in the least; he was still wearing the same raincoat with a tight belt, his jaw still twitched in the same mechanical way. I closed my eyes and tried for a moment to put my thoughts in order. It was true that he had always looked like that, but this time I thought I saw a harder expression in his eyes. I remembered my confession and it occurred to me that if the priest had spoken, as I feared he had, and Sonzogno had come to know of it, my life wasn't worth much.

This thought did not frighten me. But he, as he stood there stiffly beside me, really did frighten me — or rather, he fascinated me and dominated me. I felt I could refuse him nothing, and that there was a bond between us perhaps even stronger than the bond between myself and Mino, although it was certainly not love. He, too, must have felt it instinctively and his whole attitude to me was one of masterfulness. "Let's go to your place," he said to me after a while.

"If you like," I replied docilely, without the slightest hesitation.

Mino came up, making his way with some difficulty through the crowd, and stood just beside Sonzogno, clinging to the same seat as he did and actually brushing Sonzogno's thick, short fingers with his own long, thin ones. The streetcar gave a jerk, they were thrown against one another, and Mino politely begged Sonzogno's pardon for having bumped into him. I began to suffer at seeing them together, so close and yet so unknown to one another, and I suddenly turned to Mino, with deliberate ostentation, so that Sonzogno would not think I was addressing him. "Look, I've just remembered I've got an appointment with someone for this evening — it'd be better to say good-bye now."

"If you like I'll see you home."

"No — I'm being met at the streetcar stop."

This was nothing new. I still took men home and Mino knew it. "As you like," he said unconcernedly. "I'll see you tomorrow, then." I nodded in agreement and he went off through the crowd.

As I watched him making his way among the people, I was overcome for a moment by a vehement despair. I thought I was seeing him for the last time, but not even I knew why. "Good-bye," I murmured to myself, as I followed him with my eyes. "Farewell, love." I wanted to cry out to him to stop, to turn back, but my voice stuck in my throat. The streetcar stopped and I thought I could see him getting down. The streetcar started off again.

During the whole journey Sonzogno and I never opened our mouths. I felt calmer now and told myself the priest could not possibly have spoken. Besides, after some reflection, I did not really regret this meeting. This way I would be rid of my doubts once and for all concerning the results of my confession.

I stood up at the stop, got off the streetcar, and walked on a little without looking back. Sonzogno was beside me and I could see him if I turned my head slightly. "What do you want from me?" I asked him at last. "Why have you come back?"

"You told me to come back yourself!" he said with a touch of astonishment.

This was true, but in my fear I had forgotten it. He came up close to me and took my arm, gripping it tight and almost holding me up. I began to tremble all over despite myself.

"Who was that?" he asked.

"A friend of mine."

"Have you seen anything more of Gino?"

"Never."

He looked around him rapidly. "I don't know why, but I've had the impression lately that I'm being followed. There are only two people who could have given me away, you and Gino."

"Why Gino?" I asked in a whisper. But my heart had begun to beat violently.

"He knew I was going to take that thing to the jeweler's, I'd even told him the name. He doesn't exactly know I killed him, but he could easily have guessed it."

"Gino doesn't have anything to gain by giving you away; he'd be giving himself away, too."

"That's what I think," he said between his teeth.

"As for me," I went on in my calmest voice, "you can be sure I've said nothing. I'm not a fool — I'd be arrested, too."

"I hope so, for your sake," he replied threateningly, then added, "I saw Gino for a moment. He told me as if he were joking that he knew a whole lot of things. I don't feel easy in my mind. He's a pig."

"You treated him really badly that evening, and of course he hates you now," I said. I realized while I was speaking that I almost hoped Gino truly had really denounced him.

"It was a beautiful punch," he said with grim vanity. "My hand hurt for two days afterward."

"Gino won't turn you in," I concluded. "It wouldn't suit his purposes. Besides, he's too frightened of you."

We were walking side by side, without looking at one another as we spoke, our voices lowered. It was twilight; a bluish mist enveloped the dark walls, the white branches of the plane trees, the yellowish houses, the distant view of the main road. As we reached the street door, I felt for the first time the precise sensation of betraying Mino. I had wanted to delude myself into thinking that Sonzogno was only one of many men, but I knew this was not true. I entered the entrance hall, closed the door behind me, and there in the dark I stopped and turned toward Sonzogno.

"Look," I said, "it's better if you go away."

"Why?"

I wanted to tell him the whole truth, despite the fear that possessed me. "Because I love another man and don't want to be unfaithful to him."

"Who? The man who was with you in the streetcar?"

I was afraid for Mino. "No, someone else," I replied hastily. "You don't know him. And now, do me a favor, leave me, go away."

"What if I don't want to go away?"

"Don't you understand that there are some things you can't get by force?" I began. But I was unable to finish. I do not know how it happened, but without seeing him or his movements in the dark, I suddenly felt him give me a terrible blow full in my face with the back of his hand.

"Start walking," he said.

I hurried on to the stairs with my head bent low. He had seized me by the arm again and was lifting me up every step; I almost felt as if he were raising me off the ground and making me fly. My cheek was burning, but what alarmed me most of all was a sense of tragic foreboding. This blow, I felt, had interrupted the happy rhythm of recent days and now the difficulties and fears of the past were about to return. I was filled with utter desperation and decided then and there to escape from the fate I foresaw. I would run away from home that very day. I would find refuge somewhere else, either at Gisella's or in some furnished room.

I was thinking so intently about all these things that I hardly noticed that I was in the apartment and had passed through the outer room into my own. I found myself — I might almost say I woke up — seated on the edge of the bed, as Sonzogno was taking off his clothes, piece by piece, and placing them methodically on a chair with the precise, self-satisfied gestures of an orderly man. His fury had passed. "I would have come before," he said evenly, "but I couldn't. I've been thinking about you all the time, though."

"What were you thinking?" I asked mechanically.

"That we're made for each other." He stood still, holding his vest in his hand. "In fact," he added in a strange tone of voice, "I came to make you a proposal."

"What?"

"I've got some money. Let's go away together to Milan, where I've got lots of friends. I want to start up a garage. And then in Milan we could get married."

I felt as if I were collapsing inside and such weakness overcame me that I closed my eyes. This was the first time since Gino that anyone had proposed marriage to me and it was Sonzogno who made this proposal. The life I had longed for so intensely, with a husband and children, was now being offered to me, but with the normality reduced to a kind of empty sheath, inside which everything was abnormal and terrifying. "But why?" I said feebly. "We hardly know one another, you've only seen me once —"

He sat beside me and put his arm around my waist. "No one knows me better than you do," he said, "You know everything about me."

It occurred to me that he was moved and wanted to show me that he loved me and that I ought to love him. But this was only imagination on my part, for nothing in his behavior warranted the assumption.

"I know nothing about you," I said in a low voice, "I only know that you killed a man."

"And then," he said, as if speaking to himself, "I'm so tired of living alone. When you live alone, you end up doing something crazy."

After a moment's silence I spoke again. "I can't say yes or no point-blank like this," I said. "Give me time to think it over."

"Think it over, think it over," he said to my astonishment, clenching his teeth. "There's no hurry." Then he left my side and continued undressing.

I had been struck chiefly by the phrase, "We're made for each other," and I asked myself now whether he was not right, after all. What could I hope for now but a man like him? And was it not true that a hidden bond, which I recognized and feared, existed between us? I found I was repeating submissively to myself the words, "Run away, run away —" and shaking my head despondently.

"Milan?" I said in a clear voice that filled my mouth with saliva. "Aren't you afraid they'll be looking for you?"

"I just said that . . . Actually they don't even know I exist."

The weakness that had weighed down my limbs suddenly vanished and I felt strong and very determined. I stood up, took off my coat, and went to hang it on the coatrack. As usual, I turned the key in the lock and then walked slowly over to the window to close the shutters. Then standing straight in front of the mirror, I began to unbutton my bodice from the bottom up. But I stopped almost immediately and turned toward Sonzogno. He was sitting on the edge of the bed and was bending over to untie his shoelaces. "Just a minute," I said with assumed casualness, "someone was supposed to be coming this evening; I must go and warn Mother to send him away." He made no reply, had not even time to do so. I left the room, closing the door behind me, and went into the living room.

Mother was at the sewing machine near the window. She had taken up her work again a while ago to relieve the monotony of her existence. "Call me at Gisella's or at Zelinda's," I said hurriedly, under my breath, "tomorrow morning." Zelinda rented out rooms in the center of town; I used to go there sometimes with my lovers, and Mother knew her.

"Why?"

"I'm going out," I said. "When that man in there asks about me, tell him you don't know anything."

Mother sat there gaping at me while I pulled down her worn old fur jacket, which had been mine years before, from its hook.

"Above all, don't tell him where I've gone," I added. "He'd murder me."

"But —"

"The money's in the usual place. . . . Take care, then — don't tell him anything and phone me tomorrow." I went out hurriedly, crossed the hall on tiptoe, and began to go downstairs.

When I was in the street I began to run. I knew that Mino was at home at that time, and I wanted to reach him before he went out with his friends after supper. I ran as far as the square, took a taxi, gave Mino's address. While the taxi sped along, I suddenly realized that I was fleeing not so much from Sonzogno as from myself, because I felt myself, in some obscure way, to be attracted by that violence and furor. I remembered the piercing cry of mingled horror and delight he had wrung from me the first and only time he had possessed me, and I told myself that on that day he had conquered me once and for all, as no other man had since known how, not even Mino. Yes, I could not help concluding, we really were made for each other, but as the body is made for the precipice that causes its head to spin and its eyes to mist, until it is finally dragged toward the giddy depths.

I climbed up the stairs two at a time, arriving out of breath, and gave Mino's name to the elderly maid who came to the door.

She looked at me with a frightened air; then, without a single word, she hurried away, leaving me on the threshold.

I thought she had gone to tell Mino, so I went into the hall and closed the door.

Then I heard a kind of whispering behind the curtain that separated the hall from the passage. The curtain was raised and the
widow Medolaghi appeared. I had forgotten her entirely since the
first and only time I had ever seen her. As she rose up suddenly before me, her heavy black figure, her deathly white face with the
black mask of her eyes filled me with a sense of terror, as if I were
in the presence of some frightening apparition. She halted at
some distance from me and addressed me.

"Did you want Signor Diodati?"

"Yes."

"He's been arrested."

I did not understand. I don't know why, but I imagined his arrest was connected in some way with Sonzogno's crime. "Arrested!" I stammered. "But he's got nothing to do with it."

"I know nothing about it," she said. "I only know they came
here, searched the house, and arrested him." I understood from
her expression of disgust that she would not tell me anything.

"But why?" I could not help asking her.

"Young lady, I've already told you I don't know anything."

"Where did they take him?"

"I don't know anything."

"But tell me at least whether he left any message."

This time she did not even reply, but turning away in stiff and
offended majesty called out, "Diomira!"

The old maid with the scared look reappeared. Her mistress
pointed to the door, and said, as she raised the curtain and turned
to go, "Show the young lady out." The curtain fell back into its
place.

Only after I had gone downstairs and was out in the street, did
I realize that Mino's arrest and Sonzogno's crime were two separate facts, independent of one another. The only real link between
them was my own fear. This unexpected convergence of misfortunes was proof to me of the lavishness of a destiny that poured out
all its tragic gifts for me at once; just as a good season makes all
kinds of different fruits ripen together. It is a fact that troubles
never come singly, as the proverb says. I felt this, rather than

thought it, as I walked from one street to the next, with my head and shoulders bowed under a shower of imaginary hailstones.

Naturally, the first person I thought of turning to was Astarita. I knew the phone number to his office by heart, so I went into the first café I came across and called him. His number was not busy but no one replied. I dialed several times and at last grew convinced that Astarita was not there. He must have gone out to supper and would be back later. I knew all this, but I had hoped that this time I would find him in his office, as an exception to the rule.

I looked at my watch. It was eight o'clock in the evening and Astarita would not be back in his office before ten. I stood rigid on a street corner; the curved surface of a bridge lay before me, with its unending flow of pedestrians, alone or in groups, and they rushed toward me, dark and hurrying, like dead leaves driven by a ceaseless wind. But the rows of houses beyond the bridge created an impression of peace, with all their windows lit up and people moving back and forth among the tables and other furniture. It occurred to me that I was not far away from the central police station, where I imagined Mino must have been taken, and although I knew it was a desperate undertaking, I decided to go straight there to ask for news of him. I knew in advance that they would not give me any, but that did not matter; I wanted more than anything to feel that I was doing something for him.

I followed the side streets, keeping close to the walls, reached the police station, mounted the few steps, and entered. A guard who was leaning back on a chair in the booth by the door, reading a newspaper with his feet on another chair and his cap on the table, asked me where I was going. "Alien's Office," I replied. This was one of the many departments at the police station and I had heard Astarita refer to it one time, I do not remember why.

I did not know where I was going, but I began to climb at random up the dirty, badly lit staircase. I kept on running into clerks or uniformed policemen, who were going upstairs or coming down, their hands full of papers, and I kept close to the wall on the darkest side with my face lowered. On every landing I had a glimpse of low, dark, dirty corridors with people moving to and fro, scanty lighting, open doors, rooms and rooms. The police station seemed to be like some kind of an extremely busy beehive, but the bees who inhabited it certainly did not alight on flowers, and their honey, of which I was tasting the flavor for the first time in my life, was rank, black, and very bitter.

When I reached the third floor, I felt so desperate that I chose one of the halls haphazardly. No one looked at me, no one troubled about me. Door after door, mostly open, stood on each side of the corridor and uniformed policemen were sitting in the door-ways on straw-bottomed chairs, smoking and chatting. The view inside each room was always the same — shelf upon shelf of files, a table, and a policeman seated behind the table with a pen in his hand. The hall was not straight but curved slightly, so that after a short time I had lost my way. Every now and again it led down into a lower hallway and I had to descend three or four steps — or it crossed over other corridors that were identical in every particular, with their lights, their rows of open doors and policemen seated in the doorways. I felt bewildered. At one point, I had the impression that I was retracing my own steps and was following a corridor I had already gone down once before. A messenger passed by, so I asked him, at random, for the "deputy superintendent" and without speaking he pointed to a dark passage nearby, between two doors. I went toward it, descended four steps and entered a low and extremely narrow little corridor. At the same moment a door opened at the end, where this kind of entrail of a corridor formed a right angle, and two men appeared; they were walking away from from me toward the corner. One of them was holding the other by the wrist and for a moment I thought it was Mino. "Mino!" I cried, and hurled myself forward.

I did not manage to reach them because someone seized me by the arm. It was a very young policeman with a thin, dark face, his cap perched sideways on a mass of curly, black hair. "Who do you want? Who are you looking for?" he asked me.

The two men had turned at my cry and I could see I was mistaken. "They've arrested my friend —" I panted. "I wanted to know whether he's been brought here."

"What's his name?" asked the policeman, with an air of peremptory authority and without letting me go.

"Giacomo Diodati."

"What does he do?"

"He's a student."

"When was he arrested?"

I suddenly realized he was questioning me in this way to give himself an air of importance and that he knew nothing. "Instead of asking me so many questions," I replied angrily, "tell me where he is."

We were alone in the corridor. He looked around and then pressing close to me whispered in a fatuous tone of understanding, "We'll go see the student — but give me a kiss in the meantime."

"Let me go! Don't waste my time!" I shouted furiously. I pushed him away, ran off, entered another hallway, and saw an open door and beyond the door a room larger than the others, with a desk at the end where a middle-aged man was seated. I went in. "I want to know where Diodati the student has been taken — he was arrested this afternoon," I said without pausing to get my breath.

The man raised his eyes from his desk where a newspaper lay open before him and looked at me in astonishment. "You want to know —"

"Yes, where Diodati the student, who was arrested this afternoon, has been taken."

"But who are you? How dare you come in here?

"That's none of your business — just tell me where he is."

"Who are you?" he shouted, and hammered with his fist on the table. "How dare you? Do you know where you are?"

I suddenly realized that I would learn nothing and that I was in danger of being arrested myself, and then I would be unable to talk to Astarita, and Mino would not be set free. "It doesn't matter," I said withdrawing. "I made a mistake — I'm sorry."

My apologies made him even more furious than the questions that had preceded them. But by now I was near the door. "You make the Fascist salute on entering and leaving this room," he shouted, as he pointed to a notice that hung above his head. I nodded as if in agreement that it was quite true, one ought to enter and leave the room with the Fascist salute; and I left the room, walking backward. I went back the whole length of the corridor, wandered about for a while, and at last, having found the staircase, I hurried down it. I passed the porter's booth and came out into the open once more.

The only result of my visit to the police station was that it had helped some time to pass. I reckoned that if I were to walk very slowly toward Astarita's Ministry it would take me about three-quarters of an hour, or even an hour. When I got there I could sit in a café near the Ministry and phone Astarita after about twenty minutes, in the hope of finding him in.

While I was walking along, it occurred to me that Mino's arrest might be a kind of revenge on Astarita's part. He held an important position in the branch of the political police force that had arrested Mino; obviously they must have been keeping an eye on Mino for some time and knew of my relations with him. It was not at all unlikely that the papers had passed through Astarita's hands and that he had given orders for Mino's arrest out of jealousy. At this thought, a kind of rage against Astarita overwhelmed me. I knew he was still in love with me and I felt quite capable of making him pay bitterly for his cruel deed if my suspicions turned out to be well-founded. But at the same time I realized, with a sense of misgiving, that perhaps this was not the case and that I was preparing, with my feeble weapons, to fight a hidden foe who had no features and whose properties were rather those of an ingenious mechanism than of a sensitive man swayed by his emotions.

When I reached the Ministry, I gave up the idea of going to sit in a café and went straight to the telephone. This time someone lifted the receiver at the first ring and it was Astarita's voice that answered me.

"It's Adriana," I said impetuously, "and I want to see you."

"At once?"

"Yes, immediately, it's urgent. I'm down here outside the Ministry."

He paused to think for a moment, then said I could come. This was the second time I had climbed the stairs in Astarita's Ministry, but I now did so in a very different state of mind from the first time. Then I had been afraid Astarita might blackmail me, afraid that he might upset my marriage with Gino, afraid of the vague threat all poor people feel hanging over them where the police are concerned. I had gone there with a tremulous heart, a quivering spirit. Now, on the contrary, I was going there in an aggressive mood, with the idea of blackmailing Astarita in my turn, determined to use every means in my power to get Mino back. But my aggressiveness could not be explained solely by my love for Mino. My scorn for Astarita formed part of it, too — and my scorn for his Ministry, for politics, and for Mino himself, inasmuch as he troubled himself with politics. I understood nothing at all about politics, but perhaps it was this very ignorance of mine that made politics seem a ridiculous, unimportant thing compared with my love for Mino. I remembered the way Astarita's speech was impeded by his stammer every time he saw me, or even when he only heard my voice, and I thought complacently that he certainly did not stammer when he faced one of his chiefs, even if it was Mussolini himself. With these thoughts in my mind, I hurried along the huge corridors of the Ministry and noticed I was looking scornfully at all the clerks I happened to meet. I longed to snatch the red and green folders they were squeezing under their arms and throw them away, to scatter to the winds all their papers full of prohibitions and iniquity.

"I have to speak to Dr. Astarita at once — I have an appointment and can't wait," I said imperiously to the receptionist who came toward me in the anteroom. He looked at me in amazement but did not dare to protest and went to announce me.

As soon as Astarita saw me, he hurried forward, kissed my hand, and led me toward a divan at the end of the room. This was the way he had greeted me the first time, too, and I suppose it was the way he behaved to all the women who came to his office. I restrained the surge of anger that I felt swelling within me as well as I could. "Look," I said, "if you've had Mino arrested —

have him set free at once. Otherwise you can count on never seeing me again."

An expression of profound astonishment mixed with unpleasant reflection colored his face, and I realized he knew nothing. "Just a moment — what the . . . What Mino?" he stuttered.

"I thought you knew about it," I said. And then I told him, as briefly as possible, the whole story of my love for Mino and how he had been arrested at his house that afternoon. I saw him change color when I said I loved Mino, but I preferred to tell him the truth, not only because I was afraid of harming Mino if I lied, but also because I longed to proclaim my love to the whole world. Now, after discovering that Astarita had had nothing to do with Mino's arrest, the rage that had sustained me collapsed, and I felt utterly weak and disarmed once again. So although I began my tale in a firm, excited voice, I ended it in tears. In fact, my eyes were overflowing. "I don't know what they'll do to him," I said in anguish. "He says they beat them —"

Astarita interrupted me immediately. "Don't worry. If he were a workingman . . . but since he's a student —"

"But I don't want . . . I don't want him to be locked up!" I cried tearfully.

Then we were both silent. I tried to master my emotion and Astarita looked at me. For the first time he seemed reluctant to do me the favor I was asking him. But his unwillingness to satisfy me must have been due in part to his disappointment at finding that I was in love with another man. "If you get him out," I said, as I placed my hand over his, "I promise I'll do anything you want."

He looked at me irresolutely, and although my heart was not in it I bent forward and offered him my lips. "Well — will you do me this favor?" I asked.

He gazed at me, torn between the temptation to kiss me and his consciousness of the humiliating significance of that kiss, offered by my tear-stained face as a bribe. Then he pushed me away, leaped to his feet, told me to wait, and disappeared.

I was certain now that Astarita would have Mino freed. I was so inexperienced in these matters that I imagined Astarita telephoning a servile warder and telling him in enraged tones to free the student Giacomo Diodati immediately. I counted the minutes impatiently, and when Astarita reappeared I rose to my feet, thinking I would thank him and then hurry away to meet Mino.

But there was a singularly unpleasant expression on Astarita's face, a mixture of disappointment and malicious anger. "What do you mean by saying he's been arrested?" he said shortly. "He fired on the police and ran off — one of the policemen is dying in the hospital. If they catch him now, as they most certainly will, I can't do anything more for him."

I stood there breathless with astonishment. I remembered I had removed the bullets from the pistol — but, of course, he might have reloaded it without my knowledge. Then, on second thought, I was filled with joy and this joy sprang from very different feelings, as I realized at once. It was the joy of knowing Mino was free; but it was also the joy of knowing he had killed a policeman, which was an action I had thought him incapable of and which profoundly modified the idea I had had of him until that moment. I wondered at the aggressive, urgent force with which my heart, usually so opposed to all forms of violence, applauded Mino's desperate action; it really was the same kind of irresistible pleasure I had felt when I had reconstructed Sonzogno's crime in my own mind, but this time it was accompanied by a form of moral justification. Then I began to think how I would soon find him again and how we would run away and hide together; we might even go abroad, where as I knew political refugees were welcomed; and my heart swelled with hope. I also imagined that perhaps a new life was really about to begin for me, and I told myself that I owed this renewal of my life to Mino and his courage and I was filled with gratitude and love for him. Meanwhile Astarita was pacing furiously up and down the room, stopping from time to time to shift some object on his desk. "Obviously he rallied after he was arrested," I said calmly, "so he fired and escaped."

Astarita stood still and looked at me, twisting his whole face into an ugly grimace. "You're glad, aren't you?" he said.

"He was right to kill the policeman," I said straightforwardly. "He was trying to take him to jail — you'd have done the same yourself."

"I have nothing to do with politics," he answered unpleasantly, "and the policeman was only doing his duty: he had a wife and children."

"If Mino is involved in politics, he must have his own good reasons for it," I replied, "and the policeman should have known that a man will do anything rather than let himself be carried off to jail. So much the worse for him —"

I felt peaceful because I imagined Mino going freely about the streets of the city, and I was eagerly anticipating the moment when he would summon me from his hiding place and I would see him again. Astarita seemed to lose all self-control at the sight of my composure. "But we'll find him again," he cried suddenly, "What do you think — that we won't be able to find him?"

"I don't know anything. I'm glad he got away, that's all."

"We'll find him and then he can be sure he won't have it so easy."

"Do you know why you're so angry?" I asked him after a moment.

"I'm not angry at all."

"Because you hoped he'd been arrested so you could show off your generosity to me and to him — and instead he slipped out of your hands. And that makes you angry."

I saw him shrug his shoulders furiously. Then the telephone rang and Astarita lifted the receiver with the relieved air of a person who has succeeded in finding some excuse for breaking off an embarrassing discussion. At the very first words I saw his face, like a landscape gradually illuminated by a sudden ray of sunshine on a stormy day, change from grim annoyance to a more serene expression; and I interpreted this as a bad sign, though I could not say why. The call was a lengthy one, but Astarita never said anything except yes or no, so that I could not tell what the discussion was about. "I'm sorry for your sake," he said as he hung up the receiver, "but the first report about that student's arrest was wrong. Police headquarters had sent their men both to his house and to yours, to make absolutely sure of getting him, no matter what — and in fact they did arrest him, at the widow's house where he rented a room. But they found someone else at your place, a small, blond man with a Northern accent who, as soon as he saw them, shot at them and escaped instead of showing his papers as they asked. At the time they thought it was your student, but instead it was obviously someone who had his own account to settle with the law."

I felt faint. So Mino was in jail; and Sonzogno was convinced I had denounced him. Anyone, seeing me disappear and then seeing the police arrive immediately afterward, would have thought the same. Mino was in prison and Sonzogno was looking for me to revenge himself on me. I was so dazed that I could only murmur, "Poor me," as I took a step toward the door.

I must have gone very pale because Astarita immediately lost his dark, triumphant look of satisfaction and came up to me. "Sit down," he said anxiously, "Let's talk it over — nothing is irrevocable."

I shook my head and put my hand on the door. Astarita stopped me. "Look," he stammered, "I promise you I'll do all I can. I'll question him myself — and then, if it's nothing serious, I'll have him set free as soon as possible. Is that all right?"

"Yes, that's all right," I said dully. "Whatever you do," I added with an effort, "you know I'll be grateful."

I knew by now that Astarita really would do all that lay in his power to free Mino, as he had said. And I had only one desire — to go away, to leave his dreadful Ministry as quickly as I could. But he was addressing me again, as a scrupulous policeman. "By the way, if you have any reason to be afraid of that man they found at your place, tell me his name. That'll make it easier for us to lay our hands on him."

"I don't know his name," I said and started to leave.

"In any case," he insisted, "you'd better go on your own to the commissioner of police. Tell him what you know — they'll tell you to keep yourself at their disposal and then they'll let you go. But if you don't go, it'll look bad for you."

I replied that I would go and said good-bye. He did not close the door at once but stood watching me from the threshold while I walked away across the anteroom.

9

ONCE I WAS OUTSIDE THE Ministry, I walked hastily to the nearest piazza, as if I were running away. Only when I had reached the middle of the square did I realize that I had no idea where to go and I began to wonder where I could take shelter. At first I had thought of Gisella; but her house was a long way off and my legs were giving way under me through sheer exhaustion. Besides, I was not at all sure that Gisella would be willing to take me in. Zelinda, the woman who rented out rooms and whom I had mentioned to my mother on my way out, was the only other solution. She was a friend of mine, and, besides, her house was nearby; I decided to go to her.

Zelinda lived in a yellowish building, one of many of the same kind, overlooking the station square. This house of Zelinda's was remarkable, among many other particulars, in that it had a staircase that was immersed, even in the mornings, in an all but impenetrable obscurity. There was no elevator, there were no windows, and as you climbed up in almost total darkness you were liable to bump into the shadowy forms of people coming down, clinging to the same handrail. A perpetual stench of cooking tainted the air; but it was cooking that might have been done years before, whose odors had been decomposing all this time in the dank and chilly air. My legs trembled and I was sick at heart as I mounted those stairs that I had climbed so often before, followed closely by some impatient lover.

"I want a room — for tonight," I said to Zelinda, who came to open the door.

Zelinda was a corpulent woman, no more than middle-aged, perhaps, but looking old beyond her years on account of her obesity. Gouty, with blotchy, unhealthy cheeks, dull, bleary blue eyes, and scant dirty blond hair, which was always disheveled and hung down in tufts like the rough ends of tow ropes, she still retained in her features some remnants of affectionate grace, as a ray of sun will linger in stagnant water at sunset. "I've got a room," she said. "Are you alone?"

"Yes, I'm alone."

I went in and she closed the door. She stumbled along in front of me, broad and dumpy in her old dressing gown, with her knot of hair hanging down half undone on her shoulders, and all her hairpins sticking out. The flat was as chilly and dark as the stairway. But here the smell of cooking was recent as of good, fresh food being prepared that moment. "I was just getting supper," she explained, turning around and smiling at me. Zelinda, who rented out rooms by the hour, was fond of me, I did not know why. After my usual visits she often detained me to chat and offer me sweets and liqueurs. She was unmarried and probably no one had ever made love with her, as she had been deformed by obesity ever since childhood — her virginity could be deduced from the shyness, curiosity, and clumsiness with which she questioned me about my affairs. Utterly lacking in envy and malice, I think she secretly regretted that she had never done what she knew was being done in her rooms; and that her occupation of renting them out by the hour satisfied not so much her business sense as her perhaps unconscious desire not to feel entirely excluded from the forbidden paradise of love-making.

At the end of the hall there were two doors I knew well. Zelinda opened the left-hand one and preceded me into the room. She lit the three-branched lamp with its white glass tulips and went to close the shutters. It was a large, clean room. But its cleanliness seemed to throw into pitiless relief the worn-out poverty of the furnishings — the threadbare carpets by the bed, the darns in the cotton coverlet, the rusty stains on the mirrors, the chips on the jug and basin. She came toward me. "Don't you feel well?" she asked me as she looked at me.

"I feel fine."

"Why don't you sleep at your own place?"

"I didn't want to."

"Let's see if I can guess," she said with a fond, knowing air. "You've had a disappointment — you were expecting someone and he didn't turn up."

"Perhaps."

"And let's see if I'm right this time, too — it was that dark-haired officer you came with last time."

This was not the first time that Zelinda had asked me questions of this kind. "You're right — and then?" I replied at random, almost choking with anguish.

"Oh nothing — but, you see, I understand you at once! I guessed what was the matter at first glance. But you mustn't be upset — if he didn't come, he must have had some reason for it. Soldiers, you know, aren't always free to . . ."

I did not reply. She looked at me for a moment. Then she addressed me again in her fond, hesitant, coaxing voice. "Do you want to keep me company at supper? There's something nice."

"No thanks," I replied hastily. "I've already eaten."

She looked at me once again and gave me a little tap on the cheek in place of a caress. "Now I'll give you something you surely won't refuse," she said, with the promising, mysterious expression of an old aunt talking to some young nephew. She pulled a bunch of keys out of her pocket, went over to the chest of drawers and opened one of the drawers with her back to me.

I had undone my coat and now, leaning against the table with one hand on my hip, I watched Zelinda rummaging about in the bottom of the drawer. I remembered that Gisella often came to that room with her men friends, and I recalled that Zelinda did not like Gisella. She liked me for myself and not because she liked everyone. I felt consoled. After all, I thought, everything in the world was not police, ministries, prisons, and other such cruel, heartless things. Meanwhile Zelinda had finished rummaging in her drawer. She shut it carefully and came over to me, repeating, "Here — you surely won't refuse this," and put something down on the mat on the table. I looked and saw five cigarettes, good ones, gold-tipped, a handful of sweets wrapped in colored papers, and four little colored fruits made of almond paste. "How's that?" she asked, giving me another little pat on the cheek.

"That's fine, thanks," I stammered in embarrassment.

"Don't mention it, don't mention it — if you need anything, just call me, don't be afraid."

When I was alone once more I felt chilled to the bone and greatly troubled. I was not sleepy and I did not want to go to bed; but in that cold room where the chill of winter seemed to have been preserved for years as it is in churches and cellars, there was nothing else to do. I had never had to face this problem the other times I had come here — both the man accompanying me and I myself longed only to get beneath the sheets and warm one another; and although I felt no emotion toward those lovers picked up on the street, the act of love itself absorbed me and immersed me in its spell. It now seemed incredible to me that I had made love and had been made love to among such squalid furniture, in such a gelid atmosphere. The ardor of the senses surely created an illusion for me and my companions each time, making those absurdly alien objects both pleasant and familiar. It occurred to me that my life, if I were never to see Mino again, would be just like that room. Looking back at my life objectively, without illusions, I saw that it contained nothing really beautiful or intimate, that actually, it was entirely made up of ugly, worn, chilly things, just like Zelinda's room. I shuddered and began to undress slowly.

The sheets were icy and clammy with dampness; to such an extent that I had the impression, when I stretched myself out in the bed, that I was imprinting the shape of my body on wet clay. For a long time I remained absorbed in thought while the sheets gradually grew warmer. I went off on a sidetrack thinking about Sonzogno and lost myself in analyzing the motives and consequences of that whole shadowy affair. Sonzogno certainly believed by now that I had betrayed him and there was no doubt that appearances were all against me. But only appearances? I remembered his phrase, "I have a feeling I'm being followed," and I asked myself whether the priest had talked, after all. It did not seem likely, but so far there was nothing to prove that he had not.

Still thinking of Sonzogno, I began to imagine what must have happened at home after my flight. Sonzogno waiting, getting impatient, dressing, the entrance of the two policemen, Sonzogno pulling out his gun, shooting without warning, and running away. These imaginary visions of what had occurred gave me an obscure, insatiable pleasure, as when I had reconstructed Sonzogno's crime. Time and time again I went over the scene of the shooting, dwelling lovingly on all the details; and there was no doubt that, in the struggle between Sonzogno and the police, I was heart and soul on Sonzogno's side. I trembled with joy at seeing the wounded policeman fall to the ground; I heaved a sigh of relief when Sonzogno escaped; I followed him anxiously down the stairs; my peace of mind was restored only when I saw him disappear in the distant darkness of the main road. At last I grew tired of this kind of mental cinema, and turned off the light.

I had already noticed on other occasions that the bed stood against a door that communicated with the next room. As soon as I had turned out the light, I saw that the two halves of the door did not meet properly, so that a vertical ray of light shone through the gap. I pulled myself up onto the pillow on my elbows, slipped my head between the iron curls of the bedstead and put my eye to the crack. I did not do this out of curiosity, since I already knew what I would see and hear through that slit, but fear of my thoughts and loneliness drove me to seek companionship in the next room, even if I could do so only by spying. But for a long time I could see no one at all — there was a round table in front of the crack in the door and the light from the lamp poured down onto the table, beyond which I caught a glimpse of a wardrobe mirror gleaming in deep shadow. But I could hear voices — the usual talk that was so familiar to me, about one's hometown, one's age and name. The woman's voice was unemotional and reserved, the man's urgent and excited. They were talking in some corner of the room, perhaps they were already in bed. I began to have a sharp pain in my neck from gazing so long without seeing anything and I was about to turn away when the woman appeared beyond the table, in front of the shadowed mirror. She was standing up straight with her back toward me, naked, but visible only from the waist up, since the table hindered my view. She must have been very young; her back, under a mane of curly hair, was thin, hard, without grace, and of an anemic whiteness. She looked as if she were not even twenty years old, but her breasts were flaccid; she may have already had a child. She must be one of those starved young girls, I thought, who hang around the municipal parks near the station, hatless and often coatless, badly madeup, and ragged, their feet thrust into enormous orthopedic shoes. When she laughed she must show her gums, I thought. All these things occurred to me quite spontaneously, without reflection, because the sight of that miserable, naked back comforted me and I felt I loved that girl and understood only too well the feelings she was experiencing at that moment while looking at herself in the mirror. But the man's voice called out roughly, "Will you let me in on what you're doing?" and she left the mirror. For a moment I saw her sideways, with her curved shoulders and scraggy chest, just as I had imagined her. Then she vanished and a second later the light was extinguished.

The vague affection I had felt for the girl while I could see her was extinguished, too, and I found myself all alone once more in the big, still, cold bed, in that darkness filled with cold, worn-out objects. I thought of the two of them there on the other side of the wall, how they would fall asleep together after a while. She would lie at her companion's back with her chin resting on his shoulder, her legs entwined in his, her arm around his waist, her hand on his groin, and her fingers lost languidly in the folds of his belly — like roots seeking life in the blackest earth. And suddenly I felt like an uprooted plant myself, thrown out on smooth stone where I would wither and die. I missed Mino, and if I stretched out my hand, I became conscious of an enormous, empty, frozen space that surrounded me on all sides, while I lay there huddled up in the middle without protection or companionship. I felt a strong and sorrowful desire to embrace him, but he was not there, and I felt myself to be a widow and began to weep, hugging sheets in my arms, pretending to myself that I was holding him. At last I fell asleep, I know not how.

I have always slept well and deeply. Sleep for me is like an appetite, easily satisfied without any particular effort or interruption. So when I woke up the next morning, I was almost surprised at first to find myself in Zelinda's room, stretched out in that bed, in a ray of sunshine that had slipped through the shutters and fallen onto the pillow and the wall. I had hardly realized where I was when I heard the phone ring in the hallway. Zelinda answered, I heard her say my name, and then she knocked at the door. I leaped out of bed and ran to the door as I was, in my nightgown and bare feet.

The hall was empty, the receiver lay on a ledge, and Zelinda had gone back into the kitchen. I heard Mother's voice at the other end of the line, asking:

"Is that you, Adriana?"

"Yes."

"Why did you go away? Things have been happening here. . . . You might at least have warned me. . . . Oh, what a scare!"

"Yes, I know all about it," I said hurriedly. "It's no use talking about it."

"I was so worried about you," she went on, "and then there's Signor Diodati."

"Signor Diodati?"

"Yes, he came over very early this morning. He wants to see you urgently. He says he'll wait here."

"Tell him I'll be there right away. Tell him I'll be there in a minute."

I hung up the phone, ran into my room, and dressed as quickly as I could. I had not even hoped for Mino to be set free so quickly, and I felt less happy than I would have if I had waited for his liberation for a few days or a week. I mistrusted such a speedy release, and could not help feeling vaguely apprehensive. Every fact has a meaning, and I was unable to grasp the meaning of that premature return to freedom. But I calmed down when I thought that possibly Astarita had managed to have him set free immediately as he had promised. In any case, I was impatient to see him again, and my impatience was a joyful sensation, although it was also painful.

I finished dressing, put the cigarettes, almond sweets, and candies, which I had not touched the evening before, into my purse so as not to hurt Zelinda's feelings, and went into the kitchen to say good-bye to her.

"Feeling more cheerful?" she said. "Got over your bad mood?"

"I was tired. Good-bye, then."

"Now, now! Do you think I didn't hear you on the telephone? Signor Diodati, eh? Here, wait a minute — have a cup of coffee." She was still talking when I was already out of the apartment.

Perched on the edge of the seat in the taxi, with my hands gripping my purse, I was ready to leap out as soon as it stopped; I was afraid I would find a crowd in front of the house on account of Sonzogno's shoot-out. I even wondered whether it was wise to go home — Sonzogno might turn up to carry out his vendetta. But I realized I did not care. If Sonzogno wanted to take his revenge on me, he could. I longed to see Mino and was determined I would never hide myself again for something I had not done.

At home I met no one at the street door and no one on the stairs. I rushed into the living room and saw Mother sitting at the sewing machine by the window. The sun poured in through the dirty windowpanes, the cat was sitting on the table licking its paws. Mother stopped sewing immediately. "So here you are, back at last" she said. "You might at least have told me you'd gone out to get the police!"

"What police? What do you mean?"

"I'd have gone with you — if you only knew how frightened I was."

"But I didn't go out to get the police," I said irritably. "I went out, that's all. The police were looking for someone else. That man must have had something on his conscience."

"So you won't even tell me," she said, giving me a look of maternal reproach.

"Tell you what?"

"It's not like I'll go around talking about it — but you'll never get me to believe you went out like that for nothing . . . and, in fact, the police came just a few minutes after you'd left."

"But it isn't true, I —"

"You were right to go, anyway. There are some terrible people around here. Do you know what one of the policemen said? 'I've seen that face before,' he said."

I saw that there was no way of convincing her; she thought I had gone out to denounce Sonzogno and there was nothing I could do about it. "All right, all right," I interrupted her brusquely. "What about the wounded man? How did they take him away?"

"What wounded man?"

"They told me a man was dying. . . ."

"No, no, they told you wrong. One of the policemen got his arm grazed by a bullet. I bandaged it up for him myself. But he went away on his own two legs. Still, if you'd heard the shots! They were shooting on the stairs. The whole house was in an uproar. Then they questioned me, but I said I didn't know anything."

"Where is Signor Diodati?"

"In your room."

I had lingered with Mother for a little while because I now felt almost reluctant to go in to Mino, as though I anticipated some bad news. I left the living room and went toward my bedroom. It was plunged in utter darkness, but even before I put my hand out to the switch, I heard Mino's voice say out of the dark, "I beg you not to turn the light on."

The peculiar tone of his voice struck me; it did not sound at all cheerful. I shut the door, groped my way to the bed, sat down on the edge of it. I could feel he was lying on his side close to where I was sitting. "Don't you feel well?" I asked him.

"I feel fine."

"Aren't you tired?"

"No, I'm not tired."

I had expected quite a different kind of meeting. But it is a fact that joy and light are inseparable. In the dark like that my eyes seemed unable to sparkle, my voice was incapable of breaking into exclamations of joy, my hands could not reach out to recognize his beloved features. I waited for some time. "What do you want to do?" I asked him then as I bent toward him. "Do you want to go to sleep?"

"No."

"Do you want me to go away?"

"No."

"Do you want me to stay here beside you?"

"Yes."

"Do you want me to lie on the bed?"

"Yes."

"Do you want to make love?" I asked randomly.

"Yes."

This reply was a surprise to me, because, as I have already said, he never really felt inclined to make love to me. I suddenly felt myself growing excited. "Do you like to make love with me?" I asked him in a soft, inviting tone.

"Yes."

"Will you always like it from now on?"

"Yes."

"And will we always be together?"

"Yes."

"Don't you want me to turn the light on?"

"No."

"I doesn't matter; I'll get undressed in the dark."

I began to undress with the intoxicating sensation of having won a complete victory. I imagined that the night he had spent in prison had unexpectedly shown him that he loved me and needed me. I was wrong, as I shall relate; and although I was right in thinking that there was a connection between his arrest and his sudden surrender, I did not understand that this change in his attitude held nothing complimentary or even encouraging in it for me. On the other hand, it would have been difficult to be so clear-sighted at that moment. My body urged me impetuously toward him, like a horse that has been curbed too long, and I was impatient to give him the ardent, joyous welcome his attitude and the darkness had prevented me giving him earlier.

But when I drew close to him and bent over the bed to stretch myself beside him, I suddenly felt him grip my knees with his arms and then bite me so savagely on the left hip that it bled. I felt an acute spasm of pain and at the same time the precise sensation that the bite expressed some indefinable despair he was experiencing. It was as though, rather than being two lovers about to make love, we were two of the damned driven by hatred, rage, and sorrow to bury our teeth in one another's flesh in the depths of some new kind of hell. The bite seemed endless — it was really as though he wanted to tear out a piece of my flesh with his teeth. At last, although I half wanted him to bite me, liked him biting me, even sensing that there was little love in it, I could not stand the pain any longer and I pushed him away. "No, no," I said in a humble, broken voice, "what are you doing? You're hurting me —"

And so, almost immediately, my illusion of victory came to an end. After this, we said not one word more all the time we were making love; nevertheless from his actions I was able to guess dimly the true significance of his abandonment, which he later explained to me in detail. I understood that until that moment he had wanted not so much to ignore me as to ignore that part of himself that desired me; now, instead, he was giving this part of himself free rein, whereas before he had fought against it — that was all. I had nothing to do with it, and he loved me no more now than he had done before. It was all the same to him whether he had me or someone else, and, as before, I was nothing more than a means he adopted to punish or reward himself. I was not so much conscious of thinking these things while we lay in the dark together, as of feeling them in my flesh and my blood, just as some time before I had sensed the fact that Sonzogno was a monster although I had known nothing of his crime. But I loved him; and my love was stronger than my knowledge.

Still, I was amazed at the violence and insatiability of his desire, which had once been so grudging. I had always thought that he restrained himself for reasons of health, since he was delicate. So, when he began all over again for the third time when he had just that moment taken his pleasure of me, I could not help whispering to him, "For me, go ahead . . . but watch out you don't hurt yourself."

I thought I heard him laugh and I heard his voice murmuring in my ear, "Nothing can ever hurt me now."

That "ever" gave me a tragic feeling and so that the pleasure I felt in his embraces was almost destroyed, and I waited impatiently for the moment when I could talk to him and finally find out what had actually happened. After we had finished making love, he seemed to drop off but perhaps he did not really sleep. I waited for a reasonable length of time before speaking to him. "And now tell me what happened," I said in a low voice, with an effort that made my heart miss a beat.

"Nothing happened."

"But something must have happened."

He was silent for a moment and then spoke as if to himself. "After all, I suppose you'll have to know, too. Well, this is what happened. At eleven o'clock last night I became a traitor."

An icy chill gripped me at these words, not so much on account of the words themselves as for the tone in which he uttered them. "A traitor?" I stammered. "Why?"

He replied in his cold and grimly humorous tone, "Signor Mino, among the comrades of his political faith, was known for the intransigence of his opinions and the violence of his resentments — Signor Mino was actually considered by them as their future leader — Signor Mino was so sure that he would do himself credit in any circumstances that he almost hoped he would be arrested and put to the test — because, you see, Signor Mino thought that arrest, imprisonment, and other sufferings are essential to the life of a political man, just as long cruises, hurricanes, and shipwrecks form part of the life of a sailor. But instead, at the first heavy seas the sailor felt as sick as the basest, most stupid woman . . . Signor Mino no sooner found himself in the presence of an ordinary little policeman than he blurted everything out without even waiting to be threatened or tortured — in other words, he's a traitor. So since yesterday Signor Mino said good-bye to his political career and entered upon that of — shall we say informer?"

"You were afraid!" I exclaimed.

"No," he answered immediately. "Perhaps I wasn't even afraid. Only the same thing happened to me as happened that evening I was with you — when you wanted me to explain my ideas to you. Suddenly nothing seemed to matter at all. I almost took a liking to the man who was questioning me. He wanted to know certain things; at the moment, I didn't care about concealing them from him and I told him what he wanted to know. Quite simply, like I'm talking to you now, or," he added after a moment of reflection, "not so simply . . . with solicitude, eagerness, with zeal, you might say. A little more, and he would have had to moderate my enthusiasm."

I thought of Astarita and I found it strange that Mino should have taken a liking to him. "Who questioned you?" I asked.

"I don't know him. A young man with a sallow face, bald head, black eyes, very well dressed. He must have been one of the high-ups."

"And you liked him!" I could not help exclaiming, since I recognized Astarita from the description.

Mino began to laugh in the dark with his mouth on my ear. "Slow down . . . not him personally, but his position. You know — when you give up being what you know you ought to be, or don't even know what you ought to be, what you really are comes to the surface. And am I the son of a rich landowner or not? And wasn't that man actually protecting my interests, by doing his job? We recognized that we belonged to the same race, that we were united in the same cause. What did you think? That I liked him for himself? No, no. I liked his function — I realized that it was I who was paying him; that it was he who defended me; I who stood behind him as a master, even as I stood facing him as the accused."

He laughed, or rather, gave a coughing sort of laugh that grated horribly on my ears. I understood nothing except that something very tragic had happened and that my whole life was once more in question. "But perhaps I'm doing myself an injustice," he added after a moment, "and I only talked because it didn't matter to me not to talk — because everything suddenly seemed absurd and unimportant and I didn't understand any of the things I ought to have believed in anymore."

"You didn't understand anything anymore?" I repeated mechanically.

"No, or rather, I only understood the words themselves, as I would understand them now, but not the facts underlying them. Now how can you suffer for words? Words are sounds; it would have been like going to prison for the braying of an ass or the creaking of a wheel. Words no longer had any value for me, they seemed all alike and all absurd. He wanted words and I gave them to him, as many as he wanted."

"Well, then," I could not help objecting, "since they were only words, what does it matter?"

"Yes, but unfortunately, as soon as I'd pronounced them, they ceased to be mere words and became facts."

"Why?"

"Because I began to suffer. Because I was sorry I had said them. Because I realized, I felt, that in saying those words I had become myself that fact which is known by the word *traitor*."

"But why did you say them, then?"

"Why do people talk in their sleep?" he said slowly. "Perhaps I was asleep. But now I've woken up."

And so he went around and around but always returned to the same point. I felt cruelly pierced to the heart. "But maybe you're mistaken," I said with an effort. "Maybe you think you said all sorts of things, when actually you didn't say a thing."

"No, I'm not mistaken," he said briefly.

I was silent for a moment. "What about your friends?" I asked him.

"What friends?"

"Tullio and Tommaso."

"I don't know anything about them," he said, with a kind of ostentatious indifference. "They'll be arrested."

"No, they won't be arrested!" I exclaimed. I thought Astarita certainly would not have taken advantage of Mino's momentary weakness. But at the idea of his two friends being arrested, the gravity of the whole matter began to dawn on me.

"Why not?" he said. "I gave their names. There's no reason why they shouldn't be arrested."

"Oh, Mino," I could not help exclaiming painfully. "Why did you do this?"

"That's what I keep on asking myself."

"But if they aren't arrested," I went on after a moment, clinging to the only hope I had left, "nothing is irreparable. They'll never know that you —"

"Yes, but I know it!" he interrupted me. "I'll always know it. I'll always know that I'm not the same person as I was but someone else, someone I gave birth to the moment I talked as surely as a mother gives birth to her child. But unfortunately, it's not a person I like, that's the trouble. Some men kill their wives because they can't bear to live with them. Now think what it's like to be two people in one body, when one of them hates the other to death. Anyway, about my friends . . . they'll arrest them for sure."

I could not restrain myself any longer. "Even if you'd never spoken," I said, "you'd have been released all the same. And your friends aren't in any danger." Then I hurriedly told him the story of my relationship with Astarita, my intervention on his behalf, and Astarita's promise. He listened to me in silence. "Better and better!" he said at last. "So I don't owe my release only to my zeal as an informer, but also to your love affair with a policeman."

"Don't talk like that, Mino!"

"But anyway," he added after a moment, "I'm glad my friends will make out — at least I won't have this other remorse on my conscience, too."

"Look," I said eagerly, "what's the difference now between you and your friends? They owe their freedom to me, too, and to the fact that Astarita's in love with me."

"Pardon. There is a difference. They haven't talked."

"How do you know?"

"I hope not, for their sakes. But anyway in this case, sharing the burden doesn't lighten the load."

"But just act like nothing happened," I insisted again. "Go back and see them, without saying anything. What does it matter to you? Anyone can have a moment's weakness."

"Yes," he replied, "but not everyone can die and still go on living. Do you know what happened to me in that instant when I spoke? I died — just died. Died forever."

I could no longer bear the anguish that wrung my heart and I burst into tears. "Why are you crying?" he asked.

"Because of what you're saying," I answered, sobbing harder than ever. "That you're dead. I'm so frightened."

"Don't you like being with a dead man?" he asked jokingly. "It's not as dreadful as it seems. In fact, it isn't dreadful at all. I died in a very special way. My body's still very much alive. Feel if I'm not alive," and he took my hand and made me touch his body. "You can feel I'm alive." He pulled on my hand, forcing me to press it against him, and finally pulled it down to his groin and crushed it against his penis. "I'm alive all over . . . as far as you're concerned as you can see for yourself, I'm more alive than ever . . . don't worry, if we didn't make love much while I was still alive, we'll make up for it thoroughly now that I'm dead."

He flung my limp hand away from him with a kind of angry disdain. I put both hands to my face and gave way noisily to my misery and pain. I wanted to cry forever, to go on crying endlessly, because I was afraid of the moment when I would stop weeping and would be left empty, dazed, and still confronted by the un-changed situation that had provoked my outburst. The moment came, however, and I dried my wet face with the sheet and stared into the darkness with wide-open eyes. Then I heard him ask me in a gentle, affectionate voice. "Let's see what you think I ought to do," he asked.

I turned around violently, clung to him as hard as I could, and spoke with my mouth on his. "Don't think about it anymore. Don't worry about it anymore. What's done is done. That's what you ought to do."

"And then?"

"And then begin studying again. Get your degree. And after that go back to your own hometown. I don't mind if I don't see you again, as long as I know you're happy. Get a job, and when the time comes, marry a girl from that part of the world, a girl who loves you, a girl of your own class. What have you got to do with politics? You weren't made for politics, you were wrong ever to take it up. It was a mistake, but everyone makes mistakes. One day you'll think it strange that you ever thought about it at all. I really do love you, Mino. Another woman in my place wouldn't want you to leave, but if it's necessary, go away tomorrow. If you think it's best, we'll never see each other again. As long as you're happy —"

"But I'll never be happy again," he said in a clear, very deep voice. "I'm an informer."

"It's not true!" I answered in exasperation. "You're not an informer at all. And even if you were, you could be happy all the same! There are people who have committed actual crimes and are still perfectly happy. Take me, for example. When people say 'whore,' who knows what they imagine. But I'm a woman like any other, and I'm often even happy. I was so happy these past few days," I added bitterly.

"You were happy?"

"Yes, very. But I knew it couldn't last. And, in fact —" at these words I felt like crying again, but I controlled myself — "you imagined yourself to be someone completely different from who you really are. And then we know what happened. Now you must accept yourself as you really are, and everything will fall into place. What's making you so unhappy over what happened is the fact that you feel ashamed, and are afraid of what other people, your friends, will think. Give up seeing them then, see other people; the world's a big place! If they aren't fond enough of you to understand it was only a moment's weakness, stay with me. I love you and understand you and I don't judge you — really," I exclaimed forcefully at this stage, "even if you had done something a thousand time worse, you'd still be my Mino."

He kept silent. "I'm only a poor, ignorant girl, I know," I went on, "but I understand some things better than your friends and better even than you. I've had just the same feeling as you have now. The first time we met and you didn't touch me, I got it into my head that it was because you despised me, and I felt so unhappy, I suddenly lost all desire to go on living. I wanted to be someone else and at the same time I realized that was impossible and that I'd have to go on being what I was. I felt a sticky, burning kind of shame, a despair, a heartsickness. I felt shriveled, frozen, bound hand and foot. I even thought I wanted to die. . . . Then one day I went out with Mother and we happened to go into a church and there, as I prayed, I felt I understood that I had nothing to be ashamed of after all. That if I was made as I was, it meant it was the will of God; that I ought not to rebel against my fate but accept it submissively and trustfully, and that if you despised me it was your fault and not mine. In fact, I thought a great many things and at last my humiliation passed and I felt gay and lighthearted again."

He began to laugh with that laugh of his that froze me. "So you're saying," he answered, "that I ought to accept what I've done and not struggle against it. I ought to accept what I've become and not judge myself. Well, maybe such things can happen in church, but out of church —"

"Go to church, then," I suggested, clinging to this new hope.

"No, I won't. I don't believe in it and I'm just bored in church. Besides — what crazy talk!" He began to laugh again but suddenly stopped short and, seizing me by the shoulders, started to shake me violently. "Don't you understand what I've done?" he shouted. "Don't you understand? Don't you understand?" He shook me so hard that he made me lose my breath before hurling me backward with one final outburst, and then I heard him leap out of bed and begin to dress in the dark. "Don't turn the light on," he said in a menacing tone. "I've got to get used to being looked at in the face. But it's too soon yet. It'll go hard with you if you switch the light on."

I did not even dare to breathe. "Are you going?" I asked him at last.

"Yes, but I'll come back," he said, and I thought he laughed again. "Don't be afraid. I'll come back. What's more, here's a piece of good news for you — I'll come and live here with you."

"Here with me?"

"Yes, but I won't bother you. You'll be able to carry on with your usual life. Actually, though," he went on, "we could both live on what my family sends me. I was paying full board, but it would be enough for the two of us, living at home."

I found the idea that he might come and live with me more strange than pleasurable. But I did not dare say anything. He finished dressing in silence in the pitch dark. "I'll be back tonight," he then said. I heard him open the door, go out, and shut the door. I lay there in the dark, my eyes wide open.

10

*T*HAT VERY AFTERNOON I followed Astarita's advice and went to the local police station to make a statement about Sonzogno's case. I hated to go, because after what had happened to Mino anything that was remotely connected with the police inspired me with mortal dread. But by now I was almost resigned: I realized that life had lost almost all its savor for me for some time to come.

"We expected you this morning," said the commissioner of police as soon as I had told him the reason for my visit. He was a good man — I had known him for some time — and although he was the father of a family and over fifty years old, I had sensed much earlier that his feelings for me were more than friendly. What stands out in my memory of him is his nose, large and spongy, melancholy of expression. His hair was always disheveled and his eyes always half shut, as if he had only just got out of bed. These eyes, of a vivid blue, seemed to be peeping out from behind a mask; his thick, pink, wrinkled face was like the skin of those huge oranges, the last of the season, which contain nothing but a shriveled core.

I said I had been unable to come sooner. The blue eyes behind the orange-peel skin of his face looked at me for a moment and then he addressed me confidentially. "Well, what's his name?"

"How should I know?"

"Come on, of course you know."

"Word of honor," I said with my hand on my heart. "He stopped me in the Corso — I remember thinking there was something strange about him, but I didn't take any notice."

"But how was it you left him alone in your room?"

"I had an urgent appointment, so I left him."

"But he thought you'd gone out to call the police. Did you know that? And he shouted out that you'd turned him in."

"Yes, I know."

"And that he'd pay you back."

"So what?"

"But don't you realize he's a dangerous man," he added, looking at me intently, "and might even shoot you tomorrow, since he thinks you turned him in, just as he shot at the police?"

"Of course, I realize it."

"Then why won't you tell us who he is? We'll have him arrested and you won't have to worry anymore."

"But I've told you I don't know his name . . . Really . . . Am I supposed to know the names of all the men I take home?"

"But we do know his name," he suddenly declared, in a higher, more theatrical tone of voice as he leaned forward.

I knew he was only pretending. "If you know," I answered coolly, "why are you tormenting me about it? Arrest him and make an end of it."

He looked at me in silence for a moment. I noticed that his restless, troubled eyes were examining my figure rather than my face, and I understood that, suddenly and despite himself, his professional sense of duty had been overcome by his longstanding desire for me. "We also know that if he fired and then ran off, he must have had good reason for doing it," he went on.

"Oh, I'm sure of that, too."

"But you know what his reasons are."

"I don't know anything. If I don't know his name, how could I know the rest?"

"We know all about the rest," he said. By now he was speaking mechanically, as if he were thinking about something else, and I felt sure that in another moment he would get up and come over to me. "We know all about it and we'll get him. It's just a question of days — perhaps hours."

"Good for you."

He stood up as I had foreseen he would, walked around the table, came up to me, and, cupping my chin in his hand, spoke to me. "Come on, you know all about it and won't tell us. What are you afraid of?"

"I'm not afraid of anything," I answered, "and I don't know anything. And now keep your hands to yourself."

"Come on," he repeated. But he sat down again behind the table before continuing. "You're lucky because I like you and I know you're a good girl. Do you know what another man would have done in my place, to make you talk? He'd have had you kept in custody for a long time. Or sent you to San Gallicano."

I got up. "Well, I'm busy," I said. "If you don't have anything else to say to me —"

"Go ahead. But be careful what company you keep — political and otherwise."

I pretended I had not heard these last words, which he pronounced meaningfully, and I escaped as hurriedly as I could from those sordid little rooms.

As I walked along, I began to think about Sonzogno again. The commissioner of police had confirmed for me what I had already suspected: Sonzogno wanted to revenge himself upon me because he was sure I had denounced him. I was terrified; not for myself but for Mino. Sonzogno was a raving madman; if he found Mino with me, he would not hesitate to kill him, too. I must confess that the idea of dying with Mino was curiously attractive. I seemed to see the whole scene: Sonzogno would shoot and I would throw myself between him and Mino in order to shield Mino and be wounded in his place. But I did not mind the idea that Mino, too, should be wounded and that we would die together, mingling our blood. But I thought that being killed by the same murderer at the same moment would not be as wonderful as committing suicide together. A suicide pact seemed to me a worthy conclusion to a passionate love affair. It was like cutting a flower before it has withered; like shutting oneself up in silence after having heard celestial music. I had often pondered over this kind of suicide, which arrests time before it can corrupt and spoil love, and is willed and carried out through an excess of joy, rather than an inability to bear suffering. At those moments when I felt I loved Mino so intensely that I feared I might never be able to love him so much in the future, the idea of a suicide pact occurred to me quite naturally, with the same easy spontaneity with which I kissed and caressed him. But I had never spoken of it to him, because I knew that if two people commit suicide together they have to be in love to the same degree. And Mino did not love me; or if he loved me, he did not love me so much to want to cease living.

I was reflecting intensely on all these things as I walked home. But all of a sudden an attack of dizziness accompanied by a wave of nausea and a ghastly feeling of weakness throughout my body overcame me, and I just had time to go into a café nearby. I was not far from home, but I knew I did not have the strength to cover that short distance without falling down.

I sat down at one of the little tables behind the glass-fronted door and shut my eyes, overwhelmed by illness. I still felt sick to my stomach and giddy and this sensation was increased by the puffs of steam from the coffee machine, which were extremely upsetting although strangely remote. I could feel the warmth of the closed, heated room on my hands and face, but despite this I felt very cold. "A cup of coffee, Signorina Adriana?" called the man behind the counter, who knew me well, and without opening my eyes I nodded assent.

At last I recovered and sipped the coffee that the man had placed on the table in front of me. As a matter of fact, it was not the first time lately I had felt this kind of sickness but it had always been very slight, scarcely noticeable. I had not paid any attention to it, because the extraordinary and painful events in which I had been involved had prevented me from thinking about it. But now, reflecting on it and correlating the sickness with a significant interruption in my physical life, which had occurred just this same month, I became convinced that certain vague suspicions I had harbored recently, but had always pushed into the darkest background of my consciousness, must be founded on fact. There can be no doubt about it, I suddenly thought, I must be expecting a child.

I paid for the coffee and left the place. What I felt was extremely complicated and even now, after such a lapse of time, I do not find it at all easy to express it. I have already remarked that misfortunes never come singly; and this new fact, which I would have greeted joyously at any other time and in any other conditions, seemed to me to be a real piece of bad luck in the present circumstances. On the other hand, my temperament is such that an inexplicable and irresistible instinct always leads me to discover a pleasing aspect to even the most unpleasant circumstances. This time such an aspect was not at all difficult to find; it was the same feeling that fills the hearts of all women with hope and satisfaction when they learn that they are pregnant. It was true that my child would be born in the least favorable conditions imaginable; but he would still be my child; I would be the one who had given him birth and raised him and delighted in him. A child is a child, I thought, and no woman, however poor she is, however desperate her circumstances and uncertain her future, however abandoned and unprovided for, can help being happy at the idea of bringing one into the world.

These thoughts restored my calm, so that, after a moment's fear and despair, I once more felt as placid and trustful as ever. The young doctor, who had examined me some time before when Mother had dragged me to the pharmacy to find out whether Gino and I had been making love, had his consulting room not far from the café. I made up my mind to go and be examined by him. It was early and there was no one in the waiting room. The doctor, who knew me very well, greeted me cordially.

"Doctor, I'm almost sure I'm pregnant," I announced quietly as soon as he had closed the door.

He began to laugh because he knew what my profession was. "Are you sorry?" he asked me.

"Not at all. I'm glad in fact."

"Let's see."

After he had asked me several questions about my sickness, he made me lie down on the oilcloth sheet spread on the cot, and examined me. "You've hit the nail right on the head this time," he said cheerfully.

I was glad to have my suspicions confirmed without feeling any shadow of disappointment. I was perfectly calm. "I knew I was," I said. "I only came to make sure."

"You can be absolutely sure."

He rubbed his hands together as joyfully as if he were the father himself and swayed from one foot to the other, all cheerful and full of pleasure for me. Only one thing troubled me and I wanted to make certain. "How far gone am I?" I asked.

"About two months, I should say — more or less. Why? Do you want to know who it was?"

"I know already."

I went to the door. "If you need anything, come and see me," he said as he opened the door for me. "And when the time comes, we'll see that the baby is born under the best conditions possible." He, like the commissioner of police, was very fond of me. But I liked him, too, whereas I did not like the commissioner at all. I have already described the doctor once. He was a handsome young man, very dark, healthy and vigorous, with a black mustache, bright eyes and white teeth, as cheerful and lively as a gundog. I often went to him to have myself examined, at least once a fortnight, and two or three times I had let him make love to me, out of gratitude because he never made me pay him, on the same cot where he had examined me. But he was discreet and, except for an occasional playful gesture, he never tried to force his desire on me. He gave me advice, and I think he was a little bit in love with me in his own way.

I had told him I knew who was the father of my child. Actually, at that moment I only suspected it, instinctively rather than by any real calculation. But when I was out in the street again, counting the days and examining my memories, this suspicion became a certainty. I remembered the long, plaintive cry of agony and pleasure wrung from me in the darkness of my room by the mixture of terror and attraction I had felt for him, and I was sure that the father of my child could be no other than Sonzogno. It was dreadful to know that I had conceived a child by a brutal and monstrous murderer like Sonzogno, particularly since there was a danger that the son might take after his father and inherit his characteristics. On the other hand, I could not help feeling there was some justice in Sonzogno's paternity. Sonzogno was the only one of all the many men who had made love to me who had really possessed me, beyond any sentiment of love, in the darkest and most secret core of my flesh. The fact that he horrified and frightened me and that I was forced to give myself to him against my will did not alter but confirmed the fact that his possession of me had been complete and profound. Neither Gino nor Astarita nor even Mino, for whom I felt a completely different kind of passion, had aroused in me the sensation of such a legitimate possession, even though I loathed it. All this seemed strange and terrifying; but so it was. Feelings are the only things one cannot reject or deny or even, in a certain sense, analyze. I came to the conclusion that some men are made for love and some for procreation; and if it was only right that I should have a child by Sonzogno, it was no less right for me to detest him and flee from him and to love Mino instead, as I really did.

I climbed the stairs slowly, thinking of the living weight I was bearing now within my womb; when I was in the hall I heard voices in the living room. I looked in the door and was surprised to see Mino sitting at the head of the table talking peacefully to Mother, who was seated near him sewing busily. Only the central light was burning and most of the room was in darkness.

"Good evening," I said languidly as I came forward.

"Good evening, good evening," said Mino in a grating, hesitant voice. I looked at his face, saw how bright his eyes were, and felt sure he was drunk. One end of the table was spread with a little tablecloth and silverware for two, and, knowing that Mother always ate on her own in the kitchen, I realized that the second place was for Mino. "Good evening," he repeated, "I've brought my suitcases. They're in the other room. And I've made friends with your mother. We understand each other perfectly, Signora, don't we?" he said to her.

I felt faint at heart as I heard his sarcastic and grimly playful voice. I slumped down into a chair and shut my eyes for a moment. I heard my mother reply to him. "That's what you say. But if you speak badly of Adriana, we'll never get along together."

"But what have I said?" exclaimed Mino, feigning astonishment. "That Adriana was born for the life she leads. That Adriana thinks a whore's life is wonderful. What's wrong about that?"

"It isn't true," retorted Mother. "Adriana wasn't born for the life she leads. She deserved something better, much better, with her beauty. Don't you know she's one of the most beautiful girls in the neighborhood, if not in all Rome? I see lots of other girls who aren't nearly as good-looking as she is, who strike it lucky. But for Adriana, who's as beautiful as a queen, nothing . . . But I know why."

"Why?"

"Because she's too good, that's why. Because she's beautiful and good. If she were beautiful and bad, you'd see how differently things would go."

"Oh, stop it," I said, feeling embarrassed by this discussion and more particularly by Mino's tone of voice, for he seemed to be making fun of Mother. "I'm hungry. Isn't dinner ready yet?"

"It's ready now." Mother put her sewing on the table and went out hurriedly. I followed her into the kitchen.

"Are we running a boardinghouse now?" she grumbled. "He walked in as if he were the master, put his suitcases in your room, and gave me some money to go out shopping."

"Well, aren't you glad?"

"I liked it better before."

"Well, pretend we're engaged. Anyway, it's only a temporary arrangement, he's only here for a few days, he won't stay forever."

I said one or two other things of the same kind in order to put her into a good humor, hugged her, and then went back into the living room.

I will remember that first meal of Mino's in my own home, with Mother and me, for a long time to come. He kept on joking and had an excellent appetite. But his jokes seemed to me to be colder than ice and more bitter than a lemon. It was clear that he had only one thought in his head, and that it was lodged in his conscience like a thorn in the flesh, and his jokes only served to drive the thorn deeper and renew the agony. It was the thought of all he had said to Astarita, and really, I never saw anyone so deeply repentant. As a child, the priests had taught me that repentance washes away sin, but in Mino's case the repentance seemed to have no end, no outlet, and no beneficent result. I realized that he was suffering dreadfully and I suffered for him to the same extent, and perhaps even more, because my suffering was increased by my inability to help him or lighten his burden.

We ate the first course in silence. Then Mother, who was standing up to serve us, said something about the price of meat. "Don't worry," said Mino, raising his head. "From now on I'll provide for you. I'm going to get a good job."   .

I felt almost hopeful as he made this announcement.

"What job?" asked Mother.

"A job with the police," said Mino with exaggerated seriousness. "A friend of Adriana's is getting me the job — a Signor Astarita."

I put down my knife and fork and stared at him.

"They've found out that I've got the very qualities they're looking for in the police."

"Maybe," said Mother, "but I never liked the police myself. The son of the laundress who lives below us became a policeman, too. Do you know what the young men who work next door in the cement works said to him? 'Stay away, we don't know you anymore.' And anyway, the work's badly paid." She made a face and changed his plate, then offered him the dish of meat.

"That's not what I mean," retorted Mino as he helped himself. "What I'm talking about is an important job, something very delicate, very secret. What the devil! I haven't studied for nothing! I've almost got my degree. I know modern languages. Poor people become mere policemen, not people like me."

"Maybe," repeated Mother. "Take this," she added, pushing the largest piece of meat onto my plate.

"Not maybe at all," said Mino. "It's true."

He was silent for a moment. Then he said, "The government knows that the country's full of people opposed to it, not only among the poorer classes but among the rich, too. They need educated people to spy on the rich, people who speak as they do, dress as they do, have the same manners, and inspire their confidence. That's what I'll do. I'll be very well paid, I'll live in first-class hotels, travel in a sleeper, eat in the best restaurants, get my clothes from a fashionable tailor, visit luxurious seaside resorts and famous holiday spots in the mountains. Who did you take me for?"

By now Mother was gaping at him. She was dazzled by such splendor. "In that case," she said at last, "I've nothing to say."

I had finished my meal. I suddenly found it impossible to go on assisting at such a lugubrious comedy. "I'm tired," I said brusquely. "I'm going into the other room." I got up and left the living room.

When I was in my own room I sat on the bed and huddled over myself, then began to cry silently through my fingers, spread across my face. I thought of Mino's grief, of the baby that I was going to have, and both these things, the grief and the baby, seemed to be growing by themselves, independently of me, out of my control, and they were alive and there was nothing more to do. After a while Mino came in, and I got up at once and turned away from him so that he would not see my eyes full of tears before I had time to dry them. He had lit a cigarette and threw himself down flat on the bed. I sat down beside him. "Mino," I said, "please don't talk like that to Mother ever again."

"Why?"

"Because she doesn't understand what you're doing. But I understand, and every word you say is like a needle piercing my heart."

He said nothing and went on smoking in silence. I took one of my blouses out of the drawer, picked up a needle and spool of silk, and began to sew without speaking, sitting on the edge of the bed near the lamp. I did not want to speak because I was afraid that if I did, he would begin to discuss the usual thing, and I hoped that if I kept silent, his thoughts would wander and he would stop thinking about it. Sewing requires a lot of visual attention, but leaves the mind free, as all women who sew for a living know.

While I was sewing, my thoughts whirled around in my head, or rather, I felt as if I were mending a tear or stitching a hem in my mind as I was in the work I held in my hands, pushing the needle rapidly in and out. I, too, shared Mino's obsession by now and could not help thinking of what he had said to Astarita and the consequences it would have. But I didn't want to think about it, because I was afraid that if I did, some mysterious influence would set him thinking about it, too, and I would be responsible despite myself for having increased his sorrow and keeping it alive. So I tried to think about something else, something clear, something light and cheerful, and I concentrated with the whole strength of my mind on the baby I was going to have, which was, in fact, the only joyous aspect in my life, now so full of terribly tragic prospects. I imagined what he would be like at two or three years of age, the best time of all, when children are at their most charming and beautiful. And as I thought of all the things he would do and say and the way I would bring him up, I grew cheerful again, as I had hoped I would, and forgot Mino and his pain for a moment. I had finished mending my blouse and as I took up another piece of work I reflected that during the next few days I could relieve the tension of the long hours spent with Mino by making the baby's layette. Only I would have to hide from him what I was doing, or I would have to find an excuse. I thought I would tell him that I was making it for a neighbor of ours who was actually expecting a baby, and I thought it would be a good excuse, since I had already mentioned her to Mino and had referred to her poverty. I was so taken up with these ideas that, without noticing it, almost, I began to sing softly. I have a very good ear, although my voice is not very strong, and my accent is extraordinarily sweet, even in my speaking voice. I began to sing a song that was popular just then: "*Villa triste.*" When I raised my eyes, as I bit the thread with which I was sewing in two, I saw Mino looking at me. I thought he might reproach me for singing at a time that was so grave for him, so I stopped.

"Sing some more," he said, looking at me.

"Do you like me to sing?"

"Yes."

"But I can't sing well."

"It doesn't matter."

I took up my sewing again and began to sing for him. Like most girls, I knew quite a number of songs; in fact, I had a fairly vast repertoire because my memory is excellent and I could even remember the songs I had learned as a child. I sang a little of everything, and as soon as I had finished one song I began another. At first I sang softly and then, as it grew on me, I sang aloud with all the feeling I could muster. One song followed another, and they were all different. As I sang one, I was already thinking of the next. He listened to me with a certain serenity in his face, and I was glad that I was able to distract his attention from the remorse he felt. But at the same time I remembered that once when I was a child I had lost some toy I was very fond of, and since I could not stop crying on account of the loss, Mother to console me had sat down on my bed and had begun to sing the few things she knew. She sang badly, out of tune; nevertheless, at first I was distracted and listened to her just as Mino was listening to me. But after a while the idea of the toy I had lost had slowly begun to distill bitterness into the cup of forgetfulness that Mother offered me, and at last it had poisoned everything and had made it, by contrast, utterly intolerable. So I had suddenly burst into tears again and Mother, out of patience with me, had switched off the light and gone away, leaving me to cry my heart out in the dark. I was sure that when the deceptive sweetness of my singing had vanished, he would inevitably feel once more the same pain, which would burn even more sharply by contrast with the sentimental superficiality of my songs; and I was not mistaken. I had been singing for nearly an hour when he interrupted me brusquely. "That's enough," he said. "Your songs bore me stiff." Then he curled up as if he meant to go to sleep, with his back turned to me.

I had foreseen that he would behave in this rude way so I was not too deeply hurt. In any case, I did not expect anything else now but unhappiness, and the opposite would have astonished me. I got up from the bed and went to put away the clothes I had mended. Then, still in silence, I undressed and slipped into the bed on the side Mino had left free. We lay for some time in silence like that, back to back. I knew he was not asleep and was thinking all the time of one thing; and this knowledge, together with the sharp sense of my own helplessness, provoked a storm of confused, desperate thoughts in my mind. I was lying on my side and staring in front of me into a corner of the room as I thought. I could see one of the two suitcases Mino had brought with him from Signora Medolaghi's house, an old yellow leather case covered with the colored labels of different hotels. Among the rest there was one that showed a square of blue sea, a huge red rock, and the word *Capri*. In the half-light, among the dull, opaque furniture of my room, that blue spot seemed luminous, seemed something more than a mere spot; it was a hole through which I caught a glimpse of that strip of distant sea. I felt a sudden longing for the sea, so sparkling and lively, in which even the most corrupt and deformed object is purified, smoothed, rounded, fashioned into something beautiful and clean. I have always loved the sea, even the tamed and crowded beach of Ostia; and the sight of it always gives me a sense of freedom that intoxicates my ears even more than my eyes, as if I were listening to the notes of a wondrous, timeless music floating eternally on its waves. I began to think about the sea, yearning acutely for its transparent waves, which seem to wash not only the body but, with its liquid contact, also the soul, rendering it light and full of joy. I told myself that if I could take Mino to the sea, perhaps the immensity, the perpetual motion and sound would produce in him the effect my love alone could not achieve.

"Have you ever been to Capri?" I suddenly asked him.

"Yes," he said, without turning around.

"Is it beautiful?"

"Yes — very."

"Listen," I said, turning around in the bed and putting an arm around his neck. "Why don't we go to Capri? Or some other seaside place? As long as you stay here in Rome, you won't be able to think about anything pleasant. If you have a change of air, I'm sure you'll see everything differently. You'd see lots of things that escape you for the moment. I'm sure it would do you a lot of good."

He did not answer at once and seemed to be thinking. "I don't need to go to the sea," he said. "I could see things differently, as you say, even here. All I have to do is to accept what I've done, just as you advised, and I'd begin to enjoy the sky, the earth, you, everything, at once. Do you think I don't know the world is beautiful?"

"Well, then," I said anxiously, "accept it. What does it cost you?" He began to laugh.

"I should have thought of that first . . . do as you do — accept right from the beginning. Even the beggars that sit warming themselves in the sunshine on the church steps have accepted it from the beginning. It's too late for me."

"But why?"

"There are some who accept and some who don't. Obviously I belong to the second category."

I did not know what to say so I remained silent. "Now turn out the light," he added after a moment. "I'll get undressed in the dark. It must be time to go to sleep."

I obeyed and he undressed in the dark and got into bed beside me. I turned toward him to embrace him, but he pushed me away wordlessly and curled himself up on the edge of the bed with his back to me. This gesture filled me with bitterness and I, too, hunched myself up, waiting for sleep with a widowed spirit. But I began to think about the sea again and was overcome by the longing to drown myself. I imagined it would be only a moment's suffering, and then my lifeless body would float from wave to wave beneath the sky for ages. The gulls would peck at my eyes, the sun would burn my breast and belly, the fish would gnaw at my back. At last I would sink to the bottom, would be dragged head downward toward some icy, blue current that would carry me along the sea bed for months and years among submarine rocks, fish, and seaweed, and floods of limpid saltwater would wash my forehead, my breast, my belly, my legs, slowly wearing away my flesh, smoothing and refining me continually. And at last some wave, someday, would cast me up on some beach, nothing but a handful of fragile, white bones. I liked the idea of being dragged to the bottom of the sea by my hair. I liked the idea of being reduced one day to a little heap of bones, without human shape, among the clean stones of a shore. And perhaps someone without noticing it would walk on my bones and crush them to white powder. With these sad, voluptuous thoughts I finally fell asleep.

II

THE FOLLOWING DAY, ALTHOUGH I tried to force myself to believe that rest and sleep had changed Mino's feelings, I noticed immediately that he was the same as ever. In fact, if
anything, he seemed decidedly worse. As he had the day before,
he kept passing from periods of long, gloomy, obstinate silence to
outbursts of rambling, sarcastic discourse about irrelevant things
in which, however, the same dominant thought was always apparent, like the watermark in some kinds of paper. As far as I could
see, his deterioration consisted also of a kind of willful inertia, apathy, and carelessness that were something quite new in him, for
he had always been extremely active and energetic; it was a kind of
progressive detachment from all the things he had done so far. I
opened his suitcases and put his suits and other clothes in my
closet. But when it came to the books he needed for his studies —
I suggested temporarily putting them in a row on the marble-
topped chest of drawers underneath the mirror — he said, "Leave
them in the case. They won't be any use to me anymore, anyway."

"And why not?" I asked. "Don't you have to get your degree?"

"I'm not going to get my degree."

"Don't you want to go on with your studies?"

"No."

I did not insist, fearful lest he begin to talk again about the thing that was grieving him, and I left the books in the suitcase. I noticed that he did not think to shave and did not wash himself. Before this he had always been very clean and finicky in his person. He spent the whole of the second day in my room either lying on the bed smoking or walking thoughtfully up and down with his hands in his pockets. But he did not say anything more to Mother at lunch, as he had promised me. When evening came he said he would dine out and left the house by himself, without my daring to suggest that I should accompany him. I have no idea where he went. I was just going to bed when he came back in and I noticed immediately that he had been drinking. He embraced me in a theatrical and exaggerated manner and insisted on making love to me. I had to give in to him, although I realized that making love for him was now like drinking, something unpleasant that he forced himself to do in order to tire and numb himself. I told him so. "You might as well do this with some other woman," I told him. He laughed. "I might as well," he replied, "but you're here, right to hand." I was offended by these words and hurt even more than offended since they proved he felt little or no affection for me.

Then I had a sudden kind of illumination, and turning toward him I said, "Look, I know I'm only a poor girl like any other, but try to love me. It's for your own good that I ask you this. If you could manage to love me, I'm sure you'd be able to love yourself in the end." He looked at me, then repeated, "Love, love," in a loud, mocking voice and switched out the light. I lay there in the dark with staring eyes, feeling bewildered and embittered, not knowing what to think.

There was no change in him in the days that followed and everything continued in the same way. He merely seemed to have formed new habits to replace the old ones. Previously he had studied, gone to the university, seen his friends at some café, and

read. Now he lay on the bed smoking, strolled around the bedroom, went on making the same crazy, rambling allusions, got
drunk, and made love. On the fourth day I began to feel really desperate. I could see that his anguish was as bitter as ever, and it
seemed to me it would be impossible to continue living in such
pain. My room, which was always full of cigarette smoke, seemed
to me like a factory working day and night to manufacture sorrow,
without a moment's break; and the very air I breathed had by now
become a thick gelatinous mass of sad, obsessive thoughts. During
these times I often cursed my ignorance and ineptitude and the
fact that Mother was even more inept and ignorant than I was.
One's first impulse in moments of difficulty is to turn to someone
older and more experienced for advice. But I did not know anyone
who possessed these qualities, and asking Mother for help would
have been like asking help from one of the many children playing
in our courtyard. Aside from this, I was unable to penetrate to the
depths of his sorrow; many things escaped me; little by little, I
came to the conclusion that what tormented him most of all was
the thought that everything he had said to Astarita was written
down in the police report and kept in the archives, as a perpetual
witness to his weakness. Several things he said strengthened me in
this conviction. So one afternoon I spoke to him about it. "If
you're sorry they wrote down everything you said to Astarita —
well, Astarita would do anything I asked him. I'm sure if I ask him
he'll have the report on you destroyed."

"What makes you think so?" he said, giving me a strange look.

"You said so yourself the other day. I told you that you ought to try
to forget and you told me that even if you forgot the police wouldn't."

"But how would you go about asking him?"

"That's easy enough. I'll simply phone him and go to the
Ministry."

He would not say what he wanted. "Well — do you want me to
ask him?" I insisted.

"Do what you like, as far as I'm concerned."

We went out together and phoned from a café. I got hold of Astarita at once and told him I had to speak to him. I asked him if I

might come to the Ministry. "Either at your place or not at all," he replied in a strange, stuttering voice.

I realized that he wanted to be paid for the favor I was going to ask him to do; and I tried to avoid the point. "Let's meet in a café," I said.

"Either at your place or not at all."

"All right, then," I said, "at my place." I added that I would expect him that same day, late in the afternoon.

"I know what he wants," I said to Mino as we returned home, "he wants to make love to me — but no one has ever been able to force a woman to make love against her will. He blackmailed me once, when I was still inexperienced, but he won't be able to bring that off again."

"But why don't you want him to make love to you?" asked Mino indifferently.

"Because I love you."

"But maybe he'll refuse to destroy the reports if you don't let him make love to you — and what then?" he asked, still in a casual tone.

"He'll destroy them, don't worry."

"But suppose he didn't want to except on this one condition?"

We were on the stairs. I stood still, "Then I'll do what you want me to do," I said.

He put his arm around my waist. "Well," he said slowly, "this is what I want — I want you to get Astarita to come to your place and go into your room with you under the pretext of making love. I'll be waiting behind the door and as soon as he comes in, I'll kill him with a pistol. Then we'll shove him under the bed and make love ourselves, all night."

His eyes were shining; for the first time for days they were cleared of the oppressive mist that had obscured them. I grew frightened, mainly because I could see that there was a certain logic in what he suggested and also because by now I was resigned to the idea of ever worse and more definitive disasters and it seemed just the kind of crime that might happen. "For God's sake, Mino!" I exclaimed. "Don't say that even in fun."

"Not even in fun," he repeated. "I was only joking, as a matter of fact."

I thought that probably he had not been joking at all; but I was reassured by the thought that his pistol was unloaded, although he did not know this, since I had removed the bullets from it. "Don't worry," I continued. "Astarita will do anything I want. Don't talk like that anymore. You gave me such a scare."

"Oh, we can't even joke anymore!" he said lightly as he went indoors.

I noticed that a sudden fit of restlessness possessed him as soon as we entered the living room. He began to walk up and down with his hands in his pockets as usual. But he was moving differently, more energetically than usual, with an expression on his face that showed that he was thinking clearly and profoundly and had shaken off his usual disgust and apathy. I attributed this change to the relief of knowing that the compromising papers would soon be destroyed. "You'll see, everything will be all right," I said, hope springing once more within my breast.

He shuddered deeply, looked at me as if he did not recognize me, and then repeated mechanically, "Yes — everything will be all right."

I had sent Mother out on the pretext of doing some shopping for supper. I suddenly felt optimistic. I thought everything really would be all right, perhaps even better than I expected. Astarita would do what I wanted, if he had not already done so; and day by day Mino would become detached from his remorse, would begin to enjoy life again, and look confidently towards the future. In time of trouble we all content ourselves with merely surviving, but as soon as the wind changes we begin to construct ambitious, far-reaching plans. Two days earlier I had thought myself capable of giving Mino up for his own happiness; but now that I had persuaded myself into believing that I might be able to restore this happiness I not only renounced all ideas of leaving him, but tried to work out how I could bind him ever more strongly to me. It was not my reason that urged me to form these plans; it was an obscure impulse within my spirit, which wants always to hope and cannot bear humiliation and sorrow for long. It seemed to me that there were only two possible solutions for us, as things stood: either we must separate or be bound to one another for life. Since I did not even want to consider the first alternative, I began to wonder whether there was not some means by which I could achieve the second. I hate lying and I think I may count a sometimes even excessive sincerity among my few admirable qualities. If I lied to Mino at that moment, it was because I did not feel as though I were lying at all; I seemed to be telling the truth. It was a truth that was truer than truth, a spiritual and not a material truth. As a matter of fact, I did not think at all; it was, if anything, a kind of inspiration.

He was walking up and down as usual and I was sitting at one end of the table. "Listen," I said suddenly, "stand still. I've got something I have to tell you."

"What?"

"I haven't been feeling well lately. I went to see a doctor a few days ago. . . . I'm pregnant."

He stood still and looked at me, "You're pregnant?" he repeated.

"Yes. And I'm absolutely sure it was you."

Mino was intelligent and although he could not guess that I was lying, he immediately understood the real purpose of my announcement. He took a chair, came and sat down beside me, and caressed my cheek fondly. "I suppose this ought to be one more reason, the reason par excellence, in fact, for me to forget what has happened and go ahead with life. Isn't that so?"

"What do you mean?" I asked, pretending I had not understood him.

"Since I'm going to become a *pater familias*," he continued, "I should, for the sake of this innocent creature, as you women say, do what I wouldn't do for love of you."

"Do what you like," I said, shrugging my shoulders. "I've told you because it's the truth, that's all."

"After all," he went on in that reflective tone of his, as if he were thinking aloud, "a child can be a reason for living. Many people ask for nothing more. A child is a good justification. You can even steal or murder for a child."

"Who's asking you to steal or murder?" I interrupted him indignantly. "I'm only asking you to be happy. If you aren't — then there's nothing more to be said."

He looked at me and stroked my cheek again fondly. "If you're glad, I'm glad. Are you glad?"

"I am, yes," I said proudly and firmly. "First of all, because I like children and then because it's yours."

He laughed. "You're a clever one," he said.

"Why? What's so clever about being pregnant?"

"Nothing. But you must admit it's a good stroke just at this moment and in these circumstances. 'I'm pregnant and therefore —'"

"Therefore?"

"Therefore you must accept what you've done," he shouted unexpectedly at the top of his voice as he leaped to his feet, waving his arms wildly, "therefore you must live, live, live!"

The tone of his voice was indescribable. I felt pierced to the heart and my eyes filled with tears. "Do what you like," I stammered, "if you want to leave me, leave me, then. I — I'll go away."

Apparently he regretted his outburst, for he came up to me and caressed me again. "I'm sorry," he said. "Don't take any notice of what I say. Think about your child and don't worry about me."

I took his hand and pressed it to my face, bathed it with my tears, and stammered: "Oh, Mino — how can I help worrying about you?"

We remained silent like this for some time. He was standing beside me; I pressed his hand against my face, kissed it, and wept. Then we heard the front doorbell ring.

He broke away from me and became very pale, but at that moment I could not understand why and did not trouble to ask him. I leaped to my feet. "Go on," I said, "here's Astarita! Quick! Go away."

He went out by the kitchen door, leaving it ajar. I dried my eyes quickly, put the chairs back in their places, and went out into the hall. I felt perfectly tranquil and sure of myself once more; and in the darkness of the hall it occurred to me that I might even tell

Astarita I was pregnant; in this way he might leave me alone and if he was disinclined to do me the favor I asked out of love, he might do it out of pity.

I opened the door, and took a step back. Instead of Astarita on the threshold, I saw Sonzogno.

His hands were in his pockets and as I tried, almost mechanically, to shut the door in his face he shoved lightly against it with his shoulders, flung it wide open, and came in. I followed him into the living room. He went and stood by the table near the window. He was hatless as usual and as soon as I entered I felt his insistent unwinking eyes fixed upon me. I closed the door and spoke to him, pretending indifference.

"Why have you come?"

"You informed on me, didn't you?"

I shrugged my shoulders and sat down at the head of the table. "I didn't inform on you," I said.

"You left me, went out, and called the police."

I felt quite calm. If I felt anything at all at that moment, it was anger rather than fear. He did not frighten me any longer and I felt a great rage rising within me against him and against all those who prevented me from being happy, as he did. "I left you and went away," I said, "because I love another man and I don't want to have anything more to do with you. But I didn't call the police. I'm not an informer. The police came of their own accord. They were looking for someone else."

He came up to me, took hold of my face with two fingers, and pinched my cheek so cruelly that I had to unclench my teeth as he raised my face to his. "You can thank your God that you're a woman," he said.

He continued to pinch my face, forcing me to make a painful grimace that I knew was both hideous and ridiculous. Rage overcame me and I leaped to my feet. "Get out, you imbecile!" I cried.

He put his hands back into his pockets and came even nearer to me, staring into my eyes as usual. "You're an imbecile!" I cried once more. "With your muscles, your little blue eyes, your bald head! Get out, go away, you idiot!"

He really was an imbecile, I thought. He said nothing, but, with a slight smile on his thin, crooked lips and his hands in his pockets, approached me, staring at me fixedly. I ran to the other end of the table, gripped an iron, a heavy tailor's iron, and shouted, "Get out, you cretin! Or I'll smash your face with this."

He hesitated a moment and stood still. At the same instant the door of the living room opened behind me and Astarita appeared in the doorway. Obviously he had found the door open and had walked in. I turned toward him. "Tell this man to get out," I cried. "I don't know what he wants from me. Tell him to get out."

I do not know why the elegance of Astarita's clothes on this occasion gave me such pleasure. He was wearing a double-breasted, gray overcoat that looked new. He had on what looked like a silk shirt, with red stripes on a white background. A silvery gray twill tie was tucked into the folds of his navy-blue suit. He looked at me as I stood there waving the iron, looked at Sonzgono. "The young lady told you to go away," he said evenly. "What are you waiting for?"

"The young lady and I have several things to talk over. It would be better if you went," said Sonzogno in a very low, deep voice.

As Astarita came in, he took off his hat, a black felt with edges bordered in silk. He put it down on the table in a leisurely fashion and went toward Sonzogno. His attitude amazed me. His eyes, which were usually so black and melancholy, seemed to gleam belligerently, his large mouth widened and curled upward in a pleased, defiant smile. He showed his teeth. "Oh, so you don't want to go," he said, hammering out each syllable, "but you see, I'm telling you you're going, right now."

Sonzogno shook his head in refusal but, to my astonishment, took a step backward. And then I remembered precisely who Sonzogno was. And I was afraid, not for myself but for Astarita who was provoking him so boldly, without knowing who he was dealing with. I had the same feeling of anguish I had experienced as a child at the circus when I saw a little lion-tamer armed with a whip facing a huge, roaring lion, and teasing it. "Look out!" I wanted to shout, "he's a murderer, a monster!" But I did not have the strength to speak. "Well, are you going — or aren't you?" said Astarita once more.

Sonzogno shook his head again and took another step backward, Astarita moved one step forward. They were now nose to nose, each the same height. "Who are you, anyway?" asked Astarita with the same twisted grimace. "Your name — right now!"

Sonzogno made no reply. "So you don't want to tell me, eh?" repeated Astarita almost voluptuously, as if Sonzogno's silence was a source of pleasure. "You don't want to tell me and you don't want to get out, eh? Is that it?"

He waited for a moment, then raised his hand and slapped Sonzogno hard, first on one cheek, then the other. I put my fist to my mouth and buried my teeth in it. Now he'll kill him, I thought as I shut my eyes. But I heard Astarita's voice, saying, "And now clear out! Go on, move it!" I reopened my eyes and saw Astarita pushing Sonzogno toward the door, dragging him by his coat collar. Sonzogno's cheeks were still crimson from the blows he had received, but he seemed docile. He let himself be dragged along as if he were thinking about something else. Astarita pushed him out of the living room and then I heard the front door slam violently, and Astarita reappeared.

"Who was he?" he asked, mechanically removing a piece of fluff from the lapels of his overcoat and looking himself over as if he were afraid he had spoiled his elegance by the violent effort he had made.

"I never knew his last name. I only know him as Carlo," I lied.

"Carlo," he replied with a snigger, shaking his head. Then he came up to me. I was standing in the window embrasure and was looking out through the panes of glass. He put his arm around my waist. "How are you?" he asked me, and his voice and expression were already quite different.

"I'm well," I said, without looking at him. He gazed at me and then pressed me to him, close, without speaking. I pushed him away gently. "You've been very kind to me," I said. "I telephoned to ask you to do me another favor."

"Let's hear it," he said. He was still gazing at me and did not appear to be listening.

"That young man you questioned —" I began.

"Oh, yes," he interrupted, making a face. "Always him. . . . He didn't turn out to be very heroic."

I was curious to know the truth about Mino's interview. "Why?" I asked. "Was he afraid?"

Astarita shook his head. "I don't know if he was afraid or not. I only know that at the first question I put to him he blurted out everything. If he had denied it, I couldn't have done anything to him. There wasn't any proof."

So it really had gone as Mino had said, I thought. It had been a kind of sudden absence, like a collapse, reasonless, unasked for and unprovoked. "Well," I went on, "I suppose you wrote down what he said. I want you to destroy everything you wrote."

He smiled contemptuously. "He put you up to this, didn't he?"

"No, it's my idea," I replied. "May I be struck dead this moment if it's not true," I swore solemnly.

"They all want the records to disappear," he said. "The police archives are their uneasy consciences. When the record disappears, the remorse disappears."

"I wish that were true," I said, remembering Mino, "but I'm afraid you're wrong this time."

He drew me to him again, so that my belly was pressed against his. "What will you give me in exchange?" he stammered, trembling with desire.

"Nothing," I replied simply. "Nothing at all this time."

"And if I refuse?"

"You'd make me very unhappy because I love this man, and everything that happens to him is as if it were happening to me."

"But you told me you'd be nice to me."

"I did say so. But I've changed my mind."

"Why?"

"Because. There isn't any reason."

He pressed me to him again and, stammering rapidly with his mouth to my ear, he began to beg me to yield, at least for one last time, to his desperate desire. I cannot repeat the things he said, because he mingled his supplications with atrocious things I could not write down, things men say to women like me, things women like me say to their lovers. He enumerated them in meticulous, abundant, and precise detail; not with the shameless gaiety that usually accompanies such outbursts, but with grim pleasure, as if he were obsessed. I once saw a homicidal maniac in the insane asylum describe to his nurse the tortures he would inflict upon him if he chanced to have him in his power, and he spoke with the same scrupulous, serious, balanced tone of voice with which Astarita whispered his obscenities to me. What he was really describing in this way was his love, both tragic and lustful, which to others might have seemed mere lechery, but which I, on the contrary, knew to be as deep, absolute, and, in its way, as pure as any love could be. I felt stirred to pity for him, as I always did, since underneath all those obscenities I could sense only his loneliness and his absolute incapacity to escape from it. I let him pour it all out, then said to him. "I didn't want to tell you, but you force me to. Do what you like, but I can never again be what I was. I'm pregnant."

He was not astonished; he never deviated for one single moment from his fixed purpose. "Well — so what?"

"So now I'm going to change my way of life. I'm getting married."

My main reason for telling him of my condition had been to console him for my refusal. But I realized as I spoke that I was saying what I really thought and that those words came from my heart. "When you first knew me I wanted to get married," I added with a sigh. "And it wasn't my fault that I didn't."

His arm was still around my waist but he had loosened his hold. Now he drew away from me completely. "I curse the day I met you!" he said.

"Why?"

He spat, turning his head to one side, then continued. "I curse the day I met you and I curse the day I was born." He spoke quietly and did not seem to be giving vent to any violent emotion. He spoke calmly and surely. "Your friend has nothing to fear," he added. "The interview wasn't written down, and the information he gave wasn't acted upon. He's only noted in our archives as still being dangerous from the political standpoint. Good-bye, Adriana."

I remained by the window and returned his farewell, watching him from a distance as he went off. He picked up his hat from the table and left without turning around.

The door leading into the kitchen opened immediately and Mino came in with his pistol in his hand. I gazed at him in astonishment, feeling empty and speechless.

"I had made up my mind to kill Astarita," he said with a smile. "Did you really think I cared whether the papers dealing with my case disappeared or not?"

"Then why didn't you do it?" I asked in a dazed voice.

"He cursed the day he was born so deeply; let him go on cursing it for a year or two yet," he said shaking his head.

I felt that something was hurting me but however hard I tried I was unable to discover what it was. "In any case," I said, "I got what I wanted. There's nothing written down."

"I heard him, I heard him," he interrupted me. "I heard everything. I was standing behind the door, and the door was ajar. I saw what he did, too. He's brave," he added carelessly, "your Astarita's brave . . . pam pam! The way he slapped Sonzogno was really masterful! There are ways of doing these things, even slapping someone. He hit him like a superior hits an inferior, like a master hits a servant. And the way Sonzogno swallowed it! He didn't say a word." He laughed and put his pistol back into his pocket.

I was rather disconcerted by this singular eulogy of Astarita. "What do you think Sonzogno will do?" I asked uncertainly.

"Oh, who knows?"

It was nearly night by now and the living room was immersed in deep shadow. He leaned over the table and switched on the central light, which was surrounded by darkness. Mother's glasses and her patience cards lay on the table. Mino sat down, picked up the cards, and shuffled them. "Want to play a game of cards while we wait for supper?" he then said.

"What an idea!" I exclaimed. "A game of cards?"

"Yes, *briscola*. Come on."

I obeyed him, sat down, and mechanically took up the cards he dealt me. I was confused in my mind and my hands, I was not sure why, were trembling. I began to play. The figures on the cards seemed to me to possess a malicious, disturbing character of their own: the jack of clubs, black and sinister with his black eye and a black flower in his fist; the queen of hearts, lustful, excited, shapeless; the king of diamonds, paunchy, cold, impassive, inhuman. I felt we were playing for some immensely important stakes, but I did not know what. I was deathly sad and every now and then, even as I was playing, I sighed lightly to ascertain whether the weight that was oppressing me was still there. And I could feel that not only was it still there, but was becoming heavier.

He won the first game and then the second. "What's the matter?" he asked, shuffling the cards. "You're playing so badly."

I threw the cards down. "Don't torture me like this, Mino! I really don't feel like playing at all."

"Why not?"

"I don't know."

I got up and walked around the room, furtively wringing my hands. "Let's go into the other room, do you want to?" I suggested.

"Let's go."

We went out into the hall and there in the dark he put his arm around my waist and kissed me on the neck. For perhaps the first time in my life, then, I looked at making love as he did; that is to say, as a means to numb oneself and drive out thought, no more pleasurable or important than any other. I gripped his head with my hands and kissed him violently. We went into my room clinging together. It was plunged in darkness but I did not notice. A glowing light as red as blood filled my eyes and every movement we made had the splendor of a flame leaping rapidly and unexpectedly out of the fire that consumed us. There are times when we seem to see with a sixth sense diffused throughout our bodies and the shadows become as familiar as the light of the sun. But it is a vision that goes no further than the bounds of physical contact; and all I could see were our two bodies projected against the night like the bodies of two drowned people cast up on the shore from some black eddy.

Suddenly I found I was lying on the bed with the light from the lamp reflected on my naked belly. I squeezed my thighs together, I don't know whether from cold or shame, and covered my sex with my two hands. Mino looked at me. "Now your belly will begin to swell," he said, "more and more each month . . . and one day pain will make you open these legs you're locking together so jealously now, and the baby's head, already covered with hair, will pop out and you'll thrust it out into the light of day and they'll pick it up and put it in your arms, and you'll be happy, and there'll be another man in the world. Let's hope he won't end up saying what Astarita said."

"What did he say?"

"'I curse the day I was born.'"

"Astarita's a wretched man," I said. "But I'm sure my son will be happy and lucky."

Then I wrapped myself up in the blanket and I believe I fell asleep. But Astarita's name had reawakened in my heart the same feeling of anguish I had felt after his departure. Suddenly I heard an unknown voice shouting, "Pam, pam!" loudly in my ear, as if imitating the noise of two pistol shots; and I sat up sharply in bed in terror and anxiety. The lamp was still lit; I got out of bed quickly and went toward the door to make sure it was properly shut. But I ran into Mino who was standing fully dressed near the door smoking. Bewildered, I went back and sat down on the edge of the bed. "What do you think?" I asked him. "What will Sonzogno do?"

"How should I know?" he replied, looking at me.

"I know him," I said, succeeding at last in finding words to express the anguish that oppressed me. "The fact that he let himself be pushed out of the room without protesting doesn't mean anything. He's capable of killing him. What do you think?"

"Maybe. It's very likely."

"Do you think he'll kill him?"

"I wouldn't be surprised if he did."

"I have to warn him," I cried, getting up and beginning to dress myself swiftly. "I'm sure he'll kill him. Oh, why didn't I think of it before?"

I dressed rapidly, continuing to talk about my fear and my presentiment. Mino said nothing; he was smoking and walking around. "I'm going to Astarita's house," I said at last. "He's at home now. Wait here for me."

"I'm coming, too."

I did not insist. Truthfully, I was glad of his company, because I was so agitated that I was afraid I might be ill. "We must get a taxi at once," I said as I put on my coat. Mino put on his coat, too, and we went out.

I began to walk hurriedly along the street, almost running, and Mino lengthened his stride to keep pace with me, his arm in mine. After a while we found a taxi and I hurried into it, shouting out Astarita's address. It was a street in the Prati neighborhood; I had never been there but I knew it was near the law courts.

The taxi began to gather speed, and, as if I were crazy, I began to follow its route, leaning forward and watching the roads over the driver's shoulder. At a certain moment I heard Mino behind me say softly, as if speaking to himself, "And what if he has? One serpent has devoured another," but his words made no impression on me. As soon as we were outside the law courts, I stopped the taxi and got out and Mino paid the fare. We ran across the little formal gardens, following the gravel paths between the trees and benches. The street where Astarita lived unfolded itself suddenly before me, long and straight as a sword, illuminated as far as the eye could see by a row of large white lamps. It was a street of orderly, massively built houses, without any shops, and seemed deserted. From the number I guessed that Astarita's house must be toward the end. The street was so peaceful that I said, "Perhaps it's all my imagination. . . . Still, I had to come."

We passed three or four buildings and crosswalks and then Mino spoke. "Still, something must have happened," he said calmly. "Look." I raised my eyes and saw a black crowd gathered before one of the front doors, not far away. A row of people stood lined up on the opposite sidewalk, gazing up toward the dark sky. I was sure right away that that must be Astarita's house, and I began to run, and it seemed to me that Mino was running, too. "What is it? What's happened?" I panted to the first people in the crowd pressing around the doorway.

"It's not altogether clear," said the person I had turned to, a young blond boy, hatless and coatless, who was holding a bicycle by the handlebars. "Someone threw himself down the stairwell. Or he was thrown down. The police have gone up onto the roof and are looking for someone else."

I made my way through the crowd and elbowed myself into the entrance hall, which was spacious and well lit and crammed with people. A white stairway with an iron railing rose in a wide curve over the heads of the crowd. As I pushed ahead, almost lifted up by my own impetus, I was able to see, over all those heads and shoulders, an open space on the floor underneath the stairway. A round white marble column supported a naked, winged figure in gilded bronze, whose one upraised arm held a frosted glass torch with an electric bulb inside it. A human body covered with a sheet lay immediately underneath the column. Everyone was looking in the same direction, and I looked too, and then I saw that they were gazing at a foot in a black shoe that stuck out from under the sheet. At that moment a number of voices began to shout imperiously. "Get back, get back!" and I was pushed violently out with all the others into the street.

"Mino, let's go home," I said faintly to someone just behind me, and I turned around. I saw an unknown face looking at me in astonishment. The people, after protesting loudly and hammering in vain on the shut door, began to disperse and make their comments on what had happened. Others kept running up from other directions; two cars and a number of cyclists had stopped for information. I began to wander through the crowd in a state of increasing anxiety, looking into each face one by one without daring to speak to anyone. Certain shoulders, certain necks seen from the back seemed like Mino's; I would push my way impetuously into the groups of people only to find a number of unknown faces looking at me in surprise. The crowd was still at its densest around the doorway; they knew there was a body there and they still hoped to catch a glimpse of it. They were closely packed, with patient, serious faces; it was as though they were lining up outside a theater. I went on wandering around, but at a certain point I realized I had looked into every face and kept coming across the same ones. I thought I heard Astarita's name mentioned in one of the groups and realized I no longer cared about him at all, and that all the anguish I felt was centered on Mino. At last I convinced myself that he was no longer there. He must have gone off when I pushed my way into the hall. It seemed to me, I don't know why, that I should have foreseen his flight; and I was astonished at not having thought of it before. Pulling myself together with great effort, I dragged myself as far as the piazza, got into a taxi, and gave my home address. I thought that perhaps Mino had lost me and had gone home on his own. But I was almost certain that this was not true.

He was not at home and did not come back that evening or the day after. I shut myself up in my room, overwhelmed by such a strong feeling of uneasiness and anxiety that I could not prevent myself from trembling all over. I did not have a temperature, but I seemed to be living outside myself, in an abnormal, excessive atmosphere in which every sight, every noise, every contact hurt me and made me faint. Nothing could distract me from the thought of Mino, not even the detailed descriptions of the new crime Sonzogno had committed, which filled all the papers Mother brought me. This crime bore Sonzogno's unmistakable imprint: perhaps they had struggled with one another on the landing outside Astarita's front door for a moment, then Sonzogno had bent Astarita back against the railing and had lifted him up and thrown him down the stairwell. Such brutality was extremely expressive: only Sonzogno could have thought of murdering a man that way. But, as I have said, I had one thought only and was unable to take any interest even in the articles that told how Sonzogno had been shot dead later that night as he was escaping across the roofs like a cat. Any form of occupation, distraction, or even reflection unconnected with Mino filled me with a kind of nausea, and at the same time to think of Mino caused me unbearable anguish. Two or three times I happened to think of Astarita, and as I remembered his love for me and his melancholy, I experienced a strong feeling of

helpless pity for him and told myself that if I had not been so anxious about Mino, I would surely have wept for him and prayed for
his soul, which had never been gladdened by any light and which
had been cut off from his body so barbarously and prematurely.

This was how I passed all the first day and night and the whole
of the day and night following. I lay on my bed, or sat in the armchair at the foot of the bed. In my hands, I clutched one of Mino's
jackets that I had found hanging up, and every now and then I
kissed it passionately or bit it to calm my restlessness. Even when
Mother forced me to eat something, I ate with one hand only and
continued to grip the jacket convulsively in the other. Mother
wanted to put me to bed on the second night and I let her undress
me passively. But when she tried to take the jacket from me, I let
out such a shrill scream that she was terrified. Mother did not
know anything for certain, but she had more or less guessed that
Mino's absence had driven me to desperation.

On the third day I managed to work out an idea and I stuck to
it all morning tenaciously although I dimly felt how unfounded it
was. I thought that Mino had become scared when he found out I
was pregnant, that he had wanted to escape the obligations in-
herent to my condition and had gone home to the provinces. It
was an unpleasant supposition, but I preferred to think him vile
rather than to accept the other possibilities I could not help imagining to explain his disappearance. They were such tragic ones,
suggested to me by the circumstances accompanying his flight.

At noon that day Mother came into my room and threw a letter
on the bed. I recognized Mino's writing and my heart leaped with
joy. I waited for Mother to leave the room and then waited for my
excitement to die down a little. Then I opened the letter. Here it is.

> Dearest Adriana,
>
> By the time you receive this letter, I shall already be
> dead. When I opened the pistol and found it unloaded, I
> realized right away that it was you and I thought of you with
> great affection. Poor Adriana, you don't know anything
> about guns and you didn't know there was a bullet in the

barrel. The fact that you didn't notice it strengthened me in my decision. And anyway, there are so many ways to kill yourself.

As I already told you, I cannot accept what I did. I have realized in these past few days that I love you; but if I were logical, I should hate you; because you are everything I hate in myself, as revealed to me by my interrogation, to the highest degree. What really happened at that moment was that the character I should have been collapsed, and I was only the man I am. It wasn't a question of cowardice or treachery but only a mysterious interruption of the will. Perhaps not even so mysterious — but that would take me too far from the point. All I need to say is that by killing myself I am putting things back in the order they should be.

Don't be afraid. I don't hate you, in fact I love you so much that just thinking of you reconciles me to life. If it had been possible, I surely would have lived and would have married you and we'd have been, as you so often say, so happy together. But it really wasn't possible.

I have thought about the child that is to be born and have written two letters concerning him, one to my family and one to a lawyer friend. They're decent people, after all, and although one can't have illusions about their feelings toward you, I am sure they will do their duty. If they should refuse, which I think highly unlikely, don't hesitate to go to law. My lawyer friend will come and see you and you can trust him.

Think of me sometimes. I hug you, your Mino.

P.S. My lawyer friend's name is Francesco Lauro. His address: Via Cola da Rienzo, 3.

As soon as I had read this letter, I buried myself under the covers, pulled the sheet over my head, and cried bitterly. I cannot say how long I cried. Every time I thought I had finished, a kind of violent, bitter laceration pierced my breast and made me burst out sobbing again. I did not scream out loud, as I longed to, because I was afraid of attracting Mother's attention. I wept silently and felt that this was the last time I would ever cry in my whole life. I wept for Mino, for myself, for my whole past and my whole future.

At last I got up, still crying, and feeling dazed and stupid, with my eyes blinded by tears, I began to dress hurriedly. Then I washed my eyes in cold water, made up my red, swollen face as best I could, and went out quietly without telling Mother.

I went to the local police station and had myself shown in to the commissioner. He listened to my story and then said skeptically, "Really, we haven't heard anything about it. You'll see, he will have changed his mind."

I longed for him to be right. But at the same time he irritated me greatly, I don't know why. "You talk like that because you don't know him," I said sharply. "You think everyone's like you."

"Well, look," he asked. "Do you want him alive or dead?"

"I want him to live," I shouted, "I want him to live! But I'm so afraid that he's dead."

He reflected for a moment. Then he said, "Pull yourself together. When he wrote that letter maybe he did want to kill himself. But he might have changed his mind afterward. He's only human. . . . It could happen to anyone."

"Yes, he's human," I stammered. I did not know what I was saying any longer.

"In any case, come back this evening," he concluded, "and by then I'll be able to give you some news."

I went straight from the police station to church. It was the church where I had been held up to be baptized, where I had been christened, and where I had made my first communion. It was a very old church, long and bare, with two rows of beige stone columns and a dusty floor of gray paving stones. But in the darkness of the naves on each side, beyond the two rows of columns, were a number of richly gilded chapels like deep grottoes filled with treasure. One of these chapels was dedicated to the Madonna. I knelt down on the floor in the darkness before the bronze screen that shut off the chapel. The Madonna was shown in a big, dark picture behind a large number of vases full of flowers. She held her baby in her arms and a saint dressed like a monk knelt at her feet with clasped hands, adoring her. I bent down to the ground and beat my head hard against the paving stones. As I covered the stone with kisses, I made the sign of the cross in the dust and then called upon the Virgin and made a vow in my heart. I promised I would never let another man touch me, all my life, not even Mino. Making love was the only thing I cared about in the whole world, the only thing I enjoyed, and I thought I could make no greater sacrifice for Mino's salvation. Then, still bent double with my forehead on the floor, I prayed without words and without thoughts, from my heart. But when I got up I was dazzled. The deep shadow that engulfed the chapel seemed to break into sudden brightness and in this light I distinctly saw the Madonna looking at me sweetly and kindly, but nevertheless shaking her head, as if to say she did not accept my prayer. It lasted only an instant and then I found myself standing once more in front of the screen facing the altar. Feeling more dead than alive, I crossed myself and went home.

I waited the whole day, counting the minutes and the seconds, and toward evening I went back to see the police commissioner. He looked at me in a certain way, so that I felt as if I were going to faint and said in a ghost of a voice, "It's true then, he did kill himself."

The commissioner picked up a photograph from the table and held it out to me. "A man who has not yet been identified killed himself in a hotel near the station," he said. "Have a look and see if it's him."

I took the photo and recognized him at once. They had photographed him from the breast up, stretched out on what appeared to be a bed. Black lines of blood ran across his face from the temple where he had shot himself. But beneath these lines his face was serene, as I had never seen it during his lifetime.

I identified him in a faint voice and got up. The police officer wanted to say something more, perhaps to console me; but I paid no attention to him and went out without turning around.

I went home and this time I threw myself into Mother's arms, but without crying. I knew she was stupid and understood nothing, but she was the only person I could confide in. I told her everything — Mino's suicide, our love, and that I was pregnant. But I did not tell her Sonzogno was the father of my child. I also told her about the vow I had made, and said I had decided to change my way of life and would help her with her shirtmaking or go into service. After trying to console me with a number of silly but sincere phrases, Mother said I shouldn't make any rash decisions — what I had to do now was to see what the family would do for me.

"That's a matter that concerns my child," I said, "not me."

Next morning Mino's two friends, Tullio and Tommaso, called on me unexpectedly. They, too, had received a letter in which, after telling them he was going to commit suicide, Mino informed them of what he called his betrayal and warned them of the consequences it might have.

"Don't worry," I said sharply. "If you're scared, you can relax. Nothing at all will happen to you." And I told them about Astarita and how Astarita, who was the only one who knew anything, had died, and how the interview had never been written down and they had never been denounced. Tommaso looked sincerely upset about Mino's death; but the other had not yet recovered from his fear. After a moment Tullio said, "Still, he got us into a mess. Who can trust the police? You never know. It was a real piece of treachery." And he rubbed his hands together with one of his usual exaggerated bursts of laughter; as if it had been something really amusing.

I got up in indignation. "What treachery, what treachery," I said. "He killed himself, what more do you want? Neither of you would have had the courage to do it. And I'll tell you another thing, too — you two are worthless, even if you aren't traitors! Because you're two wretches, two poor men, two miserable creatures who have never had a penny to call your own and your families are wretched, poor, and miserable, and if things go well you'll finally get what you've never had in all your life, and you and your families will be all right. But he was rich, he was born into a wealthy family, he was a gentleman, and if he got mixed up in it, it was because he believed in it, and not because he expected to get anything out of it. He had everything to lose, unlike you, who have everything to gain! That's what I have to say to you — and you should be ashamed to come here and talk to me about treachery."

Little Tullio opened his enormous mouth as if he wanted to reply, but Tommaso, who had understood me, stopped him with a gesture. "You're right," he said to me, "but don't worry. I'll never think anything but well of Mino, myself." He seemed moved and I liked him because obviously he had really been fond of Mino. Then they said good-bye and left.

When I found myself alone once more, I felt almost relieved in my sorrow by what I had said to those two. I thought about Mino and then I thought about my child. I thought how he would be born of a murderer and a prostitute; but any man might happen to kill someone and any woman might sell herself for money; and what mattered most of all was that he should have an easy birth and grow up strong and healthy. I decided that if it was a boy I would call him Giacomo in memory of Mino. But if it was a girl, I would call her Letitia, because I wanted her to have what I had not had, a gay and happy life, and I was sure that, with the help of Mino's family, that was just what she would have.

OTHER STEERFORTH ITALIA TITLES

VENICE REVEALED
An Intimate Portrait
by Paolo Barbaro

ROME AND A VILLA
Memoir
by Eleanor Clark

The Adventures of
PINOCCHIO
by Carlo Collodi

TORREGRECA
Life, Death, Miracles
by Ann Cornelisen

WOMEN OF THE SHADOWS
Wives and Mothers of Southern Italy
by Ann Cornelisen

THE TWENTY-THREE DAYS
OF THE CITY OF ALBA
by Beppe Fenoglio

ARTURO'S ISLAND
by Elsa Morante

HISTORY
by Elsa Morante

THE WATCH
by Carlo Levi

DARKNESS
Fiction
by Dacia Mariani

THE CONFORMIST
by Alberto Moravia

THE TIME OF INDIFFERENCE
by Alberto Moravia

THE WOMAN OF ROME
by Alberto Moravia

TWO WOMEN
by Alberto Moravia

LIFE OF MORAVIA
by Alberto Moravia and Alain Elkann

Claudia Roden's
THE FOOD OF ITALY
Region by Region

CUCINA DI MAGRO
Cooking Lean the Traditional Italian Way
by G. Franco Romagnoli

A THOUSAND BELLS AT NOON
*A Roman's Guide to the Secrets and
Pleasures of His Native City*
by Franco Romagnoli

CONCLAVE
by Roberto Pazzi

THE ABRUZZO TRILOGY
by Ignazio Silone

MY NAME,
A LIVING MEMORY
by Giorgio van Straten

LITTLE NOVELS OF SICILY
by Giovanni Verga

OPEN CITY
Seven Writers in Postwar Rome
edited by William Weaver